R.K. LANDER

Copyright © 2020 R.K. Lander. All rights reserved.
This work is registered with the UK Copyright Service. Registration no.: 284734464

This is a work of fiction. All characters, names and events in this book are fictitious. Any resemblance to real persons, living or dead, is purely coincidental.

This book or any portion thereof may not be reproduced or used in any manner whatsoever without the express written permission of the publisher except for the use of brief quotations in a book review.

RETURN OF A WARLORD

THE SILVAN BOOK IV

R. K. LANDER

Edited by ANDREA LUNDGREN AND VICKY BREWSTER

Beta reader M. Y. LEIGH

Illustrated by ASHA ZNAMENSKA AND HECTOR AIRAGHI

R.K. LANDER

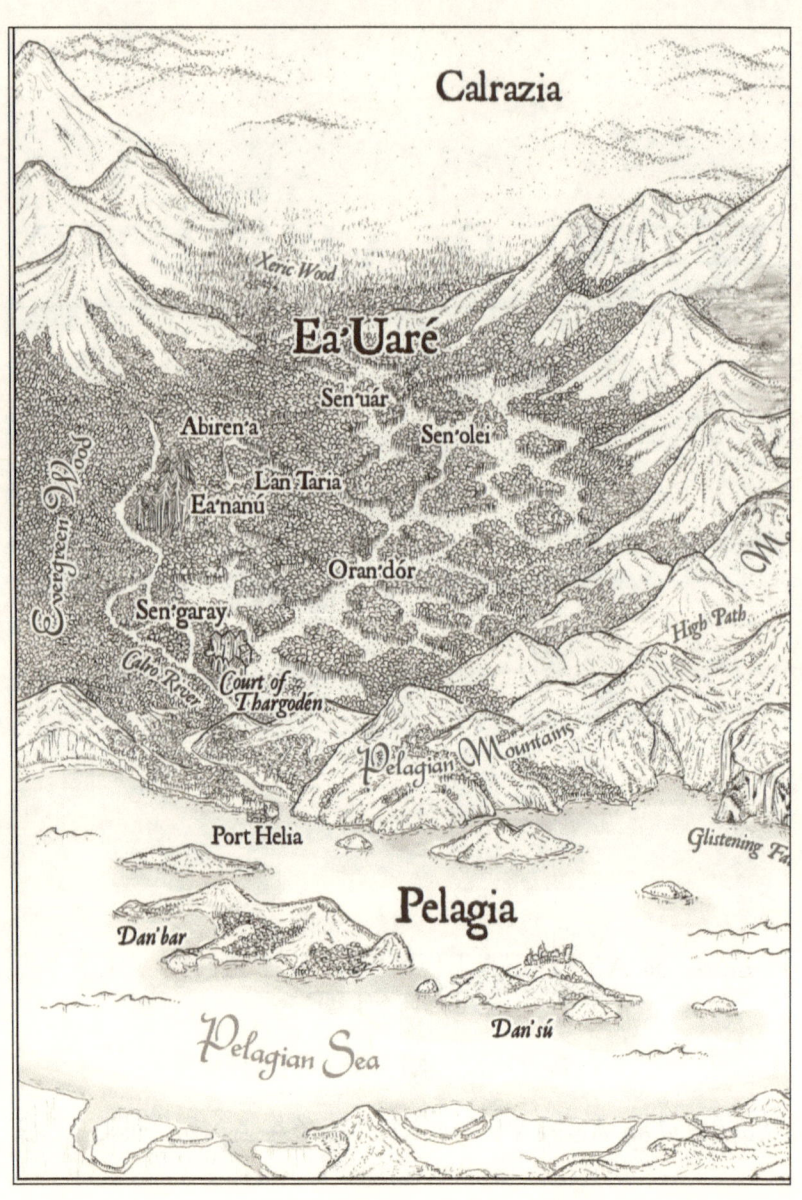

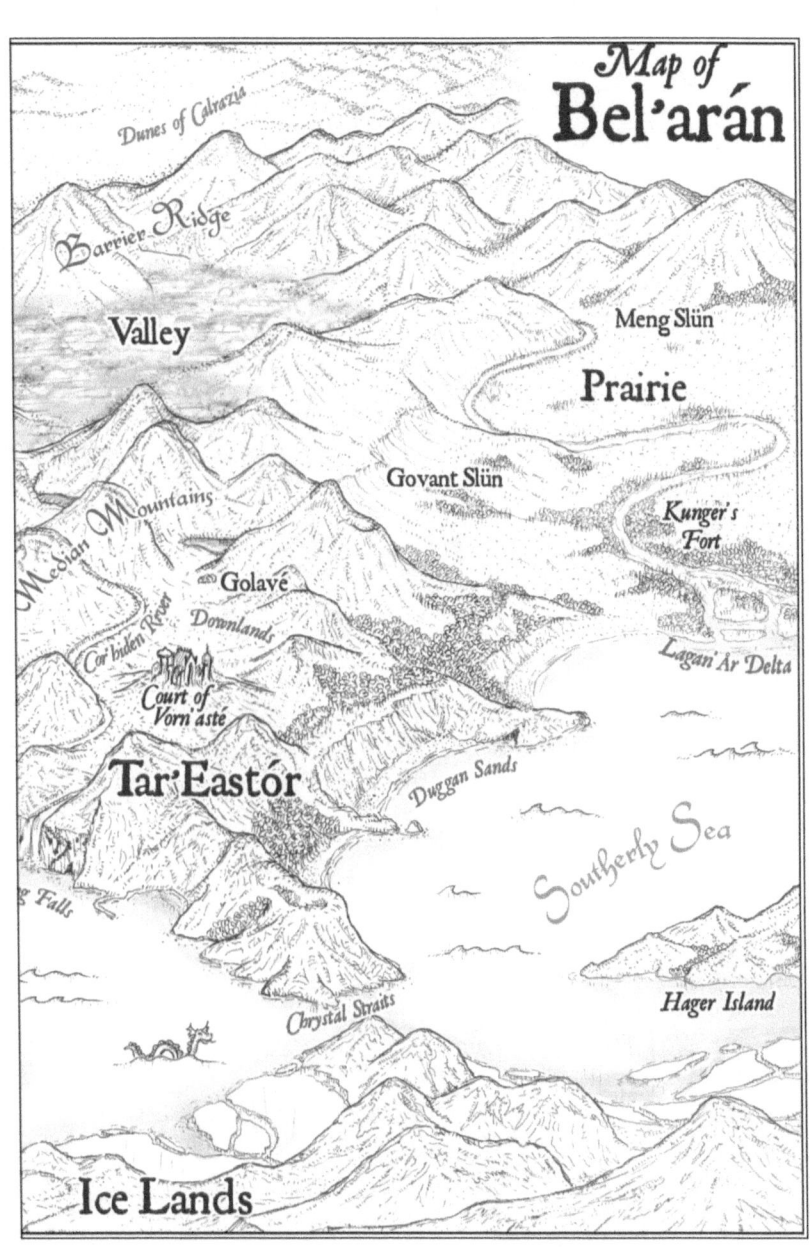

PROLOGUE

A pale hand reached up. Long, elegant fingers brushed softly over smooth, milky skin.

Unblemished. Immortal.

He traced the outline of his acutely pointed ear, finger travelling down a high, angular cheekbone until it reached a strong jaw. His glinting blue eyes strayed to rosy-red lips, delicately curved. There was life behind his eyes, despite the deathly pallor of his skin.

I am exquisite, he thought.

He waited for a soft ripple of water to steady his reflection.

Cocking his head to one side, his finger moved back up to follow the lines of his almond-shaped eyes and the long, dark eyebrows that framed them perfectly. All the while his mind grappled with the conundrum that had accompanied him for almost all his life.

A rough hand, a warrior's palm, smoothed down the silken locks of long blue-black hair. Dark silk hugged the honed muscles of his back, like liquid onyx spilt over white marble.

His eyes moved downwards, past the thick neck and strong chest, the ridges and plains of his body lending him the perfect equilibrium. He was tall, much taller than the rest of his kin, and yet he was not as stocky as his younger brother had been. He was fast, too, his reflexes almost instant, speed akin to that of the northern mountain lions. And Gra'dón had seen them; had stared, in awe of their prowess; had coveted their ruthlessness.

They, too, were predators.

He smiled, first tentatively in satisfaction at the beauty of his own face, and then in pride as his two long incisors emerged, reaching just past his bottom lip. Their pointed tips were lethal, designed for piercing, for tainting elven blood.

Beautiful, said the Deviant side.

Monster, said the Elven side.

Another ripple of water and his image wavered, distorted his jaw, twisted it. But it soon settled—it always did.

His smile widened, lips stretching tight around his teeth, jaw opening wider than any elf should ever be able to manage. It pulled on his features until he was unrecognisable.

But he *was* an elf.

This body could not be vanquished. No warrior could kill him, for he was harnessed power, pale and lethal, terrifying to look upon because he was grotesque—and he was beautiful.

Beautiful monster. *Nim'uán*.

His was a species doomed to extinction. He knew this beyond doubt. His half-Elven soul rebelled against his human side, was ashamed of its weakness, but so, too, was he ashamed of his Elven side, for had they not rejected a mother and her children in their direst hour of need? How she had pleaded, explained, begged for them to understand, but all they did was stare back at her, shake their heads and order her away. She had had no choice and left. But she took her children back another day.

Closer.

Beyond the Last Markers.

Yet still, they had been cut off, chased but not caught. Gra'dón closed his eyes and willed the memories away, conjuring instead the brother that was missing.

Xar'dón had been a good warrior, an excellent apprentice, but he had always been rash, too quick to rile. He was too much like his human father. He was fire, had burned too brightly and waged his attack on Tar'eastór before Gra'dón, Saz'nar and Kay'hán had been ready.

Xar'dón had paid the price: killed by some Alpine mage, they said, skewered on a tree branch and hoisted high above the forest.

Left to rot.

Gra'dón turned from the well, the last he would see for some time. His jaw pulsed in barely repressed ire for the terrible fate of his younger brother. It was yet another reason to wage his revenge upon the elves. They had all but killed his mother with their refusal to allow her children passage into the Source. And then they had killed his younger brother.

How *dare* they? *They* had a home, a place to go when this life no longer held meaning. All Gra'dón had were his brothers and the dream that perhaps there was a place somewhere, where he could be normal, where he could be accepted and even loved.

His own people had rejected them, feared them and had forced the king's hand. They were exiled, though they were not forgotten. Their many-times-removed nephew now sat upon the throne of Calrazia, ruled it with a stony fist and a cruel mind, and for that he, too, was respected. The four royal princes of Calrazia could never make a home in the land of their birth, despite their legitimate claims to the throne. Still, the crown had acceded to helping their exiled princes. Calrazia would be rid of its dangerous, immortal lords at last. The Sun King would have the water he so coveted, and in return, he would help them find their own lands to rule over.

Gra'dón and his twin brothers, Saz'nar and Kay'han, would not make the same mistakes as Xar'dón. They were the tacticians, the wiser brothers, more like their mother. They would find such a place for themselves, do it for the memory of their brother, and for her, the mother who had killed herself when her sons began to change—when the rot had set in and she could no longer look upon them.

She was the only elf they would ever love.

It was a beautiful place that Gra'dón had chosen to live, a place of majestic trees and deep valleys, close to the lands of his forefathers in Calrazia. It was a land soaked to the brim with water.

Ea Uaré, the Great Forest Belt. That would be their home, land of the Nim'uán and their lesser kin. Lands they now set out to conquer.

There was the promise of a good life, for they were princes, and princes were destined to rule and, one day, become king.

1
RESTORATION

"The Battle of Tar'eastór was won. Six warriors and a forest had changed fate that day, before a foe none had ever seen. Nim'uán. Beautiful Monster. But he was vanquished ... and so were the trees."
The Alpine Chronicles: Cor'hidén

To anyone else, the warrior who wielded his blades on the field was perfection. To anyone except a master of the Kal'hamén'Ar.

Fel'annár was *very* good, but Gor'sadén of Tar'eastór saw the details, the small things that would one day make him excellent. He was capable, more than any other apprentice he had seen, and Gor'sadén had seen many. He could count them, still see their faces, remembered their weapons of choice, and would sometimes even contemplate them upon the battlements. They were all there, forever suspended in the Dance.

All Fel'annár needed now was the guidance of his Kah Master, the wisdom of the Kal'hamén'Ar and its teachings. Then, he would be great, perhaps even the greatest of them all.

But Gor'sadén was crippled.

Be it temporarily or permanently, the Nim'uán had incapacitated him, driven his oversized sword straight through his thigh, severing tendons and muscle. The beast had wrought damage that Master Healer Arané said he had fixed, even though he could not say if Gor'sadén would ever completely recover.

"Patience," he had said. But Gor'sadén had never been good at that. Whichever way he looked at it, it would surely be years before he could fight as he once had, dance the Kal'hamén'Ar as he once had.

Fel'annár, too, was still recovering from the horrific bite of the Nim'uán, the one that had scarred him for centuries to come. Gor'sadén could see the over-compensation, the slightly higher left side, how his elbow protected the healing ribs. But he was still good enough to take this test and become a Blade Master.

He was good enough to pass it.

Gor'sadén felt Pan'assár's presence at his side but he didn't take his eyes away from his Disciple as he fought with Captain Sorei for the privilege of sporting another armband, his second.

"Has sleep brought with it some clarity?" asked Gor'sadén. Not that either of them had slept much. They had sat well into the early hours of the morning together with Prince Handir, discussing the finer points of a plan Fel'annár had revealed to them that very evening.

"Some. I admit this plan of Handir's seems optimistic and, dare I say, out of character? I had not thought him that invested in the Silvan people."

"You had not thought him capable of such a thing?" It was not really a question, and Pan'assár's hesitation was testimony to the truth.

"No. And that is more to do with me, I suppose. It is *me* that has changed. Now, I see a prince who wishes to pull our people together, strengthen his father's position on the throne and be rid of those Alpine Purists that Band'orán leads. I see a *prince*, Gor'sadén. I always discredited him for not being a warrior, underestimated him because he could not fight."

"Yet fight he must if he is to achieve all that. I had thought the conflict was among the Inner Circle, but he suggests it is the Royal Council itself that is turning against the king."

"I understand warriors, Gor'sadén, and warriors defend the land. We don't make the rules. If our Royal Council is tainted, then Handir is right to be worried. Thargodén has not exactly been a strong king these last years. He is vulnerable and the vulture surely circles his prey."

"Band'orán?" asked Gor'sadén.

"Yes. Who would have thought? My memories of him here in Tar'eastór are good, if not distant. He loved his brother back then."

Gor'sadén nodded, remembered him well.

"Fel'annár calls this plan *the Restoration*," mused Gor'sadén as he watched his Disciple miscalculate his defence, earning a tear in his pants. Gor'sadén's eyes narrowed, but it was Pan'assár who spoke, words that brought satisfaction to Gor'sadén.

"Careful, boy."

Careful, yes. Because Sorei was not in the slightest bit concerned for the integrity of her opponent's breeches, nor the further injuries she may inflict. She bore down on him, pushed him back, but Gor'sadén could see Fel'annár was no longer surprised. He could see his control.

"I had no idea the situation was as bad as it seems to be. I cannot fathom where your prince means to start in all this," he murmured. Gor'sadén had thought his journey to Ea Uaré would be one of teaching his Disciple the ways of the Kah Warrior, and those of the captain he strove to become. He meant to stay a while as Fel'annár met the family he did not know—his real father, his older brother, perhaps even his enigmatic sister. But now, he was left with the sensation of voluntarily walking into a volatile world of bigoted Alpine lords and angry Silvans, under the rule of a failing king.

A collective gasp from the onlooking warriors and civilians brought Gor'sadén back to the present. His eyes focussed on

Fel'annár as he parried Sorei's vicious onslaught. She was not holding back, even though Fel'annár *was*. He thought perhaps that his Disciple did not want to use the unfair advantage of the Kal'hamén'Ar. He wanted to face her on equal terms. He still didn't understand, realised Gor'sadén. The art was an integral part of the warrior, could not be separated from the individual. It was why he had failed that previous move. Discerning eyes registered every mistake and then committed them to memory, for later when they were alone.

The duelling elves came together, swords locking at the hilts, guards crossed and faces almost touching. Sorei's lips were moving and Gor'sadén could only imagine what she said to his Disciple. He smirked, wasn't wrong, and in three moves, Fel'annár held his long blade firm and steady over her right shoulder.

Enha'rei. Disarm, or lose your limb.

It was a move Fel'annár had learned just recently. It had cost him sleepless nights and obsessive repetition, and still, he did not always execute it correctly. Even now, Gor'sadén could see the blade a little too far to the right. Should he slice through her arm, it would not be a clean amputation. Still, it was enough. He had bested a Blade Master.

A call from the side lines and they stepped apart. Gor'sadén watched as Captain Sorei lifted her blades and slid them into the sheaths strapped to her back. She was a cool one—cool, foul-mouthed and stone-faced.

He didn't envy his poor Disciple. He would be holding his breath, wondering if he had passed.

"Foolish child," he muttered fondly.

Sorei bowed before her opponent. Fel'annár returned the reverence, and when he righted himself, he saw it. A leather armband, at the centre of which were two crossed blades. She smiled as she held it out to him, blue eyes glittering with emotions Gor'sadén could well guess at. Fel'annár plucked the band from her hand and then turned to his Kah Master, the brightest of smiles upon his extraordinary face.

Gor'sadén's heavy thoughts retreated and his own lips curled upwards. But before he could limp forward and congratulate his disciple, The Company converged upon Fel'annár, slapping and hugging him with their boisterous play and words of congratulations. He had passed the test for Blade Master, a necessary requisite for a Kah Warrior.

Gor'sadén damned his weakened leg. It should have been him standing there, congratulating his Disciple. Now, he would have to wait to tell Fel'annár that he was proud, later, when he could sit and rest his confounded leg that throbbed and ached incessantly.

He saw Prince Handir and Llyniel standing to one side of the crowd, clapping as they, too, watched The Company celebrate Fel'annár's achievement. Llyniel hooted in pure Silvan fashion, while Handir struggled to hide the look of pride that threatened to shatter his practiced, princely veneer. But Gor'sadén suspected he wouldn't have cared much, had it indeed cracked.

Sorei approached the two commanders, her step sure, almost predatory. They saluted.

"Commander. I have heard rumour that the Silvan warriors will be leaving soon." Her eyes drifted to Pan'assár beside him, who nodded.

"It seems likely, Captain."

She nodded curtly. "If you are still here, with time enough for another patrol, I would take him out under my lieutenant. The experience will do him good."

"It would," agreed Pan'assár. "But that is unlikely, Captain."

"A pity then," she said, eyes returning to Gor'sadén. "Still, should there be a change of plan, I ask that you remember my timely request." Nodding and saluting, she turned and strode away in a flurry of black and silver.

"How many *requests* does that make?" asked Pan'assár with a quirk of his lips.

"Twenty-two, or perhaps twenty-three." He shook his head and continued on the path towards the palace and the Healing Halls. "Comon lost Captain Rainor in the battle. Sorei is his closest collaborator now."

"She certainly has a commanding presence," murmured

Pan'assár, watching Gor'sadén, knowing he was trying not to limp.

"We will ride for home soon and I cannot help but wonder what has happened at court—how much the situation may have deteriorated; whether our forest still *has* a king. It is time to plan our return, Gorsa."

"How long before we ride, do you think?"

"Ten days I would say. After tonight's celebrations, we must study our route back and then leave. The weather is fine enough for the time of year."

"Ten days. I would not hold you back, Pan." He wondered if he should step back, allow Fel'annár to leave without him and travel later. But then he wouldn't be at Fel'annár's side when he needed him the most: when he met his father.

"You can walk. You can run. You can still fight better than any other warrior I know. Besides, Arané has said you can go, and you have me, for whatever I can do to help."

"I know, brother," said Gor'sadén tiredly, raking one hand down his face. "But how am I to teach the boy like this?"

"By teaching him. You could do it sitting down, with my help."

Gor'sadén's head shot to Pan'assár, eyes moving from one side of his face to the other. "You would do that for me?"

"And for him. He deserves this. I will no longer hold him back."

Gor'sadén nodded and smiled sparingly. "Then I will endure my daily torture with Arané. I will see you later, brother. Perhaps we can all just enjoy the evening. I have a feeling that from tomorrow, we will not get many more chances for a while."

Pan'assár nodded, leaving Gor'sadén to venture inside the all-too-familiar Halls, boots thudding irregularly upon the wooden floor. Yes, Gor'sadén would endure anything, for as long as it took, so that he could continue upon the road he had chosen for himself. To train Fel'annár in the Kal'hamén'Ar. To make of him the leader he was born to be. To accompany him back to a land that stood upon the brink of rupture and perhaps even war.

∼

THAT NIGHT, the newly elevated Blade Master stood high upon the balustrades, where the dead stood frozen in the Dance of Graceful Death. Only *he* was alive, and he looked down upon the people of Tar'eastór as they finally allowed themselves to celebrate their victory over the Nim'uán. Swirling lights, swaying bodies. The smells of roasting meats and fine pastries, rich wine and heady mead. The merry sights and the cloud of tantalising aromas wafted upwards and Fel'annár breathed them in.

His smile was sparing, indulgent, but his own festive mood would not come. Indeed, he had melted away from the merrymaking to stand here and look down on the world, to cast his eyes upon the ruined forest that had saved them all from the ravages of the enemy.

But *dead* forests did not whisper.

He listened to the timid voice in his mind, allowed the underlying emotions to seep into his own complex web of feelings. Grief and sorrow, and yet there was no regret, no echo of blame. Only finality.

It had been only yesterday when Fel'annár and The Company had taken to the devastated woods with spades and saplings brought from further afield, as per his request to King Vorn'asté. They had spent the entire day in the company of grateful Alpines, who had eagerly learned how to plant a tree, together with what had seemed to be the city's entire stock of children.

It should have been done before spring, Fel'annár knew. But then no one had wanted to touch the decomposing carcass of the Nim'uán. The gruesome sight and putrid smell had kept them all away, until a group of brave souls had beaten it down with sticks, wrapped it in filthy cloth and taken it away, off the path and out of sight. They had burnt it. A tainted patch of land no one would approach.

Carefree laughter, excited cries and cheers, merry music and clapping, and Fel'annár's mind turned away from the Nim'uán and to the Alpine people. They had bided their time, as no Silvan ever could. They had waited for news that Fel'annár would live, that Commander Gor'sadén would not lose his leg. They had waited for Commander Comon to secure the land, and they had waited for the hundreds who had died to be sent on their glorious path along the

Short Road to Valley. They had given time for grieving families to mourn, and then, they had heeded Fel'annár's call for their lost forest to be repopulated.

Fel'annár had then been summoned to speak at the Inner Circle, to answer the questions the captains had respectfully waited to ask. What had happened to the trees? What could he tell them of the Nim'uán? Of the Gas Lizard?

The best scholars had set to studying the Nim'uán's sword and its many etchings and engravings. There was script, symbols they did not understand, that would, perhaps, give some insight into where the beast had come from. Idernon himself had requested time with the blade, so that he could draw it and take a diagram with him. He wanted to study it, he said, decipher it if he could, and Sontúr had nodded enthusiastically at the challenge. But every time he mentioned it, Fel'annár would frown and Gor'sadén would turn to some other chore.

Finally, with the land secured, the dead mourned and the trees replanted, they had celebrated, and The Company had been honoured with more than thankful eyes and respectful bows. It had been Sontúr to pin the Silver Mountain upon their high collars.

Fel'annár's right hand reached up to the collar of his own tunic, index finger smoothing over a single sapphire. The king had named it Blue Mountain, the highest expression of bravery; a token of the gratitude of his people for acts of extreme heroism. It had not felt that way to Fel'annár at the time, yet even so, it made his heart swell. He had done his duty—nothing more, nothing less.

His finger moved forwards until it felt the cooler touch of silver. One long strip that occupied the rest of his collar, to the front of his neck. Pan'assár had given him this as a sign of office. The sign of a lieutenant. Silor had worn this and shamed it. Fel'annár swore *he* would do it justice.

He smiled, breathed deeply, felt the cool air fill his lungs.

He had felt it—the moment he had died. That timeless, breathless moment in which his own end had seemed so clear. He remembered a bone-deep sadness, for himself and his young, soon-to-be-sundered life. It had been too short, full of flighty dreams, few of which had become a reality. Funny. He had felt wise in that moment in which his heart still beat and yet his breath had ceased, lungs inert. His mind—all his memories and all that he was—had concentrated into one pinprick of light, heavy with sorrow, light with hopes for the future.

Questions.

And then he had seen her. She had bent low, and knowing blue eyes gazed down upon him for the first time in the waking world. He had only ever seen her in his dreams.

Aria had surely come to shepherd him upon the Short Road.

That glowing ball of emotions and experiences that was himself had shattered into a thousand shards, not icy cold like death but molten with the heat of life.

It was then that his lungs twinged and a long rush of cool air filled them. The light of his life was back inside him. Even as she smiled, he could feel it slipping into place, wherever that was. No, he would never forget that dawn, for in a sense it *was* a death—the death of Fel'annár the child, the inexperienced warrior, the resentful son, the angry boy with no father and a dead mother. He had come back a changed elf, for he had seen himself, seen it shatter and disperse and then regroup—differently—inside him.

He felt different because he *was* different. He had seen the face of Aria, protector of this world, and Fel'annár, as her servant, had finally understood what he was, who he must become.

He knew. But Llyniel didn't. Gor'sadén didn't.

Fel'annár's eyes fell on a lonely tuft of clover, growing through a crack in the stone. He reached out, took it between his thumb and forefinger and rubbed gently. His mind focussed and he remembered how he had decided that no one save The Company needed to know about the divine nature of the Restoration. But now, he knew it was wrong, an error born of weakness, a fear of rejection he no longer felt.

He had told Pan'assár of the Restoration and now, he would tell Llyniel, tell Gor'sadén what he had kept from them.

"Skulking in the shadows, Hwind'atór?" A mellow voice spoken through a smile.

Fel'annár's mouth twitched, eyes only half travelling to the newcomers, and although one of them was overly large, they made no sound at all.

"You should be down there, celebrating our victory," Fel'annár said, not quite out of his musings.

"As should we all. But you know the ways of The Company. We would sit together this night; it seems fitting."

"And you would know, Wise Warrior," murmured Fel'annár, striking green eyes finally landing on his childhood friend, Idernon the Wise. His smile widened fractionally and then he turned, first to Ramien the Wall of Stone, and then to Carodel the Bard Warrior. Beside him stood Galadan the Fire Warrior, and then Galdith the Fierce. Sontúr, Alpine prince of Tar'eastór, recently named the Winged Warrior, stood watching, mouth half-up-turned, eyebrow riding high on his forehead. They were seven warriors from three different races, but all with the same giving heart. They were brothers in every way that mattered, and Aria knew, Fel'annár would need them in the months to come.

He felt whole. He felt sure of himself and his duty. He felt wiser and calmer, even though he knew there was still a part of himself that was not complete.

He had not yet met his Alpine family in Ea Uaré, nor his Ari family in Abiren'á.

But he was not angry, not apprehensive or defensive about it as he had once been. All that had been washed away by battle, by the duty that loomed before him.

He was curious, he realised. Curious and willing. He *wanted* to meet them, however much he could not predict his own reactions when the time came.

Fel'annár's hand rested on one of the carvings beside him, wondered what the subject's name had been, how they had died. He felt like a living ghost amongst the glorious dead, one soul that strived to mastery in the Kal'hamén'Ar. But he still had one more weapon to dominate. Fel'annár had chosen the double-edged spear, much to the surprise of his Master.

He breathed deeply, gaze back on the mountains beyond. They were a reflection of his own life, the ups and downs, the hard rock, the cold snow and the odd smattering of green goodness.

Idernon broke away from the rest and came to stand beside Fel'annár. He looked down on the festivities, eyes alight with contemplative thoughts.

"Are you ready?" he asked softly.

Was he? he wondered briefly. Ready for what? The Restoration? Their return to the forest and his family? Ready for the Kal'hamén'Ar? And then he realised it didn't matter. Whatever Idernon had been referring to, there was no reserve, no trepidation at all, only quiet resolve.

"I am." He turned his head to face Idernon. He smiled as the rest of The Company joined them.

"Where's Llyniel?" asked Galdith.

"Down there," said Fel'annár, pointing with his chin. "Having fun with Handir."

"Are you jealous?"

"Not anymore."

"And are *you* going to have fun with her later?" asked Carodel with a snicker.

Fel'annár held his gaze and Carodel's grin faltered for an instant. "Perhaps," he said, turning away after a while, and Carodel shrugged.

He still hadn't told her that he was Ari, that he was Ber'anor. He hadn't found the right moment. But then, he realised, there had been many right moments and just as many failed attempts.

"I wonder what forest we return to, brothers." He walked forward and reached out to touch one of the crenellations, face cast outwards, a feast below and the still snow-capped mountains beyond. "It may shun the Alpines amongst us, turn against those who have ruled so unjustly these past years—and who would blame them? Pan'assár was complacent and those Alpine sons of lofty lords are the ones who have truly commanded our army. My only question is, will the

Silvans turn their backs on the king? Will they claim their independence?"

"That cannot be predicted. Not until we're closer."

"But the possibility must be contemplated, Idernon. The Silvans have been down-trodden for many years but that doesn't mean they're beaten. It's not our way; it's not the way of the forest. *They* fought for us." Fel'annár gestured to the recently reforested woods. "They fought and it was terrifying, but should I call on them once more, should I need them in Ea Uaré, this forest is minute in comparison to the vastness of the Great Forest Belt."

It was a sobering thought, and the ensuing question was whether Fel'annár would be able to control them, should it indeed come to more than words.

"One step at a time," said Idernon. "First, we must return home and find out what has transpired in our absence. It may not be as bad as all that. Common sense often prevails, in the end."

"Aye, but the question is," asked Sontúr, "how long will it take to prevail? And what will happen in the meanwhile?"

Idernon held the prince's gaze and nodded silently, conceding the point.

Fel'annár turned to The Company. "The night is still young. Shall we return to the celebration? Drink and dance away the night, leave our hefty thoughts for tomorrow at least?"

"That sounds just about right." Ramien smiled, slapping Fel'annár on the shoulder. The rest nodded and together, they left.

Just for today, this one night, he would seek nothing more than his own pleasure, together with Llyniel and The Company, in a land he never thought he would love. A land he had once hated, but was now sad to leave behind.

The Motherland. His father's land.

∼

Deep in the forest of Ea Uaré, on the road between Lan Taria and Oran'dor, three Alpine merchants struggled with their wagon. It was filled to the brim with forest produce they were transporting to the king's palace. One wheel was stuck between two rocks and they had dismounted, guiding the horse backwards and forwards in an attempt to loosen the trapped wheel. Others worked to keep the stacks of goods from sliding off the back. These goods had cost them good money, money they could not afford to lose.

"Push harder!"

"We're trying, Seila," ground out one of the three Alpines, pushing the back of the wagon with his shoulder. Their horse whinnied, disturbed at not being able to move forwards, even though an elf was tugging hard on her reins.

Seila turned to the sound of thundering hooves behind them. "Help at last!" he said, drawing himself up and waiting for the approaching group. But his face dropped no sooner he caught sight of them.

Bare chests and leather skirts, some with breeches. Painted faces and ornate bows jutting skywards from behind their shoulders.

Silvan rebels.

They had been warned of this itinerant group that had been hampering Alpine merchants, confiscating goods and threatening them, should they return and 'steal' from the Silvan people. But Seila and his associates had had no choice. They were not rich lords but humble merchants that needed to feed their families.

Seila stepped forward, an appeasing hand before him. "We need help, brothers. We cannot free our wagon."

"A wagon full of *Silvan* produce you have surely paid a paltry price for." A Deep Forest accent, sure and accusing.

"We paid what was asked of us. We are honest merchants, not thieves."

"You're Alpine," explained the leader as he slung one leg over the saddle and dismounted. His ten companions followed suit and they walked towards the small group of merchants. They were a daunting sight, feral and tribal in their scant clothing and colourful beads. "You're Alpine and you're not welcome in these lands you think you rule. Go back to your stone fortress and your puppet king and tell them. Angon of Ea Nanú will suffer no Alpine thieves in the hallowed forests of the Silvan people—not while they think to rule over us without our consent."

"We are not politicians, Angon. We are peaceful folk making an honest living," said Seila, hands out to either side.

Angon's jaw pulsed and his eyes narrowed. He walked until he was before the merchant, eyes glittering in mounting anger. "You do nothing while your leaders tread on my people. By doing nothing you are just as guilty as they are. You're happy to sit back and watch your Alpine rulers take what's not theirs. It doesn't concern you; it doesn't *move* you. You are not welcome."

Seila turned to his companions who stood staring at the group of strange Silvans. They had never seen the like and they were not about to intervene. Seila had been brave enough to confront them but none would gainsay the imposing leader.

"May we at least take our wagon and horse with us?"

"We'll help you with your horse, but the rest is ours." With a jerk of his head, the Silvans set to work and had soon freed the wagon of its confines and handed over the skittish mare. Hooking the cart up to one of their own steeds, Angon turned back to Seila.

"Where did you get this?"

"Lan Taria," replied Seila, rubbing a shaking hand against his thigh.

Angon gestured southwards with his chin. "Leave these forests, merchant. And don't come back. Remember. You're not welcome."

The group cantered away, their wagon clattering behind them and Seila turned to his companions, kicking at a bucket that had fallen from their confiscated wagon and sending it clattering into a tree. Blowing out a long breath of utter frustration, he scratched his head, and then turned to one of his two colleagues as he spoke.

"It gets worse by the day. First we're pelted with acorns and stones and now this. It's as if they've gone wild, reverted to elder days and ways. We must inform the Merchant Guild. This place is no longer safe."

∼

"Three merchants dead." Huren stood a general, boots planted firmly upon the fine rug beneath. There was no hint on his face of the blatant lie he had just told his king.

"The merchants resisted them?" A thoughtful voice from the wall of shutters that looked out over the Evergreen Wood.

"We don't know. Only that they were attacked on the road between Oran'Dor and the city. Our merchants may soon have to hire mercenaries if they are to extract produce from the forest and escape those Silvan rebels."

"Does Erthoron condone this?" asked Crown Prince Rinon from where he sat before the hearth.

Huren turned to the crown prince but it was the king who answered. "He can't contain them for much longer." Thargodén turned from his favourite spot at the window. "He is a good leader, but the Silvans have been pushed to the limit. The people demand action and yet we must wait for the votes to take place, try to contain this escalation as best we can."

"And meanwhile, Band'orán uses the situation against you. To many, it is the perfect reason the Warlord must not be allowed to return." Aradan paced, one hand swiping down his face, over his mouth.

"The Silvans were already turning on us," Huren said. "What will they do with a Warlord to fight for them?" He watched and waited for a reaction to his words.

"And I would tell our people that *we* turned on the Silvans first. It falls to *us* to fix this." Thargodén faced his general, eyes gleaming, crown glittering in the morning sun. Huren controlled his impulse to step backwards. He had seen Or'Talán, the king's father, for just a moment. But he would never tell Band'orán that.

Aradan closed his eyes and heaved a deep breath. "This is just what Band'orán needs. Conflict. This *Angon* has played straight into his hands. I would speak with Erthoron once more."

"He will not come," said Rinon. "He made his position clear. The

Night of a Thousand Drums was much more than a tantrum. It was a declaration of intentions. The time for talk is over. They wait for us to vote, and by the Gods, it must be for equality, for the return of the Warlord." Rinon stood and walked towards the general. "Because if it isn't ... we may be facing civil war."

Huren answered carefully. "Yes. I believe we will."

Rinon turned away from him, walking towards where his father stood. The forbidden Evergreen Wood sprawled away into the southern sky until the sea barred its journey, somewhere beyond the horizon. He almost startled when his father spoke, softer now, and Rinon wondered if Huren could even hear him.

"We need Handir here. We need all our assets, all our skill and all our wits if we are to pull this land back together; heal the damage I have done."

Thargodén's profile was strong once more, and yet there was a bone-deep sadness in his eyes—not for his lost soulmate but for his years of aimless wandering, years that Band'orán had used to grow strong, weave his lies, his half-truths. It was regret, and something else.

Rinon thought he knew what it was. Something he had never seen before in his father's eyes.

Fear.

Huren's status report had not been comforting, and later that afternoon, King Thargodén and Councillor Aradan sat on the lawn on the highest rooftop of the Royal Palace of Ea Uaré.

The king's private garden looked out over the Evergreen Wood, Or'Talán's gift to the Silvan people. It was their own piece of paradise, he had said. A forest prohibited to all save the Silvan foresters and those their leaders allowed inside. It extended from the back of the palace, beyond to the mountains and then the cliffs and the Pelagian Sea. It was a constant bone of contention with the Alpine Purists. They had once moved to keep the gates open to allow at least Thargodén's court to venture inside. But Thargodén had never allowed that, had never even agreed to discuss it.

No Deviants. No Sand Lords. Only Aria's creation, free to live and die as nature dictated. Perhaps that was why it was so beautiful, mused the king. Indeed, this was his favourite place, save for one. He would never go back *there*, not physically, because there was something missing. In his mind, though, he visited every day, because *she* was still there.

Lássira would have been happy here.

He felt the velvety skin of a cool leaf as he rubbed it between his fingers. It was a habit he had always had. His mother used to laugh and his father stare but Thargodén never worried about it. It comforted him, brought things into perspective.

Aradan stirred at his side, apparently tired of the report he had been reading. He breathed in and threw it on the lawn in front of him where he sat. Not tired. Angry.

"If only we knew *why*. He has no legitimate claim, cannot take the throne unless you and all your children are dead or incapacitated, and although I do not trust that snake, I refuse to believe he would go that far. He has always adhered to the law, though he manipulates it well, and makes a travesty of it at times."

"Rinon said as much. And if you were speaking to *him* now, he would tell you that Band'orán has not always followed the rules. He suspects him of much more than just conspiracy, Aradan."

"Rinon is quick to anger, sceptical beyond reason at times."

"And yet, he has come a long way these past few months. He smiles sometimes, even at me." Thargodén smoothed his finger over the leaf and felt peace settle around him.

"That is progress, yes. And I dare say he has shown where his loyalty lies. Before, in his need to reject you, his words were meant to hurt and to worry, where now he thinks and speaks wisely. Just yesterday he was telling me of what he had heard at the barracks. The same things I hear in our streets, the same lies Miren tells me of. Your son was angry, Thargodén. Offended, even."

"What do they say? Apart from that I am weak and lovesick."

"That your heart is not in it. That all you want is to take the Long Road and be reunited with Lássira. They say the kingdom needs a stronger ruler, that change must come if we are to stop the Silvans from rebelling and turning against us."

"All this from Lord Draugolé, I assume."

"Naturally. Alarm the people with talk of a weak ruler. Show them that chaos is coming. Frighten them into believing that change is *necessary*. A classic technique."

"It is working."

"Only if we let it, Thargodén." Aradan's eyes were lost for a moment, back to the days when Or'Talán was still king and his own master, Ileian, was Royal Advisor. "Your father used to walk the streets every Friday evening. And every Sunday he would ride out to Analei, stop along the way and speak to merchants. He knew everything that went on in the city, in the forest." Aradan stared at Thargodén's profile, waiting for him to react.

"I am not my father."

"No. But he was well-advised. He was loved in part because he was humble, spoke to the workers, not just the lords. He was invested in their problems, however trivial they were. They not only accepted him as a leader, they felt it too."

Aradan had loved Or'Talán, but the advisor knew not to mention him too much. Thargodén had worshipped his father, then hated him when he had prohibited his love for Lássira. No, he knew Thargodén could never forgive Or'Talán, but there were precious lessons to be learned, ones he knew his friend would understand. Still he watched carefully for the signs that his words had been well-received.

Thargodén smiled sparingly at his friend, understanding his trepidation, wondering what he would have done without him all these years. "Tomorrow. I will ride out tomorrow, with you at my side. And Turion. He has been involved in our plans from the beginning, knows about Fel'annár. Ask him to arrange a retinue."

Thargodén's lips twitched at the sudden turn of Aradan's expression. From satisfied to panicked. Still, the councillor nodded bravely in spite of the prospect of horseback riding. This was something the king had to do, and if his presence could somehow help his friend, then Aradan would do it gladly.

"Show them that Band'orán lies. Show them you are not weak and you are not pining. Show them you will not leave and that you will rule them, strong and steady, just as Or'Talán did. Whatever is happening out there, one thing remains, my friend. Our people are still loyal to the House of Or'Talán, even the Silvans. You can still turn this around."

Perhaps he could, so long as Band'orán adhered to the law. But Rinon did not think that he would, did not even think that he had. And maybe Rinon was right. Thargodén would play his uncle's game: appear to play by the rules, even if he did not. Sooner or later, someone would cross a line and the game would end. The question remained: how far would one elf go to gain absolute power? How far would the other go to stop him?

OUTSIDE THE CITY GATES, the Great Forest Belt pressed in on three sides. Well-used roads streaked here and there, wearing away at the forest floor. One led due north, the main route to Oran'Dor. Another led north-west and to Sen Garay. But the path eastwards led to the foot of the Median Mountains. It was a well-worn road, the main route the warriors would take towards the Motherland.

An hour's ride away, just off that path and hidden by a thick copse of beech and oak, sprawled a mansion of dark stone and carved timber.

Analei. Forest's Edge.

It had once been Or'Talán's second residence, one Thargodén had never wanted to use. Too many memories, he once said, and Band'orán well knew the power of those.

Inside the manor, grand stairs led down into storerooms, and a smaller spiral stairway led further still. Down and down they climbed, and then walked to the very end of a long passageway, until there was nowhere else to go. And yet, beyond the walls, was Band'orán.

He stood naked, save for his dark breeches and black boots. It didn't matter here, where no one except himself and his personal guard ever came. Upstairs he would entertain his lordly friends, all noble and ambitious. He would dress as was befitting his station. The finest cloth and leather, suedes and silks. Upstairs he was a lord destined for a throne. But down here he was already a king. King of black rock and crystal pools, commander of his own army, an army ready to lead him into the city in victory. They, too, were invincible.

He carefully placed the jewel he held upon a stark wooden table against a wall of bare rock. The reflection of candlelight in water dancing upon it, like a kaleidoscope, mesmerising and lovely. One finger brushed over the polished sapphire and he turned to face his underworld kingdom where everything echoed, his own memories and his own desires. Even time.

Lips stretched tentatively, eyes dancing over a statue of polished bronze that stood upon the gently lapping shore, icy waters beneath her feet. Colourful stalagmites jutted from it, like faithful worshippers. He walked towards her, one hand brushing over a cold limb, the purple sash of a Kah Master swaying around his black-clad knees.

Good morning, my queen.

2
GUIDING LIGHT

"A Divine Protector is gifted with a Guiding Light. It is another sense, a surety that cannot be explained."
Book of Initiates, Chapter IV. Sebhat

Splayed hands beckoned the dawn, called to its light. It seeped through the fingertips, up his arms and to his centre. He listened to the still tenuous voices of the distant forest, calm and serene; and then the stronger voice of the Winter Sentinel, deep and powerful.

Fel'annár had died there.

Green, purple and blue, subtle streaks of fleeting light, vaporous trails chasing around arms and legs as he moved, slow and precise. He saw everything, nothing.

Someone approached.

Knees bent, arms to his sides, head tilted to the emerging sun. He bowed to Aria, took a deep breath and brought the world into focus. With it came his own thoughts, their voices breaking the silence of the Kah Warrior.

He knew the lights were becoming stronger. Every time he weaved the Dohai they were more visible, and he felt stronger, moved more precisely the slower he performed the stances. But there was another development. The pain in his chest eased with every dawn, and he wondered. What would happen if he could somehow channel the lights, use them consciously? Could he heal himself?

There was the rhythmic clank of wood over stone, uneven steps, and the deep drone of energy that always seemed to accompany the one who approached. Fel'annár did not turn. He simply waited for Commander Hobin to stop at his side. Something moved in his chest, surged into his mind, and he wondered if it was Lainon.

"You dance with magic."

"Not magic. Energy. Aria."

Hobin did not react, and Fel'annár wondered if he thought them two separate things.

"We will soon be gone from here," said the Supreme Commander of the Ari'atór. "You to Ea Uaré and your destiny, and I to Araria, to investigate the Nim'uán. It has been an honour to serve in such times as we have shared."

Hobin had been central in his own transformation. Himself a Ber'anor, his purpose to help others understand their paths, help them to accept their destinies, and at the same time, allow them to reject them if they so wished. But Fel'annár hadn't, couldn't.

He half-turned his head, eyes registering the dark, severe features and the unnatural brightness of his eyes, the swirls and dots of dark ink that trailed down his chin, over his nose and across his forehead.

"I must bid you farewell now, Ber'anor. I leave for Araria tomorrow."

Before the battle, Hobin had said he would tell Fel'annár about Zéndar when the time was right. Surely this was the moment? He would not see the commander again any time soon, and he opened his mouth to speak. But then Hobin smiled and Fel'annár closed it, a soft scowl on his face. Hobin had every intention of telling him.

"I know you have questions—about your family, about your grandfather, Zéndar. Back when I first told you of him, you had yet to accept your duty. There were many things on your mind, many ways you could have interpreted my words." Hobin waited for a reproach, but it did not come. "Zéndar died performing his duty. He made the ultimate sacrifice, much as Lainon did. On the battlefield. Protecting me."

A wave of cold needles broke over Fel'annár's skin. Hobin was Ber'anor ...

"Yes. Zéndar was Ber'ator, *my* Ber'ator. A strange whim of fate that his Guiding Light should be here." He gestured to his head. "He would be proud of you, as are all the Ari'atór."

Fel'annár's eyes flickered wide. There was nothing but truth in Hobin's eyes. Truth and grief.

"When did he die?"

"Long ago, before you were born."

"And he's found himself?"

"Yes. Yes, he found himself many years ago. He gave his Guiding Light to me, just as Lainon gave his to you. I have learned to live with its presence, use it even. For you it is still new, but with time, you will learn. Zéndar was a great elf, Fel'annár, hardened though he was by the fate of his daughter, your mother. He struggled with his fealty to a king who had caused such suffering. Indeed, I know his entire family left Ea Uaré to take up residence in Araria. He lived there with his Connate, Alei, and his son, Bulan."

"And when Zéndar died?"

"They returned to Abiren'á, where I believe they remain. I have not heard from them in many years."

"Does his Connate blame you?" The words had tumbled from Fel'annár's mouth without his permission, but he wasn't sorry. He wanted to know.

"She did, at first. Once her grief was tempered, I believe she forgave me. But I knew then that the friendship we had once shared would forever be overshadowed by Zéndar's duty, the one that led him upon the Short Road."

"Tensári must feel the same about me."

It was Hobin who turned to face Fel'annár now, met his gaze for the first time since their conversation had begun. "She did," he confirmed. "But she is Ari'atór. She feels Lainon in her mind now that he has found himself. Alei is Silvan. She never had that comfort and never will, not until she passes through the Veil."

"Will you give Tensári my regards?"

"I will." Hobin's eyes seemed to flare, and the cold needles were back. "Have you told her? Have you told Llyniel that you are Ari'atór? That you are Ber'anor?"

Fel'annár froze. "Not yet."

"You already know that she needs to know. You must give her the choice of accepting you together with your circumstances, for they are inseparable."

"I know."

Hobin's stare lingered, knowing full-well how difficult it was going to be.

"So, unless they have taken the Long Road, I have a grandmother, an uncle, perhaps even cousins in Abiren'á."

"Alei and Bulan must surely know of your presence. That you have never met seems ... unlikely. And yet, that is the case. How your aunt achieved that I cannot say."

"Amareth hid me away."

"They *all* did, I wager. But when all this is over and you are free to meet them, I hope you will give them *my* regards."

"I will." He would. Well he understood the sense of guilt that lingered when a Ber'ator gave their life to save the one they were destined to protect. Hobin had clearly felt guilty, and Alei had scorned him for it. Tensári's face lingered in his mind, sharp features, eyes that spoke of grief and resentment. "Safe journey, Hobin."

"I will send word, once I have found the origin of the Nim'uán. I am unsure of where you will be, or how safe my message will be, so I will send it to the Ari'atór of Abiren'á. They will find a way to forward it to you."

Fel'annár nodded, but Hobin had not finished. "Your task is important to us all. A war between elves will give strength to the common enemy. You must not allow it, Fel'annár. Should you need aid, should you need warriors to see it done, you must call on me. Araria will ride in your name."

Fel'annár told himself it would never come to that. Once they were home, Handir would find a way to stop the conflict and restore peace.

And then the enormity of what Hobin had said hit him. The Ari'atór of Araria would heed his call for aid as if he were a general, a commander even. But he wasn't. He was a trainee lieutenant, and proud of that. He didn't know what to say, so he took one last glance at the lightening sky.

"Thank you, Hobin, for guiding me. For teaching me."

The commander nodded slowly, and Fel'annár returned the gesture. Unspoken words lingered in their eyes, some affinity they shared, some surety that they would see each other again. And so Fel'annár left in search of Llyniel, and Hobin watched him.

Tensári's face came to his mind's eye, and he murmured softly into the breeze.

Have you solved the puzzle, lieutenant? Have you understood your purpose at last?

Have you found your Guiding Light?

THE COURTYARD WAS QUIET. Many were still abed, and those who were not wandered about their business with puffy eyes and pasty faces. Some had not even made it to their beds. Llyniel hadn't. Fel'annár grinned, because after a night of drinking, dancing and fooling around, they had made for *his* bed ... only to fall asleep. She had not been there when he had finally awoken. It was not difficult to know where he would find her.

The sky was a dark blue, contrasting with the orange glow of candles upon windowsills. Soon they would be drenched in sunlight, the magical moment lost until the following dawn.

He ducked inside the Healing Halls, waited for his eyes to adapt to the gloom inside. Then he saw her from afar, bending over a patient, helping him to drink. He watched and smiled when she turned and caught his gaze.

Wiping her hands on her long, black apron, she approached him, head cocked to one side. "What is it?"

"Can we talk?"

She looked about the Halls, saw Mestahé sitting in a corner. "It's quiet enough. I won't be missed."

Grabbing her shawl from a hook beside the door, she fell into step with him, tired eyes on the path towards the trees. They walked to the one they both knew well. But as time passed and Fel'annár remained silent, she realised it was something important he wanted to tell her, something he did not quite know how to approach. "Breakfast will be late this morning. Perhaps now these people can find their peace once more. Move forwards."

"The trees have been replanted; the land restored as best it can be. But the memory of war lingers. It will take them a while."

She nodded, and then realised Fel'annár had come to her alone. He hardly ever was. "Where's The Company?"

"Ramien is probably stalking us even now. Idernon is studying, obsessed with the Nim'uán and its origins. He's made a drawing of its sword, a fine one mind. He stares at it, Sontúr at his shoulder." He smirked and Llyniel's eyes laughed with him.

"There's more though, isn't there?" she asked. Watchful.

Fel'annár nodded slowly. How he had tried to tell her before, so many times, but he had not dared. Telling The Company had been hard enough. Indeed, in the end, he'd had to show them.

"Come." He invited with a hand. She took it, and together they climbed the tree where they had first met, back when she had called him *Silvan* and he had called her *Healer*. They climbed until they were half-way up and out of sight, sitting opposite each other upon a bed of criss-crossing branches which made a natural platform, strong enough for them both and more. Around them, the branches seemed to close in, protecting them from the outside world, shielding them from prying eyes. Llyniel caught Fel'annár's downcast gaze.

"How many times does this make—five? Six?"

Fel'annár huffed as he smiled, shaking his head. "Was it that obvious?"

She lifted an imperious brow but her humour was fleeting.

"There is something you must know—about me—before we can move forward. It affects our relationship in a singular way. You may not even believe me, and this is why I hesitated."

She said nothing, but stared placidly back at him. It was time, to whatever end.

"I am Ari'atór." He said it so fast he had almost sounded annoyed, his words echoing in the space between them, even here amidst the boughs. He could see their meaning did not quite penetrate her mind. He knew why. She saw the pale face and silver hair of an Alpine elf, not the copper skin and black locks of a Spirit Warrior. "I am not mistaken, Llyniel. Commander Hobin has confirmed it, has welcomed me as a brother."

"Sweet Gods." A soft mutter meant only for herself.

"*Sweet* may not be the word. Why they saw fit to make me *pale* I cannot say. Still, I am Ari'atór and, as such, my duty stands before all else. Even my own life."

"Even before me."

"Yes. That, too."

She looked down, to the side and then back at him. "I've already accepted that, Fel'annár. Even had you not revealed this to me, I knew from the moment the Nim'uán came that I never had a choice in this matter. I love you and I can't change that, however important or otherwise I am to you."

He watched her eyes grow heavy, needed to correct her mistake. He leaned closer. "It is not about how important you are to me, Llyniel. I am Ari'atór and that makes you my Connate. What I feel for you goes far beyond the bond between soulmates. I can't change that, in spite of my duty, and even if I could, I never would. You see why I had to speak with you before we deepen our relationship?"

"Yes. Yes, I do," she said, rubbing at her forehead, struggling to accept what Fel'annár was telling her. "Although it's a little too late for that." She shrugged. "You have a penchant for surprising me. Is there anything else I should know?" she asked, eyes boring into him, but they were kind, if challenging. Fel'annár's hesitation froze her features. Her brow twitched, mouth slack.

A noisy breath. He dragged a hand over his face and then over lips. He looked at her, looked away and spoke. "We have never discussed faith, you and I. Do you believe, Llyn?"

She stared back at him and contemplated the odd question. "I believe there's a collective goodness, some energy I don't understand." Her gaze wandered to the wall of leaves around her, the incommensurate beauty of nature. "I sometimes think there's a higher entity, one that's good. At other times I say it's simply some inbred necessity we are born with, to do good, to be kind. And then I think of Sand Lords and Deviants, about the suffering they cause." Her eyes snapped back to Fel'annár. "I don't think that was the answer you were hoping for."

Fel'annár nodded slowly. He remembered having thought much the same himself. But it was one thing to accept the existence of an energy, or an entity as she put it, but quite another to accept that there was a thinking mind behind it. He was at the crux of the question.

"The Ari'atór believe that energy, that Aria, is a conscious entity whose purpose is to protect and to guide us. While you may not believe that, we do. And in that belief, we hold that there are those who do her bidding."

"You speak of the Ber'ator and the Ber'anor. Ari folklore."

"Not folklore, not to us. It's fact. Commander Hobin is Ber'anor."

"I don't ... I can't ..." She stopped, huffed and started again. "You're saying that there is a conscious, living mind behind the goodness. It implies purpose, Fel'annár. You are speaking of a *person*."

"I know. Believe me, Llyn. I've struggled with the concept for months now. It isn't necessary that you believe all this. But I do need to tell you."

"That Hobin is Ber'anor ... tell me, why is this so important to you?"

Fel'annár could see her eyes, questing for some knowledge she might read from him, to understand. He needed to speak more clearly. "He came to me, as is his duty as Divine Servant. His purpose is to guide others upon their path of service to Aria. He came to help *me*."

Her lovely honey eyes bulged, filled with unshed tears of shock for the sheer enormity of what he had said. She swayed backwards. "You believe yourself a Divine Servant?"

"I believe it. Hobin confirms it. Llyniel. I have seen the face of Aria. How can I deny her existence? How can I refuse the call of divine duty? I've always felt it, for as long as I can remember. I've always seen her in a tree, looking down on me, myself nothing but a babe. At first, I thought she was my mother but then I saw her, too, and they were different."

She stared back at him, and for the first time Fel'annár struggled to understand what she was thinking. For the first time he truly contemplated the thought that she might not accept him. That she might walk away from him. His stomach plummeted, almost felt sick, for the wait was unbearable. This very thing had happened between Lainon and Tensári, had separated them for a century. He startled at her soft and careful words.

"I understand that you believe, Fel'annár. You are Ari'atór. Faith is in your blood but I … I can't just believe it. I cannot conjure the image of an all-powerful entity that watches over us with a conscious mind. A divine queen, her divine servants … there's too much suffering in the world."

"Llyniel. Stop. It's not necessary. You don't have to believe it, but I did have to tell you. I've not lost my mind and I love you. It's why I hesitated to tell you before: because I understand your reaction and I was afraid to lose you."

He leaned back a little, felt the familiar warmth of Lainon's Guiding Light in his eyes. He braced himself for how she would answer his next question, now that she knew. "Do you accept me as I am? All of me, as your soulmate?" His voice was nothing but a whisper, the flow of power collecting at the doors of his mind, of his eyes, begging for freedom. The pressure was almost unbearable, the need to hear her answer agonising.

Her eyes danced from one side of his face to the other, eyes that were wide and bright with wonder and dawning understanding. Then he saw tiny pinpricks of light in her eyes, knew she saw them in his. He had no control over this rush of raw power that had invaded him. He stood on the brink of some bottomless chasm, or was it a roofless sky? His soul pounded inside him—agitated, desperate, and the lights shone brighter in her eyes. And yet she moved forwards, unperturbed, breeching the gap that separated them.

One, hot hand seemed to burn into his cheek.

"I accepted you upon the slopes of Tar'eastór, the day you would have selflessly given your life in service, even though I thought I knew I would never see you again. You have me, Fel'annár. My love for you is stronger than my own mind, stronger than my ability to stop this ... this force that is sweeping me away with you. I can't stop it. I don't want to."

He lifted a hand to cover hers, still on his cheek. He turned to kiss her palm, heart taking flight and soaring upon the currents of her answer. She shifted forwards until her knees touched his, her hands coming to rest on his thighs. His eyes burned hotter, a green haze falling around them, but she didn't turn away. She gazed back at him, and although he knew her doubts about Aria, so too did he see her love for him. Love and acceptance.

And wonder.

"We leave soon, and well you know there will be no time for us on the road. It'll be dangerous and we must all keep our wits about us. I cannot lose myself in you once we step out of those gates," said Fel'annár.

She leaned forward, pulling his face towards hers. Her lips were so supple, so slow as they moved over his. "Then lose yourself in me now, Ari'atór. Show me how you love your Connate. Bond with me."

His heart burst with joy and he wondered how it would happen— how exactly their souls would join. Was it enough to simply desire it? He looked at her with hopeful eyes, questioning eyes, saw her own doubts. She was just as lost as he was, and so he captured her lips once more. Soft at first, then hard and needy, driven by a soul-deep need for acceptance, a quest for that part of himself that would reach out to her. He could feel himself, body impossibly stretched, searching for her essence so that he could swallow it, feel her in his mind, bind her to him. He had never understood the concept of soul-mates, had never understood the nature of Connates. Yet now, all he could do was marvel at the power that surged, slowly vanquishing his will and pushing him dizzyingly towards a light that pulsed ever brighter.

A rush of something primal seemed to flow from him. She gasped and pulled away, eyes wide and disbelieving. Then she kissed him, pulling him against her, pressing their bodies as close together as she could. She was not Ari'atór, but she seemed to feel at least a part of what he did. They were so close Fel'annár could no longer focus. He leaned back a little until her features sharpened.

One hand was on his shirt, unclasping it, pushing it apart. His own hands were on her, loosening the laces of her simple dress, and when skin was upon skin and they sat entwined, Fel'annár looked at her through the haze in his eyes. He could see the same heat in hers, the same desire, the same storm that was wresting their control. He needed to see her eyes.

"Don't look away. Come bravely to me."

"You have all of me."

He could see the moment she steeled herself, opened herself to the energy that pulsed around them, and when it breeched her lowered defences, Fel'annár felt bliss as he never had done before. It engulfed him, cocooned them both, swirled and whipped around them until there was nothing else. Only pleasure.

He felt himself sink into her, her mind, her essence. All that she was opened to him. There was a bridge before them, one he knew he would never sunder, and he gasped at the rush of emotions. Her light penetrated his mind, shredding it, flinging it into the air, and he was changed. As the pieces fell into place, a surge of utter bliss carried him away.

Overwhelming.

Tears leaked from his eyes but he could not stop. His arms pressed around her as if he could push his whole body into hers, skin and muscle, blood and bones, and when she cried out, he followed, enduring the merciless storm that engulfed them both. It was mindless, primal, frightening and then uplifting.

It was sheer bliss.

She lay below him, chest heaving, brow furrowed, and in her honey-coloured eyes there was love mixed with confusion. Something beyond her conscious mind clamoured at the doors of comprehension. He knew this because he felt it too.

One hand reached up to smooth down one side of her head, swiping at the tears that had run down her temples. His own eyes searched hers, the lights now gone, and he wondered if she could see his own questions, his own confusion. She must have because she smiled up at him, then pulled him down for another deep kiss, and he lost himself in her once more.

It was akin to nothing either of them had experienced before. Strange that the simple desire to bond could elevate pleasure, turn it into bliss. That power he had felt, had weathered but had not been able to control. It was inside him, inside them both. How could he resist her now that she was inside him? How could he face the journey home without feeling this all-encompassing passion once more? And yet he knew he must. They had come together, sealed their bond with this act of love, the sweetest promise of a life together sometime in the distant future. To the Silvan side of themselves, they were wed, missing only the feasting and the celebration.

Was this what Tensári had felt with her Connate, Lainon? And his own parents, they had surely wanted this, but Or'Talán had forbidden it. Now that he had felt it for himself, his rejection of his grandfather, the elf he so closely resembled, grew even stronger.

To deny the union of two willing souls ... he could not fathom the cruelty. What had moved that king to destroy his own son's happiness?

He had been *Prince* Handir for two days, parading in his finest robes and his circlet of office. First had been at the medal ceremony, then at the reforesting and finally at yesterday's feast.

It was the end of weeks of the aftermath of the Battle of Tar'eastór. He had stood at Vorn'asté's side as he organised his kingdom, Lord Damiel never far away. He had listened to his father's commander general, made decisions, learned more of statesmanship in those few weeks than he had in the last six months. He had visited with Fel'annár on many occasions, their bond slowly forming, and he had even seen Llyniel, albeit on rare occasions when she was not required in the Healing Halls.

How different things would have been had that first kiss felt right. And yet he no longer wondered why it hadn't. She loved Fel'annár, and Handir ... perhaps one day he would find his own partner and understand what all the fuss was about.

He was exhausted, had hardly slept since the night of celebrations. He could have stayed in bed, of course—half of Tar'eastór had. But he had always been an early riser and so, in spite of the lingering dizziness from the wine and the liqueurs, he had risen from his bed to start his day. Gods, but had he danced last night? He thought he may have, repressing a shudder at the thought.

He threw himself into a comfortable chair, not far from the fire that always crackled in the hearth of his well-appointed guest rooms, and then cast an almost baleful glance at his desk and the work that had accumulated there. He hadn't touched a single parchment these last few weeks.

Guilt prevailed, and he stood with a groan of fatigue. Making his way to his desk, he sat in the leather-bound chair, back hunched and his head resting on the palm of one hand. His eyes focussed on the stack of long-abandoned parchments. The off-white, richly decorated sheets were his own, full of flowing dark-green script—ever careful, well-crafted. But the piles were not as neat as was his wont.

Not as neat as he had *left* them.

He frowned, leaned forward and peered closer. Between those familiar pages were lighter, thicker sheets, dotted with flecks of blue ink. His frown deepened, and he reached for the pile, hand peeling back the top layers to reveal the one sheet that had caught his eye. There were more underneath. Setting the other papers aside, he reached for the foreign parchments and brought them before his eyes. The warm, fuzzy feeling of having imbibed too much wine was suddenly gone, replaced by the tingle of icy needles as his eyes read, though his mind was slow to interpret the words.

'My Lord ...'

His breath froze in his mouth. He reached for the candle that burned steadily in the lightening dark, pulling it as close as he could without burning his own hair.

'We have yet to carry out the deed. There are certain elements we had not accounted for, some skill that helps our common enemy, and our best elves are changing their tactics to accommodate for this. Did you know, my lord? Did you not know he is a Listener?'

The frigid wave of some impending dread tore down Handir's limbs, burning his scalp and robbing his breath. Blood roared in his ears, and his heart hammered for freedom in his chest.

He stood in a flurry of fine robes, his frown turning into an expression of horror, and then glittering fury. Everything they had suspected ... His eyes read over the rest of the missive and to the end:

'My own son is overseeing the particulars. Once it is done, my colleagues and I will join you in Ea Uaré, pledge our allegiance to you as was our accord.'

It was not signed, but Handir was sure that, should they compare this script with Lord Sulén's, it would match. This paper, too, was not easy to come by. The mark of the House of Sulén was clearly visible in one corner.

He threw it onto the table and began on the next.

'My dearest son ...'

His father's script.

'There is a dilemma before us, a vote that must be taken, and I pray our Royal Council will indulge the demands of the Silvans for they are just ...'

He shuffled through the parchments, read the next one—Sulén's ink again.

'I have it, Ras'dán. I will bring it with us, for although it burns all those who touch it, it is our guarantee, should our new lord find fault in our deeds.'

Page after page, different dates, different dispatches.

'They call it Night of a Thousand Drums. It is the dawn of a Silvan insurrection. If those votes are not approved ...'

Handir called upon all his training, all his acumen and his self-discipline. He banished the haze of wine and feasting, and even as the sun rose, still he read. A servant visited, left, returned with breakfast and left again, and still, his eyes did not leave the papers that filed before him, one after the other.

Finally, he leaned back in his chair and stretched his sore muscles, breathing deeply as he smoothed one hand over his tousled hair.

Is it too late? he pondered. *Is my father still king?* How long did he have before Band'orán made his final move?

So many questions; only one surety.

They needed to leave.

Now.

The Company sat in stuffed chairs before the hearth in Fel'annár's rooms, just as they always did before breakfast.

"Where's Fel'annár?" asked Galdith.

Idernon turned to him, unconcerned. He knew his friend had slept here last night, with Llyniel, and knew he had left, Ramien in tow and out of sight. "He'll be standing before the sun, or with Llyniel."

Galdith nodded and then stretched. "Thank the Gods we're not on duty today. I feel like a squirrel caught in a dust devil."

Carodel wanted to cover his ears at the terrible simile, the ridiculous image it conjured, but his arms were not cooperating. "That's one way of putting it," he said, fingers rubbing at his temples. "The whips of Galomú are slashing at my brain. I can feel my own teeth in my head, throbbing in time with my eyeballs. They may explode and—"

"That's nothing compared to my belly."

"That's quite enough, Galdith, Carodel," interrupted Galadan. "We should find Sontúr and then get to breakfast. Commander Pan'assár will soon call for our return, and there is plenty I would do before we leave this place."

"The last time we made plans like that, we ended up fighting a battle with an elven Deviant," pointed out Galdith. "Perhaps we should stay indoors."

"The Nim'uán is gone. One less threat at least," said Galadan.

There was a tentative knock on the door. Galdith rose and opened it, coming face to face with a young guard. He smiled, then remembered that he shouldn't and schooled his face, embarrassed.

"A message, sir. From Prince Handir for The Company."

Galdith nodded, took the note and waited for the guard to leave.

"We have a message from the prince."

"Sontúr?" asked Galadan.

"No. Handir."

"Read it," said Idernon, turning from the fire.

Galdith opened the note and then looked up to the expectant Company.

"We are summoned to Prince Handir's quarters immediately."

Idernon glanced at Galadan and then at the rest. "I told you. Time to return. I wager they are giving us a week."

Carodel shrugged, and Idernon said nothing, but all of them smoothed down their dishevelled hair while Carodel swayed and grasped the back of a chair. And still, they said nothing as they made their way outdoors in search of Fel'annár.

They had just stepped over the threshold of the palace when they spotted him. For one moment, Idernon almost forgot the prince's summons. His best friend's face was glowing and at his side was a smiling Llyniel. His eyes travelled downwards to their intimately clasped hands and then upwards, to the braid each had woven in the other's hair, at the very front. Two twisted threads wound around each other, and to seal it, the Seven Wheels. Sontúr, one brow raised high on his forehead, was versed enough in forest law to recognise the Bonding Braid. Galdith grinned, while Carodel hooted, and behind the newly wed elves, Ramien beamed like a schoolboy with a honey cake.

Galadan just smiled. Alpine that he was, he had adopted the forest as his home, and he knew as well as the rest what this meant to the Silvan people. There was no law that could separate Fel'annár and Llyniel now. Even if their parents objected and denied them the bonding ceremony, in the eyes of Aria, they were already one.

THE GUARD at Prince Handir's door granted them entry, and The Company were soon standing in the living area.

The prince stood at the window, his back turned, and beside him stood the two commanders. Gor'sadén turned to Fel'annár, his greeting frozen upon his tongue. His eyes strayed to Llyniel at Fel'annár's side, watching as she moved away from him and made for the hearth.

Fel'annár crossed gazes with him, allowing his Master's scrutiny. It was something he and Llyniel would have to endure. That and the questions that would surely come. *Where is your ring?* The Alpines would ask. *Why didn't you celebrate?* The Silvans would ask. They would all just have to wait until there was time for a ceremony. It mattered little to him at that moment, whatever Gor'sadén might think. He had all he wanted: her love and her acceptance, in spite of her doubts. He jumped when Handir spoke.

"Please sit." Handir turned from the window to face them, and Fel'annár's heart lurched. Handir was not worried; he was shaken and, for the first time, dishevelled. "Every one of you here is sworn to secrecy, answerable to the crown of Ea Uaré. I want your oaths, all of you. What is discussed in this room will stay in this room."

Fel'annár frowned and watched as one by one, the commanders, Llyniel and The Company nodded. He, too, bowed at Handir and then watched as the prince stepped forward. Fel'annár could see creases in his tunic, the messy braids, and his heart sank even further. He chanced a glance at Llyniel and saw her confusion.

"I am an early riser, and perhaps by some trick of the light, my eye was drawn to my admittedly cluttered worktable. I found *these*," he said, holding up a number of parchments in one hand. "Letters from my father, from Lord Aradan, Captain Turion and Lord Erthoron. It is the correspondence we have been waiting months for."

Handir's audience remained utterly silent, watching as the prince stepped further towards them. "There are other missives, unfinished correspondence I believe to be from Lord Sulén. He speaks of a target not yet dealt with. A target who is a *Listener*. He speaks of a pledge he has given to this unknown lord he writes to, and he speaks of some item, a guarantee, should his deeds be judged insufficient."

Pan'assár was almost as rigid as Gor'sadén, but Handir had not finished.

"Commander Gor'sadén. Can you arrange an extensive search of Lord Sulén's residence? In answer to any questions, we must simply say he is suspected of some malpractice, nothing more. It is my hope that more papers such as these may be found, something that may show beyond the certainty of my mind that the receiver of these letters is Lord Band'orán."

"And what of Sulén himself, Prince?" asked Gor'sadén, eyes blazing.

"He is not here, Commander. I have made some preliminary enquiries. Neither he nor his son, Silor, have been seen for many days. Lord Ras'dan is also missing. They must be aware of the theft, and I wager they are already on their way to Ea Uaré to fulfil this pledge—to Band'orán, we must assume. In any case, Sulén will be frantic, wondering who stole these documents and why. He will be concerned at not having fulfilled his part of the bargain. For not having killed Fel'annár."

Fel'annár stared at the prince, mind struggling to piece together what he had said, the implications. He needed to ask. "Why is my death so important?"

Handir nodded slowly, walking towards Fel'annár. "During the first Forest Summit, which took place in our absence, the Silvan people brought forward two requests. One was for equal Silvan-Alpine rule on the Royal Council. The other was the reinstatement of the *Warlord*. They want Fel'annár to be that figure."

Llyniel and The Company gasped, while Fel'annár stared back at him, eyes cool yet full of questions.

"Those votes are imminent. The Silvans understand that both their requests may well be denied. Lord Aradan says they linger outside the gates, that they refuse to leave until the votes are taken. Lord Band'orán realises that Fel'annár is the unifying factor, a figure who will make the Silvan people strong, give them a power Band'orán does not want them to have. *This* is why they want him dead. A unified Silvan front is not what Band'orán needs. And so he orders his conspirators to kill him."

Fel'annár slowly shook his head while Idernon's hand rose to the pommel of his longsword. Llyniel looked at her lover in concern, his own eyes latching onto hers.

Galadan spoke up. "My prince. Whoever put those missives on your desk may be able to provide us with names. Is there any indication as to who it might have been?"

Handir smiled tightly. "I don't know. Your guess is as good as mine. Obviously, it was someone who was angry with Sulén, someone skilled in the arts of theft and stealth. Whoever it was, their argument was our gain."

There were nods around the room, but Fel'annár was only half listening. The Silvans had requested the return of the Warlord. They had named him specifically, and the suspicion was firmly planted in his mind. How long had the Silvans been planning it? Was that why Amareth and everyone else had lied to him? Not to protect his life, but also to protect their own futures?

Pan'assár's voice was strong and assertive enough to pull him out of his dark thoughts. "If Sulén is travelling to Ea Uaré, he has a head start, and he surely knows his correspondence is missing. He has fled to his lord in Ea Uaré and has failed in his attempt to kill Fel'annár. I do not think he will simply walk in and tell Band'orán this. He will endeavour to carry out that promise to his lord before Fel'annár can return to the forest. Otherwise, he will return a failure."

"Agreed." Gor'sadén nodded. "We cannot take the main road back."

"No. Now listen carefully," said Handir. "We need time to prepare, to understand how we must travel and what route to take. Under different circumstances, I would suggest a forward scouting party to determine the situation, but we have no *time*. I must be back before those votes take place. We need to plan a route, but we must ask ourselves, how far gone is the conflict between Silvans and Alpines? Will we be free to travel through the forest? Is it even safe to do so?"

Pan'assár nodded. "My prince. I suggest we meet at sundown. We need maps, we need the latest reports on the two major routes back to Ea Uaré, and once we understand which is our best road, we need provisions. Commander Gor'sadén?"

"You will have them, Commander, Prince."

"And I must speak with King Vorn'asté and Councillor Damiel," said Handir. "But heed me, all of you: I would leave Tar'eastór in three days or before if we can."

As preparations for departure began, Sontúr, Pan'assár and Gor'sadén stood in the library of Lord Sulén's abandoned residence. Sulén, Silor and Ras'dan had, indeed, already left, and had an unknown head start on them. It was enough to ensure that the missives could not be used against them, at least not here in Tar'eastór.

They had seen signs of panic. Displaced books, papers strewn about the place. They found burnt parchment in the grill and empty drawers left open. This was no planned absence but a hasty retreat.

It had been Sontúr himself who climbed the mobile ladders that reached up to the highest level of the vaulted ceiling. He had stayed there for hours, pulling out books, reading their titles, looking behind them while Gor'sadén and the other guards searched the furniture and the many nooks and hidden doors they had found. They discovered a trap door, which Gor'sadén had ordered searched and then Sontúr had called down at them from the heavens.

Maps. Maps of Ea Uaré, villages, their population, the ruling house of its leaders and the natural resources in the area. Important buildings were marked and connecting roads clearly drawn. But it was the village of Oran'Dor that had drawn Pan'assár's eyes especially. Through its name, a long, stark line had been drawn, and over that, another replaced it.

Sulén'Dor.

There were notes in the margins, of thanks to Band'orán for his generosity, of his ongoing loyalty. It was one more indication, one more incriminating circumstance; but it was not proof of Band'orán's treachery, not quite.

Pan'assár shook his head. They were planning to carve up the forest, take it from the natives and reshape it, rename it, suck it dry. They had never understood why Or'Talán had ridden that day, in search of new lands to colonise. But Pan'assár had known the mind of he who would be the first king of Ea Uaré.

He had never wanted to dominate the natives. He had never wanted to take anything away from them, but rather to give them what he could. Roads, buildings, a new way of legislating, of commanding an army and defending the lands from an enemy that sought to overrun them.

It had never been about gain or power.

Sulén, the thought of what he was trying to do, how he would make a mockery of those honourable intentions ... it boiled Pan'assár's blood. He could still see the faces of those captains who had followed Or'Talán. Dinor, Bendir, Ileian and a young Captain Band'orán. How he had looked up to his mighty brother. How he had loved him. How he had betrayed him.

He closed his eyes. Felt sick.

Why did Or'Talán's brother now covet the throne? Did he not have all the wealth and renown he needed? Why would he turn against the legacy of his kingly brother and strive to oust his own nephew from the throne? Was it simple lust for power? But Pan'assár already knew the answer.

They *were* missing something.

3
THE MIND OF GODS

"All Ber'anor have a purpose, but that purpose is always to protect. That is the nature of Aria. To unite a forest at war was an admirable goal, just and good. But what was Aria thinking? Was there a purpose beyond the Restoration?"

The Alpine Chronicles: Cor'hidén

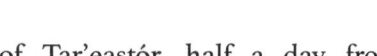

To the south-west of Tar'eastór, half a day from the Glistening Falls, Lord Sulén sat in his tent.

They had fled in haste, had shoved anything and everything of importance into cloth satchels and loaded them onto their horses. Everything except his most prized possession. One hand reached up to his chest and patted the object under his tunic.

He still remembered the day on which the Gods had seen fit to reward him, deliver him. It was the day on which his father died.

The venerable Lord Ileian had bid his son come to him alone, and in those final minutes of his life, Ileian handed him the journal. Sulén had taken it in his hands and his father, with a strength that belied those last moments of life, had bid him listen well.

'Guard this with your life. Let no one know what it is. This is your lifeline, Sulén. If you are to follow Band'orán, remember this: he is not Or'Talán. Your new lord will be generous with you, so long as you are useful to him. Loyalty means nothing to him except as payment for your service. But should he turn away from you ... if you must follow Band'orán, this is your lifeline, Sulén.'

He hadn't understood at the time. His father had passed, and he had inherited everything—everything except his loyalty to the king of Ea Uaré. He had thought it was his father's own journal. How wrong he had been.

Not Ileian's, but Or'Talán's.

Precisely, it was Or'Talán's fourth and final journal. The last words of the great king before he had been cut down at the Battle Under the Sun. It had taken Sulén a while to work out its importance, but he had done, eventually. It was, indeed, Sulén's lifeline; his guarantee that Band'orán would not harm him should he fail to kill the bastard, should he fail Band'orán in any way.

Still, he would not tempt fate. Silor had failed to kill the Silvan in the city, but the bastard could not escape Sulén's mercenaries. The time it had taken him to see to things had been a risk but a worthy one.

They had stopped at Senge. Sulén did not care much for its lord. Tenbar was a soppy old fool with the face of a child. Still, he was a respectable Alpine with more money than he and Ras'dan put together. Why he had accepted the government of that river village that smelled of fish and rotting vegetation he could not quite understand. Still, Sulén had needed those few days to coordinate his efforts, send his elves out and issue messages to others further afield.

By the time Sulén took ship to Port Helia, the boy would be dead. Even now, they were watching the path over the mountains, down the river, lying in wait and upon the shores of Tar'eastór and Ea Uaré. They sat in taverns and mixed with the underworld, listened to every piece of gossip and hearsay.

He watched his own group of mercenaries from the open flap of his tent, saw Ras'dan's identical tent just over the way. They sat around fires, cooking and eating, grunting and shoving at each other. Elves of few words, ruthless and unscrupulous. All they cared about was money—money and reputation, because their successes meant a higher cache for the next bidder. He knew them well, or thought he did until Macurian had turned on him. The Shadow had stolen his jewels and his papers. Band'orán had it right, secretly training his own warriors, his own army for what was to come. But only *he* had the skill to achieve that. Sulén had never been good with a blade.

He shut the tent flap and turned to the table laden with sumptuous goods. Exotic fruit and tangy cheese. A bottle of his finest wine lay open, half-consumed. Sulén always travelled in luxury, even when he was fleeing.

He reached for the wine, poured it into his jewelled goblet, and then started at the yell of a guard. His wine sloshed dangerously, and he frowned. Standing, he made for the entrance, irked at the interruption, and peeked outside.

His mercenaries were scrambling to their feet, strapping on their weapons. He saw Silor rush past the tent, shouting his own orders.

Ras'dan was nowhere to be seen.

He backed away, looked around him. They were under attack, and Sulén was no warrior. He saw a knife on the table, sitting next to a hunk of his favourite cheese. He lunged for it. Then his back hit the tarpaulin, and he stood on shaking legs. He could hear shouting and the clashing metal. And then he heard it. The unmistakable wailing of Deviants.

He paused, breath uneven, noisy, heart banging against his ribs, stupid knife in his clenched fist. The battle beyond the tent was frenzied. The screaming and wailing chilled him, the shrieks as his mercenaries fell. And then there was nothing but a ringing echo.

Silence.

His heart beat wildly. He was panting, sweating, staring wide-eyed at the tent flap. The off-white cloth, expertly oiled, was pushed aside by a grey and mottled hand. A towering figure stepped inside. The stench made his eyes water, but so, too, did his fear. The blurred

Deviant stepped closer, head cocking from side to side as if it struggled to understand something. It raised one hand, clutching at the blond hair of a head it had severed, and held it up for him to see.

The face of his son swam before him, words of grief upon his tongue, refusing to spill over quivering lips. But then fire seared his neck, heat spread down his front. He was choking, and couldn't understand why he could see the fire vent through the roof.

The Deviant watched as the elven lord's head slipped backwards and his body fell to the floor. He grabbed Sulén's head and left the tent, turned to his tribe and watched them work for a while. It was a glorious sight that made his black heart sing. Immortals, dead and mutilated, headless. It was just as exhilarating as his commander had said it would be.

They hoisted the bodies up into the stinking trees and impaled their heads upon wooden stakes driven into the ground. A whole line of them, and behind, their bodies hung, just as the warriors of Tar'eastór had done to their own kind.

He spared one last look at the elven lord's head, bloody mouth round with surprise. He smiled, wanted to laugh but couldn't.

His beautiful commander would be pleased.

As the sun began to set, Handir, Llyniel, the commanders and The Company stood around a large table that had been set up in the prince's sitting area.

"I wonder at the wisdom of returning over the High Path," began Pan'assár, turning to Gor'sadén, Handir and The Company. "It takes us into the heart of the forest. There will be little escape should the situation escalate. Our company is predominantly Alpine, not to mention we travel in the company of princes of the Motherland and Ea Uaré. If the Silvans have turned hostile, that route is unsafe." He leaned over the large table on which a detailed map had been spread, held down by stones and candles.

"But surely they would not rebel to the point of conflict," said Fel'annár.

"Why so sure, Lord Fel'annár?" asked Handir, turning from the hearth and approaching the table, eyes fixed on the Median Mountain range. "To me, it is clear that it is in Lord Band'orán's favour to instigate violence. By destabilising the kingdom, he will strive to show my father's incapacity to deal with it, and we all know who he would propose as an alternative. But the Silvans cannot see this. They do not know Band'orán as I do. They will rise to the bait, believe those lies, because there is no reason not to."

Pan'assár's gaze lingered on his prince for a while before he nodded and continued to reason out where and how they should return. "Well said, my prince, and I concur. I would suggest avoiding the Path and travelling further south, along the Cor'hidén to the sea. From there, we take sail westwards to Port Helia."

"But that is a busy place, Commander," began Sontúr. "We will surely be recognised. And the descent from the Glistening Falls is, shall we say, renowned for its perils. The human bones that litter those shores are a testimony to that. And if that were not enough, those lands are riddled with jewel bandits, thieves, pirates further down the cliffs. There are also Cave Deviants. Oh, and *Hounds* towards the end of the descent here."

"Hounds are better than mercenaries, Prince," said Pan'assár.

But Sontúr was not convinced. "If we take the High Path, we will find Mountain Deviants along the way. It will lead us to the heart of a forest that may not welcome Alpines, and true, Fel'annár here will be recognised. If we travel the Cor'hidén and to the Glistening Falls, we risk the wiles of nature, Hounds and human bandits. And still, Fel'annár will be recognised. At least in the forest he will have allies, where in Port Helia, it is the Alpine merchants who will recognise him. Allies, I think not."

"The risks are balanced, Prince. But the southern sea route takes two weeks off our travelling time. The question is, do we risk it for the sake of arriving sooner?" asked Pan'assár. He barely had time to rake his eyes over Gor'sadén, The Company and his prince, for his answer lay in Handir's eyes.

"We must. These missives were written some time ago. That vote is imminent, but with some luck, we will arrive in time. Time is the key to our success. Risks must be taken for the stakes are as high as they can be. I say we travel south, and we do it unannounced, anonymously. An Alpine lord and his retinue of courtiers and warriors, or perhaps merchants, travelling together for added security."

"And if the Alpines recognise Fel'annár?" asked Galadan.

"Then we are lost," said Handir. "As long as we hide that face," he pointed at his brother, "then the sea route is our best option." He turned to Pan'assár. After a while, the commander nodded.

"We will need civilian clothing and travel horses, not chargers; and coin to commission boats. We will be merchants, cartographers, craftsmen come together to make the trip from Tar'eastór to Ea Uaré in search of new trade. Travel time ... say eight days to the cliffs and then another to safely descend the Glistening Falls. From there, we commission a boat from Bulls Bay—here—to Port Helia—here. Three days aboard will see us there. We find discreet lodgings and horses to navigate up the estuary and to the city. If we are lucky, three weeks will see us home."

"And once we are there, how do we get in? Do we show ourselves or spirit in unannounced, with a prince of the realm, a son of King Vorn'asté, a Silvan would-be Warlord and two of The Three?" asked Sontúr, one brow acutely arched.

"I do not think we can decide on the manner of our arrival just yet," replied Pan'assár, resisting the urge to snicker at the prince's sarcasm. "Perhaps once we are closer, the information we are missing will tell us the best way. Publicly or secretly, to the palace, to the Silvans, or perhaps even separately."

Handir nodded. "Then we have a plan, at least until we are in the forests once more. We travel in the hope that more will be revealed to us as we progress. We may be able to arrive normally, report to my father and prepare for the votes, if they have not yet taken place. But should the conflict be worse than we imagine, then we enter in secrecy and gain the upper hand from Band'orán. The element of surprise may prove pivotal."

"I will see to our provisions, Prince," said Gor'sadén. "You are sure you do not wish for more warriors?"

"I am sure, Commander. We need to pass unnoticed without drawing attention to ourselves. We need to move fast, mingle into the crowds at Bulls Bay and Port Helia. Guards would give us away." Handir's gaze crossed with Pan'assár's. The commander nodded.

"I will prepare the medical supplies for the journey," said Llyniel. Handir nodded at her and then turned to face them all.

"We must move quickly, and although I understand the need for safety, the news we bear must reach my father before Band'orán makes his final move. There is no guarantee it will be enough, but it will be sufficient to cast serious doubts on Band'orán's motives. He must be stopped, else we return to a forest in which I am no longer a prince; in which a tyrant rules. That will bring war to Ea Uaré. Of that, I have no doubt."

"We will make sure that does not happen," said Pan'assár, stepping forwards, and Fel'annár nodded, The Company steadfast beside him.

And so, their path had been set, as much as it could be with so much uncertainty. Fel'annár watched quietly as the commanders left, met Gor'sadén's inquiring gaze as he passed, smiled at Llyniel as she made for the Healing Halls once more, or so he supposed. The Company made for the door, but they stopped and turned, wondering why Fel'annár had not moved. He gestured to them with his head, watched them leave, knew that they would be right behind the door.

He turned to Handir and found him staring back.

"You could travel without me, Handir. I can take an alternative route. My presence on this journey will place you in danger."

"I am already in danger, Fel'annár. And yet I think your presence will be more of a benefit than a hindrance. You, together with the commanders, are our best warriors. I believe we should weather that danger together."

Fel'annár nodded. He made to leave, but Handir spoke again. "And I would be there ... to introduce you to our father when the time comes."

Fel'annár searched Handir's eyes, but all he saw was quiet resolve and a subtle smile.

"Congratulations. You have bonded with an extraordinary elf."

Fel'annár's smile was so wide his cheeks ached, and for one moment he wanted to step forward and hug Handir. But he stopped himself and instead, he stepped back, bowed in heart-felt thanks. And then he left.

THAT NIGHT, Fel'annár and The Company sat at the fire, talking quietly of Handir's revelation and what it meant. But Fel'annár was restless and did not hear Galadan's question.

"I think he'd rather be somewhere else," said Carodel, gesturing with his head to Fel'annár, watching as he shrugged.

"I spoke to Llyniel yesterday," he said absent-mindedly.

"You did more than that," said Carodel with a soft snort.

Fel'annár's grin was fleeting. "I told her. Everything."

"Oh." said Ramien, nodding slowly. "Well, she seemed to accept it well enough."

"She doesn't think me mad, at least." He stood, unwilling to share her scepticism with The Company. "I am going to Gor'sadén's chambers."

"Not alone."

"Of course not." He was peeved and wanted Idernon to know it, but the Wise Warrior said nothing. He simply followed his friend as he made his way to the commander's quarters. Once there, Idernon arranged himself on a bench outside, stubbornly watching as Fel'annár disappeared into the room.

He found his Master sitting in his favourite chair beside the hearth, staring into the fire he had just stoked.

"How is the treatment progressing?" asked Fel'annár, watching as

Gor'sadén leaned back, stared up at him, then gestured to a chair opposite. Fel'annár sat, enjoying the warmth of the fire for a while.

"The treatment is painful. Granted, it is fleeting, and tomorrow it will be somewhat better. You, however, do not seem so troubled with your injury anymore." The commander looked at him with appraising eyes.

"It does bother me, but I swear there's something about the Dohai that is mending it. In fact I wanted to ask you about that. When the lights come, it's as if they flock to the damaged muscles and bone. I can almost see it in my mind, like a cauterising fire, like a soothing balm. And then I wonder if it's just my imagination, fooling my mind into thinking these lights have some real impact on my recuperation."

"It is an interesting theory," said Gor'sadén. "There are stories of the elder days, of Kah Masters who could ease the passing of fatally wounded brothers with some sort of energy transfer. But that was before my time. There are some mentions of it in the Warrior Code, in the annexes, I believe."

Fel'annár committed that comment to memory, for future research.

"There may not be time to continue with your training until we are on the road. There are arrangements to be made at the Inner Circle before I hand my duties over to Comon. But we must not forget the Enha'rei. It is not yet right."

Fel'annár knew that. The flurry of movements that were required before the final strike always left him a little unbalanced, enough to displace his blade over bone instead of cartilage. He almost jumped when Gor'sadén spoke.

"Why did you really come?"

He blew out a breath, squared his shoulders and looked straight at his Kah Master. "I ... I've held back from you, partly because circumstances did not permit and partly because I needed time—to come to terms with something I learned only recently."

Gor'sadén nodded encouragingly, although a slight frown marred his brow, eyes searching his Disciple's troubled face.

"Despite appearances, I am ... *Ari'atór*." Fel'annár kept his eyes trained on his Master, watching his frown deepen as the news sank in. In the silence that followed, while Gor'sadén pondered, Fel'annár studied the view of the mountains beyond the windows, resisting the urge to fidget.

"How did you discover this?"

"It was Commander *Hobin* who told me," he began. His gaze shifted from the mountains to Gor'sadén. Whatever he had expected to see, it was not this.

Dawning understanding.

"And you agree with Hobin?"

"There can be no doubts, in spite of the colour of my skin. My dreams, my traits as a child, even my hair." He huffed. He was talking too much. But Gor'sadén said nothing, and so he continued. "I don't doubt it. And yet, can you imagine, Gor'sadén? Thinking you are Silvan when in fact you're Alpine; thinking you're male, only to realise you're female? Or believing you're a bear only to grow wings and discover you are an eagle? It's disconcerting. Passing strange."

"I can only try. I do understand, I think." Gor'sadén turned to the fire, his face unreadable. "I wish you had found the time to tell me sooner."

Fel'annár turned his eyes to the ground and nodded. Gor'sadén was right. "And for that, I am sorry. When I gave you my promise of honesty, I never thought I would be told I was Ari'atór. I could never have imagined that."

"It was certainly unlikely. Is that why Hobin came personally to Tar'eastór?" Even as he asked the question, something dislodged in Gor'sadén's mind and floated to the surface. It carried with it remembered words from the night Fel'annár had asked him to be his father.

It is the dawn of a legend.

He hadn't understood why he had thought that at the time, but now he knew his own destiny was about to be unveiled.

"In part." Fel'annár paused and swallowed. "It's taken me time to understand—to believe, even—and yet the implications of my own words frighten me. I don't want to lose your regard ..."

"You won't," said Gor'sadén, impatient at last, cutting off Fel'annár's words. "You won't. We are past that, Fel'annár. We died together, in a sense. There is little more intimate than that. You called me *father*."

Fel'annár smiled sadly, eyes back on the land over the commander's shoulder, though not really seeing it. "I meant it."

"Then you must also feel it, Fel'annár. Whatever you say cannot change my regard for you. I am here to listen, to understand if I can, but not to judge. That is what fathers do."

The world felt lighter to Fel'annár in that moment. His burden of responsibility somehow lessened as he thought of the steadfast presence of this mythical warrior who had somehow, to his own great fortune, accepted him as a son. Whatever happened now with Thargodén, Fel'annár would hold on to this, remember this. It was time to speak.

"Hobin is Supreme Commander of the Ari'atór, but he serves another purpose, has another duty—one Aria has charged him with."

Gor'sadén stared back at him, eyes moving from one side of his face to another. "Hobin is Ber'anor?" he asked softly.

Fel'annár held the commander's gaze, now steady and confident, relieved that his mentor understood Ari lore, that he didn't have to explain. "Yes. You once told me that you trusted me, and I ask you to remember that now. I need your implicit trust. I need your silence to all save The Company and Llyniel."

Gor'sadén looked at him as hard as he ever had. "You have both."

"Hobin came to Tar'eastór to help me. Inquired as to whether I knew. It is his task, you see, to guide others on their path of service to Aria."

A cloud of brilliant blue passed over Fel'annár's left eye, and Gor'sadén swayed backwards, eyes wide. Then a rush of scenes and words, of expressive eyes and careful tongues, came to him. He saw Hobin in the Map Room, skirting around his questions. He saw

Fel'annár's thoughtful face and the lights in his eyes. But mostly, he remembered the next part of those words he himself had uttered.

'It is the dawn of a legend. I will see it done.'

"Holy Gods ... you, are Ber'anor?" he whispered, eyes overly bright in the gloom. Thoughts rushed at him, flowed from his mouth. "So Lainon was your Ber'ator? And that blue light in your eyes is his Guiding Light?"

Fel'annár nodded slowly. "This is all so ... illogical. Gods and divine tasks, dreams, apparitions. A web of unlikely coincidences. My mother's father was Hobin's Ber'ator; my grandfather's presence in the eyes of a Supreme Commander, Lainon in mine. I sometimes wish I was more like Idernon and Sontúr. Sceptical, devoid of faith, so that I could search for a more plausible explanation for all this."

"But you can't."

"No. There is something in my nature that does not permit it."

"No Ari'atór questions faith, Fel'annár. As a Spirit Warrior, it is beyond your ability."

"Not faith, perhaps, but the existence of the Divine Servant and Protector? I understand how all this sounds to others, but especially to those who are not Ari. It's why I didn't tell you."

"But you told The Company."

"Yes. But that's because they follow me. I cannot drag them into this dangerous game without them knowing the truth. I only told my Connate this morning. Not telling them would have been deception. Not telling you would have been cowardice."

Gor'sadén understood, and all he could do was nod, even though his head seemed ready to explode with questions, with the implications of what Fel'annár's purpose was. All Ber'anor had a purpose. "And what are you to achieve, Fel'annár? Has Aria revealed it to you?"

Fel'annár licked his dry lips, nodded. And then he told Gor'sadén everything he knew.

∽

Much later, after Fel'annár had left his rooms, Gor'sadén sat in the same chair before the fire, palm holding up his chin.

He had known. All this time, ever since that day Fel'annár had first come to him and asked about his own father. He had seen some greatness in the boy, a greatness that had played out on the battlefield. The boy had become a legend, and Gor'sadén had known—known that there was more.

And now he knew what it was. The Gods themselves had taken notice. They understood the importance of a unified forest, had chosen Fel'annár to achieve it. But why? Was it for the simple justice of it? To right a wrong that Band'orán had instigated? Propagated? Or was there some other reason?

Rhetoric, fancy words that Lord Damiel would appreciate. But Gor'sadén was a warrior. All he knew was that Aria was the Guardian. Everything she did was to protect. She was not responsible for the evil in this world. She was charged with avoiding tragedy, not righting it. She was not concerned with consequences, only that they should never come to be.

And therein lay his answer. Aria had charged Fel'annár with uniting the forest so that something else would not come to be. But whatever that something was, it had yet to be revealed, even to Fel'annár.

If there was one thing clear in Gor'sadén's mind, it was his own part in this destiny. He was the anchor. He was the rudder that would guide Fel'annár upon that path. He was the experience his Disciple had yet to gain. He was the calming presence, the encouraging hand and the soothing shoulder. Gor'sadén was the Kah Master who would take Fel'annár to the next level of warriorhood, not only with his skill at arms but with his ability to lead. Crippled leg be damned, it would not stand in his way. It couldn't, because Aria knew Fel'annár would need him in the weeks to come.

Swords clashed in the growing dark. The last vestiges of sunlight dipped under the horizon and cast a bluish-grey hue over the still arid lands of southern Araria.

A lone Ari'atór hefted her sword high over her head and then sliced sideways, taking with it the half-rotten head of a towering Deviant. Its body lurched sideways, but she was already fighting another. A body crashed to the dry sand, and another, younger and less experienced, took its place. No less frenzied, its onslaught pushed her backwards. She ducked, and the beast staggered forward. Whirling around, her sword cut from bottom to top, through its belly, and it shrieked then thrashed where it had fallen. She drove the tip of her blade through its neck to shut out the terrible screaming.

She fell to her knees, chest heaving with exertion. She was out of shape, she realised, the result of long weeks of quiet contemplation in the wilds. She had overestimated her physical form, had meant to neutralise this small group on her own and had almost paid the highest price.

Using her sword for leverage, she hauled herself to her feet with a groan and hastily wiped the steel across the back of a dead Deviant. She would burn the carcasses and then find water and a safe place to rest for the night. This area was not safe. She had already spotted larger groups of Incipients, returning from Valley in search of refuge in the Median Mountains until their transformation was complete. This group had come down from the mountains.

She constructed a pyre, watching as the smoke snaked upwards and then dissipated. Ignoring the stench, she turned to the still distant Citadel of Tar'eastór. She needed to see Commander Hobin, explain why she was leaving, and then garner his blessings. But above all else, she needed to know if Prince Handir's group was still there, or whether they had already left for Ea Uaré.

The first leg of her journey, at least, would be quick. It was early spring and the Median Mountains, although dangerous, would be forgiving, if wet from the thaw.

It was all that mattered to Tensári now.

Find Fel'annár.

A nudge in her mind, an answering twitch of her lips. For the first time in too long, her duty was once more at the very fore of her mind. It was carved in flesh and blood, emblazoned on her soul, painted on her face in secret runes only the Ari'atór understood.

Protect the Ber'anor, just as Lainon had done before her.

Had Commander Hobin known, she wondered? Did he know that she was Ber'ator? Had he truly sent her into the wilderness so that she could accept Lainon's passing, come to feel his presence in her mind? She was not convinced. And yet, if Hobin *had* known, the implications were intriguing.

She turned, skin over-sensitive. There were only two who could answer her questions. Hobin in Tar'eastór, or Fel'annár, wherever he was.

But did the Silvan even know what he was? She prayed that he did, because how else could she justify her appearance? But then, what did it matter? she realised.

She had no choice.

4
LEGACY

"Or'Talán had died at the Battle Under the Sun. Mourned. Remembered. Missed. The troops they had called for never arrived, and few escaped the cruelty of foreign blades. But those who lived to tell the tale of that last, desperate stand would never forget the horror of it. Mighty king fallen; his screams still echoed in dreams."
The Silvan Chronicles, Book II. Marhené.

In Acting Commander General Huren's private offices, many eyes, all of them blue, gleamed with the promise of wealth and power. Before them was a map held open with stones of different sizes and colours. Ten captains nodded in satisfaction and agreement as Huren continued to explain.

"Dinor here, see? The land is fertile and not far from a stream that runs through here. Taking down these trees will make the perfect spot for your manor."

The captain nodded, the insignia of his noble house shining upon his breastplate. Dinor, lord and captain, one of the original fathers of the colonisation, together with Bendir and Huren. They were the only ones still alive, save for Pan'assár and of course Lord Band'orán himself.

"Bendir. This sector is yours. A similar structure, only here there is a valley rich in ore. Your father will exploit it well."

There were murmurs of agreement and pleasure. Huren's reasoning was sound. Each of the lordly captains had been assigned their own sectors of the forest, based on the ancestral skills of their families. Merchants, jewel smiths, warriors or artists; all of them had a place in the forest, one they would be granted in exchange for their loyalty—not to Thargodén but to the future king of Ea Uaré.

"What news of how we are to take possession of our lands?" asked Dinor.

"Our lord will inform us shortly. The final votes are still to be held on schedule, three weeks from now. Once the council is secured and in our favour—specifically, the return of the Warlord overruled—we will be told. I will, however, ask you to brace for unexpected developments. You must show surprise, show that you are loyal to Thargodén until our lord declares otherwise. For now, know that these lands are yours when that time comes. You have earned them."

There were nods and approving murmurs, speculation as to what these *surprising developments* would be. Huren watched them all with a trained eye. These captains had much to gain from this new order. Their powerful families were weaving their rhetoric with the indecisive, be they on the Royal Council or the Inner Circle. Lands, raw materials, unlimited Silvan hands to mine them. New trade routes, new opportunities to gain coin, chests full of it. It was only a matter of time before common sense prevailed and more joined their cause—Band'orán's cause. They had expected it of Or'Talán, but all they had gained was title and privilege. No lands.

Of course, there were those of the Inner Circle that Huren knew would never be swayed, those still loyal to Or'Talán's house. Their refusal to collaborate, actively or passively, was a risk Huren was well aware of, one he would find a way to neutralise. He knew who they were, knew how to manipulate them. He would deploy them here and there, anywhere but within the city. Turion was one such captain, as was Dalú, who fortunately had already done him a favour and deserted.

"Commander. We all know the Silvans will not allow this lightly. How far will we be expected to go, should they resist this change?"

"That is for our lord to say. However, should it come to force, he will not falter. His personal guard cannot be vanquished, not by Thargodén's warriors."

The captains nodded but said nothing. They had heard mention of this personal guard before, and well understood that it was not a question to be voiced. It was prohibited to speak of those soldiers.

Huren shared a passing glance at Captain Bendir, commanding officer of the Outer City Barracks.

"And what of Pan'assár?" asked another. It had not been formally announced within the small circle of chosen captains, but they all knew what the future held for him, once Band'orán rose to power. Huren would command the army, not Pan'assár.

"Pan'assár is finished. He is mostly unconcerned with the Silvans and their cause. He blames them for the death of his lord, his brother. The fight is gone from him. He delegates command to me. However, should he, too, resist change, there is a plan."

The circle of captains grew silent.

"All who have opposed our lord have learned the hard way that he was born to rule these lands."

The captains nodded, not in satisfaction but understanding and some trepidation. They knew Band'orán had a way with people, was persuasive. He was also the brother of Or'Talán. Strength came naturally to him. But Huren well knew that, had Or'Talán lived, they would never have acceded to participating in the Renewal, would never have shown disloyalty to *that* king. Band'orán knew that, too. It was why he never spoke ill of Or'Talán. It was why they could never know. Only he, Dinor and Bendir knew the truth.

Huren had not lied. Band'orán suffered no opposition. Or'Talán had known that, had died for his folly. This new lord offered them a whole new world, one which most would not resist. Thargodén was weak, pining for his Silvan love. Rinon, too, would fall, a victim of his own anger. And Handir was nothing but a novice councillor. Pity, mused Huren, that Pan'assár had not died with Or'Talán that day. Still, what did that matter now? There was always a second chance, and Huren would seize it while Pan'assár was at his weakest.

Meanwhile, they would continue to suck the hope from the Silvan people. Draugolé was a master weaver of lies. Fel'annár was not here, either because he did not care or he was dead. Either way, he told the people that he wasn't coming back. The lies would spread, he said, and Huren did not doubt Draugolé's word on the matter.

And then Band'orán had bid Huren pit Silvan against Alpine, create conflict because it worked in their favour now, in *his* favour. And so, Huren would continue to stage the deaths of Alpine warriors, blame it on the Silvans until the rope snapped and the fighting became real. And he would not bat an eyelid as he watched them fight.

Everything was in place, the odds in their favour. Band'orán would activate the final stage of his century-long plan. All that remained was to find out if Sulén had finished the job. If he hadn't, then it would fall to Huren to stop the Silvan bastard from returning. Stop him from uniting the Silvan people.

THE SILVAN ENCAMPMENT that stood before the gates to Thargodén's fortress had grown in size and complexity since their arrival for the first Forest Summit. That initiative had ended with the Night of a Thousand Drums, a declaration of intention. They would no longer be ignored, excluded, discriminated against.

And so, they had formed their own Council of Elders. Lord Erthoron was their leader, native of Lan Taria. Lord Lorthil of Sen'oléi, Narosén the Ari'atór, and Lady Amareth, also of Lan Taria and Abiren'á. The Silvans had rejoiced in the decision, would abide by their rulings. But they would not leave the encampment until the votes had taken place. They would stay until they knew whether the

Alpines would allow them to live in peace, or whether they forbade the Warlord, forbade equality on the council.

Should the votes turn against them, they would declare their own independence, make it known to the Alpine people. They did not want conflict, but neither would they continue to be denied equality, denied their own say in the military strategy that was decimating their folk in the Deep Forest, leaving them vulnerable to the attack of Sand Lords and Deviants.

And then Angon had deserted, and with him, a good number of Silvan troops who believed the time for talk was over. Erthoron and his newly formed Council of Elders was hard-pressed to keep them at bay. They had, though, arguing that it was just a few more weeks. Let them vote, and then let them face the consequences of their own actions, he said.

This place almost felt like home to Amareth, save that monstrous battlements loomed over them. The mighty walls blocked half of the fortress from sight, but the domes and spires were still clearly visible, jutting into a clear blue sky. She felt like an ant contemplating its oversized world. The camp was a symbol, one last, stubborn stand. One that would mean nothing if Fel'annár *were* dead. If he was, she would leave these lands and venture through the Veil.

But she did not believe it. The rumours were simply that, born of malicious lies spread by the Alpine Purists. Fel'annár was alive, and when he finally came, she would beg his forgiveness for what she had had to do.

Pulling her eyes away from the foreign construction, she allowed her gaze to drift over the morning activities. Bakers pulled steaming loaves from their clay ovens, handing them to all who flocked there. Further along, fish were skinned and boned, and mighty pots bubbled with water and brews. Elves stood around, warming their hands before fires or around their steaming mugs and talking quietly. The subject was always the same. Would the king convince the council? Would the Inner Circle be swayed to accept their Warlord? Was Fel'annár alive? And where was Angon?

But Amareth knew Angon was not the solution. He was loved and he was criticised. His ability to inspire loyalty was not strong enough, not to rally an army. It was still Fel'annár who would unite them. She had done what Lássira had asked of her, protected him, prepared him. And so too, had she conspired to hide him so that he could fulfil this destiny the Silvan people had imposed upon him. He was Lássira's child, the king's child. Who better to serve as their Warlord than the son of their rightful queen?

Not a bastard. A legitimate prince.

Still, there had been times when Amareth had regretted her actions, had pleaded for Fel'annár to stay away, prayed that he would not come back. But then she would cast her gaze over her people and see their hopeful, wishful eyes. She would remember the injustice, bolster her belief in their cause.

She waited her turn for a cup of redberry tea. A kindly woman extended her hands with a smile and a respectful nod. Touched, Amareth took the cup with a nod of her own. She had cared for Fel'annár all his life, loved him as a son. She was the sister of the one who should have reigned at Thargodén's side. They had always shown her deference, even though they had hidden it in the presence of Fel'annár.

The tea slid down her throat, a warming stream of tangy goodness, and she closed her eyes for a moment. It was early spring, but still cold in the mornings.

Sniffling, she turned towards the tent the Silvans used as headquarters. Inside, candles flickered in the soft drafts that wafted through the cracks in the oiled cloth. Erthoron's silhouette danced oddly behind him as if it didn't belong to him but to some playful, invisible sprite.

"Amareth."

She nodded at Erthoron, the elf who had always been at her side, solemn and wise, gentle and respectful. But his brow was furrowed with deep lines of concern.

"Lady Miren has brought news," said Lorthil from the other side of the tent, Captain Dalú standing just behind him. "She says three Alpine merchants have been killed by Silvan rebels."

"Surely not," said Amareth, eyes momentarily catching those of Captain Dalú. He was angry.

"It's a lie, lady. Angon wouldn't do that."

"It may have been an accident, Dalú," murmured Lorthil.

"No. Angon is vocal. He can be rough, agreed. But he would not have killed them, lady. My oath, he would not."

She nodded. "But he is leaving himself open to Band'orán's lies. By waylaying those merchants, it is all too easy for the Alpine people to believe those lies."

"Pah," huffed Dalú. "If he hadn't decided to ride and bring some justice to our people, someone else would have done it. Isn't it clear by now that Thargodén is not going to do anything about it? That he won't stand up to his own Royal Council? He's nothing but a puppet in Band'orán's hands."

Dalú had loved Or'Talán, had almost died for him. His face had been cut open, nearly lost an ear, and the evidence of that sacrifice would be with him always. Thargodén ruled, and Dalú had followed —but Lássira's absence turned that reign dismal. He had become impatient, eager for change, whatever form it took.

Amareth walked towards him. "You don't know our king at all, Captain. You know only what others tell you and what you want to believe. Anger leads you astray. He is no puppet, not to anyone."

"He let Pan'assár do whatever he wanted at the Inner Circle, cared nothing for our warriors, for our villages. We can't forget that. It's why Angon is the way he is, why two hundred Silvan warriors have left the barracks and come here to serve their own people."

"It's not a question of whether the king cared or not, Dalú," said Amareth. "It's a question of understanding *why* he faltered. He *does* care, always has, but Lássira's absence was an impossible wall for him to climb. His *bond* was broken. That doesn't make him weak, especially not now that he knows Fel'annár lives."

Dalú's frown deepened, the silvery scar pulling at his features. Narosén stepped from the shadows, placing a hand on his rigid shoulder. "There is still a chance for peace, Captain. Your time, Angon's time, has yet to come."

Dalú nodded abruptly. Amareth knew he did not agree, thought that it already had come. But in this tent, he was outnumbered and had wisely decided to bide his time. Out there, though, she knew the rebels were gaining popularity. Angon said the things they all thought, inflamed their people with rumour and hearsay, and Dalú seconded him.

"This propaganda that Band'orán is spreading must be counteracted." Erthoron paced, clasping his hands before him. "They say the king has no sway over the council. They say that Fel'annár is unconcerned with our plight, perhaps even dead." He turned and caught Amareth's gaze. She held it.

"And why are you all so sure it *isn't* true? The fact is that he's not here, and there has been no correspondence." Dalú rounded on Erthoron, startled when Amareth banged her cup on the table and walked towards him. Her head barely reached the centre of his chest.

"You're a faithless fool, Dalú! This forest means everything to him. He understands this place better than any of us. He hears it, *speaks* with it. He's not dead, and he does care. It is easy to intercept correspondence, Captain, and then claim that silence is due to indifference. You must tell our people that, not perpetuate those Alpine lies Band'orán is feeding you, the ones you are hungry to believe. You think war will solve our problems? You think killing Alpine warriors is the solution? Dalú ... it's not the warriors we must stop. It's their leaders. And to stop *them*, you must first understand them; understand Band'orán."

"Can you not see how our warriors look to us? To *you*?" said Dalú, eyes travelling over the Council. "They trust us to reclaim these lands and they must be able to see that you—that *we*, are achieving just that."

"But not at all cost, Dalú. Not yet," said Amareth.

"For how much longer, lady?" The fire in the captain's eyes was dimming.

"Until the return of the Warlord. Only that."

Satisfied at the concession in Dalú's eyes, she nodded. Amareth of Lan Taria was no meek and frightened mother who had contrived to preserve Fel'annár's life in Lássira's memory. She was the daughter of the great Zéndar, aunt to their future Warlord. She was strong, empowered by years of caution, close observation and careful planning. None of what she had done had been cowardice. It had been strategy, heart-breaking and soul-shattering but brave, relentless.

Yes, she had done it for Lássira, but so, too, had she done it for her people.

ANGON AND HIS SILVAN WARRIORS, or rebels as some called them, galloped into the village of Lan Taria. Seila's bulging wagon rumbled behind them, piled high with the wares and produce they had confiscated just days ago. They reined in their horses and dismounted.

The town folk smiled at the brown leather skirts and harnesses that crossed over their bare chests, and for a moment, it seemed they had been transported to the elder days. To many of them, it brought fond memories of easier times, a more just society. Others, though, watched them warily.

Angon breathed in the fresh forest air and gestured to his warriors that they should follow him. Slinging their sacks of goods over their shoulders, they made their way to the town square, and with every step they took, the crowds grew thicker and louder.

By the time they finally arrived at the ring of trees that marked the heart of Lan Taria, it seemed like the entire town had gathered around them. The warriors threw the sacks of goods to the ground and then pulled the fabrics away. Resins and herbs, honey and medicinal roots, even glow moss. The people murmured, but quietened as Angon turned with open arms and spoke to them.

"These assets are Silvan, not to be shared for two coins with greedy Alpines. They have taken away our voice in our own homes —and in return, we take away the forest goods we know they need. We should not deal with those who despise us. We should not take money from power-hungry lords who would take everything we have and drive us into the hands of Sand Lords and Deviants. Have a care, brothers and sisters. Alpines are not welcome in the Deep Forest."

"And so says Angon!" The voice of an angry Silvan who stepped forward, unafraid of the imposing Silvan warrior. "Who chose you, Angon, to speak for the Silvans? How come you speak for us without our permission? That is what the Alpines have done. You would mirror them? Even though you despise them for doing the very same thing?"

"It is not the same!" thundered Angon, stepping closer. "Sometimes, words are not enough, forester. Sometimes, the hateful and the greedy need to be shown the fruit of their wrongdoings. I am here to do that, to show them they must not cross the natives of this land. We will not tolerate it. It is what the Warlord would do!"

There were murmurs of approval, but many remained quiet, looking now at Thavron of Lan Taria.

"I do not follow the Alpines because they took away our voice. I will not follow Angon, who also seeks to take away my voice. I am not a warrior. I cannot stop you from this madness, this terrible *waste*." He pointed with his finger at the bruised produce, the broken packages and the cracked vials. "What will you do with the money that was given in exchange for this? Will you seek out the sellers and rattle them? Will you confiscate the money and use it for your cause? Since when do Silvans steal from others?"

Thavron braced himself as Angon stepped closer to him, the appeasing hand of a fellow warrior on his arm. Even so, his eyes bore into Thavron, seething and barely controlled. Eyes that had seen too much. Eyes that had waited for too long.

"I do not steal," Angon hissed. His eyes narrowed, a vague memory surfacing. "You are a friend of his." Thavron nodded. "Then heed me, forester. Your friend is not coming back. Fel'annár of Lan Taria is unconcerned with the plight of our people. Either that or he is dead. Why else does he not come? Why does he not send news?"

"You are *wrong!*" shouted Thavron. "He's not dead. It's what they want us to believe. He will come back. He'll find a way."

Some were nodding, but Angon shook his head. "Wishful thinking. *Now* is the right time and *he* is not here, forester. The Alpines prepare for a vote and we all know what the outcome will be. The Inner Circle acts out its pantomime, and again, we all know what their answer will be. They will not give us our Warlord. Pan'assár won't allow it."

The shouts were louder now, and Thavron closed his eyes. "Stop this, Angon. Stop before it is too late. Fel'annár will come back, and when he does, what will you do, warrior? Will you step aside? Or will you push *him* aside?"

Absolute silence fell about them, and Angon brushed off the restraining hand. "I met the boy, served with him. He's a good lad and wears his honour stone proudly, but he's not here! I will do what I must, for my people. For my forest and the trees of my birth. It is that simple."

"And Fel'annár will do the same, as will I, just as Erthoron and Lorthil do. *They* are our rightful leaders, Angon. Let them act. Let them finish their mission and come back to us. Only then can we decide a way forward. But do not pre-empt the worst possible outcome. It has not come to that, not yet." Thavron dared another step towards Angon, eyes begging him to understand, to listen. "He *will* come back, and when he does, he will do right by us, you'll see. Wait for the return of the Warlord."

Angon's nostrils flared and his chin jutted skywards. "We will not stop in our efforts to show the Alpines our produce is not for sale. I will not stand by and watch as they take our homes away from us. You should come to the encampment in the city. See for yourself how our people clamour at the very walls of King Thargodén's city. It *is* time, forester. Now *is* the time to act when others talk. To show when others negotiate. The time for words has passed."

Some cheered Angon but many others looked to Thavron.

"To *act* you must first understand. To *show* you must have it clear in your mind. The time for words never passes, Angon. Don't jump ahead of everyone else and make all our efforts these past fifty years nothing but a fanciful dream. This is not for you to decide. It is for our Elders, for our people to decide, as one!"

The cheers were deafening, fists held high, and Angon stood livid. But Thavron the forester had not finished. "If you must confiscate goods from the Alpines, do not waste them. Do not spoil them. Treat them with care, for they were grown with love and with hours of hard work. They are a part of the creation and must be handled with respect. Don't let your anger turn you away from our most sacred of beliefs."

The warriors behind Angon nodded, eyes roving over the resins and powders, the nuts and the dried hedgeberries. It was not the Silvan way, and who better than a forester to remind them of that? Angon knew this, too, just as he knew that it was useless to continue arguing, here in Lan Taria.

He turned and left the Warlord's village in search of his next Alpine victims. Thavron felt comforting hands on his shoulders. He had done what he could, but he had seen the divide, straight down the middle of the Silvan people. They applauded Angon's initiative, identified with his no-nonsense approach to Alpine domination. They were convincing themselves that Fel'annár would not come back, that he did not care, or that he was dead.

But Thavron knew differently.

TEN HORSES AMBLED along the Eastern Road, the two foremost riders side by side, their faces similar. They were talking of horses, of the hunt and the crop of mushrooms that awaited them for dinner. Nothing extraordinary, save that this was Captain Barathon and his father, Lord Band'orán.

Barathon couldn't believe it, couldn't remember the last time they had discussed nothing in particular. Neither could he remember returning home with his father like this after a council meeting. Together. True, the last time he could remember, they had not been surrounded by guards. Back then, there was no strife. They lived in peace with the Silvan people.

They were approaching the foothills and the turnoff to Analei,

Forest End, their residence. It was a sprawling mansion that backed onto rock, but the façade was a beautifully crafted thing. All vines and trees and the most intricately sculpted wood he had ever seen, save perhaps for the workmanship of the king's throne.

Or'Talán had commissioned it, Alpine king who had loved this forest almost as much as he had loved his son, Thargodén. Barathon still remembered the great king's face, its strength and determination, the light in his eyes and his up-turned lips. So different to his own father's face.

Band'orán took this road to the city every day. At a steady canter it could be done in half an hour, but today, Or'Talán's brother was contemplative and uncharacteristically talkative. Barathon wasn't complaining. He didn't want their ride to end because once they were home, they would dine, and then his father would disappear into his study. There had been times when Barathon had not seen him for days. But he knew better than to ask him what it was he did in there.

"We have guests tonight."

Barathon was startled out of his musings. He turned to his father.

"We have captains Dinor and Bendir. Sar'pén and Emor. Huren, of course. I have invited Draugolé and his dear Poronir. And then Melu'sán. She is a fine match for you, Barathon. Make an effort at least, will you?"

Barathon nodded. The moment had been fleeting, his father's final words marking the onset of normalcy. Melu'sán was head of the Merchants' Guild, a shrewd and cunning woman with a plain face and overly large breasts. Not his type at all. At least Dinor would be there—small mercy. He liked Draugolé, too, but there had been times in his life when the councillor had rescued Barathon from more than a few uncomfortable situations. Draugolé knew things about him, things he did not want to share with others. It made him feel inadequate, he supposed. Even more so than when he was in the presence of his father. At least he had been accustomed to that since childhood.

Always lacking. Never enough.

That evening, Barathon changed out of the uniform that marked him as a captain of the Inner Circle and into his velvets and brocades, the opulent attire of a privileged Alpine lord and councillor. Suitably decked, he joined their guests below, naturally gravitating to Dinor who sat chatting with Bendir, and for a while, he simply listened.

They talked of the Elder Days, when Or'Talán had first colonised the forest. He had promised them the moon and more, they said. Yet he had given them nothing. No lands, no manors, no ore to mine or estates to handle. They had felt cheated, and wanted what they felt was theirs, in return for their pledge of loyalty. Yet they recognised the worth of that king. Band'orán was quick to agree. He had indeed been great, he claimed. But his son was not. Thargodén was weak, the unfit scion of such a glorious king.

It was when Melu'sán herself spoke that his father's face changed and his own stomach flipped inside him.

"Thargodén is not weak, Band'orán. Not anymore. Did you not see what he did just yesterday? He walked out into the market, spoke to the people as he bought goods. He knows what they say: that he is finished, that he is a mewling, love-sick ruler that would be better off taking the Long Road to his Silvan bitch. He is showing them they are wrong. And it's working, I tell you. My nephew's latest fancy was gushing about it, saying how healthy he seemed, how handsome, how strong."

Barathon knew his father as well as any other, which was, admittedly, not much. But he knew when he was angry, and he knew when the strangeness came. Just as he knew it, so did Draugolé. Indeed, the evening had wound down soon after, and Barathon had made himself scarce, leaving his father in the presence of Draugolé, who had sent Poronir outside to wait for him. But it wasn't until the following day that Barathon was told the news.

It was time.

That was all his father said to him at breakfast. And Barathon knew exactly what he meant.

~

That night, while Analei slept above him, Band'orán stood upon the shores of the dark lake, still empty. Later it would fill with crystal clear water. It would shimmer and shine, reflect the gems and the ore that lived in the walls, in the bed of this underwater lagoon that ebbed and rose like a constant every day. As constant as his love for her.

He turned to the stone statue of Canusahéi beside him. Band'orán had loved her, ever since he had seen her at the tender age of fifty-five, when the world was still green. When his heart had still known goodness, its beat still steady.

Her mere existence had awoken him to a world he had yet to enjoy. Duty, proving himself to others, defending himself ... it was all he had ever known. Her face had made him dream.

And Band'orán had dreamed wildly.

He would learn the ways of the Kah Warrior, marry his love. It was all that had mattered to him. Or'Talán had known. His own brother had seen the love in his eyes for a nobleman's daughter, had approved and even jested, for Band'orán was besotted. He smiled at the memory of how she had affected him. Those distant days momentarily filled the hole in his soul, the rent in his mind.

Or'Talán himself had married, and a son was born. An heir to the throne of Ea Uaré. Thargodén grew strong, was a passing warrior, but never showed an interest in the Kal'hamén'Ar.

But Band'orán had. He trained so that he could qualify, and over the years, he became an excellent warrior. With Canusahéi still unwed and his own dreams driving him forward, he had approached his kingly brother, told him that he wanted to be a Disciple.

Or'Talán had refused.

He could not understand it. For a warrior to become a Disciple, the Masters must agree unanimously, and all of them did, even two of The Three. But not the king. Why had his beloved brother betrayed him? Band'orán had begged him for a reason, but all his brother would ever say was that two Kah Masters in the Royal Family was an unnecessary risk. Or'Talán had an heir, but he was still unwed. Until such time as the succession was guaranteed, he would not allow it.

Yet Band'orán had never believed him. There was some other reason.

Frustration, incomprehension, the injustice of it. And then, Canusahéi, too, had refused him. She would not walk with him, rejected his offer of courtship.

He knew why. He had waited too long. She did not want the lesser brother, the simple warrior that had been forbidden the teachings of the Kal'hamén'Ar by the mighty Or'Talán. She wanted to marry a future king.

She wanted Thargodén, crown prince of Ea Uaré. Or'Talán's son.

He closed his eyes, breathed deeply. Damned Or'Talán and damned his son.

And then, Band'orán had come to understand it all. It was then that his world began to change. It was all about power.

Or'Talán had refused to train him because he could not share his own glory. Could not abide the thought of his brother eclipsing his light. Canusahéi did not want him because he was not bound for the throne. He would never be a king.

But they were wrong. Both of them. He *was* worthy of the Kal'hamén'Ar. He *was* worthy of her love. Band'orán was a *warrior*. He would not yield, would never give up his dreams. He *would* be a Kah Master. He *would* marry Canusahéi ... because he would be a *king*. And with that conviction, he had set his plan into motion.

Slowly. Carefully. Over the passage of years, Band'orán followed the road his mind had shown him. He would create a reason for others to follow him. Make them feel special. Give them something that they yearned for. His own motives, his real reasons would no longer matter to them.

Pride. Land. Power.

This was his recipe. This was his path to kingship. And once he had achieved that, then Canusahéi would want him and Or'Talán would be gone. He would be free to train in the Kal'hamén'Ar, no longer an illicit Master, no longer doomed as he was to practice the art in secrecy.

But it no longer mattered to Band'orán, not really. He had become accustomed to doing things alone. He was reminded, then, of one such time when he had taken to the forest, in search of answers. He had witnessed a scene he could not have imagined. He always blessed that fortuitous day.

He had seen his nephew, Thargodén, and his lover, Lássira. He had heard them speak of the future, together, and he remembered his own love for Canusahéi. But as he watched and listened, he realised that he could never allow them to be wed. There was a power about them, some strength that, should they reign together, they would have been great.

Too great.

Thargodén would have followed in his father's glorious footsteps and she ... she would have united the Silvan and Alpine people. The people he had worked so hard to separate.

He had acted then, had demanded that Or'Talán forbid the marriage of Thargodén and Lássira. It was not fitting, not acceptable to the Alpine nobles. She was *Silvan*.

The father had refused. And then Band'orán had stepped upon a road with no return. He had explained the consequences of the king's refusal. Or'Talán had toiled over it, he knew, but after days of turmoil, he finally yielded.

Then the unthinkable happened. In his vengeance for forcing his son away from his soulmate, Or'Talán chose *Canusahéi* to be his heir's bride. He had chosen the only one Band'orán could ever love.

He had wanted to concede. Let Thargodén marry the Silvan bitch then, he had thought. But how could he? When so much hinged on the crown prince's downfall; when his plan relied on division between their people. Band'orán would never rule if he could not break Or'Talán's son.

It was no longer about Canusahéi alone. It was no longer about not being a Kah Master. It was about *him*. Somewhere along that long and strange road, his own dreams had died, and in their place, a new one reigned. He would be king.

And so, Band'orán had chosen power over love. He had continued, implacable with his plan, one Huren had so deftly brought about. Or'Talán perished upon the sands of the Xeric Wood. The great king was gone, one of only three remaining Kah Masters. With one of them in Tar'eastór and the other broken by the death of his king, Band'orán was free to learn the Kal'hamén'Ar. But he did so in secret. That, too, was a part of his plan.

He should have been encouraged by the new state of things. Thargodén, even though he was king, was broken. Killing Lássira was a masterful move, one of the best he had ever taken. All that was left to do was remove an already failing king, weaken and discredit his children.

And then it would be time. At last.

He was distantly aware that he had lost something along the way. Something had dislodged itself. Something that, at times, he could not hide. It was why he sometimes hid himself away, here, in the place only he was allowed to visit, he and his personal guard. This was his dark kingdom, a secret realm of underground caverns and crystal lakes. Here he was already a king, and Canusahéi was his queen. As was befitting an Alpine queen, there were jewels, those of his family and others he had managed to collect over the years. There were works of art and exquisite sculptures. There were prized weapons of old and the most priceless of books, which the scholars of Ea Uaré would kill for.

He gazed at her sculpture, standing life-size on the shores of the slowly rising crystal lake. The glittering reflection of rippling water played over her fine features. It was almost as if she were alive, speaking with him, telling him that she loved *him*, not Thargodén.

Should his plan fail—should Band'orán die and find himself on the other side—would she still speak to him? Would she still love him for the things he had done, in her name? He cocked his head to one side. Could she forgive him, he wondered? Would she understand why he had done it?

Blue eyes glittered in the flickering candlelight. His jaw clenched, he had all but turned to stone himself.

Anger seared through his blood, sudden and odd. Anger at Or'Talán for his terrible revenge. At Thargodén for the queen who stood at his side, unloved. Anger at himself for accepting the sacrifice of his love. At her, too, because she had never told him that she loved him, though he knew it was true.

Band'orán had once loved Or'Talán. But he never regretted killing him.

He wrenched his eyes away from her, straightened his hunched shoulders, smoothed his wrinkled brow. He closed his slack mouth and shuttered his volatile emotions with cool eyes.

It was time to train. Alone. Just as he had for the past century. And soon, it would all become real, at last. He would be king, just like Or'Talán.

Better than Or'Talán.

5

A HUNDRED AND ONE SWORDS

"Fel'annár and The Company left Tar'eastór on the eighth day of spring. It was the day 101 Alpine swords gleamed under the sun."
The Alpine Chronicles: Cor'hidén

The day had finally come: the day they would leave the Motherland, the day the Restoration began, at least in Fel'annár's mind.

He had been granted an audience with the king. He stood in the doorway, watching as Vorn'asté carefully placed a book back on a shelf. He turned, smiled at Fel'annár in the half-light. "Come. Sit with me before you leave." He gestured to a long, rectangular table before a towering wall of books.

"Thank you for finding the time to see me, sire."

The king nodded. "Now that the way to Ea Uaré is clear, I have sent news to your king. We must assume any former correspondence has not arrived. They may not know of the battle or the attempts on your life. I am also sending messages with Prince Sontúr for your father. If there is something you would send, I will gladly add it to the dispatch. Prince Handir has already prepared a good number of messages."

He briefly considered writing to Amareth or to Erthoron, but what would he say? There was far too much to express and no time in which to do so. And what was the point, if he couldn't see their eyes? Besides, he didn't even know where they would be. Lan Taria? Or were they at the Silvan camp that Aradan had told Handir about.

"No. There is nothing I would send, sire."

"You will not answer your father?"

"No. We'll meet soon enough, although in what circumstances I cannot imagine. Will he even still be king by the time we arrive? The missives Handir found paint a dismal future for my home, for my people."

"And they look to you, Fel'annár. Sometimes, it takes one elf to change the course of history. One elf and his circumstances—a catalyst, if you will."

"I won't be alone, sire. I have Prince Sontúr and The Company. And I trust Prince Handir will use those incriminating missives well. We have a chance of stopping Band'orán, but it will take a skilled statesman to do so. It falls to him to make things right in the city, while I and The Company must bring the Silvans together and rally them behind their king. Assuming they are still loyal, still willing to give him a second opportunity."

"It is their obligation, Fel'annár."

"I don't believe that, sire. Still, if the question of discrimination is addressed, if they're given equal opportunity and respect, there's a chance at least."

"You have it all clear in your mind, do you not?" said Vorn'asté, suddenly closer to Fel'annár than he had been before. Curiosity, confusion. Fel'annár could see it, almost hear the king's mind as it worked. He wondered if he had said too much, but then Vorn'asté smiled.

"I have much to thank you for. You and The Company accepted death to defend my lands—Alpine lands—and for that, you will be remembered and always welcomed as beloved sons of the Motherland." The king sat in his high-backed chair, gesturing to Fel'annár to join him in its twin by his side.

Fel'annár remembered that he had once considered staying in Tar'eastór, back when he had been ignorant of his race and purpose, before the battle and Llyniel. That he could return, serve here and make a life for himself was gratifying. But the forest was in his blood, and now more than ever, there was a reason to return. A duty to fulfil.

"I will cherish my time here," said Fel'annár softly, his eyes lazily travelling over the shelving, the art upon the walls and the soft flicker of the fire. "Here I became a lord, a Kah Disciple. Here I learned of myself, became a Blade Master. I lost a brother, and then gained one."

"My son carries a new light in his eyes." Fel'annár watched the king, the shrewd eyes that would not lift from him. "Crown Prince Torhén is due back from Prairie in a few days. He will take up his duties, and Prince Sontúr has my leave to join you, for a while at least. It is a token, perhaps, of my interest in the Restoration your brother has told me about. The Motherland does not condone treason and the presence of my son will be testimony to that, for whatever difference it may make to your people."

"Sontúr always makes a difference." A smile tugged at Fel'annár's lips at the thought of his sarcastic, witty brother, an elf who had given him empathy from the very start. "He is a part of The Company, for as long as you allow it. We are all grateful for that."

"I wish you luck, Aren Or'Talán—for the journey back, for the family you have never met. May you be happy, warrior. May you find your peace at last."

Fel'annár wondered if the King of Ea Uaré was like this—or if he had been, before he was separated from Lássira.

Fel'annár stood, bowed low. "Thank you, King Vorn'asté. I hope we will meet again when everything is done."

He glanced at the life-sized portrait of Queen Lerhal, the woman who had sacrificed herself so that her warriors would live. She had found herself in Valley. Fel'annár had seen her through the Winter Sentinel, although the king said he could not bring himself to believe it.

Vorn'asté followed Fel'annár's gaze, knowing, perhaps, what he was thinking. But he said nothing, and it gave Fel'annár pause. In those shrewd blue eyes was a light, a kind of wonder, as if he *had* believed what Fel'annár claimed but dared not admit it.

Fel'annár smiled, stepped backwards and then left. As he navigated the corridors, he thought he would have preferred the king to call him Ar Thargodén instead of Aren Or'Talán. He had met neither, but Or'Talán had ruined his son, and Fel'annár felt nothing but shame for the name he carried, for the face he bore.

He did not notice the bows and the soft smiles from those he passed. Servants and scribes, attendants and messengers, warriors and musicians. They remembered the great lord, the great king. They knew nothing of broken hearts and forbidden love. All they knew was that Or'Talán had been great and his grandson would be just as great.

FEL'ANNÁR MADE his way to the Healing Halls, a heavy travel bag slung over his shoulder and Carodel just behind him.

"Where's that new lyre of yours?"

"In the prince's chest. I will not lose another to battle, or to Ramien's backside."

"He sat on one?" Fel'annár chuckled.

"He did. Broke my heart."

Inside the Halls, Fel'annár made his way to the end and then right. Llyniel's rooms were there, and he turned, nodded at his friend and then knocked. He didn't wait for her answer but slipped inside.

On the table was her own travel bag. Her medical journal would be inside, wrapped in protective oilcloth, just like his own diary. He smoothed a hand over the rough cloth and then turned to the sound of her steps.

Before him was the elf that he loved, and in her hair, the Bonding Braid, tied at the end with the Seven Wheels. With his eyes fixed on the spirals of cloth, a memory surfaced, of his youth in the Deep Forest and the Spring Festival ...

One for the sun that gives light
One for water that gives life
One for the earth that yields growth
One for the trees that give air
One for the stars that bring dreams
One for Aria who feeds the soul
And one for love that binds the world together.

He lunged forwards, pulled her into his arms and cradled her head against his chest, clutching hands desperate. He felt her warm against him, safe in his embrace, and he squeezed his eyes shut, heart so very full. Then he lifted her off the ground and spun her around. Everything behind her blurred, ceased to make sense. There was only her smiling face and the Bonding Braid flying around her head, his own dancing about his face. And then her laughter, hand batting at his arm in mock anger to let her go.

They stood before each other, panting and smiling and blessing the Gods that they had each other. Their bodies leant forwards, unable to stay away.

But a knock at the door reminded them both that it was time to leave. Fel'annár scowled and Llyniel laughed.

Slinging their bags over their shoulders, they left the room and made for the Halls with Carodel. They found Master Arané and Head Healer Mestahé on the threshold before the main courtyard.

Fel'annár came to stand before Arané, smiled at him. "I have no words to express my gratitude. You saved my life, and I am in your debt, Master Arané."

"There is no such debt, my lord. The service a healer lends has no price, requires no payment. It is done from the heart, and in this case, I am honoured to have preserved your life, Aren Or'Talán." The healer stepped closer to Fel'annár, so that no one else could hear. "You have many names, Fel'annár: The Silvan, Hwind'atór, and another I know you do not use. But whatever your purpose, I know it is a good one. So I bid you serve well, stay safe. I pray we meet again, outside these Halls for once." His mouth quirked on one side, but there was a shrewdness in that ancient gaze. Arané *knew*, had no doubts as to what he had seen upon that extraordinary dawn, and had come to his own conclusions.

Fel'annár stepped away, turned to Mestahé while Llyniel said her own goodbyes. He watched as they spoke, and then the Master Healer gave her a scroll. Fel'annár wondered if it was a commendation. He smiled as she turned to him.

"Are you ready?" he asked her.

She smiled back as she opened her bag and placed the scroll safely inside. Together, they walked towards the rest of The Company, as close as lovers could, Carodel behind them at a discreet distance.

Horses stood patiently by, laden with the provisions they would need for the journey to Ea Uaré. On the largest of their mounts, Prince Handir's fine wooden chest sat in all its graceful strength. Leather straps had been tied around it, buckled tight, and inside the well-protected bowels, their greatest treasures lay. Messages from Vorn'asté to Thargodén, and the missives, proof that would see them rid of Sulén and perhaps even Band'orán for good.

There were other items inside, too. Things that they could not carry in their bags for fear of damaging them. Handir's princely regalia, books Lord Damiel had gifted him, even Idernon's book on Calrazian history and his drawing of the Nim'uán sword and its yet undeciphered script. Carodel had seen his opportunity and asked if he could stow his lyre inside and then Llyniel had included her bulky medical journal. There was plenty of room, and Handir had not objected.

They had been provided with civilian attire. Black and blue breeches, muted green and blue tunics, leather chest protection and vambraces of the finest quality. Their cloaks were black, their design long and ample, the hoods wide and concealing.

Mounting, they made their way to Handir's side. At the fore, the two commanders rode, although they, too, wore simple clothes and little armour. Fel'annár thought their disguise altogether inadequate. Power seemed to roll off them, magnified when together.

Gor'sadén gestured with his head that he should join them. It was Fel'annár's first mission as a trainee lieutenant, and he glanced over his shoulder at The Company. He found them staring back at him with smiles, even Galadan. At his side, Pan'assár murmured, "Give the order, lieutenant."

Fel'annár was stepping upon the road of leadership, and although he had never been happier, there was a sadness about the moment—like a fond farewell, to a life he had somehow outlived. He smiled, even as his eyes felt full and his chest heavy. "We ride for Ea Uaré. Our mission: to protect our prince and that which he carries. King Thargodén is grateful for your service."

Idernon was the first to raise his fist in salute to a superior officer, and the rest followed suit. Pan'assár sat taller in his saddle, and Gor'sadén's eyes gleamed.

They spurred their mounts to a gentle walk, eyes scanning the crowds that lined the way towards the open gates. Fel'annár spotted Comon's old patrol, and he lifted his hand in farewell to Pengon, who returned the salute with an ample smile.

At the gates, Commander Comon himself stood in his new uniform that marked him as Acting Commander General. Captain Sorei was at his side, and behind them, the entire Inner Circle. They drew silent steel, held their blades to the sky in solemn salute. Fel'annár's breath was short, and all the nerves in his body seemed to come alive. He had never seen such a glorious thing, had never felt so worthy. His cause had been stamped in stone, sealed now with these Alpine blades. Unyielding. Unbreakable.

As they filed through the gates, under the Kah Warriors of old, Fel'annár twisted in the saddle. He saw King Vorn'asté standing high upon the walls, one hand extended in farewell to his son.

With the warmth of an early spring sun on his back, he thought he would never forget this place and the swords of gratitude that still glinted, unmoving, even as the gates began to close with a deep groan and then banged shut.

~

BAND'ORÁN SAT at a large desk strewn with papers and books.

Against one wall was a line of bottles. Inside one a chunk of mealy moss. Next to it, whole, dried hedgeberries, a deep purple fruit from the north and then another jar, filled with a dark grey powder. A dozen candles illuminated the workspace, stuck to its surface, the wax almost invasive.

Glass clinked behind him, and he turned. "Why did you never contemplate the teachings of the Kal'hamén'Ar?"

Huren considered the question, placed a goblet before his lord and sat in a chair beside the desk. His eyes roamed over the fascinating collection of herbs and berries, books and scrolls. "I'm not sure. Perhaps it is the solemnity of it, the philosophy that accompanies it, that I cannot abide. Forgive me, my lord, but perhaps it is a lack of patience. Or perhaps I simply do not understand it enough to want it. It never really touched me, save for the beauty of the Dance and my respect for the skill it requires."

"Indeed, you do not understand it. Still, you are a good enough Blade Master. Good enough to be my Commander General."

Huren nodded slowly in thanks, eyes watching his lord carefully. Small carving knife in hand, Band'orán whittled away at a piece of softwood, painstakingly emptying the pliant inside and making for himself a small, cylindrical receptacle. He raised his eyebrows, wondering what in Aria Band'orán would use it for.

"You have been here for many days, my lord."

Band'orán reached for his wine, drank some, took his time answering Huren. "What Melu'sán of the Merchant Guild said about Thargodén is true. He is regaining his popularity, becoming strong again. Too strong." He looked down at the parchment before him, the seal of Sulén in one corner. Picking it up, he held it to the flames and watched it burn. "Sulén is on his way, come to help his lord, cast his greedy eyes upon his new lands. He hasn't mentioned the Silvan at all."

"Still alive, then." Huren watched as Band'orán put down his wine and reached for the bottle of hedgeberries. He dropped four into a pestle and mortar, bent over it and smelled, eyes closed.

"It would seem that way. That fool and his idiot son have failed me, and still he thinks of his lands rather than his service to me. No sooner he steps inside this forest, I want him here, Huren, alive but out of sight."

"Of course. And the Silvan?"

"We must first wait for news from our Shadows abroad. Our contingents at the High Path and Port Helia may be our last chance. After that, should he step one foot inside this forest, I will deploy my personal guard."

"You would expose them?"

"If that is what it takes." Band'orán's eyes were on him, heavy with unspoken words. Huren nodded briskly, sipped his wine again. Band'orán turned back to his desk, picking up his pestle and pressing down on the berries, twisting and grinding.

Despite Sulén's coin and his endless supply of Shadows, the boy had eluded them all. And if Huren, too, failed him, then he would show the world that the Kal'hamén'Ar had returned. His personal guard, his hidden army, was loyal to *him* and they were unbeatable. Four hundred Kah Warriors could take on a thousand-strong army. Thargodén's had once been twice that number but now, with three hundred Silvans gone and many others deployed unnecessarily into the forest and to the sea, the final preparations were coming together.

"I want a daily report, Huren. Things will happen, and soon. You must be ready."

Huren stood, finished his wine. "Lord." He bowed as he would to a king, turned, and began the long trek back to civilisation.

Soon, Thargodén would keep Band'orán company, down here where no one except Huren and his personal guard were allowed. He would entertain the monarch only until the Silvan was dead, until he had shown Rinon's incompetence, until the people finally understood that there was only one way forward. *His* way.

And then, when Thargodén had seen it all, understood it all, he would die.

He poured the purple powder into his small wooden cylinder and then covered it with a piece of cloth. He had perfected the art, and soon, perhaps, he would have reason to use it and see the consequences of his skill.

He sat back and smiled.

MIST LINGERED over the damp ground. The heady smell of soil and foliage was familiar and steadying. Fel'annár filled his lungs and fixed his gaze on a distant tree.

His waking body was reaching out, stretching its senses, leaning towards the forest and its welcoming voices. The two masters beside him could not hear what he did. They could not hear the whisperings, the gentle words and the ever-present hum of power pulsing through roots, in his own veins. They did not understand the magic that was his life now, even though they, too, felt it pooling in their bodies, unaware of what it was, how it worked.

He extended his hands, straightened his back and reached out, knees bent, ready. They began in almost perfect synchrony, their slow movements and accurate grace mesmerised those who watched from afar. They boiled water and prepared food, but their eyes would not be parted from the dawn spectacle of the Dohai, a Kah Warrior's greeting to a new day.

There were no words when the three returned and sat at the fire, even though it was the first time Llyniel and Handir had seen it. Idernon was the only one who had been otherwise occupied, his head in the book on Calrazian history and an open parchment in his lap.

"Any findings?" asked Fel'annár as he ate.

The scholars of Tar'eastór had concluded that the sword was

most likely of Calrazian origin. But so little was known of that culture, of its language, and their studies were ongoing.

Idernon nodded, but he didn't look up, and Sontúr beside him peered sideways at the page he was studying.

"Is that the diagram of the sword?" asked Fel'annár, pointing to the curling parchment.

"Yes," murmured Idernon, irritated at the interruption, and Fel'annár thought he would get no more from him.

Indeed, the Wise Warrior said nothing for the entire day as they travelled, and by sundown, he was once more immersed. The Company were used to Idernon's obsessions, and while Sontúr admired his tenacity, Pan'assár found it odd. As for Gor'sadén, Fel'annár could only guess at what he was thinking.

They could see the still distant lights of Senge. There would be fresh fish for dinner tomorrow, mused Fel'annár. He was suddenly reminded of how he had prepared fish and come face to face with the prince, his brother, for the first time. Lainon had told him who he was that night. His smile faltered.

With the guard set and the fire blazing, Galdith chuckled at a comment from Carodel, who was patting at a dough he had made. Stretching it, he placed it over an upside-down pan. After a moment, he turned it. The smell of hot bread accompanied the tantalising aromas of Ramien's broth which bubbled away on the other side of the fire. The smells drowned the by now familiar scent of herbs that always seemed to hang about Llyniel, Sontúr and Gor'sadén.

"Have you managed to make any sense of that gibberish, Idernon?" asked Pan'assár.

"Not yet, sir, only that it *is* Calrazian, as the scholars suspected. There is precious little on their history. Captive Sand Lords don't speak, this we know, but their language has been heard, and some scholars have, at some point, tried to make sense of it. We also have Canter's intrepid account of his captivity. I read that before we left."

"Well, if it is about what that script means, why not go straight to those references on their language?" asked the commander, accepting a hot bread and ripping it open, nose flaring at the waft of steaming goodness.

"I have, sir. But there is hardly anything, and what there is, I've already read. It helps little, although it does give some insight. No, it's in the other reading that clues may come to light—if they ever do. Linguistically, all we know about the Calrazian language is that it is highly inflected, and phonetically, it is ... exotic, in that it uses a series of clicks and trills that sound passing strange."

"I can see that may be fascinating to one such as you. But tell us, Idernon, is there anything that we can use to decipher it?" insisted Handir.

Idernon placed the diagram on the ground before him, close enough to the fire pit to make it visible.

"For instance, this word here?" Handir pointed at the diagram.

"I'm not certain, but my guess is *family*, *friend* or perhaps *owner*. I am still working on that."

"And this drawing here?" Carodel pointed.

"This is interesting, yes. It is a symbol of some sort, perhaps even a family emblem, and that doesn't surprise me. This sword was the weapon of a lord."

"What do we know of their political system, Idernon? How do they live?" asked Llyniel, wiping her mouth on a napkin.

"The Sand Lords have a tribal society, not unlike the Silvans of centuries past. They have a king, this we also know. In turn, the king has his overlords who rule over a limited number of territories. Within each territory, each overlord has a chieftain who will defend those territories. As an example, our commander, Pan'assár, would be the overlord and Fel'annár, if he is Warlord, would be his chieftain in the forest."

"But why are they so reclusive?" insisted Llyniel.

"They are natural enemies of the Silvans. They lack water, and we have much of it. It is generally assumed that they wish to gain territory in the northern reaches, push the Silvans back, and slowly populate those areas. Perhaps they would build a piping system from our water supplies to the closest settlements in the south of

Calrazia. Slowly but surely, they would take away our territories and make their own greener, from south to north. It's logical that the less we know about them, the better they can achieve that goal."

"Why do you think they cloak themselves?" asked Carodel. "I mean, it's hot in Calrazia."

"They wear black because it seems to protect their bodies from the heat. Admittedly, we don't understand why that would be. As for their physical qualities, they are dark-skinned, as you know, but a different shade to that of an Ari."

"Well, except for Fel'annár," snorted Ramien. And then he froze, eyes swivelling to the side and Idernon, who glared back at him. Pan'assár was staring back at them in confusion, but Handir was shocked. The prince tore his eyes away from Ramien, slowly sought out Llyniel, who was studiously examining the ground beneath her feet. Not so Fel'annár, who was staring right back at him.

He stood slowly, crumbs falling to the ground. "A word, *brother*."

Llyniel watched as Fel'annár rose to his feet, gaze lingering on Ramien who would not return it. Instead, he fiddled with his mug, lips pulled into a tight line. With a loud exhale, Fel'annár followed Handir, well aware of Pan'assár's gaze that almost seemed to burn.

Inside, the oil lamps lent Handir's tent a cosy warmth, a stark contrast to the ice in Handir's eyes.

"Why didn't you tell me?"

"Why should I have?"

Handir had not expected that, and he quelled his rising temper. Instead, he nodded slowly. "Alright. I can see there was no obligation for you to do so. Yet it seems inherently wrong for you to hide your very race from me. Tell me, am I the only one who doesn't know?"

"No. Pan'assár didn't."

"So The Company, Llyniel, Gor'sadén—there were reasons for *them* to know?"

"Yes." Fel'annár turned slightly, walking to one side of the tent and perching himself upon a wooden chest. "Llyniel is my Connate. For this reason, she had to know before she accepted me."

Handir raised an eyebrow, forcing himself to focus on the question at hand.

"The Company needed to know because they follow me. That is a great responsibility and honour for me. I couldn't have kept it from them. They are my family."

Handir straightened.

"And Gor'sadén is the father I never had."

That was the plain truth, Handir knew. Idernon, Ramien, Carodel, Galdith and Galadan. Even Sontúr, a foreign prince, was more of a brother to Fel'annár than he himself was. Handir had his answer, and the tension in his body eased as he watched the Silvan stand and slowly walk towards him.

"There was no reason for me to tell you, and yet I would have, given time."

"Of course," he said placidly, once again the statesman. "You may leave, Fel'annár," he said, watching as his brother bowed and left. There was no apology in his eyes, just as there was no anger in his own now—not towards Fel'annár, at least. All that was left was acceptance.

He had *wanted* to be told, and for some reason, it angered him to have been left for last.

As Fel'annár made his way back to the fire, he passed Llyniel on her way to Handir's tent. He reached out and stroked her hand and then joined the others at the fire. The awkward silence was broken only by the rustling of Sontúr's hand inside his stuffed bag as he rummaged for some such envelope of herbs to treat Gor'sadén's leg. The prince stood, pulled at the commander's boot, and then pulled again. He caught himself from falling on his backside with one hand, Gor'sadén's boot in the other. Ramien snorted but quickly turned away when Fel'annár's gaze fell on him.

Turning back to the tent, Fel'annár saw the orange glow from behind the flaps, warm and inviting. His heart bid him go there, to his wife and the brother he was slowly coming to know. He had seen the surprise and hurt so clearly, it had taken him aback. He meant what he had said, though; there had been no practical reason to tell Handir that he was Ari'atór.

But the nagging voice in his mind told him it was not about practicality. He silenced it. Distraction was his worst enemy now. He returned his gaze to the fire and Gor'sadén's knowing eyes.

A HOODED FIGURE snatched a paper from his second in command. Flicking it open, he read and then strode to the fire pit, looked down on his elves and throwing the paper into the flames. They watched him, expectant.

"They are making for the river, avoiding the mountain passes."

"Senge then," said his second, watching, waiting for the order.

"Senge. Once they are away from the town, as they rest upon the riverbank. That is where we will take them."

He turned and walked towards the rocky outcrop that looked out over the lower land. Still open, still Tar'eastór.

Their quarry was elusive, had some affinity with trees. Sulén had told them, and none had doubted it. They had all seen the forest fight. They respected him, the one they would kill. But money was money, and besides, trees couldn't swim. The leader sniggered.

6

FOUR PRINCES

"An elf once asked why he should learn philosophy. 'Was it not as clear as day, that without philosophy, one could not rightly justify one's deeds?' The others stared back at the outspoken elf, as did the schoolmaster. But Idernon simply shrugged and then called them all boil-brained. He had been ten years old."
The Silvan Chronicles, Book III. Marhené

∾

With Handir's tent packed away and their horses saddled, they mounted and continued on their journey. Today they would arrive at Senge, and from there, they would commission boats for the journey down the River Cor'hidén. It was a well-worn path that led into Senge, lined on both sides with trees, and only a narrow shoulder of grass and loam for carts to pull over, should the space be needed.

Gor'sadén glanced sideways at Fel'annár, knew he was listening. But the Silvan said nothing. Yet, as the morning wore on, his frown persisted, and the commander turned to Pan'assár, gesturing with his head towards Fel'annár.

"Something worries him," he murmured. But before he could approach his Disciple, Fel'annár trotted towards them, eyes brighter than usual.

"We have company, a few minutes north and moving fast. Not the enemy."

"Friends?" asked Pan'assár, but Fel'annár was shaking his head.

"They don't know."

"Hoods," ordered Pan'assár, ushering them to the side of the path. Moments later, they heard galloping horses and saw three riders coming towards them, bent low over their lunging mounts. Their leader held up a hand and pulled back on his reins. The others slowed behind him.

Pan'assár registered the panting animals, the dusty riders, the uniform of Ea Uaré. Whatever their mission, it was an urgent one. He nudged his horse forward, saw Fel'annár approach from the corner of his eye. Not ready for battle, but neither had he said they were friends.

"Messengers?" asked Pan'assár, watching as the foremost warrior nodded and pulled his hood back, waiting in vain for the one before him to do likewise.

"From Abiren'á. We carry urgent messages for Prince Handir. Will you not show yourself, *Pan'assár*?"

The commander bristled. These were Silvan warriors from the army he commanded. They had not saluted, and he wondered how had this elf known it was him? Were they rebels? But Fel'annár was beside him, sat calmly in the saddle. He did not seem concerned.

Pan'assár pulled his hood away, narrowing his eyes as they travelled over the warrior, committing his face to memory. The other two warriors revealed themselves. They stared at their commander, daring him to discipline them.

"Who do you answer to?" asked Pan'assár.

"To King Thargodén. We are loyal to the line of Or'Talán. Many Silvans still are, lord."

"And yet you do not salute your commander general, brother as he was to our first king."

Handir had ridden up to Pan'assár's other side, but he remained cloaked, wary.

The Silvan's face hardened, but he said nothing. He flinched when Pan'assár moved towards him, close enough to strike if he so desired. Close enough to see the light in his eyes. Pan'assár scowled, half-turned towards Fel'annár, but still he sat quietly, and so he nodded at Handir.

The prince lowered his hood. The three messengers bowed respectfully. But there was no surprise in their eyes at all. Handir held out his hand to take the scroll the Silvan warrior held out to him, then nodded his thanks.

"What is your name, warrior?" asked Handir.

"Yerái, Prince." Handir watched him turn to the still hooded figure of Fel'annár. The messenger's eyes suddenly seemed to reflect too much light, like a cat in the dark.

"There are Listeners amongst you?" asked Yerái, almost in a whisper.

"Why do you say that?" asked Handir.

"Because *I* am a Listener. I feel their presence."

So that was how they had found them, mused Handir. And if this warrior was a Listener, it would be useless to deny it, yet he was unsure if revealing Fel'annár's presence would benefit them. He did not expect the warrior's next question.

"Is it him? Is it our Warlord?"

"That vote is yet to take place," said Handir, glancing at Pan'assár beside him.

"Not for the Silvans, Prince."

"Yerái. If he *were* here, he would not be in danger. I know you are wary of Commander Pan'assár, but remember this, warrior: my oath —*his* oath—is to the line of Or'Talán. The line you serve. When you leave this place, do so in hope."

Handir's eyes burned almost as brightly as Yerái's.

"Your Warlord is safe, and will remain that way, so long as I am alive," added Pan'assár.

The messenger looked from prince to commander, and then at

the still hooded figure he could feel in his mind, even as he spoke. "We must now ride to Tar'eastór with missives from our lord to King Vorn'asté. Once we have fulfilled our duty, we must return to Abiren'á and await instructions. That is the only safe route for urgent missives now. Is there anything we can take with us?"

Handir considered the question. They carried urgent correspondence from King Vorn'asté to Thargodén. It was possible these messengers could get them to the city before he could. "How safe is the passage from Abiren'á to the city, Yerai?"

"It is safe until just beyond Oran'Dor. From there, Silvan messengers are often confronted, their missives confiscated. If you carry something urgent, Prince, I can take it as far as that village with my personal guarantee."

"Carrier birds?" suggested Pan'assár.

"We have lost almost fifty in the last few months. They say it is furtive hunters, but the Silvans don't believe that."

"Then we must take our chances and continue on our path, Yerái. Farewell. Ride in hope, and in *silence*. 'Tis not a time for revelations," said Handir.

The Silvan nodded, turned once more to Pan'assár, and to the commander's utter surprise, he saluted. "It may not be time for revelations. But it is time for *returns*, would you not say, Commander?"

The messenger turned back to the one he knew was Fel'annár Ar Lássira, allowing himself the slightest and most fleeting of smiles. Eyes back on Pan'assár, they saluted respectfully this time. Kicking their mounts into a canter, the three warriors clattered down the path, towards Tar'eastór.

HANDIR IGNORED the questioning glances from his companions, just as he ignored the scroll that sat half inside his tunic. Meanwhile, Fel'annár tried not to think about Yerái, a Listener like himself. He had never met another. He had wanted to stop him and ask how it was for him. But there was no time for that. Still, he would remember the name and search for him when all this was over.

Their path soon widened, and the riverbank came into sight. Pan'assár signalled for them to stop and dismount. He shoved his hand into his saddlebags and pulled out a fistful of coins. Handing them to Galadan, he instructed him and Idernon to venture into the town and commission the boats they would need for the journey towards the Glistening Falls. He would not have his prince linger near the town for longer than necessary. He had no way of knowing if Senge was safe; the quicker they passed through and took to the boats, the better.

Handir settled upon the bank of the Cor'hidén and pulled out his scroll. The others kept a respectful distance, even Llyniel who sat talking quietly with Sontúr, whiling away the time before Galadan and Idernon were back, and they would walk into Senge.

In the town proper, Galadan searched the riverbank. It was lined with long, narrow jetties, and along them were poles to which small boats and larger rafts were tethered, bobbing on the placid waters. On one such jetty, he met Talen, a veteran River Master who introduced his friend, Deron, who had his own boat up for rent. With half their fees satisfied in advance, Galadan and Idernon took the path back, well aware of the stares and murmurs from the villagers. Silvans were obviously not common around these parts.

Not an hour later, they were back, and the entire group made for Talen and Deron's jetty. But as they approached, what seemed like the entire village of Senge had congregated there, including Lord Tenbar himself. It was not that Idernon had been Silvan; it was because he and Galadan were members of The Company. They had not passed by unnoticed.

"Prince Sontúr. It is an honour." The leader of Senge stepped forward and bowed low.

"Lord Tenbar. I hope you and your people are well."

"Like many villages, Senge is recovering from the battle as best it can. We lost many of our sons and daughters that terrible day. We would have lost more, had it not been for your companions," he said, eyes straying to Fel'annár and The Company.

The villagers talked quietly, nodding, but their eyes were riveted on the warriors who had stood before the horde—especially on Fel'annár, or was it Or'Talán returned, as some speculated? This was the one who had moved the trees, bid them fight.

"Please accept these humble offerings, a small token for the road." Tenbar nodded at his people. They laid their gifts before Sontúr and his companions.

"These gifts are most appreciated." Sontúr smiled, his poise and manner gracious and commanding. Fel'annár had rarely seen this side of his friend, the public figure, respected warrior prince. He was leaving all this behind to join them on their quest to the forest.

"Safe journey, then, and know that we are grateful," said Tenbar, eyes straying again to Fel'annár. "We are most thankful for the sacrifices made."

Tenbar and the village of Senge smiled and nodded, watching from a respectful distance as the warriors began to load their belongings onto the boats. But a small child broke free of his father and dashed straight for Fel'annár, a wilted-looking potted plant in his hands, a silent but desperate plea for help on his face. Skidding to a halt, he looked up at the towering warrior he knew was The Silvan. Timidly, he held out the plant. Fel'annár knelt and cocked his head to the side in thought.

"What's so special about this plant, sprout?"

"My mother. My mother gave it to me before she left for the battle. She told me to care for it but *look!*" he said, bottom lip quivering and his eyes welling with tears which he struggled to hold back.

Fel'annár breathed deeply. "Then care for it you must." He poked a finger into the water-logged soil and smiled tightly, eyes moving from the plant to the boy. "You're trying too hard, see? There's too much water, and that makes the leaves yellow. Every morning, lay your fingers over the soil like this and bring them away. If the soil sticks, don't water it and if they come away clean, then you can give it a little water. When the roots come out of the bottom, you must plant it in the ground or give it a bigger pot. This is your mother's tree, and her spirit will be inside it, but heed me, sprout. Should it die, don't fret. She'll live on. This is but one sapling amidst a whole *world* of trees; trees that share one mind. If she is in one, she is in *all* of them."

The boy's eyes widened, his childish misconception dawning on him and lightening his heart. Before Fel'annár could stand, the boy wrapped one arm around his neck and nestled his tiny head in the crook of his shoulder. The warm breath brought with it a jolt of memory, of the Battle of Sen'uár and the babe that had died in his arms. He repressed it with a slow blink, squeezed the little body and then looked down at the child, very much alive.

He gestured with his head that he should return to his fretting father. The boy scampered away and all but barrelled into his father's legs. As the group left, the boy's remaining family looked back over their shoulders, nodding slowly at Fel'annár as they left. He watched them leave, and then stood and turned, almost colliding with Pan'assár. The commander's eyes bored into his, but they no longer intimidated him and he returned the gaze, unwavering.

With a curt nod, Pan'assár turned away, unvoiced words of praise stuck to the back of his tongue. As for Galdith, his eyes had been on the boughs above him, unable to watch the young orphan with his dying plant. It reminded him of his own lost family, dead at the Battle of Sen'uár.

Galadan squeezed Galdith's shoulder, pushing him along towards the edge of the pier where their two boats bobbed in the water, tied to a wooden post. Ramien smiled as he hefted the chest onto one of the boats all by himself. To one side, Handir and Llyniel talked quietly. Her eyes crossed with Ramien, a smile lighting her face. He mirrored it, winked at her then felt Idernon's elbow in his ribs.

The boats were bigger than Fel'annár had expected. There was room for three aside and enough space in between for luggage. At the back was a long rudder that jutted out way past the guides' shoulders, and around the entire structure was a low wall of logs, on top of which sat three paddles on either side. The wooden benches along each side did not look comfortable, but he supposed three days on the river was better than two weeks in the saddle. He turned back to the commanders and listened to Pan'assár's brief.

"The River Masters require that we all listen to their instruction today. The waters are calm so they will show us the proper use of paddles and some safety measures should we run into difficulty. From tomorrow, it seems the currents will be stronger and the ride rougher. I want both princes and that chest duly protected. I will travel with Handir and his chest, Fel'annár, Ramien and Idernon. Gor'sadén will travel with Sontúr, Galdith, Galadan, Carodel and Llyniel."

Gor'sadén nodded, satisfied at the distribution of their group, save that he would have preferred Fel'annár in his own boat.

"Should we run into problems, we make for the eastern shore, before the Horizon Falls and then the cliffs beyond and the Glistening Falls." The commanders and lieutenants nodded their understanding, and Pan'assár gave the order to climb aboard.

Talen ushered Handir to a spot at the back, just beside the rudder that he himself would be steering. There were two coils of thick rope, on top of which lay a bright red buoy. He could only guess what that might be used for. Handir swallowed thickly and reached for the criss-crossing ropes that held down their chest of most precious belongings.

Along the port side, the guide placed Fel'annár at the bow and beside him on the right, was Ramien. Behind Fel'annár was Idernon, and beside him, Pan'assár would sit. Paddle in hand, Ramien smiled over at Fel'annár, excitement on his face, and for a moment, Fel'annár was back in the Deep Forest, up to some mischief. It was a welcome distraction from his slowly growing anxiety of what awaited in the forest. It was a moment of boyish adventure they had not felt for too long, and Fel'annár turned, only to find Idernon smirking back at him.

There were many rivers in the Deep Forest, but none of them as wide as this one. The biggest could be forded in five strides, and the water was rarely deep enough to swim. Granted, there were a few canyon pools that were almost always full of swimmers. But they had heard the tales of the vast expanses of water in these parts, and the rapids. And then, of course, there were the falls. On their way to Senge, Idernon had teased the Silvans amongst them. He had spoken of the roaring waters, the clouds of mist and the dangerous undercurrents. He had then answered the questions Galdith, Ramien and Carodel had asked him. With relish, he had exaggerated the dangers, enjoyed their round eyes and slack mouths far too much. Unfortunately, Handir had also heard it all.

On the other boat, Gor'sadén stood by his own guide, watching his group organise themselves.

"You must put words to a melody of our adventures on the Cor'hidén, brother," said Galdith, clapping Carodel on the shoulder. "I hope you've wrapped and stowed your baby well."

"I slipped it inside our prince's chest," he murmured.

"Well, it will be safe there, yes." Galdith nodded, duly impressed with his friend's audacity, unaware that Handir had given him permission.

"Here we go!" said Sontúr as their guides gave the order to row and they floated away from the jetty.

"Reach out with your hands and feel the ropes along the outside of the craft," instructed Talen while Deron did likewise on the other boat. "These ropes are for your safety. Should you fall into the waters, you must swim hard back to the craft and hold on to these ropes. If any member of this vessel is thrown into the water, it is your priority to aid them in returning. If you fall and cannot return, you should float upon your back and follow the current with your feet before you. This will allow you to kick away from rocks, boulders and other hazards. If you are thrown a rope, take it and swim back towards the vessel, not forwards or you will get more than just a mouthful of frigid mountain water. If you are being swept by the current, do not attempt to stand. Swim to the vessel or the eastern shore if you can; we will find you."

Pan'assár turned to his warriors and watched as they nodded their understanding. Handir swallowed, his hand grasping the inner safety ropes a little tighter. From the other boat, Llyniel pulled her face into a mock panic and then smiled fondly at him. She knew him well, and Handir didn't mind, so long as it was just her that had noticed his fear.

His eyes travelled to the chest that sat at the centre of their boat, strapped down with ropes. The missives were inside, carefully wrapped in oilcloth. They must not be lost for they were the unequivocal evidence of Sulén and Silor's treachery, and of course, they pointed at Band'orán's instigation of it. They were the weapon Handir would use to discredit him. Such a precious cargo they carried, and for the first time, he wondered at the wisdom of taking this route. Was two weeks less travel time worth the risk?

"Row!" came two commands, and after some angling and seesawing, the boats slipped into the soft current that took them at a leisurely pace down the centre of the river. The tree-lined shores were close enough to see the faces of those who fished or washed or simply sat and waved as they passed. All the while, their guide explained how to paddle forwards, then backwards, to the left and right, and with every instruction, he made them carry out the movements and observe the results.

Ramien was fascinated, claiming that river boating was the best thing since smoked sausages, and Idernon was taken with the kinetics of movement through water. Carodel was whipping up a song in his mind, while Galdith scowled at the waters, saying they were starting to make him queasy. As for Fel'annár, he scanned the shores as he listened to the guide, the song from the trees peaceful and welcoming, while Sontúr and Galadan enjoyed the ride, accustomed as they were to river navigation.

Handir, though, seemed unimpressed. His critical eye searched the structure for signs of ill-use and fatal flaws. He found none, but the sour lemon Fel'annár rather thought was in his mouth did not disappear. He turned to his wife in the other boat, a little behind his own, and watched as thin wisps of hair floated around her face, framing her placid smile and dreamy eyes.

It was a miracle they were here, mainly whole and hale. It was such an unlikely thing that, in spite of what awaited them—the prospect of war, of meeting strangers that were his father and brother —he could enjoy this moment. But with Aria as his witness, he *was* enjoying it. It was a brief, wonderful interlude in which everything else faded away, and he was free; free to row and laugh and contemplate his love on the river.

The day passed far too quickly for Ramien's liking, but the day dragged on endlessly for Handir. He was no good out here. He was a liability, incapable with a sword, a slow runner, vulnerable to the wiles of nature. The others were warriors, except for Llyniel, but even she was accustomed to the outdoors and enjoyed it.

THIRTY MINUTES LATER, Handir's tent stood upon dry ground, and two fires cast warmth about the camp. The warriors fetched water and collected more wood, as the sun hung low on the horizon. Soon, the smell of smoke mingled with the heady perfume of Sontúr's special brew of tea. The aroma of roasting fish made their mouths water and their tongues tingle. Handir watched them all as he knelt before the larger fire, observing the still unfamiliar routines of a military camp and its workings. It was a welcome distraction from his growing anxiety, the need to be home.

Opposite, Gor'sadén sat with his leg stretched out before him, absently rubbing his thigh as he, too, watched the camp settle. Beside him, Sontúr mixed a concoction. Smelling it, he turned and placed it under Llyniel's nose. She nodded, satisfied.

"My nightly torture approaches," murmured the commander.

"You seem steadier on your feet," ventured Sontúr.

"Perhaps." The commander shrugged as he blew hot steam from the surface of the brew, knowing what awaited him afterwards. He watched Fel'annár as he approached the fire.

"I have sent Galdith and Carodel to forward scout along the riverbank." It wasn't a question, but Galadan knew Fel'annár needed his approval.

"On what grounds?"

"The trees are tense, expectant. But I can't fathom the nature of their worries."

"Not Deviants? Hounds?"

"No."

"Then you have done well. Have you set a time limit?"

"One hour."

"Inform me when they are back."

Fel'annár nodded and then left to make another round of the camp.

"He will make a good leader." Galadan nodded.

"If this idea of the Warlord comes to fruition, I wonder where his loyalties will lie," said Pan'assár as he watched Fel'annár leave. "It will be his duty to defend the best interests of the Silvan people, but if it comes to it, should he ever have to decide between his people and his father, what will he choose, I wonder?"

"He will do the right thing."

Handir's gaze lingered on Gor'sadén, saw the certainty in his eyes and the doubts in Pan'assár's. Handir understood him. Thargodén had reached out to Fel'annár, and he had acceded to meeting him. But the king was nothing but a stranger to him. At the end of the day, it would come down to loyalties. Or'Talán had chosen the welfare of his people over the love he held for his son. Would Fel'annár do likewise?

"Prince. Will you tell us of your father's missive?"

Handir looked up from the fire and nodded slowly, knowing all eyes were upon him—all except those of Fel'annár, Galdith and Carodel. "The enemy is closing in. Band'orán is manoeuvring his assets, moving in on the throne. The king calls for our urgent return, in silence. He asks us to take the Dark Road."

Pan'assár nodded, but he said nothing, in spite of Gor'sadén's insistent stare.

"What's the Dark Road?" asked Ramien.

Sontúr stifled a chuckle, and Idernon pursed his lips.

"Nothing you need worry about," said Pan'assár.

And so they sat, the chunks of fish crackling as they roasted, spitting juices, impregnating the humid air with their irresistible smell. Ramien watched, fascinated as the translucent flesh slowly turned white and flaky. Idernon sat cross-legged, once more engrossed in his readings on the Sand Lords and the open scroll he had copied from the academics at his side. He did not look up when Fel'annár returned, sat beside Llyniel and turned to Galadan.

"There is something unsettling, Galadan. But for some reason, we cannot fathom what it is. From experience, I would say that if it *is* danger, then whatever or whoever it is, is inside the rock."

"How close would you say this danger is?" asked Pan'assár, leaning forward.

"If I am right, we may have a little time should they wish to attack."

"Enough to pack up our camp and escape?"

"I believe so, Commander."

"Suggestions?" prompted Gor'sadén.

"I would double the guard, rotate every two hours. I have spoken to Talen and Deron. Our boats should be ready to leave at a moment's notice. I will not sleep."

Gor'sadén nodded slowly at his Disciple, turned to Galadan as he spoke. "And neither will I."

Silence fell over them. It was not unexpected. They were past Senge and the safe zone. To the warriors this was routine, but to Handir and Llyniel it was unsettling. They were anxious, and so Fel'annár turned to Idernon in search of a distraction. "Any developments, Idernon?"

"This. This is ... interesting," murmured Idernon, his book open on his lap and a stick of fish in the other. Sontúr peered over his hunched shoulder, eyebrows rising. "This diacritic is repeated here, and here." He pointed. "And then in this phrase here." He shuffled to another extract of the Calrazian language. "See? It is the same, and because we know the meaning of this word..." Idernon's brow furrowed even more deeply, a sudden agitation in his questing fingers. He shuffled through the book more roughly than he ever had. It surprised Fel'annár because Idernon never mistreated books.

"You have lost me, brother. What is it?" asked Sontúr.

"A moment," ground out the Wise Warrior, Sontúr's question an unwanted distraction. "And take this bloody skewer off me," he said, shoving it at Ramien who shrugged and began to eat it.

The rest of The Company sat forward while Llyniel took the spits out of the fire and lay the second batch of fish to one side, smoking and untouched. Only the sound of rustling parchment joined the crackling fire. The hoot of a nearby owl was loud enough to startle.

"Ab, en, or, di ..."

"What?" asked Ramien through the fish in his mouth.

"Ab, en, or, di—one, two, three, four," said Idernon curtly as he flicked through the pages. "Ebanuk, San Ebanuk, King Ebanuk ..."

"'San' is 'king'?" murmured Sontúr.

"I believe so, but look here." He pointed to the scroll with the copy of the Nim'úan sword. "*Here.*" He tapped roughly on two words along the curve of the sword.

San dir.

"The name of the king?" suggested Sontúr.

"No. Not capitalised."

"Look here, Prince." He tapped again, this time to a word in his book. "This we know is the name of a Chieftain."

Batún.

"See here?"

Batún dir.

"Some sort of suffix," said Sontúr, shaking his head.

"Son of Batún, Sontúr. 'Dir' means 'Ar'—'son of'."

Their eyes turned back to the sword.

San dir.

"Son of a *king*, Sontúr? This blade belonged to the son of the king of Calrazia."

"Oh Gods," muttered Sontúr, lifting his eyes from the book to The Company and Llyniel who sat frozen.

"That thing was a *prince*?" asked Galadan.

"It would seem that way," confirmed Sontúr, but Idernon's head was back in his book.

"Wait." Picking up the scroll once more, he pulled it closer and then swayed backwards, eyes wide, body stiff. "Di san dir … commanders." He turned gleaming eyes on Gor'sadén and then Fel'annár.

"Translate it for us, Warrior," said Pan'assár carefully.

"Di san dir. Four princes."

Their fire crackled, sparks rising upwards. The flapping of some night bird sounded not far away, the rush of flowing water. Their thoughts remained unspoken. Four brothers. Four princes.

How many of them were Nim'uán?

WITH THE WATCH set and rotating every two hours, Fel'annár meant what he had said. He would not rest. He sat, half way between the camp fire and the perimeter, cross-legged and with his back against a birch tree. Galadan knelt close by, hands on his thighs.

"Well, trainee-lieutenant. How have these first days been as a commanding officer?"

"It has been easy so far. Our warriors are my brothers, I know them well." He turned to Galadan. "And then I have you, should I do something stupid."

Galadan turned to him. "You will not. And yes, you have me. But there is little I can teach you, Fel'annár, save perhaps for my experience. You know the Code, you know the theory, and you have a natural disposition towards command. All you lack is experience; the anticipation of strife, the sometimes unlikely turn that events can take. Only experience can foresee what may or may not happen. Although in your case, you have the trees."

"They are not infallible. But yes, I have the trees. The problem is sometimes convincing others that there is a danger they cannot perceive. With The Company it's not a problem, but with those that don't know me … it comes down to a question of trust – faith, even."

"Then it is up to you to kindle that faith, that trust. That is the mark of a commander, Fel'annár. Warriors will throw themselves into the face of danger at one word from you. They will not question your motives or your reasoning but simply trust that it is sound. If you can achieve this, then you will know that you are a commander."

Fel'annár let Galadan's words settle. It was not about how skilled he was as a warrior. It was not how well he knew the code, or how efficiently he set up a camp and set a guard. It was not even about his ability to strategise. The key, according to Galadan, was his relationship with his warriors.

"Perhaps I will achieve that one day, become a captain." He smiled. Fel'annár had never relinquished that dream, never would.

"You have already achieved it, Fel'annár. All that is left is to test you at the command of unknown warriors. I look forward to the day we arrive, when the Silvan warriors will look to you. And still, I will be there to help you, if you need it."

"I will always need you, Galadan."

The lieutenant who had never wanted to be a captain, smiled softly into the night, head turned away from the trainee lieutenant who did not seem capable of seeing himself as others did. He would though, soon enough, because if Galadan was right, the Silvan warriors of Ea Uaré would follow him willingly. They had proclaimed him Warlord and the challenge for one such as Fel'annár, would be the greatest he would ever face.

7

FLIGHT TO INFINITY

"Water can soothe, cleanse, quench thirst and feed nature. It harbours life, gives life, as easily as it can take it."
The Alpine Chronicles: Cor'hidén

∽

At dawn, Carodel and Galdith once more reported to Fel'annár and Galadan. They, in turn, spoke discreetly with the commanders and the rest of The Company. They had nothing to report, except that Galdith had seen a flash in the night. Carodel said it was moonlight, reflecting on steel. Fel'annár thought it could have been many things. Still, he was uneasy, the trees restless. Something was wrong, but it was as if some distant danger was being magnified, more than it should.

They pushed away from the shore and navigated into the very centre of the river, Talen crossing gazes with Deron. They moved faster than they had the previous day. But yesterday's excitement of navigating the river had turned to tense silence. Between the unknown threat that Fel'annár spoke of and Idernon's discovery, there was plenty to consider.

The Nim'uán they had vanquished had three brothers. Were they alive? Were they Deviant, too? Fel'annár, for one, didn't understand. He knew Deviants and Sand Lords were enemies, and yet their own prince was a Deviant? An *elf*? It didn't make sense, but he wasn't going to question Idernon's findings. He wondered if, perhaps, Hobin would be able to shed some light on the matter.

But of all of them, it was Fel'annár and Gor'sadén who had seen the beast up close. Only they knew of its strength, its beauty, that velvety, hissing voice and the perverse gleam in its eye.

Under normal circumstances, the commanders would send urgent missives to Comon in Tar'eastór and Huren in Ea Uaré, to warn them that there may be more Nim'uán, that they may be allied with Sand Lords. But these circumstances were not normal. There were no messengers to send. They were nowhere near a military outpost and wouldn't be, not until they were in Bulls Bay and even then, it would not be safe to approach the army.

Fel'annár's arms burned, but he welcomed it. The rhythmic movement helped him to focus, and his eyes were back on the river and the now murky waters they sliced through. The Cor'hidén was wider here, the distance between them and the shore greater. Should the enemy attack, they would not be so hard-pressed to escape. Still, Handir sat with one hand wrapped tightly around the ropes that held down his luggage, though whether that was due to the rapid waters or the threat of attack, Fel'annár couldn't say.

With an order from the guide to correct their direction, Ramien dug in and rowed faster towards the right. The boat lurched sideways, sending Handir's other hand to the safety ropes. Pan'assár saw him but said nothing. Handir had proven himself an outstanding statesman and a better tactician than he had ever given him credit for. He had been a pleasant surprise to Pan'assár on this mission. Yet one thing was crystal clear to him: Handir was not an elf of action.

The current was strong, pulling them to the left, and their guide held fast to the rudder, leaning against it. Water splashed over the sides, and before long, they were all drenched, and the roar of the river was almost deafening.

Talen's voice broke over the tumult of angry water warring with stone. "Row hard—*hard!*"

Ramien and Fel'annár picked up the pace, digging their paddles deep into the water, hands disappearing beneath the surface. The boat rocked and tipped with the ever-higher waves, and then the bow would plunge back into the river, sending sheets of frigid water over them all.

Handir spluttered, his hair plastered to his head and neck, and he turned to the other boat a distance away. He could see Llyniel clearly enough, saw that she was smiling into the breeze, eyes wide and mouth open. He had always known she had a mad streak in her.

They hurtled down the river, seemingly out of control, and Handir thought it best to watch the guide. If he was worried, then Handir would know there was something wrong. He watched as the elf leaned into the stern, watched the others as they rowed. Their muscles bunched and braids flew about their heads and all the while, their lips were upturned and exhilaration danced in their eyes. He wished he could share their glee as they battled the power of nature. But he couldn't. He sat in his corner and fixed his eyes on the undulating horizon. He told himself it would soon be over, and his feet would walk on solid, unmoving ground.

Thank the Gods.

HANDIR RETCHED AGAIN, one hand pressed against the bark of an accommodating tree. Only Fel'annár stood close by, guarding him from the sight of others. They had come ashore not minutes ago and Handir, pasty-faced, had walked hastily away from them. Pan'assár had gestured to Fel'annár to follow him, and now he stood by, waiting for Handir's bout of sickness to pass.

After moments of silence, he turned, only to find Handir sat upon the ground, legs apart and elbows resting on his knees, head bent between them. Waterskin in hand, Fel'annár approached and looked down upon him. "Here."

Handir looked up into the clear gaze of his brother. Reaching with a hand he took the skin, uncorked it and drank, spitting out the water and then drinking again. Fel'annár took it back and offered his other hand to the prince. After a while, Handir took it and Fel'annár pulled him up.

"I am ... *unaccustomed* to life outdoors," he said, eyes not quite focusing on anything.

"As I am unaccustomed to life at court. I will need you in the weeks to come."

Handir's gaze shot to Fel'annár. He searched for a moment, and then his taut features relaxed. Handir's stomach rebelled against the unnatural movements of their boat, while Fel'annár's stomach would perhaps churn at the political machinations of life at court. His still did sometimes.

"Thank you."

Fel'annár nodded briskly. "We should return to the others."

Soon they sat with the rest, a moment of respite before they set up camp once more.

"Talen informs me that the temperatures are unusually high for this time of year. The melts are abundant. Should this heat continue, we may find ourselves on an overly swollen river tomorrow. He believes we may have to continue on foot a while."

"Lieutenant. Do you sense anything out of the ordinary?" asked Galadan from Pan'assár's side. He started at Fel'annár's hesitation.

"They're still concerned, still confused. There is something I cannot quite grasp. Too much rock ... or perhaps there is more than one danger."

"Is there a danger of attack?" Pan'assár persisted, silence falling around him. Even the River Masters stared from afar.

"There may be. But if that is the case, they are still a way off."

Galadan nodded. "Set a healthy perimeter guard. Status every fifteen minutes."

Fel'annár nodded in return, briefly catching Llyniel's gaze. She watched him leave and then helped those not on guard duty to set up the camp. Finished, she caught Handir's gaze, knew him well enough to know he was dwelling on something. She cocked her head, and together they made for the tent.

It was cold inside, and Handir wrapped his travel blanket around himself. He sat on the chest where Sulén's scrolls lay. He gestured with his head for Llyniel to join him.

"How bad is it really, Handir? What exactly does your father say?"

"Here," said Handir, pulling a scroll out of his tunic and passing it to her. He would place it in the chest once she had read it.

Llyniel pulled it open and read.

My son.

Unaware as we are as to what you know, what you do not, I write in the hopes that you are well, and that Fel'annár is with you.

Band'orán is closing in. In these days that lead to the votes for equality and for the return of the Silvan Warlord, he moves his allies skilfully. He propagates falsities, says Fel'annár is dead, wrests the hope from Erthoron's people, drives them to questionable acts in the forest. They are divided in their loyalty to their leader, have closed the forest to the Alpines, and clamour at our very doorstep. Band'orán does nothing but encourage the chaos.

If Fel'annár is with you, you must bring him with all haste but have a care. Band'orán will not welcome him. Your return will be fraught with danger. He will be hunted by Band'orán, hailed by the Silvan people.

Come swiftly and in stealth. Walk in anonymity and deliver him here. Bring him upon the Dark Road. Band'orán must not know when or how you return.

It is not my intention to cut your tutorship short. I know how much it means to you, but I need you here at my side together with Rinon and Aradan. We must appease the Silvans, give them their Warlord and convince the Royal Council that equality is the only way to maintain this realm, as it is, under my rule. We must show Band'orán's treachery, yet the way to do so eludes me.

We have until the fourth day of April. That will be a day marked by history. Trust no one, save for Pan'assár. He will see you safely home.

Safe journey, my son.

"I can just see my father, standing beside yours, urging caution."

Handir huffed. "And Rinon all riled and ready to slice Band'orán up." He smiled, turned to his friend. "I'm glad you're here."

She smiled back at him but hesitated. "What's the Dark Road?"

Handir snickered and thought about whether he should tell her. He shrugged. "It is an underground road. A safe passage for the royal family, should some danger threaten them. It runs from the palace to a place beyond the gates."

"You're not going to tell me where, are you?"

It was not really a question, and Handir smiled, saying nothing.

"Report."

"Sir. They have camped on the eastern shore. Three hours' trek if we were to leave now, at night and through the wilds."

"That will make engagement at first light. We must make it before if we can. See to it."

The scout nodded, tucking his hair behind a somewhat rounded ear. He turned to leave but hesitated. "Sir. My bones tell me there is a storm coming."

The leader scowled. "The skies are clear. Go tell your half-caste suspicions to those fool enough to listen."

The scout shut his mouth and left. He would never press any point where his captain was concerned. Still, he was right. His right ankle throbbed worse than it had done for decades. And he had seen some mighty storms in his time.

Birds were calling out, screams echoing off the stone walls of the canyon through which the river ran. Galadan sat up, blinking hard. It was too early. He jumped at a presence crouched at his side.

"Sir, the enemy approaches from the north and west. A large group of some fifty elves," said Fel'annár.

"Get up! Break camp now! Leave the tents!"

"Sir, to the boats or on foot? The land is sodden, the water has risen."

Galadan cast his eyes around them. Indeed, water lapped at the grassy shore, the level rising before his very eyes, breaking over the banks. Shrugging on his cloak, he strode towards Pan'assár, Gor'sadén and Talen. Fel'annár walked at his shoulder while the others scrambled around them to pack up their camp, pulling on their harnesses as they worked.

"Commander. Lieutenant Fel'annár reports fifty hostiles from the north and west. But the water is rising at an alarming rate, some freak flood. We either risk it on foot or take to the boats."

Pan'assár looked around him, too calm even for Galadan's liking. The commander faced Fel'annár, expression as hard as stone. "Fifty, you say. Do they carry bows?"

"Yes." Fel'annár's eyes were bright and Talen dared not move.

Pan'assár turned to him. "Your thoughts."

"The river will be furious. The melt must be huge for the water to rise so quickly."

"Fel'annár. Can you tell what kind of bows they carry?"

"Longbows. Three hundred and fifty yards with precision."

"Load the boats! Move!" shouted the commander, then stifled a cough, the first any had heard since his recovery from the Gas Lizard.

Fel'annár looked at Galadan in alarm, then at Talen who stood shaking his head. "This is madness, commander. Navigating that river now is sure death for us all."

"So is staying on land, Talen. At least in the boats we have a chance."

Talen turned, dread on his face, but still he shouted his own orders.

While they boarded the crafts, Fel'annár stood upon the water-logged shore. He did not know if Pan'assár's decision was the right one, but he felt nothing but respect for the calm and calculated way he had made it. Time would tell if the boats were, indeed, their best chance.

He heard trampling boots, heavy boots. Not shadows—mercenaries. He heard the tenuous warnings of the trees. Sparse and spindly, but clear nonetheless. And then he realised. They were not accustomed to elves hunting elves. That was why they were confused.

The voices were louder. He could see distant figures between the trees, cresting the rocks, almost within shooting distance. He turned, ran and then helped push the boat into the dirty waters with Handir already inside it, clutching the ropes and crouching low. Fel'annár jumped over the edge and grabbed for the oars. "Out, now. Thirty seconds for range."

"Row!" shouted Pan'assár, Gor'sadén echoing the command close by.

As their speed picked up and the current began to pull them further from the shore, Pan'assár saw what Fel'annár had warned them of. No uniforms, no concealing cloaks. Mercenaries. Far too many of them to have faced on land with their backs to the water.

The enemy archers drew and fired, but their arrows splashed into the deepening water, out of range, and the two boats continued towards the centre of the swelling river.

"Row! Row!"

Fel'annár and Ramien at the bow, Idernon and Pan'assár himself behind and at the stern. At Talen's feet sat Handir. With both hands holding on to the safety ropes on either side, he gave the strange impression that he was lounging, when in fact he was rigid as a novice before the king, knuckles even whiter than his face. His eyes moved from Talen to Pan'assár to the chest. He wanted to check its bindings but daren't let go of the ropes. It was a hot morning, and he looked up to the slate-coloured sky. It was just past dawn and steely clouds puffed towards the zenith, towering over them, singing their song of coming storms.

The Gods help us, he thought. They were escaping the mercenaries and riding into battle, not with Deviants or Sand Lords, but with nature herself, and he thought there was nothing quite so terrifying as that. Turning his head to the shore they had just left, he saw their pursuers, standing still, bows in hands and clay-coloured water up to their knees. He could no longer see the riverbank where their camp had been.

Handir turned to Talen, watching as he struggled with the rudder and glanced at Deron in the other boat to their right. Handir, trained statesman that he was, watched their eyes. He saw their dread as surely as he saw the surety in Pan'assár's eyes. It was a skill worked and honed and yet not attainable to any and all. Pan'assár exuded confidence and strength. It rippled over every word spoken, every command obeyed, never questioned. One mind and many bodies had delivered them from the mercenaries, into the hands of the Cor'hidén, and yet, despite their dire circumstances, Handir thought they may have a chance.

But then his eyes were back on the raging river that ran dirty and greedy over everything in its path. His hands were so tightly clenched he wondered if he would be able to let go later. All he could do was pray that the melt would let up, that they would find a way out of the torrent to dry land. He knew what lay at the end of the canyon, as well as the rest of them did.

Horizon Falls, the last frontier before the Glistening Falls, where the land gave way to the sea. It would be a sure and swift route to Valley for them all.

TENSÁRI GALLOPED over the High Plains, the citadel of Tar'eastór looming over her. One more day and she would stand in the presence of Hobin. One more day and she would tell Fel'annár her thoughts, tell him what she had come to understand.

All breath left her. Eyes bulging, she heaved desperately for air, pulling sharply on the reigns and coming to a halt in a cloud of dust. Gasping, she held one gloved hand to her armoured chest, but it seemed to move too slowly as if she were underwater. She needed to calm her breathing ...

Water. She had been underwater, unable to breathe.

A sense of danger slammed into her. Pulling on the right rein, she spared one last glance at Tar'eastór and Hobin, who was surely still there, and then cast her gaze westwards.

Forgive me, Commander.

A subtle yet discordant note. It echoed strangely, its melody playing too slowly. It was muffled and muted, but she heard it just the same, and she knew.

Water. She needed to follow the water.

"Pan'assár! Heave right! Right!" He gritted his teeth, battling with the water that pressed relentlessly against the right side of the boat, pushing them away from the eastern shore. Fel'annár roared, poured all his energy into his arms. Water rushed wildly past, and for the first time, they saw rocks beneath the surface, water churning around them. Above them, the sky exploded. A blinding flash lit up the towering clouds.

Talen looked up, and Handir saw what he had most dreaded to see. Fear.

Fat drops of water began to fall, until one morphed with another, and it was almost a constant flow.

"Watch for the rocks!" shouted Talen over the splitting crack of lightning overhead. The grey around them turned blinding white, the smell of rotten eggs, of lightning too close.

The canyon was closing in, the river narrowing. Before, the current had been their constant enemy, but now it was the rocks. Talen needed to see so that he could navigate between them and get them all to shore, but the sheet of heavy rain, the frothing water and the spray all around them made his job almost impossible.

Handir sat petrified beneath a constant gush of water that ran down his face, spluttering in his mouth where it met with his harsh breaths. He could no longer see the other boat, but he could hear distant shouts. His body lurched left, then right, and he tried to use his legs to jam himself in place. He could hear the wood beneath him sliding over rocks and wondered how long it would be before one of them split the boat in two.

A grey bulk loomed to Idernon's left. "Brace for impact!" shouted the Wise Warrior.

"Brace!" Fel'annár's strangled word came just before the painful jolt of wood impacting with stone. Talen flew upwards, out of the boat, and splashed into the water a distance off to the side. He was soon lost to sight as their boat yawed to the left, coming to lie flat against a gigantic bolder. The current rushed around them, holding them in some deathly embrace.

"Talen!" shouted Pan'assár. But there was no answer, and even if there had been, he would not have been able to hear it over the churning waters and the booming sky.

Idernon had just enough time to see the water as it snaked around the right lip of the boat, where Fel'annár, Handir and Pan'assár sat. "We're capsizing!" he shouted. He and Ramien clung to their own side which began to rise out of the water. Pan'assár jumped towards him, meaning to lend his weight but Fel'annár lunged sideways, one hand finding the ropes that secured the chest to the boat, the other grappling in the water where he had seen Handir fall.

"Handir!" Pan'assár screamed, coughing.

"I have him!" called Fel'annár.

Idernon, Ramien and the commander leaned over the left side, desperate to counter the force of the water that was sucking them under the rock. If any of them moved, they would capsize. All they could do was crane their necks as below them Fel'annár, legs in the water, clutched at the ropes with one hand, while the other bunched at Handir's collar.

"Handir. Reach for me. Get a hold!"

"What's happening. Fel'annár?" Pan'assár's frantic call between dry hacking.

"He's in the water! Can't get his arms up. The backwash ... too powerful. He's going to drown ..."

"I need rope!" shouted the commander. "Idernon, can you reach it?"

It was close. There were two lines which Talen had tied to the iron ring before they left, just where Handir had been sitting. Idernon reached out, fingers brushing over the sodden fibres, but the boat tilted and he pulled his hand back in alarm. He caught Pan'assár's gaze.

"Handir. Bring your arm out of the water. Bring it up. Find something to hold!"

Only Fel'annár heard the sounds of water muffling speech. He didn't need to hear the words, though; he could see for himself that the current which had wedged them up against the rock was too strong. It had found a route around the boat, around Handir's body, and held him in a powerful vice he could not escape from. He could not even raise his hand.

"*Reach!*" Fel'annár's panicked voice called as he pulled with all his might. But his own legs were in the water, sucking him downwards, shoulder screaming at him to let go of the prince. They couldn't reach the ropes without tipping the balance and capsizing.

"Ramien. Hold on to the safety ropes and climb over the side. We have to right ourselves." Idernon's eyes shot to Pan'assár, and then to Ramien, who was already tucking his hands between the ropes and the wood, pulling himself upwards as gently as he could. The boat tilted even further. Fel'annár shouted, but then the Wall of Stone made it over the side, his legs in the water. He leaned back as far as he dared, and felt the boat right itself only marginally.

Handir's head was barely above the water. The current buffeted his face from all sides, and Fel'annár knew he had to act now lest the prince drown right before him. But he couldn't move. He was trapped, held down by the backwash. Handir was going to drown.

"Fel'annár?" Pan'assár couldn't see them, but Idernon could.

"Hwindo. Don't let go. I'm coming."

Idernon moved his left hand, reaching for Fel'annár, for anything he might latch on to. A cape, even hair, something to anchor his friend. The boat rocked, and he froze, turning to Pan'assár once more. But all he saw was the face of fear, and for the first time, there were no orders, no ideas.

Idernon reached out again, questing fingers feeling the wooden chest, further down the ropes, and then flesh—a hand. Just a little further ...

The boat lurched, and Fel'annár's head shot to Idernon, eyes turning from fear to realisation. Handir was under the water. If he couldn't pull him up, he had to let go of the boat. The prince would not survive in the river and he himself had little chance—but together, however remote ...

One last glance at Idernon above him, and he released his grip on the ropes.

Idernon screamed to the thundering heavens.

"No! Hwindo *no!*"

"*Handir!*" Pan'assár's cry was raw, dread from his very soul given voice for only the second time in his life. With the weight of two suddenly gone, the boat almost righted itself, enough to escape the backwash.

With burning eyes, Idernon turned to where Ramien was pulling himself over the side. Pan'assár was beside him, helping him. A sopping Ramien rolled over, spluttering as he took hold of one of the two paddles that were still attached to the boat. They slipped into the current, wordless, speechless, until they were once more hurtling down the canyon, Pan'assár at the stern, Idernon and Ramien on either side at the oars.

"I want everything you have! Idernon, Ramien. The crown requires all that you are. Show me your worth and *row*. We find our princes, bring them back. By my oath we bring them back. Row hard!"

Pan'assár was pure fury as he led them on, was as angry as Idernon himself. They had lost Handir, lost Fel'annár, had not saved them, and ultimately, Idernon knew it had been *he* who had tipped the boat. Pan'assár, likewise, knew it had been his decision that had brought them to this moment. Yet still, he guided them through the gullies and around boulders as best he could, but they could hardly see through the spray and the foaming water, the churning eddies.

They no longer knew where the other boat was, or even whether it was still afloat.

How could they possibly distinguish two silver-haired elves in this? How could they possibly survive it? Still, they strained their eyes as they battled the white waters and their own mounting panic.

Fel'annár was needed if the Restoration was to ever have a chance. And Idernon knew that without his childhood friend, his brother, his own life would lose its purpose. No. He would not lose Fel'annár. The Company stayed together. Wherever one went, the others would follow, even to Valley.

He would find Fel'annár and drag him to safety before it was too late. Before they reached Horizon Falls.

FEL'ANNÁR HURTLED DOWN THE RIVER, Handir in his clutch and flailing at his side. He angled them onto their backs, but it was not easy. Handir fought to keep his head forwards, an instinct he knew. But Fel'annár remembered their guide's warning. Feet first would help to push away from obstacles, and there were plenty of those.

Rain continued to pelt down, splashing into the raging current. Their speed picked up, and a grey shadow loomed to their left. Kicking out, he pushed them away from the boulder, and they slid downwards, backs brushing over the rocks below them. They sped through a tight gully with rocks on both sides, and at the end, Fel'annár felt himself pulled beneath the surface. His left hand clutched tightly to Handir. Bubbles flew past him, and all he could see was grey fog and silver hair.

The opaque turbulence lightened to silver. His face broke the water, Handir's head appearing in a spluttering, strangled shout. The prince coughed, but he held on, and they were once more hurtling down the canyon, at the mercy of wild waters, desperate, it seemed, to reach its destiny: the sea and freedom from its rocky confines.

They smashed into a smooth rock, and they dipped under once more. Waterweeds thrashed wildly, straining against their roots.

Kicking out, the brothers broke the surface, and Handir's coughing and retching was weaker. He was losing strength. Fel'annár was not surprised. He was exhausted himself, and Handir had not been trained for endurance.

Fel'annár's eyes made quick work of their options as they rushed past the obstacles. There was nothing he could cling to, no footholds, only smooth, slippery rock. He braced for impact once again, protected himself as best he could, and then smashed into a slab of granite with a soppy smack. The river was spinning before his eyes, and for a moment, the tension left his muscles. He felt his body move like a cape in a mountain-top breeze.

He blinked furiously. White froth and diamond water drops rained before him, tinged pink. He blinked again. The blur sharpened and a silver head streaked across his peripheral vision.

"Handir! Han." His voice was silenced by a mouthful of water, which he choked out and then tried again. "Handir!"

The blond head turned, wide eyes watching as the other hurtled towards him.

"Handir!" A desperate cry, or perhaps a goodbye. Either way, although the river jostled and pushed, Fel'annár felt he was floating towards Handir.

He had let go of the prince and not realised.

He reached out, but then almost overtook Handir. Lurched sideways, one fist latched on to cloth, and they crashed together. Just for a moment, he allowed the current to carry them where it would. Fel'annár held his brother against his chest, powerful arms reaching around him.

"I see them. Left! Row hard left!"

Ramien dug his oar into the current while Idernon lifted his. The craft angled sideways and then was pulled forwards once more. They could see the two heads now, miraculously together. Pan'assár wanted to scream his joy, but the other side of himself silenced it, told him they would both die, together at least.

"Row! Row!"

The river's roar was louder now, and Idernon turned back to Pan'assár as he rowed, eyes wide. But the commander said nothing. What was the point? The Wise Warrior knew what was coming, as surely as he did. At the end of the canyon was Horizon Falls. It was here where they should have taken to shore, camped and then climbed down the cliffs and to the sea.

They could see the horizon through a natural doorway of rock, cut from years of frenzied currents. It was fuzzy with mist, and the roar drowned almost every other sound, except for Pan'assár's now raw and hoarse voice, and the terrible beat of his own heart in his ears.

"Row! All hands!"

Ramien set the pace, arms and shoulders working to full capacity. The two brothers raced down the river, dipping under but always rising again, sooner or later. The current only seemed to increase, and yet another decision loomed before Pan'assár; follow until they themselves were trapped and doomed to ruin on the falls, or retreat to shore and perhaps regroup with whoever had survived this madness. One way or the other, Pan'assár would find them, and if they were dead, then he would have failed in his promise to Or'Talán. He would take their bodies to their father and then step upon the Long Road in shame.

They seemed further away now, and the weight of the world all but squeezed his heart to a shuddering halt. They could go no further.

And then he saw the others on the shore; saw Deron throwing a buoy, rope snaking through the air. The buoy missed the two figures in the water and he pulled it back, then ran along the shore and threw it again. They saw a hand reach and catch, saw the rope tense. Their hopes flared and then snapped, as surely as the rope slid from Fel'annár's hand.

"One, last chance, warriors! Row, row, row ..."

"Commander." The urgent voice of Ramien.

"Row! Row!"

"Commander!"

The bright red buoy was streaking towards them. Holding his paddle in one hand and reaching with his other, Ramien fumbled with the oval-shaped buoy. He dropped his paddle and quickly wrapped it around the helm. Still, it tensed before he had secured it and he cried out, gritting his teeth as their craft turned sideways. With one last effort, the buoy was in place.

"What are you doing? We row!"

"*Commander*! Idernon, we can't. It's too late."

"No. Ramien. You row. We go after him. Release the boat!" Idernon was still rowing, even as Ramien grabbed the floundering rudder. Wood groaned, and the Wall of Stone shouted at Idernon, at Pan'assár.

"Stop! He wouldn't want this. Brother, he wouldn't."

Idernon's face snapped to Ramien. Fury swirled in his eyes—fury and agony. He turned to Pan'assár, but he was watching the shore and had seen Gor'sadén signalling at him. To continue was suicide, but as Pan'assár watched the rope tense and creak, he thought it a lifeline back to a shameful existence. He didn't want it, but he was a commander.

"Stop rowing, Idernon. That is an order. Stop!" he yelled.

Ramien's hand was on Idernon's forearm. "Stop, brother. It's over."

"Never," growled Idernon, eyes brimming with tears. He knew Ramien was right. They would never reach Fel'annár now.

No one would.

Angling himself as best he could, Fel'annár moved right and felt the current pulling at his legs. They hurtled past a boulder, feeling a downward tug, and then his shoulder smashed into the unyielding rock. They were under again, strangled, releasing muted moans of frustration and pain.

An arm surfaced, grappling for some purchase, anywhere. They rounded another boulder and Fel'annár kicked away from it with both feet. They picked up speed again, slammed into another obstacle. Struggling for breath, Fel'annár's eyes searched for anything to latch on to.

He could go no further. With Handir in his arms, he knew that. He was too tired, too far gone. That buoy had been their last chance.

They emerged from the gorge, the froth and foam gone. In their place, teal waters that stretched to infinity. There was a sense of weight, of such openness he wanted to bury his head beneath the water. Everywhere he turned was water and sky, almost indistinguishable. Only Handir's face broke the illusion.

"Han?" His voice was quieted by a mouthful of water which he coughed out, neck angling to see over the edge. "Handir!"

"I know. I'm sorry."

"I'm sorry too." He hadn't the strength to say what else was in his mind, to face the consequences of it. He was sorry, though, sorrier than he could ever have imagined.

And then he was floating upon a cloud of water-logged mist, silent save for a distant cry of despair, the trumpets of distant trees. He tilted his head back and saw the heavens speed away from him. All weight had lifted from his body, even from his mind, and he closed his eyes and waited for the impact that would break them both. Cocooning his brother's flailing body, he sent a prayer to Aria. Something tightened around his waist. The last thing he saw was Llyniel's face and a tree racing towards him, closer and closer until he could no longer focus.

8
THE SEARCH

"Faith and guilt. Hope and concern. Surety and scepticism. So many emotions in so few souls. None of them knew what they would find, but all of them feared the consequences."
The Silvan Chronicles, Book V. Marhené

The rustle of fine cloth and the muted clink of metal reminded Thargodén that he was not alone, even though his companions had remained silent for many long moments.

"I have arranged for extra vigilance on incoming birds, but there is still nothing. Handir would have written many times by now, as would Lainon. Whoever is intercepting their communication does so skilfully and has the upper-hand."

Aradan crossed his legs, one arm resting over the back of the sofa he sat on. Shrewd eyes fell on his friend, knowing from experience what came next.

"Gods, I should never have let him go," murmured Thargodén. "I should have seen the danger."

Aradan made to answer, but he started when Rinon spoke.

"How so? How could you?"

"Band'orán. We know he schemes, have known for an entire generation. He bides his time, waits for opportunities such as these to push forward with his plans to usurp the throne. I should have known."

"And you would keep your son imprisoned as a consequence? Handir needed to go. He needed to learn of statesmanship from the best. Every decision encumbers risk, father, and you took one in the hope that the results would outweigh those risks."

Thargodén held his son's stubborn, unyielding eyes, eventually nodding and turning back to the missive in his hand.

"What news of the investigation, Aradan?"

"Today, I received a financial report on Captain Dinor. He is certainly wealthier than he was. I also have reports on his movements. He spends much time searching the Silvan archives for maps and landmarks."

"For an Alpine Purist, that is a *strange* pastime indeed," said Turion, one brow cocked as he drank from his goblet.

"Captain Dinor was one of my father's closest advisors," said the king softly.

"We were right," said Rinon. "They plan to recolonise. They are watching and assessing what it will take to claim those lands." He turned to the councillor and the king, lip twisted in disgust. "They dream of ruling their own lands under our very noses, even as they command our warriors." His voice turned into a feral growl, and Thargodén's eyes flickered. "They have the best residences, more servants than they need, yards of silk and velvet, and they occupy the highest positions within our society. Captains, Royal Councillors ... still it is not enough. They want land, the power that comes with it."

Turion, Aradan and the king remained silent, Rinon's hostile words ringing off the stone walls. Aradan drank. Turion watched him while the king reminded himself that it was Rinon who had spoken. A wave of pride dampened his indignation at what his captains and councillors planned to do. He turned from the window.

"Captain Dinor will unwittingly lead us to the others, I am sure. We must continue with our investigations, but it is only a question of time before we have all of our traitors. Then we drag them before this forest and make them pay for what they have done," said the king.

"Band'orán is nothing if not careful, Thargodén. They will not be discovered easily," warned Aradan.

"And what of the Silvans, Aradan?" asked Rinon. "Our army is dwindling by the day. We have but a third of the numbers we boasted only a month ago. That rebel Angon is drawing them outside the city, inciting them to desert. That camp grows ever bigger, stronger. I don't think Erthoron is capable of pulling them together again. He cannot control them, but this Angon may. And it is not only the Silvans who are abandoning their posts," emphasised Rinon. "Many Alpine soldiers are leaving, in search of safer lands for their families."

Turion shook his head. "Angon is a good warrior, a loyal soldier, but bitter—bitter at the Alpines for his lot and for what happened to Fer'dán. He lost an arm, in an area where there should have been an outpost. Angon says things that others dare not, but they think them all the same. He stirs them, but he will not be able to organise them."

"You commanded him?" asked Rinon.

"I did. He was in the same patrol as Fel'annár."

"It is, indeed, a worrying development, Prince," said Aradan. "Have you asked Huren to step up his vigilance on them? Report to you of any mass movements within the camp?"

"Yes. Although he claims it's dangerous business sending Shadows into the camp."

"Does he have no dark-haired ones, then?" Aradan shook his head, tapped his chin with his forefinger. "No, Angon will not rally them to war, not before the voting."

Turion scowled, watching Aradan thoughtfully. "How do *you* know that?"

Aradan turned to him, face utterly blank, save for his eyes that shone with secret pride. "I have my contacts, Captain."

Turion raised both eyebrows, turned to Rinon for help. He saw the same cool regard there.

He shrugged, drank more wine.

"I wish Pan'assár were here," murmured Aradan.

Turion almost spat his wine while Thargodén raised his eyebrows. "Never thought I would hear that from you, my friend."

Aradan snorted, but Rinon almost seemed to snarl. "He's a Purist."

"Are you saying Pan'assár is with Band'orán?" The king turned threatening eyes on his son.

Rinon took his time answering his father, and when he did, it was careful. "I am saying we should be wary. Things have changed, and until I can see Pan'assár here, I will not be making assumptions as to his loyalty, whether to you or to Band'orán."

"Turion?" prompted the king.

"Pan'assár is ... negatively predisposed to the Silvans. However, I believe he is loyal. I have seen no evidence to the contrary."

"Then, for now, we must wait for news from abroad; from our Shadows. And we must keep Huren's eyes trained on the Silvans. We have little time to find the evidence we need to invalidate the votes of the Royal Council and the Inner Circle, but if Handir has received our message, he may just be here for it. Pan'assár, too."

Rinon was sceptical and worried. But he couldn't tell his father that. The king needed to cling to his hope—believe that Handir was well, that Fel'annár was well, that Pan'assár was loyal—so that he could continue on his road to recuperation and pull their people back from the brink.

But Rinon truly believed what he had said. The situation had changed. Band'orán had changed, upped his game, and Rinon no longer knew what he was capable of. Just how far he would go to take control.

Not for the first time, Rinon wondered why Band'orán even wanted the throne. He had no institutional right to it, and the rightful king had three heirs. What was he thinking? But then a sinking feeling invaded him. Maeneth was not here. Handir was not here. For now, only Rinon would be left, should something happen to his father. Had Band'orán planned that, too?

A stupid question. Rinon knew he was right. It was the reason this was the best time for him to strike, but his father was being king once more. He was ruling, out in the streets, at the barracks. He was at the Inner Circle and the Merchant Guild. He laughed and encouraged, showed himself to be strong, and Rinon rather thought he was spoiling Band'orán's plans.

His gaze happened upon Aradan, and Rinon startled. There was a deep wisdom there, one he himself did not possess. Rinon had intuition, but Aradan's mind was a calculating machine, one equipped with an ample baggage of experience and knowledge. Had he come to the same conclusion? Did Aradan feel it, too? That he was standing upon the brink of a chasm?

THAT NIGHT, Rinon sat in his private rooms, hair wet and loose, clad only in a silken gown he had acquired in Abiren'á many years ago. He knew this letter would be long, but he had not realised how hard it would be to write. Even as he penned it, the reality of what had happened, what could happen, seemed all the more real.

> *Band'orán is pushing. The Silvans are rebelling. Our army dwindles, and Band'orán makes his final assault. We need strength now, Maeneth, on the dawn of decision, as we sit on the brink of civil war or freedom from tyranny.*

He leaned back, placed his palm over the still drying ink and pulled his fingers closed, crumpling the parchment in his fist and shoving it to one side. He couldn't tell her his heart. If he did, his brave sister would come. He couldn't allow that. He couldn't allow Maeneth to be caught up in this web of intrigue. He somehow knew that it would soon turn from a play of wits to a royal hunt, with his family the prey. Band'orán would have no scruples about drawing her in and squeezing her dry, using her and tossing her aside on his path to the throne. But he wouldn't have her, not his twin.

Rinon would kill Band'orán should he destroy the other side of himself.

A weight is lifted from our father, sister, and he is well-advised by Aradan and Turion. When Handir returns, we will restore these lands, make them greater than they ever were. We must only win these votes and keep Band'orán in his place.

How goes your life in Pelagia?

He couldn't tell her they were fighting against the tide, that Band'orán was throwing everything he could at them, waiting for them to falter while baiting the Silvans into action. It had already come to blows and would soon become a rebellion. And then Band'orán would stand before his puppet council with all the ammunition he needed.

He took up his quill once more, took a deep breath and continued to write to the sister he had not seen in over fifty years, though he wrote every month.

Lady Jer'asir has inquired as to your efforts with the bengewood flowers. She wonders if you will finally make the perfect bud. And Lord Fengwin was most gracious in his fond memories of you.

I think he fancies you.

~

"Damn it all, Fel'annár." Galdith spat and then sniffled in the cold mist. Beside him, Ramien shuffled closer to their fire and held out his hands to warm them, rope burns stinging under the soaked bandages around his palms.

Galadan said nothing. His gaze was fixed on the flames but from time to time he would turn to Llyniel, who sat alone, far from the fires, far from their warmth and light. Sontúr had sat with her for a while and then came to join The Company, grey hair loose and slowly drying. The river still flowed strong beside them, but the banks had become visible once more. Most of the melt was now a part of the Pelagian Sea.

"Someone had to go after our prince," said Ramien, wincing as he massaged his shoulder.

"Had I stayed still. Had I not reached out ..." mumbled Idernon to himself.

"Then someone else would have," said Ramien. "Something had to change, Idernon. We couldn't have stayed that way for much longer."

Idernon knew Ramien was right. But it had been *him* who precipitated that moment. He had moved forward in an attempt to anchor Fel'annár, and that had been their downfall. He had tipped the boat and left Fel'annár with no other choice but to brave the river.

He gathered his feet below him and rose stiltedly, eyes fixed on nothing, and Sontúr made to follow him. But Ramien placed a calming hand on his forearm. He shook his head and gestured for the prince to sit once more.

Mud squelched beneath Idernon's boots, splattered against his leggings and cloak, but still he walked, past the boulders and then some, until he came to a mighty tree. He stopped and looked up. What did it say? he wondered. Did it know? He mused, head cocking to one side. Did it know that he had killed its lord?

"Return to camp, Warrior."

Idernon turned, only to find Pan'assár standing a distance away from him.

"And what would the point be? With Prince Handir gone. With ... with Fel'annár gone. What is the *point?*" he asked as he walked towards the commander, eyes searching, anger surfacing.

"They may yet be alive. If anyone can retrieve our prince, it is your friend."

"The one you left to *drown*? The one you could have followed and did *not*? The one you have always *despised*? You would not even have tried had he not been holding on to your precious prince."

"He is your prince, too, Warrior. You serve him." There was a warning note in Pan'assár's voice, one Idernon couldn't care less about. His voice rose, words too fast, faster than his rational mind, surging straight from the soul.

"Not anymore. His carcass is floating amid the timber, lapping against the shores of the Crystal Straits. He's dead." Idernon could no longer contain himself, stopped trying. With every word that left his mouth, he came closer to boiling over.

"You don't know that."

"I do. It is common sense, Commander. Common sense you do not wish to see, for if you did, you would have to face the truth. You failed to keep him safe, just as you have failed to lead our troops these past years. *You* are a failure, a racist, bigoted fool who lives off his past glory. You are nothing, Pan'assár. Time has whittled away your glory, has diluted your blood and made of you a useless relic."

Pan'assár's fist slammed into his cheek, and Idernon fell backwards, landing heavily on his side. Mud splashed on his smarting face. He looked up at the elf who towered over him, but there was no anger on his face. He crouched low so that he was as close as clear vision permitted.

"And yet it was *you* who tipped the balance, wasn't it? You know this and it angers you, but heed me, Warrior. Had Fel'annár been Gor'sadén, or Or'Talán, I would have done likewise. I would have risked a small movement for a greater chance of keeping him safe. I would have rowed that boat to infinity, over the falls and to Valley. I. *Me*. But as commander, it is my duty to see beyond the bond of brotherhood, beyond everything that is not the preservation of life."

Pan'assár watched the young warrior, his heavy, gleaming eyes so eloquent. "Your love for him is as strong as mine for my brothers of The Three. You hate me for what I became, but you forget the wherefore of it. The death of Or'Talán, the nature of his end. Will you wander the same path, Warrior? Will you, too, become a bigoted fool? Will you live your life a failure, driven by anger? They may still be alive, and I will hold to that. Have *faith*," he said, and then stood. "These shores are treacherous in the dark. You should see to that." He pointed at Idernon's cheek. With that, he was away, and the Wise Warrior lay silent, a wretched fool in the mud.

'*Have faith*,' the commander had said. But Idernon had none. He had read of Horizon Falls, knew the river's capacity, its speed and the height of its drop. He knew what would happen to a body falling from that height, in that volume of water. It would crush them both. The impact alone would surely be enough, but if by some miracle it wasn't, the injuries they would sustain would not allow them to swim to safety. It was not about *faith*. It was about *physics*.

Fel'annár and Handir were dead.

Light, just light, until a dark cloud blocked it out.

He was sinking. He couldn't breathe. All he wanted was a last glance at the sun, but his body was a reed, limp and malleable, his only movement was thanks to the current that held him back from the light. A sadness so deep it hurt.

He was dying. He couldn't see the sun.

Tendrils of bright hair snaked around his drifting body. It fascinated him. This would be his last glance at life, he thought. He had to breathe, he did. Searing pain sliced through his chest. His body jerked, arms floating at his sides. Pain, frigid weight, his last, watery breath.

Darkness.

Warmth.

I am dead, aren't I?

Light, opaque. Empty save for a dark shadow.

Pain, weight. His body was moving, twitching; or was he gasping?

There was a surge of hot liquid through his body, splattering over his face. His chest expanded, and dizziness sent his eyes spinning out of control.

He couldn't breathe, and yet air filled his wet lungs. He struggled and then sucked in a rattling breath. He coughed, more liquid in his mouth. He scrunched his eyes closed in pain, against searing agony in his chest.

He was alive.

His body lurched from side to side, floating. From the heavens, a hazy face looked down upon him.

"Handir? Brother?" A breathless, desperate question, one he could not answer. He was starving for air, panting and shivering. He wanted to ask his own questions. Where was he? What had happened? *Is this Valley, brother?*

No. My brother's eyes are blue ...

"Handir? *Prince?*"

FEL'ANNÁR'S VOICE WAVERED, barely controlled, panic receding. And he *had* panicked.

Stones dug into his knees. Hands clawed at the stony sand around him. He could hardly breathe, rasping exhales and trembling limbs.

Gods, but he hurt, his body and his mind. Salty tears mixed with sweet water, water that had filled Handir's lungs, almost killed him— still might. But sweet Aria, he could not move. What he had done, what he thought would happen.

He rocked on his heels and regretted it; filled his lungs with air and regretted that, too. He leaned forwards, all but collapsing onto his hands. A body lay before him, half in the water, once dead. They should both be dead. He turned his head sideways, to the magnificence of an ancient tree, and heard its last thoughts. He felt them echo across the land, far away.

Long years, time to leave. To die and live again.

He closed his eyes, grief and gratitude emanating from his soul, whispering away on the breeze. He turned back to the body.

He and Handir had gone from cold indifference, spite even, to a stilted impasse in which warmer feelings were slowly growing, as surely as the need to hide them. He felt himself shaking, not just from the screams of his body but those in his mind.

What had almost come to pass.

He had never had a family, save for Amareth, had never needed one, so why were his eyes so hot and full? Why was his heart swollen to the brink of shattering?

A rasping breath, not his own. He looked up at the softening sun, felt the creeping darkness of night and what it may bring. He needed to move, find shelter. All he had to do was understand, at last. Had he been that bereft? Had he hidden it so well, even from himself? He had convinced himself so utterly that he didn't need a family. He had all he had ever wanted in Llyniel, Gor'sadén and The Company.

He dragged a tattered sleeve over his eyes, repressed a sob of utter exhaustion, pain, relief so great.

He thought Handir had died.

He thought his *brother* had died.

THAT AFTERNOON, the commanders had put the warriors to work. They checked the integrity of Handir's chest, checked their own bags and harnesses, and recoiled the rope they would use later for the descent down the cliff face.

They would walk along the river edge until the Horizon Falls and then descend. There they would search and then continue to the Glistening Falls. Beyond that point, nothing had been discussed, for to do so would be to contemplate the possibility that they could find no trace of Thargodén's sons.

The chances of Handir and Fel'annár surviving, of Talen making it out, were slim to none, but perhaps by some miracle, they had freed themselves of the current before they went over the edge. In this case, they may have taken refuge away from the flooding. If they *had* gone over, they were surely dead, but at least Pan'assár would retrieve the bodies if they had not been carried away to the sea.

Pan'assár had offered Deron a fistful of coins as the last payment for both his and Talen's service. Deron took it with a tight smile, telling the commander that he would give it to Talen's wife. He would tell her only that he had gone missing, to leave her with a spark of hope he himself did not feel.

With Handir's chest tightly secured once more, the party continued along the riverbank. Gor'sadén joined Pan'assár at the fore, while Galadan brought up the rear, and between them, Llyniel walked amidst The Company. Anger still glittered in Idernon's eyes, and the stark bruise on his cheek drew the eyes of the others. But it wasn't enough to break their collective silence. It wasn't enough to make them feel anything at all.

It was not easy to walk in mud, and by midday, they were tired. Gor'sadén had been struggling for hours and predictably remained silent. He would not hold them back when Fel'annár was missing, when his fate was uncertain. And so, Pan'assár called for a brief stop, a strategy forming in his mind. With a fire now cracking and smoking heavily, he told it to the rest.

"We must find our prince and warrior with all haste. If—" he held up a hand, anticipating their reactions. "If by some miracle they are alive, they may be injured and unable to find shelter, in which case the elements may be the death of them. They may have washed up on the shore, and so we scour it, every inch until the point of no return. Past that, we can be sure they journeyed to the sea and Valley. Once we are satisfied they are not there, we venture inland. They may have been well enough to find shelter, so we continue our search along the rocky base some two leagues east of the shore. There are caves, crevices, places a warrior would go to protect himself from bears, Hounds, brigands.

"It should take us a full day to cover the distance to the descent and down, then another day and night to cover the area inland." Pan'assár drew a heavy breath. "The task ahead requires endurance and a strong mind. I pray Aria has kept them safe, that she has found a way. But if they *are* gone, if we *have* lost our prince and warrior, then let us at least send them off with honours. This is your most important mission, warriors. Keep your hearts here," he said, tapping his finger against his temple. "There will be time enough for mourning, should it come to that. But now is the time for faith and strength."

They nodded in silence, even Idernon, and then Pan'assár turned to Llyniel. "Are you well, Healer?"

Her sluggish eyes drifted towards him, stayed there as she pondered the commander's question. "No. I am cold, tired, worried."

Pan'assár nodded and made to stand. She leaned forward to stop him. "He's not dead, Pan'assár. Fel'annár is not dead," she whispered.

He started, wondering if she was simply finding her own way of coping with the uncertainty, or whether she truly knew. Fel'annár was supposedly Ari'atór, in which case he would know if his Connate had passed, but she was Silvan and did not have the same connection.

"I will hold to that," he said, turning his eyes to Idernon and the purple bruise on his cheek. "He is a Kah Warrior, Wise One. We do not die easily." Glacial eyes pierced through Idernon's cloudy gaze. The commander watched as they cleared and focussed. Nodding, he left to take up the fore, the others following.

As The Company organised themselves around Llyniel once more, Idernon bent his head to speak to her. "How do you know?"

Llyniel shook her head. "I don't know. But I feel no sorrow, Idernon. Only concern."

Feel. She felt no sorrow, she said, claimed that she didn't understand why not. But was it even possible to feel if you could not understand the wherefore of your emotions? He told himself that what she had said meant nothing. Fel'annár was dead and all they would achieve this day, if luck graced them, was to find the dead bodies of his friend and the prince. Sontúr likely thought the same, and Idernon studiously avoided Galadan and Ramien's gleaming eyes.

It was soon time to leave once more. There were still two or three more hours of light left, time that could prove vital.

The trek was not easy. The incline down the Horizon Falls was treacherous, especially for those who carried the chest. But as the land began to flatten, they were able to inspect the calmer shores. They found floating timber in the shallows, pieces from their damaged boats. And then, a little further along, they found the first body.

A mercenary, floating face down, with one hand caught between two rocks. They left him there but soon found another, and then another.

"Did they follow us in boats?" asked Pan'assár.

Gor'sadén shook his head. "No. I saw some of them running along the banks, following our progress for as long as they could, but they fell behind. You made the right decision, brother."

Pan'assár heaved a long, noisy breath. "I dread what we may find amidst the reeds, Gorsa. If Handir is dead, I will leave these lands."

"And perhaps I will follow you. Perhaps it is time," he whispered, eyes cast upwards to the slate-coloured sky.

Pan'assár smiled. "Always together," he murmured, casting his gaze sideways to his friend, aware that his limp had become more pronounced. "You should have seen Idernon, Gorsa. He would have rowed to infinity, down the very falls and to his death. When he finally stopped rowing, it cut his very soul."

"Calrazia ..."

"Yes. For a moment it was me, watching as Orta met his death."

"And he is angry," added Gor'sadén. "Enough to lose his focus and slip on those treacherous rocks he so deftly navigates now."

"Yes. A misstep for sure. I steadied him in his fall."

"He blamed you?"

"Indeed."

"And why *did* you stop?" Gor'sadén was looking straight at him now, but Pan'assár didn't have to return his gaze to know there was no accusation in his eyes.

"Because it was right. It was my duty to preserve their lives, and even if it hadn't been, Handir would not have wanted our sacrifice. Neither would Fel'annár. Ramien reminded us of that."

Gor'sadén's eyes flickered momentarily, and then a sad smile pulled at the corners of his mouth. He said no more. His left hand tingled, and in his mind's eye was an ashen face, a last smile at the living world from a warrior too young to die.

If a son could choose a father ...

A call from further ahead, loud, disbelieving. "Here! Over here!" Galdith was beckoning to them from a little further along the shore.

Before them, a mighty tree had split down the middle, almost in two. It lay on its side, the roots stuck into the air like pikes on a battlefield. It reminded Pan'assár of a dead sea creature the mariners had once caught and taken to shore.

They ran towards it, stopped just behind Galdith. Gor'sadén gritted his teeth against the ache in his leg. His gait was awkward, arms moving to compensate, but he didn't care.

Galdith was peering into the nooks and hollows of the tree, while the others joined him. Carodel smoothed his hand over the bark and gave voice to what they were all thinking.

"It looks like it's been pulled out by the roots by some giant."

"A freak storm, the sheer volume and speed of the water ..." Idernon was shaking his head, but Llyniel stepped towards it, eyes registering the split wood, the mangled roots.

"Sweet Aria," murmured Galdith, reaching into a crack between the trunk and a thick branch. Pulling his hand back, he turned to Llyniel beside him, utter shock on his face. Holding out his hand, he turned it palm up. There, a small amber river stone lay, and through it, a white water line. She reached out, plucking it gently from Galdith's hand and smiled. She could feel him, on some unknown plain, in some unexplained part of herself.

Fel'annár's honour stone.

She closed her fist around it, eyes drifting over the others, daring them to gainsay the facts.

"He's alive," declared Gor'sadén, breathless, eyes wandering over the fallen tree. He marvelled at its sheer size, the length of its roots. An unbelievable suspicion nagging at him. He watched as Llyniel placed a hand over the dead tree, and then the other Silvans did likewise, all of them except for Idernon. Where wonder and thanks shone in the eyes of Carodel, Ramien, Galdith and Llyniel, in Idernon's there was only confusion and reluctance.

"Over here!" Pan'assár's voice jolted the Silvans from their thoughts and they rushed to where the commander was crouching.

"There is a disturbance in the gravel," said Pan'assár, pointing to the tracks he had found. "It looks to me as if someone has lain here, then been dragged away—but I can't be sure."

"Over here!" came another shout from Galadan, further ahead. Pan'assár was smiling even before he arrived, The Company, too, but Sontúr and Llyniel saw nothing but sticks and stones in the sand.

"Tell me it's tracking code," murmured Sontúr.

"It is." Pan'assár reached out, following the symbols with his fingers. Two dots under a line, a semi-circle and two sticks. "There are two of them, both injured. They are moving south-east, searching for a cave on high ground."

Idernon snapped his eyes away from it, straight to Llyniel, who was staring back at him. He had doubted, of course he had; there had been nothing to suggest Fel'annár had survived until they had discovered the tracking code. In hindsight, he had been wrong, and confusion stirred in his mind. But it was not strong enough to overcome his joy, to stop his lips from stretching wide, his smile generous, bruised cheek smarting. He felt the heavy weight of Pan'assár's hand on his shoulder. A fleeting, voiceless moment. The commander understood him, was glad for him.

"Finish scouring the shallows," called Pan'assár. "Fel'annár is one of the two alive—he's the only one who would have known these symbols. The other is either Handir or Talen. Ten minutes, then we travel inland."

A sense of urgency invaded them as they finished combing the base of the falls and then moved into the treeline, in search of Fel'annár and whoever he was with.

It was more dangerous than ever now. If Fel'annár had survived, it had surely been by some miracle. But Gor'sadén could not rule out the possibility that some of the mercenaries may also still be alive. He did not want to think of the other things that lingered in these lands. Pumas, Hounds, bears and even brigands. Two injured elves were an easy target, and he could only pray that Fel'annár would hide away to wait for help to come.

We're coming, Green Sun.

9
WARRIOR

"The Alpines of Tar'eastór wrote the Warrior Code, but the Silvans had their own law, unwritten save upon the hearts of their fighters. Yet both said the same thing. To fight for yourself is a reflex. To fight for others is the highest, purest form of sacrifice."
The Alpine Chronicles: Cor'hidén

~

It was a cave. He knew that now. And as his awareness came ever sharper, Handir pieced together the events that had taken place since Fel'annár had let go of the boat and they had been washed away.

He wasn't sure if it was night or day. To find out he would have to turn his head to the entrance, but he didn't want that. Not yet. He just wanted to watch as Fel'annár worked; watch and remember.

Understand.

The fire was big and bright, and something smelled sweet and tangy. He had awoken to a grating sound, and his eyes moved to the warrior's hands. They were wrapped in cloth, save for his fingers. In one he held a long piece of wood and in the other an object Handir could not quite fathom. And then he realised.

He was making a weapon.

Tired eyes travelled to the warrior's head. The mass of silvery locks and braids was filthy and loose, and dark cloth was woven around his temples. Further down his bare chest, Handir's eyes lingered for a while. It wasn't the horrific scar that the Nim'uán had bequeathed Fel'annár, but the bruising there had blossomed into a myriad of colours like some macabre flower. There were crisscrossing lines of dark purple, stretching the entire way around his body. He frowned.

They had both plummeted over the Horizon Falls, and Handir knew he had only survived inside the protective embrace of his brother. Fel'annár's body had taken the brunt of it, and he thought there must have been more damage than a split head and bruising. Around his waist was what looked like his shirt, and with another glance away, he spotted their clothes, drying close by.

He could not fathom it. To understand, he would have to ask. But would Fel'annár share with him? Not only how, but *why*.

He had surely done it out of duty to his prince. Fel'annár had an acute sense of duty. He'd seen that often enough. He had protected his prince, cared for him so that he could deliver him to Pan'assár once they were found. But then he dared wonder, had there been another reason? He remembered those terrifying moments in which he had been caught in the current, trapped under the boat, unable to move at all. He remembered the strong hand bunched in his clothes, the grunts and cries of exertion. How Fel'annár had battled to pull him back into the capsizing boat. But when it had become too much, when he could no longer breathe, Fel'annár had not let him go. He had let go of the boat.

The warrior shifted on the ground, and then his movements stopped as his face contorted into a grimace. Closing his eyes, then opening them, he continued his slow, careful movements. It was a spear. Fel'annár was making a spear.

His half-brother's face was drawn into a frown as he worked.

Whether that was from pain or from concentration, he couldn't say, but every now and then he would turn his head to the entrance and wait, only to continue once more. Handir wondered if he was listening.

This young warrior knew exactly what he was doing. He seemed so at home here in the wilds. He had made a fire, found or caught whatever it was that smelled so good, was making a weapon and guarding them from the dangers of the night. Handir could do none of these things. He realised he felt safe, as safe as he could be, with this warrior that was his half-brother. It was comforting and disturbing because this was all his own fault. He had dedicated his life to learning, had never listened to his tutors who had told him it was fitting for an Alpine prince to learn at least the basics of warrior training and survival. He had never seen the point, had never thought to find himself in a situation such as this.

The warrior shifted, moaned, closing his eyes and slowly opened them, only for his gaze to land directly on Handir's watchful eyes. "Handir."

"Are you alright?"

Fel'annár didn't answer. Instead, he stood. Handir knew that he wasn't, wanted to help him, but he felt so weak. He watched as he bent carefully and filled what Handir could only describe as a leaf cup. Sitting awkwardly at the prince's side, he deposited it before him. Sweet-smelling steam wafted into his face, and for the first time, Handir moved, pushing himself up onto one elbow. He coughed and winced at the heaviness in his chest.

He was naked. Looking down at himself, all that covered him was a long brown cloak—Fel'annár's cloak. But Handir wasn't cold.

"Drink it."

His eyes left Fel'annár and looked at the steaming brew, marvelling at the expert way in which the leaf had been folded into a cup. He reached out towards it, arm like lead. He drank, the comforting warmth seeping into his fingers, up his arm and down his sore throat. The brew was almost too hot, but the burn was welcome while he was so very thirsty. Fel'annár watched him. Even so, Handir didn't care that some of it dribbled down his chin, and he drank until there was none left. He wanted more but didn't want to ask. It was painful just watching Fel'annár's movements. Still, his wishful eyes must have been eloquent enough, for his vessel was soon refilled, and Fel'annár sat still at last.

"For tonight we rest, recover as much strength as we may. Tomorrow we must venture out and find the others, if they survived the wash. If they did, they will be looking for us. They will think us dead probably until they find the marker."

"If they saw us going over, I am sure they do." Handir winced at his gravelly voice. He didn't know what a marker was. But he did know that Llyniel would be frantic and Pan'assár would be in a terrible rage. "How long have we been here?"

"This is our first night."

"We fell just this morning?"

"Yes."

Handir frowned. It felt as if he had slept for a week and his brother's knowing eyes looked back at him.

"You were unconscious for a while. Sometimes that slows the perception of time. Other times it is as if seconds have gone by."

He spoke from experience, realised Handir, and he was once more struck by how prepared he was. How tough and skilful the warriors of Ea Uaré were. He had always appreciated their service, but he had never really understood their sacrifice, the hardship of it; until now.

Fel'annár made to stand, but Handir stilled him with his voice. "Thank you."

Fel'annár stared back at him, unwavering. "No thanks, prince. This is my sworn duty."

"Then thank you for that oath, Warrior."

Fel'annár remained silent for a moment. Those anguished moments of just this morning when he had thought Handir dead; the emotions that fear had garnered. He needed to lock them away. He needed to bolster his discipline if they were to survive in the wilds with nothing but this makeshift spear. Distraction could mean death. He turned, rose stiffly, and took up his place before the fire.

Yes, it was his sworn oath, but Handir was observant indeed. His own hair had been released from its braids. It was clean and loose. The cuts and bruises that littered his own body had been cleaned and washed with something that pulled at his skin. His head was cushioned with every piece of dry cloth to be had.

Would Fel'annár have done this for anyone? Did his actions transcend the duty of a warrior towards those in need?

Not only owls hoot in the night, and distinguishing a call from a Silvan warrior was not easy if you weren't from the Deep Forest. Pan'assár had always been in reluctant awe of their ability to mimic birdcall.

After the discovery of the marker that afternoon, they had travelled for the rest of the day, leaving the river some two hours ago and scouting every rocky outcrop, everywhere a warrior may seek shelter. Not far to the east was an elevated ridge that hosted a cave system. That was Pan'assár's objective.

The lilting song of a hermit thrush made Pan'assár start. A proximity warning. He raised his hands, produced a flurry of hand signals. Weapons ready and lips sealed, The Company took up their positions in silence, keeping Llyniel at their centre, together with Carodel and Galdith who carried the chest.

Even before they had left Tar'eastór, Sontúr had warned of the dangers of this area. Cave Deviants, Mountain Hounds, this was their domain, and Pan'assár had sent Idernon and Ramien ahead to scout. Through their birdsong, they had kept the commander informed. Hounds were ahead of them, following some scent that was not them.

That was when they had begun to hope. And to fear.

Minutes later, they were so close they could smell the foetid hides of their quarry. They didn't need light to know their tracks would be deep, long, curved claws that could scrape an elf's face off in one strike. Fel'annár knew this enemy intimately, had fought with them on their journey to Tar'eastór.

DANGER.

Fel'annár's head shot up from his peaceful whittling and turned to the entrance of their cave.

Move.

"Get dressed. Stay inside. Don't let them see you."

"Mercenaries?"

"Hounds. Keep out of sight. Whatever happens, Handir. You must live."

"What are you talking about?"

"Hounds have caught our scent. I must face them on the slopes. It is our only hope."

"Oh, *you* who can hardly stand, and that *stick*. Do you mean to smack them on the backside with it?"

"Obey. You are no good to me in a fight."

That much was true, and Handir shrugged his way into his now dry tunic and leggings, desperate to smother a cough lest he attract the Hounds' attention. Tying his cloak around his neck, he shuffled into one dark corner, light-headed and heaving. Sweat beaded on his upper lip. Too hot. Still, his eyes wandered to a number of sizeable stones littered around the cave floor. He would use them if it came to it.

But Fel'annár had other ideas. "See that rocky shelf?" He pointed to the very back of the cave. "Let's get you up there, in case any of those Hounds get past me."

It was absurd. He could not possibly get up there, but Fel'annár was pulling on his sleeve. Handir climbed onto a boulder, felt Fel'annár pushing him up. He scrabbled up another, Fel'annár behind him. Reaching up, Handir was just about able to haul himself over the rocky ledge. Stones, pebbles and sand skittered down the wall as he clambered upwards, then sat awkwardly on the ledge, panting, sweating and coughing. He was higher up than he had first thought, and the cave swayed before his groggy eyes.

"Use those stones if they get too close," Fel'annár said, pointing to a crumbled part of the ledge further along. "Aim for the eyes."

Fel'annár climbed down. With his bruised feet back on the ground, he leaned against the wall and closed his eyes, hands clutching at his sides.

"Fel'annár?" A distant, whispery echo. He turned, looked up at Handir and smiled crookedly.

"Stay safe, my prince. Commander Pan'assár will find you."

"*You* will find me, Fel'annár."

But he was gone, and all Handir could do was watch as he walked towards the cave mouth in ragged clothes with a would-be spear in his right hand. His left hand was oddly splayed as if he searched for something, his gait awkward but determined. Handir moved further back into the darkness, pulling his legs up. All he could do was wait —wait and listen for a sign that Fel'annár had beaten back the Hounds.

Wait for his brother to come back.

He felt like a child, powerless and desperate. And then he prayed to Aria for the first time in years, for the first time with conviction in his heart.

Protect him.

SILHOUETTES MOVED IN THE DARK, blocking the silvery barks of the birch in the near distance. Fel'annár stood still on the slope, the terrain his only advantage. Their prowling was impatient, repetitive. They grudgingly awaited the signal from their leader to attack.

A growl, low and menacing, broke the silence, followed by more as the pack became agitated. So eager for the kill, to lap at his blood. He had faced these beasts before, on his way to Tar'eastór. It had been the trees that had rescued him then. Here, though, all he had were the spindly birch spread wide and, perhaps, too far away for rescue. They screamed, though, for him to run, to climb.

But he couldn't. When they finally found a path upwards, to the ledge and then the cave, they would find Handir. And then they would rip him to bits.

He focussed on his surroundings, heard their tongues lapping at saliva. He trained his ears on the trees and centred himself. He called on the energy he had stored from the Dohai, conjured it from the depths of his core, felt it pool in his damaged chest and back and then seep into his blood. Thoughts faded away. Pain receded, leaving behind only his body and its preparation for defence.

A howl split the night, and the growling and snapping of the pack followed it. Their leader had given the order, and as Fel'annár readied his stance, the voice of the trees turned from alarm to hope.

Friends.

But it was too late. The largest Hound stalked forward, haunches rising and falling with each careful step. Perceptive yellow eyes appraised him, calculating its moment to attack, but Fel'annár stood so still it became curious.

The Hound sniffed noisily, snout bobbing in the air. Lips curled back, proudly displaying its teeth, designed for ripping and gouging. *Look what I have*, it seemed to say, and Fel'annár felt his rudimentary weapon, heavier now in his hand.

The other Hounds were behind their leader, but not too close. It was his prerogative to engage, to be the first to rip into the prey and perhaps kill it, so that all of them could feed. It was the confirmation of his leadership to do so. He fought and killed, while the others ate thanks to him.

The only warning Fel'annár had was the tensing of its back quarters. As it pounced into the air, Fel'annár shot to one side, his spear before him. The body grazed his shoulder, sending him stumbling to one side, but he soon regained his balance.

The beast landed gracefully, turned and then took a running jump. Fel'annár dodged again but not quick enough and he was thrown back by the force of its body, only narrowly missing its gaping jowls. He landed hard on the rock, gasping at the pain in his chest, his back and his feet. He rolled away, just in time to avoid the Hound as it jumped. He stood, breathing hard, and the Hound circled him, calculating, aware of its companions closing in.

It sprang, paws splayed, and Fel'annár brought up his spear, driving the head into the beast's side. But it didn't break through the tough hide, and the beast landed with a yelp and then a roar of primal rage as it turned back to him, eyes slanted and glinting. Claws skittered over rock, and it pounced, baring its chest to Fel'annár's crude spear. He drove it forward with all his might, feeling a sense of utter relief when the tip sank into the hide and then slipped its entire way in. A high-pitched squeal sent the rest of the pack into silence, but Fel'annár knew it wouldn't last.

Stepping on the dead leader's chest, he tugged hard on his spear and turned to the rest. One jumped with a yelp, and he swiped his spear across its snout. It stumbled away, and another jumped at him. He repeated the movement, but the beast ducked under it and landed both paws on his shoulders. He fell back, hitting the rock hard, breath escaping him.

Gathering his legs, he placed his feet between him and the silvery pelt and pushed hard. The hound fell sideways and rolled down the slope. He had only managed to get to his knees when the next one was pushing him back down on his back. It roared its stinking breath into his face, and Fel'annár gagged. He grabbed its ears, pushing with all his might. The head thrashed from side to side, jaws gnashing, and his grip slipped. Hands pushed at its throat as it bit the air, teeth clapping loudly as it sought to bite his face off.

Fel'annár roared in desperation, shaking arms trying to push the beast away but failing. Its jowls were ever closer to him. His eyes widened in realisation. He couldn't hold it back for much longer. The beast was stronger than he was. Black lips opened wide, a gruesome smile of victory, for a new leader had emerged.

Then blood streamed from its jowls and splattered him. He gasped. One last stream of hot, stinking air and the body slackened. The face of the hound fell to one side, and in its place, a dark angel stood. Glittering blue eyes and black locks sprang into motion as she turned and took on the Hounds.

Two jumped at her. One was dead before it thudded to the ground, and the other lost its head. She drove the tip of her sword through its writhing body.

Pan'assár, Gor'sadén and The Company came crashing through the tree line, swords and bows drawn, chests heaving from the exertion of sprinting through a dark wood for long minutes. Three arrows whooshed through the air and thudded into the Hounds. The pack erupted into yelps as the warriors formed a circle around the Ari'atór and the fallen warrior behind her.

The remaining Hounds were leaderless and disorganised, too few left for any surety of sustenance, and so they backed away, slinking into the shadows.

Tensári stood, chest heaving and blades dripping. All around her lay the bodies of the Mountain Hounds they had been tracking. She nodded at Pan'assár, and then turned to look down on Fel'annár. He simply stared up at her, his head covered in the blood of the Hounds, but she read his eyes well enough.

Before she could bend down and hoist him up, The Company were there, surrounding him. Fel'annár could see the panic in their eyes. They would be thinking half his head had been chewed away. Indeed, he could see Ramien's questing eyes and his ensuing relief.

"You lucky, lucky bastard."

Fel'annár wanted to laugh, but instead, he passed out.

"Retrieve the chest," called Pan'assár. He turned to the figure in black. "You have our thanks, Spirit Warrior."

She nodded, face utterly straight, and then turned to the sound of running. A woman, not a warrior, hair flying about her, Silvan Bonding Braid bouncing around her shoulder.

"Tell me this is not *his* blood," she said, not panicked but urgent. A healer, then.

"It's Hound blood, although he was already injured," she said, looking down at Llyniel, watching as she checked for a pulse and then nodded at the large warrior close by. He picked up Fel'annár without help and walked up the slope to where an orange glow told them there was a camp.

Pan'assár gestured for them to stop while he and the other warriors went ahead to ensure there were no more Hounds to deal with. Then they would surely discover who was with Fel'annár. Was it Talen? Was it Handir?

Pan'assár stood at the cave's mouth, eyes searching for his prince but not finding him. His heart plummeting, he stepped forward and then froze.

"Pan'assár?"

He looked around but saw nothing. Then movement caught his eye at the very back of the cave, half-way up the wall. Stones and dust clattered and hissed as Handir moved in the near darkness.

"I need some help, Commander."

Pan'assár rushed forwards, Galadan beside him. Together, they pulled him down, steadying him when he swayed and held out an arm. They guided him to the still burning fire.

"By all the Gods, Prince, but I thought you had perished." It was a rare show of emotion from Pan'assár, Handir knew. He could only imagine what they had thought as they searched for them on the river. "As did I, Pan'assár."

The commander watched as Handir's cloudy eyes landed on Fel'annár, now lying on the ground before the fire with Sontúr, Llyniel and Idernon around him.

"How bad is it?" he murmured.

"We shall see. Come, Prince. You have a story to tell us."

Handir did not move immediately, and Pan'assár waited, allowing him this moment he seemed to need, to simply watch and assure himself that Fel'annár was not dead.

"And it will be *told*." There was an intensity in Handir's voice, a gleam in his fevered eyes. Pan'assár suddenly wanted that story now, in spite of everything that needed doing. Handir grabbed his sleeve, pulled him close. "Tell me you have the chest?"

"We have it, Prince." Pan'assár almost smiled at Handir's utter relief, and then startled as Llyniel skidded to a halt beside him. She crashed into Handir, hugged him close.

Soon, they were all sat around the fire, except for Fel'annár who lay between Sontúr and Llyniel, now clean and with his bare and bruised feet on display. It had taken an extra trip to the nearest water source to provide the healers with enough of it to wash away the Hound blood. There was murmuring, and then Sontúr shoved his travel pack under Fel'annár's head as he began to stir.

Just opposite, Handir sat, face flushed as he cleared his throat. He had a fever, no doubt from the effects of the river water. But he was well enough for now, and Llyniel looked down on Fel'annár, his still groggy eyes fixed on her. Sontúr was crumbling herbs into a cup he had salvaged from his pack.

Cuts and bruises marred his face, older ones down his body. She wondered how he had acquired the strange lines of bruising that coiled up almost his entire body. She started, frowned, and then she realised. The tree, the image of airborne roots still floating in the water. Had it reached out, broken their fall and left these marks? She glanced at Sontúr, saw him shaking his head, silently denying what she herself could hardly believe. And yet what other explanation was there?

She bent down and stroked Fel'annár's loose but messy locks. "Look at this," she tutted, but her hands would not cease their wandering, their need to touch and feel his warmth. She bent closer, words soft, meant only for him, and she felt Sontúr shuffle backwards.

"I didn't grieve," she whispered into warm skin. "I couldn't feel your presence, but neither did I feel your loss."

Fel'annár smiled. "You can't escape me, Llyn."

"How do you feel? You were already injured ... "

"Nothing you can't fix."

From across the fire, Pan'assár watched them, eyes drifting to

Handir. He had not lied. He would have taken the Long Road had the prince been lost. But he knew now that he had not wanted that. Life meant something to him now. There was a road ahead for him, of atonement and achievement. There were still things he could do. His oath to the line of Or'Talán still drove him.

He glanced sideways at Idernon, faithless and wise, eyes full of his friend, the one he had convinced himself had died. He could see regret. Perhaps because he had not believed. Sorrow, perhaps for himself and his sceptical ways. Relief for the return of his friend. And he saw thanks, although he wondered who Idernon gave it to.

But above all, he saw love. Love for a brother. The same love he felt for Gor'sadén, still felt for Or'Talán.

THE GLOWING EMBERS of their fire contrasted with the dark sky beyond their cave. Handir coughed, trying not to breathe too deeply.

"Alright?" asked Llyniel from beside him at the fire.

"Just about. I will never again impersonate a fish underwater. It hurts." His voice was nothing but a husky whisper, a light sheen of sweat beading on his upper lip.

"You breathed water?" she asked.

"I did. I remember it vividly."

She looked carefully at her friend, thinking that perhaps she should not yet insist. Whatever had happened, Handir had surely almost drowned. "You must tell me about that later."

He nodded and then turned to Fel'annár, who was stirring. "Is he alright?"

"I will be." The words were strangled and strained. Handir's lips twitched at the stubborn sound of his words. It was Sontúr who answered as he rummaged through his pack.

"There are four damaged ribs and several bruised bones in his back. That knock on the head and all this bruising. His feet are particularly bad; walking is going to be a trial. Ideally, I would have him ride, or better still rest for a few days at least. But we do not have that luxury."

"I don't need it. Stop fussing," said Fel'annár, trying and failing to sit up. Llyniel pushed him back down.

"We are not fussing. You will remember our words soon enough when we are back on the road." She filled one of Fel'annár's leaf cups and helped him drink from it. "And while we are on the subject, how in the wilds did you fight in this state?"

Gor'sadén leaned closer from across the fire, caught Fel'annár's gaze. "The Dohai."

The word echoed around them. Pan'assár's brow twitched.

"The Kah Warrior draws from that strength to fight, to intensify his power. But you surely had none. We have not weaved the Dohai for days." Gor'sadén was confused.

Fel'annár nodded slowly, grateful that Sontúr had helped him into a half-reclining position. "There is ... there is a way to draw strength, the same strength, without performing the Dohai itself. Or perhaps," he winced, "perhaps it is the same thoughts that render similar results."

"You drew energy without the Dohai," murmured Pan'assár.

"I think ... I think it *is* the Dohai ... but a different method." He finished with a groan and Sontúr pushed him down.

"Enough." Sontúr silenced them, and Handir admired the prince's tone of command.

He felt exhausted, both physically and with the sheer relief that he and Fel'annár had survived the night, that Llyniel was alive, the chest intact. While The Company guarded them outside, Handir watched as Sontúr and Llyniel took up their silent vigil over Fel'annár. The commanders sat together silently, and Tensári, perched upon a rock at the cave mouth, cared for her blades. She was another enigma that surrounded Fel'annár. Her presence was no coincidence, just as Handir knew Commander Hobin's visit had been purposeful. The common factor was Fel'annár.

But what was it that he still didn't understand? What was Fel'annár hiding from him? He turned to where Gor'sadén sat beside

Pan'assár. *Do they know?* he wondered. *Does Llyniel know?* For some reason, he realised that they did, although perhaps not Pan'assár. He and the commander were not close enough, he thought. Fel'annár did not trust them enough to confide in them, and Handir wondered if he ever would.

JUST AFTER DAWN, Tensári approached the fire pit, depositing a string of skinned and cleaned rabbits and behind her, the other half of The Company came to take some respite after their night guarding the cave. She lay the rabbits carefully upon the stone, passing a hand over them and murmuring a prayer. She turned, black cloak fanning close to the flames, and then took up her chosen place by the cave mouth. No one spoke to her, though her presence remained unexplained. She knew they had questions, especially the forest prince.

It had been a close thing; she had almost lost Fel'annár. It was something she would have to learn. The Guiding Light was, as yet, intermittent, and her ability to understand it still nascent. Still, she had found him, and he was, for the most part, intact. But he was not prepared for what she had to say. Even if he had been, she needed privacy for the revelations she would make. Not for the first time, her eyes landed on the Silvan healer, the one she now knew was Fel'annár's Connate. Did she know? wondered Tensári. Did she know what Fel'annár was? What Tensári was?

Fel'annár sat up with a miserable moan and then waited for the dizziness to pass. His head felt heavy, and his back and feet sent needles of pain through his entire body. "Shite," he mumbled, taking a hand to his cut and bruised cheek.

Sontúr handed him a brew. Blowing on it, he sipped. His gaze landed on Ramien, who was watching him.

"Still think I look like a lucky bastard?" he asked miserably.

The Wall of Stone's eyebrows lifted. Then he threw his head back and laughed, the noise resounding off the cave walls and drawing the attention of all. It brought smiles to their faces.

Llyniel reached into a pocket. "Galdith found this. He gave it to me."

Fel'annár's hand shot to his hair. The familiar stone was missing from his front braid. He had not realised its absence, and he stared back at Llyniel and Galdith. The others watched Llyniel extend her hand. Sitting in her palm, the amber river stone that Alféna had given him for saving her children's lives. Fel'annár's eyes glinted in the half-light, and he gently took it. He slipped it into his own pocket, nodding at Galdith. He almost jumped when Pan'assár began to speak.

"The Glistening Falls are half a day's trek on foot. We should reach them by midday. The key to successfully navigating the rockface is patience and care. The stairways are narrow but safe enough if we travel in single file. The weather is on our side, but we must make it to the shores before nightfall. Pirates and smugglers frequent that place, and we cannot discard the possibility that some of those mercenaries survived the flood. We must not be caught on those cliffs at sundown."

"Then we have no time to lose," said Gor'sadén. "When we are all safely walking over the fine sands of the Pelagian Gulf, the fires are lit and our bellies full, we will tell our stories." His heavy gaze landed in turn on Fel'annár, Handir and Tensári.

"Break camp," ordered Pan'assár.

They stood. Fel'annár swayed but was safely guarded by Ramien and Idernon on either side and behind him, Tensári. And then Gor'sadén was before them.

The commander gestured for the others to walk ahead, and soon, he was alone with his Disciple. He rested one hand on his shoulder, lightly lest he hurt him. Fel'annár's pale and pinched features softened, and colour seemed to infuse his skin. He raised his own hand to his master's leather-clad shoulder. They stayed that way for a moment, and then Gor'sadén spoke quiet words.

"I have heard about what happened, how you followed Handir into the torrent. You protected him with your body, sheltered him from harm, and then guarded him here before Tensári found you."

Fel'annár opened his mouth, but Gor'sadén's hand squeezed

tighter. "Pan'assár is most grateful. And I am proud." He pushed away from Fel'annár and turned, almost abruptly, to the bustle of the breaking camp, and Fel'annár watched him walk away.

He knew why Gor'sadén had left like that, and was glad of it. Emotion welled in his own eyes. He breathed as deeply as he could, stepped out of the cave and smiled into the sun.

AN HOUR into their morning trek, and Gods but his feet were on fire. Still, Fel'annár forced his mind to concentrate, to listen. There were no Hounds about, but there was a lingering sense of something not quite right.

His uneven step faltered, the voices around him changing.

Pity.

He stopped in his tracks, Sontúr beside him. "Commander?"

"What is it?" Both commanders turned to face him.

Fel'annár shook his head and regretted it when a lance of pain shot through his temples. He closed his eyes, opened them. "Something has happened. Some malice passed this way."

"Is there danger?" asked Gor'sadén, stepping towards Fel'annár, reading his face.

"Not anymore." Fel'annár gestured with his head towards the trees.

Pan'assár continued to lead them forwards slowly, cautiously. They could all smell it now, that familiar stench that meant only one thing to a warrior, to a healer. To Handir, though, it meant nothing other than a smell of putrefaction.

They stepped out into a small glade. Carodel shouted in surprise. He jumped back while Ramien screwed his face up in disgust. Before them, a row of ten stakes had been driven into the ground, slanting towards them. Crowning each of them, was an elven head, the tips of the stakes through their mouths. Handir covered his, turning away from the gruesome sight.

"Silor," said Galadan, stepping forwards but not touching.

"Sulén," said Sontúr, touching the late lord's forehead. Cold.

Pan'assár gestured them on, into the ruined camp. A mist lingered over the ground, over the hearths and the cold bones inside them. Blood splattered the half-collapsed tents, old and rust-coloured. There were tracks everywhere, and Galadan turned to Pan'assár.

"Deviants."

Pan'assár nodded and then started when Fel'annár spoke. "And Nim'uán."

The rest turned to him, but Gor'sadén simply stepped up to Fel'annár's side and followed his line of sight, to the trees and the terrible spectacle that hung from them. Headless corpses hanging from the branches.

Sontúr approached, Llyniel beside him. "Since when do Deviants torture their enemy?" murmured the prince.

"They don't." Llyniel saw the bruises, the marks, the discolouration. "All this was done after death."

Idernon shook his head in confusion. Gor'sadén explained. "The way these wretches were slaughtered ... this is not a coincidence. This was how the Nim'uán died. A stake through its mouth, skewered by the trees and hoisted aloft. This is *revenge*."

"No. Not revenge," said Fel'annár. "It is a *warning*."

Pan'assár was not sure he believed that. It was easier to believe an evolution of sorts, some new trait the Deviants had acquired. Still, he was commander enough not to discard the idea.

He ordered the camp be sanitised at least. The heads were piled up, still burning now, even as he stood before the line of headless bodies lying on the ground before him.

He knew which one was Sulén. His expensive clothes and golden buttons gave him away. Despite the river of blood down his front, he could still see the silver inlay and exquisite embroidery around the hem of his tunic. He knelt at Sulén's feet, cocked his head. One of those fancy buttons had popped, and from it, the corner of some object was poking out. He pushed the stained cloth back, had to undo another button, but then he pulled it out. High-quality oilcloth, he mused. He ran a finger down it and then peeled it open. Inside was a book.

Not a book. A journal.

There were two buckles around it, holding it closed. He pulled and loosened them, heard them clink as they fell away. He opened the front cover of hard, worn leather. This must be Sulén's journal, he thought.

But there, on the first page, the name of its author was revealed.

He read it. Read it again.

Or'Talán.

Or'Talán.

PAN'ASSÁR SLIPPED the journal underneath his cuirass. He said nothing to anyone, not even Gor'sadén, and soon, they had resumed their path towards the Glittering Falls.

That smell of death was dissipating, but it still lingered on their clothes, in their hair, and Handir seemed even paler than he had been before. Fel'annár soldiered along, Sontúr at his side. In all their minds hung the significance of what they had found.

Fel'annár said that the pitted heads and the hanging bodies had been a warning from the Nim'uán, and Gor'sadén had agreed. Idernon's suppositions, his translation of the script along the creature's sword—it all seemed to make sense. There *were* more Nim'uán, and the question was, *where* were they?

Now, it was the smell of salt that began to dominate. The Silvan members of The Company stood taller. Even Fel'annár's eyes were thirsty for their first sight of the sea. In spite of the river, the Hounds, the horror of what they had found; despite what awaited them in the forest and the tales that had yet to be told, it was the promise of the sea that occupied their minds. It was the thrill of the unknown.

It was the smell of adventure.

They were Silvans of the Deep Forest, and they had never seen the sea.

Band'orán read the missive before the windows of his official study, in his forest residence. Behind him, Draugolé and Barathon stood beside Captain Bendir and General Huren. They waited and watched for a sign that it was good news.

It was Macurian, our best Shadow. He grew greedy, robbed me of my family jewels, took my letters and unfinished missives.

A surge of rage rippled through him, repressed with years of practice. Sulén was a fool. This Shadow could blackmail him.

My family searches for him, but Shadows are not easy to find, as I am sure you are aware. We are watching Prince Handir for any signs that he may be in possession of those papers. We have seen no evidence that he is.

Thrice damned fool. Nobody took papers unless they mean to use them. No, not a fool. Sulén *did* know this, meant to fool him, thought him a lackwit. Memories stirred from their cage in his mind, and the surge of anger was back, hardening his muscles. Just what had Sulén written? What had he *said*?

The Silvan is hard to kill. They say he is a Listener, but he is more than that. He is a mage, some sort of forest demon. The only way to be rid of him is to overwhelm him in battle. Take him as far away from the trees as possible.

Band'orán's lips twisted into a strange smile-come-snarl that no one else could see. He straightened his face and turned.

"Sulén has failed to kill the Silvan, just as we suspected. He has also misplaced incriminating messages, half-finished missives to me. He doesn't say what was in them."

"How can he fail to kill a *boy*!" said Captain Bendir. Huren shot him a warning glare.

"He speaks of a forest demon, some sort of mage, to justify his failure."

"Ill news, lord," murmured Draugolé.

"He is on his way, claims he is still trying to carry out the deed. However, Huren has warned of a recent surge of incoming missives from the Motherland. We must be prepared for news from Handir himself to his father. It may be difficult to continue intercepting them."

Draugolé frowned, watching Band'orán's hands—warrior hands. He was nervous, could see the ligaments too clearly. He braced himself.

"The time has come." It started as a murmur, eyes lost to some thought or perhaps memory, but as he spoke once more, his gaze sharpened, focussed and glittered, words dripping conviction. Then he saw it: that deep-seated suffering he knew had never left his lord, not since he had become an adult and had been free to seek retribution for what others had done to him. What he perceived they had done.

Band'orán stood tall, regal, almost as regal as his brother. "The second era is about to begin, with us, we few founding fathers. It is time to renew your oaths, show your worth, and when it is done, reap your rewards."

Bendir nodded curtly. Barathon stared back at his father and Draugolé braced himself for the second time.

"Huren. Find them. Find them and kill them. Kill them all before they step inside this forest."

"All of them, lord?"

"All of them, General. The bastard, the prince, the commander. Bendir, make sure Rinon is duly occupied. I want you and your lieutenants here tonight. Huren, I want to know when the king's next scheduled visit outside the gates will take place. Draugolé, take care of Aradan."

Barathon wanted to talk. Draugolé did, too. But Huren was dreaming of power, Bendir of his purple sash and his stately home in the woods. Band'orán himself was dreaming of kingship. Yet more than this, he was dreaming of retribution, for the past, for what others had done to him. What he had done to himself.

Wisely, they left him alone.

No more waiting, no more butter on a lord's bread. It was time to reap what he had sown. It was time to rally his followers and take this forest for himself, a worthy king, fit for the worthiest of queens.

But she wasn't here. Or'Talán had seen to that, and Band'orán would punish him for it. He would punish his dead brother by shaming his son, wresting the crown from his brow and the power from Rinon's hands. Shame the son, kill the grandchildren, destroy his entire line. From the ashes, a new king would rise. A better king, not a lesser brother.

There would be no turning back. Ea Uaré would be his and Or'Talán's heirs would be dead.

Or'Talán would be dead.

10

THE CALL OF THE SEA

"To Fel'annár, the sea was a barrier, an unwelcome blade that severed his connection to the forest. To Ramien, it was the most beautiful thing he had ever seen."
The Silvan Chronicles, Book IV. Marhené

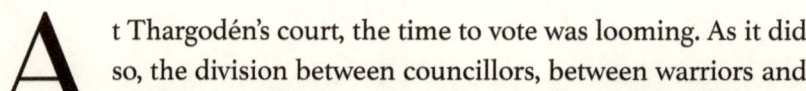

At Thargodén's court, the time to vote was looming. As it did so, the division between councillors, between warriors and between workers, became more and more apparent.

Their hearts had been stirred, their fears stoked, and their apprehension was written on their faces. They wanted a return to the days of Or'Talán; they wanted prosperous trade, and many told themselves they needed a submissive forest in order to achieve it all. It was what Band'orán told them. Others, though, listened to what the king told them in his many forays into the surrounding villages, into the markets and the very streets of the city. Everyone wanted the same thing, but they were divided in how to achieve it.

All the while, the Silvan people waited outside the gates. Some told themselves it was their right to rule beside the Alpines. They wanted equality, at the Council and the Inner Circle. Others, though, said that independence was the only future, and commended Angon for his confiscations and his warnings to the few Alpine merchants that still ventured into the forest. Erthoron struggled to maintain a united Silvan front, while the Silvan troops came to pledge their service to the Council of Elders.

In the king's study, Rinon sat before a table strewn with papers. Reports from the field, from the city. Movements and purchases, visits, times and dates, library registers. Rinon knew what they were doing. The pattern was clear, but still, it wasn't evidence. Aradan could not use this chain of circumstances to bring down Band'orán. It was not enough, and he knew it.

And damn it all, but where was Handir?

He rubbed at his temples, feeling his thudding pulse there. His eye roved over a report from the Inner Circle. Rinon thought he had convinced at least a handful of captains to vote in favour of the Warlord. But now, they said that if Lord Fel'annár were allowed to become the Warlord, the forest would turn against the Alpines. They would rebel. It was happening already, they argued. Even those sympathetic towards the Silvans had been convinced it was the wrong thing to do, or perhaps the right thing at the wrong time.

Standing, he slammed the reports on his desk and closed his eyes, willing his rising temper to calm. Turning, papers in hand, he threw them on the fire and waited for them to be consumed, knowing that his father watched him and felt the same.

Behind him, the door clicked open. Aradan strode towards the king. Thargodén stood.

"We have news. A missive, at last! From Vorn'asté himself."

They made for the table. Rinon's eyes automatically searched for Turion, but did not find him.

"Open it and read," ordered the king.

Aradan nodded, broke the ornate wax seal that held the scroll together, and pulled it open.

Gracious king of Ea Uaré, Thargodén Ar Or'Talán.

I send tidings from Tar'eastór and news of your sons, both of whom are well.

"Thank the Gods," muttered Thargodén.

Prince Handir has concluded his fruitful tutorship with Chief Councillor Damiel, who has reported that your son excelled in his studies. He recommends Prince Handir for the role of Advisor, and I urge your own Lord Aradan to continue his studies to this end. A gracious and duteous son, Handir will be welcome in my realm whenever he sees fit to return.
You may already know of the Battle of Tar'eastór.

"What? What battle?" barked Rinon.

A new foe, the Nim'uán, led a mighty host of Deviants to the very doors of my court. Your warriors, under Lord Commander Gor'sadén, shone in their duty and have been personally commended. I congratulate you, Thargodén, on an excellent militia. The Alpines of Tar'eastór are grateful. Your own Commander Pan'assár will brief you in full.

"Nim'uán? What the hell is that?" Rinon was striding around the desk, but Aradan continued reading, unperturbed.

I wish to extend my own invitation to you, to visit the Motherland at a time circumstances permit. I would speak with Or'Talán's son once more.

"Signed, etc.," concluded Aradan, allowing his arms to drop. His eyes flitted from the king to the prince.

"What, no more? Is that *it*?" asked Rinon with a scowl. He wanted the details. He wanted to know about the battle, about this Nim'uán.

Aradan brought the paper back to his eyes and scanned it once more. "The date ..."

"What about it?"

"Vorn'asté states the date of the battle. It was nearly two months ago." Aradan nodded as he turned the parchment in his hands. The king watched him. "Heavy paper ..."

"Aradan?"

The advisor strode to the door and pulled it open. "Send for Lerita. Now." One of the guards strode away, and Aradan turned back into the room, made straight for the king's desk. "I believe there is a cypher."

"He knows," concluded Rinon. "Vorn'asté knows there is danger. But *how*? Handir can't possibly know what has happened in his absence, and certainly not Pan'assár."

The king nodded. "But he knows our correspondence was not arriving, that it was intercepted." He turned to Aradan for confirmation.

"It would seem that way, yes." He wandered to the window, aware that behind him, Thargodén was pouring wine.

"How do we know we can trust this Lerita?" asked Rinon, accepting the goblet the king handed him.

"She was Or'Talán's most trusted scholar. They would sit for hours, talking and postulating. Your father will remember her."

"I do." Rinon turned to the king as he spoke. "She almost died for me once, many years ago. A story for later."

Rinon turned to Aradan, saw his thoughtful eyes. Whatever had happened, his father's advisor knew what it was.

"Well, she surely knows the consequences of betraying our trust. If word gets out, she knows she will be held responsible." Rinon was sceptical, but his father seemed as sure as he could be.

Minutes later, the doors opened, and a short woman stood in expectant silence before them. A stranger face Rinon had never seen. It seemed almost flat, her eyes the shape of almonds and her mouth as thin as a bowstring. It was almost a cruel face, he mused.

"Lerita of the Academics' Guild," declared Thargodén, smiling at the utterly still woman with the stoniest face he had ever seen. It was even worse than Rinon's. Still, he knew her well, though they had not spoken much through the years of his wanderings.

"My king, my prince, lord," she said, eyes fixed upon the king.

Thargodén saw it, something he knew the others would not. Fondness. The same he felt for her.

"We call upon you for a task that is of the utmost delicacy. As such, you are under solemn oath to not repeat what happens in this room today, unless I should personally require it of you," said Thargodén.

"You have my solemn oath, my king."

All three watched her, but Rinon was fascinated with the odd woman. Lerita was a cool, strangely hard presence in the room. Like a stone in winter, as toughened as any veteran warrior, thought the prince, and he could only wonder at the things she had seen and read.

Aradan held out the missive, and she stepped forward. Taking it, her eyes roved over the paper, fingers brushing over the smooth surface. She turned it, felt it, smelled it, and then looked at her own fingers. "There are multiple cyphers here, my lords. The sender wished to ensure the messages within could not be easily decoded. I will need some time and provisions."

"You have it all, but you must not leave this room," warned Thargodén.

She nodded. "May I sit?"

The king gestured to the table. She sat. "Can this be cleared?" she asked, pointing to the piles of paper the king had accumulated. The prince raised an eyebrow at her gall, but Aradan was already clearing it away, piling it neatly on the bookshelves behind. Thargodén watched Rinon with distant amusement.

A pale hand reached for the ink well and straightened it, then smoothed the paper out before her. "I need paper, charcoal, water, scally moss and," her eyes narrowed as she peered at something in one corner, "more candles."

With a gesture from the king, Aradan was away in search of the items Lerita had requested. Before long, her work began.

King, prince and advisor sat in silence as she worked. They sipped wine, sat rigid, waiting for her to say something. But all they heard was the scratching of a quill over paper, the scrape of a candle holder, the slosh of water in a bowl.

The dinner bells chimed, and Aradan arranged for food to be brought to them. The trays were taken from the servants at the door, which was then promptly closed. They ate as they watched Lerita work, her own food untouched. She sat there, thinking and scribbling.

Hours later, a chair leg scraped over stone. A low hiss and the sound of a quill moving rapidly over parchment.

Rinon's head slipped from his hands, jolting him awake. He rose, joined Aradan and the king at the table where Lerita now stood.

"I have it."

They looked down at the mess she had made. Sheet upon sheet of scribbling or drawings sat between wet patches of red and green. The parchment itself was damp in some parts, mottled with patches of purple.

"There are multiple cyphers. Substitution, graphic, concealment. Whoever did this is highly skilled. First, note the date stated for the battle and the date of the missive itself. They are far apart. I found a reference to this. This parchment is the fifth to be sent, by carrier bird. Second, with reference to the battle. There is some ... some startling news."

For the first time, Rinon saw emotion in Lerita's otherwise impassive countenance. She was shaken, and he bolstered himself for what she would say. What could possibly startle one such as her?

"A high lord stoops, seeks the end of the sun. Twice the sun rose above."

"What?" Rinon was so impatient he was angry. Lerita was not moved.

"There is a name, scrambled and numbered. The name is Sulén."

"Sulén ... Ar Ileian?" asked Aradan.

"Presumably," said Lerita. "To clarify, lords, King Vorn'asté tells us that Sulén is conspiring to kill the sun."

"For the Gods …"

"Rinon." Thargodén's stern eyes turned back to Lerita. "Go on."

"Of course," she said blithely, moving to the next set of notes she had made.

"The sun did set and Aria brought the dawn. A dawn of green leaves."

Rinon blew out, pulled a frustrated hand down his own face, distorting it, but Thargodén was too shocked to laugh at the comical result.

"Green Sun. Fel'annár."

She nodded. "Sulén tried to kill him twice, tried and failed. I admit I do not understand the reference to Aria." Papers shuffled in her hand, and she continued to her next set of notes. "It is here, my lords, where the greatest news lies. The battle the king refers to … it came upon them unawares. The thousands-strong Deviant army would have breached the walls of the citadel. But six *objects* stood in its way," she whispered, eyes shining as they flitted from her notes to the drawings, simple lines and symbols she now knew told a story of extreme bravery.

"A wall of stone and a lyre, a fierce face and a fire. A book and a green sun. These objects represent people, I am sure of it."

Thargodén stepped forward into the blazing halo of light around his desk, eyes on the strange markings, and specifically on one: a tree inside a circle.

"Continue," said Aradan.

"Magic comes to Ea Uaré. I cannot decipher what exactly, but this image seems to refer to trees."

"This doesn't sound like a king's missive, but more like a bard's eulogy," said Rinon.

"It is often the case, Prince. A cypher is never obviously a report. It is one more ploy to mislead any who stumbles across it. The words may be interpreted literally or symbolically."

"Continue, Lerita," said Aradan once more, hand waving about in the space before him.

"Travellers left Tar'eastór two weeks ago. You must look to the sea. Now, this list was especially difficult to decipher, my lords, but it reads like this:

> Prince Handir travels with the sun. The commander with his warriors and dignitaries from Tar'eastór. But the spirit flew."

"The spirit flew ... Lainon?" asked Aradan.

"May be dead," murmured Rinon.

"There is one more sequence. It is a warning.

> Twice the darkness struck the light. Again the darkness seeks the sun.'"

The king's voice jolted them all from the strange words and the equally strange scholar that had uttered them. "They are being followed. Sulén Ar Ileian still seeks to kill Fel'annár."

"Band'orán," spat Rinon. "Sulén is doing Band'orán's bidding."

"Aradan, we must send Turion to Port Helia. If anyone can see them safely back, it is him."

Aradan smiled grimly, for he was almost as insightful as Lerita. "I already have."

IT WAS CLOSE, they could all feel it. The smell, the air that pulled their skin tight, the taste of salt upon their tongues. The sea lay just over the cliffs, not yet visible.

Pan'assár explained the dangers of the Glistening Falls, and as he did so, he handed the rope he had salvaged to Ramien. He was to keep it safely tied to himself and Ramien could guess why it might be needed. To Gor'sadén, Sontúr and Galadan, it was the most natural of things for a warrior to carry rope. They had been born to the mountain, climbed slopes as easily as Silvans did the trees. But to the Silvans among them, it was nothing but a reminder of the danger they would face.

Closer to the cliffs and their destination, Prince Handir coughed, Gor'sadén limped and Fel'annár wore a perpetual frown. But they did not slow their pace, not even when the first sliver of silver appeared above the green and below the blue of a clear, early spring day.

The air was tangy with salt and Ramien breathed it in. There were no trees here, only grassy plains. It was too open. There was nothing to hold on to and he felt heavy, as if the skies pressed down on him. As they came closer, the sliver became thicker, a band of hazy metal that flickered and sparkled. It lay across the entire horizon and his step quickened. It surely wasn't so big as to encompass his entire vision, he mused, but as he walked and the expanse grew, he knew that it would. When they came to a halt near the edge of the cliffs and the sea stood before him, Ramien struggled to understand.

The rest of The Silvan Company gathered beside him but nobody spoke, and behind them, the Alpines and Llyniel watched. They had seen the sea many times, especially Llyniel who had lived for ten years on the island of Dan'sú. But there was no denying its impact on one who had never seen more than a forest river, or the occasional lagoon.

Ramien let out a shuddering breath. He thought he had never seen anything so wild, so harsh or so powerful. Pinpricks of emotion and sensation danced over his skin, sending his heart into an unfamiliar rhythm. He wanted to reach down and clutch at the grass, anchor himself, and yet he wanted to fly over this blanket of liquid silver.

"We descend!" called Pan'assár, and while the others moved away, organising themselves as the commander bid them, Ramien lingered. This was a new world and it had taken his breath away, though his mind still struggled with the immensity of it.

All it took was that first glimpse of the Pelagian Sea and Ramien, Wall of Stone, knew that he would always love it.

Two arduous hours later, they continued the descent, keeping as close to the rock face as they could. Their shoulders grazed over the black stone as they navigated the narrow stairs that led downwards.

When cave mouths loomed, Idernon, Galdith and Galadan would walk ahead and scout inside before the rest could pass, in case some hidden enemy lay in wait for them.

Some of the openings were shallow, meant only for resting, while others led into the mountain, gaping holes with hidden treasures that humans would die for. Elves had perfected the art of mining precious metals and stones. Their forays into the bowels of the earth were well-organised and always accompanied by guards. They were also expert climbers, well-equipped with ropes and tools. But humans would sneak in at night and hack at walls and underground riverbeds, stash their treasures and then make for Port Helia, the centre of elven trade—and human contraband. Not so skilled, their white bones sat crumpled, on display to all who passed by.

Behind their three scouts, Carodel and Ramien carried the chest, Fel'annár and Tensári just after, and behind them, Gor'sadén and Prince Handir. Their right hands were always on the rock face, eyes cast towards it and never to the left and the sheer drop that led to the rocky shore below. Handir did not mind Pan'assár's hand gripping his belt from behind, perhaps hadn't even realised he was doing it.

The sun was well on its way to its western cradle, and the light had turned golden, the yellowish tinge lending the party a false sense of warmth as they continued their downward trek. A few hours to go and exhaustion was beginning to take its toll.

A scuffle and a muted yelp. Carodel slipped, dropping his side of the chest, and Fel'annár steadied him with a steely grip to his tunic sleeve. Behind, Ramien chuckled as his friend straightened his twisted tunic with a scowl. He himself wanted to stop and stretch his aching back, but they were at the centre of the line. He would just have to wait.

A small stone hit the top of the chest, bounced off it, and then a flurry of dirt and grit. Ramien looked up, then startled at Idernon's warning cry.

"*Rockslide!*"

They lunged for the rock face, stones and rocks clattering around them. Pan'assár pushed Handir so hard it knocked the wind out of him while Gor'sadén's open hand pressed on Sontúr's chest quite unnecessarily.

A boulder fell too close to Fel'annár's foot and a part of the path crumbled beneath his feet. With a cry of surprise, he fell, forearms smashing into the rock edge. He was holding himself up by the elbows, body dangling over the cliff face.

"Fel'annár!" screamed Llyniel.

"Hold on!" Tensári lunged for him, but Idernon called a warning. Two arrows hurtled towards her, and she rolled away, then scurried back to the rock face. "Rope! We need rope!"

Ramien was uncoiling it, readying it to throw to Fel'annár, while Idernon peered over the lip of the rock. He saw two heads, and another two arrows skittered over the stone, far too close to the struggling Fel'annár.

They had been followed, attacked when they were at their most vulnerable.

"There are two of them."

"You are the only one with a line of fire, Idernon. The path is too weak to risk stepping out." Pan'assár was searching for a safe way to join him but found none.

The Wise Warrior pulled out his bow, strung it and notched an arrow.

"Careful," warned Pan'assár.

Idernon nodded, then jumped out and fired, but his aim flew wide. An arrow clattered over his vambrace and scratched his face. He threw himself back against the wall, closed his eyes and blew out.

Beside him, Ramien threw one end of the rope, making sure not to hit Fel'annár in the face. But as the rope sailed towards him, he slipped and with a strangled yelp, he disappeared, all of him except for his hands.

"No, no, no!" called Carodel, a high-pitched shriek from Llyniel. More stones rained down on the crumbling path.

"He can't let go to get the rope." Tensári was inching out again, but another arrow hit the stone just before her face.

"Brothers!" Fel'annár's wavery voice came from beyond the ledge. He felt his fingers slipping, feet dangling, with no footholds, no trees. "Can't hold ... much longer."

"Idernon," warned Gor'sadén, eyes darting from the Wise Warrior to Fel'annár's grappling fingers.

Idernon reached back, notched his bow once more, not with one arrow but two. Pan'assár and Gor'sadén watched him. He was trying something only few could achieve.

Idernon walked out, turned and aimed. He held for a moment, saw movement, and then another. He had failed Fel'annár in the boat. He would not fail again. He adjusted his fingers, heard the enemy release their bolts.

Hold steady. Don't move.

He released, then felt the tip of a bolt pierce his arm from front to back. He staggered backwards.

And then two bodies fell from the heights, plummeted past them. One crashed into the ledge just beside Fel'annár and then fell over it.

A dry crack and Tensári lurched forward, reached out and bunched Fel'annár's tunic sleeve in one fist.

Then the ledge disappeared.

She grit her teeth as Fel'annár's weight pulled her towards the chasm, but then she heard shouts and felt hands around her ankles. Still, she had slid far enough to see over the side and down, to Fel'annár's wide-eyed stare. With nothing under his boots, his left hand searched for anything to latch on to.

She didn't know what was happening on the ledge behind her, but she felt herself held in place. Even if that weren't the case, she needed to believe that.

"Take my other hand!"

Fel'annár moved his legs like a lever, his other arm coming up, but the sound of tearing cloth made him stop. Slower, he reached. Tensári stretched her arm, fingertips grazing over his hand.

"Just a bit more," she ground out. "Just a bit."

Fingers scratched over a palm, felt cloth. She closed her fist. She had him.

"Up! Pull us up!"

Yelling behind her, grunts of effort, her tunic bunching around her middle, but soon, Fel'annár was half over the ledge. With one more heave from behind he was back on the ledge, rolling onto his back. He stared at the sun, half-shocked, and then some bulk shadowed it. Ramien.

"Get away from the edge."

He rolled, staggered to the rockface and then crashed to the ground, back to the wall.

"Dear Gods," he muttered, rubbing his forearms as he watched Llyniel inspect the arrow through Idernon's upper arm.

"Nice and clean," she murmured, breaking off the shaft in one expert movement. Sontúr raised his brow as he opened a jar and scooped out a thick dollop of something that smelled of alcohol. He smeared it over the broken arrow and then placed a short piece of leather in front of Idernon's face. He bit it and pressed his back against the rock. Ramien winced, Carodel looked to the skies while Fel'annár looked straight at his friend.

"Ready?"

"Y—agh! *Bugger!*" hissed Idernon, scrunching his eyes shut and releasing a long groan.

"Nicely done," drawled Sontúr as he staunched the flow of blood, cleaned the wound and bandaged it.

Llyniel leaned in close. "Thank you, Wise One."

Idernon slowly opened his eyes, saw hers so close, saw the flecks of gold in them. He had once disliked her but had come to respect her. Now she was a friend, no longer a threat to The Company. Gods, but he had almost killed her soulmate, his closest friend, when he had tipped the boat. Now he had saved him from sure death, and the guilt had gone at last. He smiled at her, then turned to Pan'assár's outstretched hand. He took it with his good hand and pulled himself up.

"With Aria as my witness, I have only ever seen that done twice. You have passed the test for Bow Master. I will register your feat at the Inner Circle upon our return. You have gained your first armband, Warrior."

Idernon smiled, turned to Fel'annár who was grinning back at him. Ramien slapped him on the shoulder, wrenching a low moan from Idernon. Mortified, Ramien patted him lightly and turned away, taking up the chest once more together with Galdith.

Fel'annár caught Llyniel's eyes, blew his cheeks out and then lent her a lop-sided smile at the frown she wore. She was not happy with him, and who could blame her? She was meticulous with her healing and her bandages. He had likely ruined her work and would surely pay the consequences later, willingly. Still, he had heard her cries, knew he had frightened her again.

He turned to Tensári, nodding slowly in thanks. Her face was utterly straight, as it almost always was, but the gleam in her eye brought a smile to Fel'annár's lips.

An hour later, they finally set foot upon the pebbled shore at the base of the Glistening Falls. Llyniel stretched her back painfully, eyes on Fel'annár as he winced and sat gingerly upon a large rock. Her eyes turned to Handir, watching as he coughed, and for a moment, could not stop. Neither were well enough to continue their journey, but there really was no choice. Idernon cradled his arm while Ramien's face was turned to the sea and the sprawling shoreline that led to the still distant town of Bulls Bay.

Pan'assár gave them a few moments, watched as they each sank to the ground with a chorus of groans and grunts—but they could ill afford anything more. It would not do to be trapped upon the shore at nightfall without a suitably guarded camp. He gestured to Galadan, and together they scouted the area in search of a safe place to stay for the night, if there was such a place.

Fel'annár watched them leave, and soon after, Gor'sadén appeared from behind the rocks. The pain must have been intolerable, he mused, but he knew better than to enquire about it. He did catch his gaze, though, the stubborn glint unmistakable. Like father like son. Fel'annár smiled to himself.

The shrill squawk of a gull echoed strangely off the cliff face, the unlikely trill of a thrush following. Galadan was Alpine but had mastered Silvan birdcall well. Sontúr pulled Handir up while Fel'annár stood carefully, holding his hand out to Llyniel. He scowled when she grinned at him, gave him one of her looks. She took the offered hand, but she bore her own weight, her grin now a fond smile. As if he would be able to pull her up! They followed after the commanders, keeping close to the cliff face lest someone once again spot them from above.

Galadan had found a cave and deployed Galdith and Carodel to guard them.

Inside was weathered stone, but there were no passageways leading further inside the rock. This was a natural cave, too shallow for hiding a pirate's stash. Pan'assár nodded at Galadan and Ramien, who set to lighting a fire at the very back.

With Sontúr in charge of it, he left to scavenge for dry wood. He found plenty of it, wondering if it had come from ships wrecked upon the jagged shore. He waved at Galdith who had climbed a way up the boulders, and then at Carodel who sat upon the shore, out of sight from the cliff tops.

Soon, water boiled over the fire and Sontúr sat talking quietly with Handir as he searched for his sachet of dried eucalyptus. The commanders sat on the other side of the fire, and Gor'sadén watched as his friend took a hand to the centre of his cuirass ... again. He frowned.

Ramien sorted through their now scant supply of food, rationing it out as each elf held out their hands. Dried meat and nuts were the only things that accompanied their dwindling supply of fresh water. Still, the promise of fish or even meat stood just half a day's trek away in Bulls Bay.

After they had eaten, the three original members of The Company and Llyniel left the cave to watch the sunset that Ramien so wanted to see. They passed Tensári on their way out, sitting upon a high boulder, legs crossed, long sword in her lap. She nodded.

"In all my years, scant though they may be, I have never seen such a spectacle," murmured Idernon as he watched the overly large sun sail towards the horizon.

"I wonder what's inside. Fish, yes, but what else? What are the colours of that world? What other beasts swim in its depths?" asked Fel'annár. "Are they gentle, or are they predators?"

"Both, I suppose. I wonder if we'll see a Rainbow Giant."

Fel'annár ripped his eyes from Idernon and then back to the sea. It wasn't Idernon who answered.

"We will. And when you have seen one, your life will change. There are other creatures, too. Smaller and yet still the size of any elf, even of Ramien here." Llyniel smiled. "This is a place of wonder. The sea that can calm and yet exhilarate, can ease your pains and stir in you the deepest of emotions. In this water live beasts of colour and of the strangest shapes and appearances you can imagine. Most of them are friend, but some are foe, and will break upon the ships and smash them for the sport of it."

"I like it already." Fel'annár smiled, but of the four, Ramien had yet to speak. He couldn't, for the sea had woven a spell on him. He was not excited, expectant or even curious. He was enraptured.

"Come, Fel'annár, Idernon. To the healers now."

Idernon frowned, and Fel'annár pursed his lips and nodded. He felt her hand in his, grasped it tight, pulled her close and the three left Ramien alone, to contemplate the ocean in silence.

LIGHTS SHONE in the watery distance, and Llyniel smiled at the many memories of navigating around the Pelagian Gulf. Princess Maeneth loved sailing, and Llyniel had often accompanied her.

She wondered, then, how Fel'annár would take to the sea, with no trees to communicate with. She watched him now as he stretched his legs out before him, bare and bruised feet to the fire. They were blue, and she knew it must have been agony to keep the pace, to descend the stairs and then school his face as if it had been nothing at all. He thought he hid it well, and he did, but not from her. She wished with all her aching heart for a moment alone with him, so that he could stop pretending, so that he could relax, and she could soothe those bruises and over-taxed muscle. But that seemed unlikely now.

Pan'assár leaned forward, his uncharacteristically soft voice pulling her back to the present.

"The watch is quiet. Whatever danger found us on the river and pursued us down the cliffs seems to have gone, thanks to the flood and Idernon's aim. For now, it seems our backs may be safe, but not so the road ahead. It is a matter of time before others pick up our trail. I want you all to understand that the danger has not passed. There will be distractions ahead, but you must all stay focussed, keep your identities hidden."

He leaned back. "Galadan. The watch?"

"Remains quiet."

Pan'assár nodded. "Well, then. There are stories to be shared." His eyes glistened in the gloom, looking straight at Handir.

No one spoke. The only sounds were the scrape of cloth over stone, the clank of a cup and the distant hiss of saltwater over pebbles.

"The last thing I remember is weightlessness. I remember wondering if I was falling or shooting upwards. And then I remember being thrown sideways. Next, it is all a blur of Fel'annár's hazy face, the smell of earth and streaks of bright colour. I remember heat and then cold. I woke in a cave, well cared for and guarded. I don't know how we survived that fall, but I do know that he bears the bruises and I almost drowned."

A cough interrupted his words, and Sontúr gestured for him to swallow more of the tea that he had brewed. "You must have swallowed more than a mouthful of water," said Sontúr.

"I breathed it. I will always remember the feeling of weight and cold; the surety of my own demise." Sontúr's brow twitched, gaze crossing with that of Llyniel.

"I should not have moved." Idernon shuffled, uncomfortable.

"It was inevitable. In order to help us, it was inevitable." Handir looked through the fire, at Idernon's downcast face. "I could not have survived unless something changed that frozen moment in time, Warrior. I would have drowned right there in Fel'annár's grip. I couldn't breathe, couldn't even call out. Only Fel'annár could see that. Nothing you did could have changed that."

"So, you resuscitated the prince, left a tracking code and then dragged him inland. You found a cave, set up camp and then fought the Hounds," said Pan'assár, almost no intonation in his voice.

Fel'annár nodded his aching head. "I almost failed." Fel'annár turned his head a little, chancing a furtive glance at Handir, found him staring back.

Galadan slowly shook his head. "But how did you escape the falls? We thought you both dead—you *should* be dead." Gor'sadén nodded at the observation, turning to his Disciple expectantly.

Fel'annár smiled, eyes sad. "We had help."

"The tree," said Llyniel, eyes wide.

"No," said Sontúr, shaking his head.

But Fel'annár just smiled. "It was a hard fall, nonetheless. But we would have died had it not helped us into the water."

"Helped you?" asked Ramien.

"It broke our fall, at the expense of its grip on the land."

"Did you ... did you conjure it?" asked Ramien.

Fel'annár shook his head. "I didn't even see it. I prayed in those final moments ..."

Handir, sat forward. "All I remember is soaked cloth and sopping locks, your green eyes and arms pressing painfully around me."

Nobody spoke. Water broke upon the shore beyond the cave mouth, and the fire flickered in the draft.

"That was my sworn duty." Fel'annár returned Handir's weighty gaze stubbornly, but Handir would not look away. Llyniel knew Fel'annár's mind. He would have them all think it was simple duty. But it wasn't just that. Fel'annár had been protecting his *brother*. She knew it, and she rather thought Handir did too.

"What happened after the fall?" asked Idernon. "How were you not swept away in the current towards the Glistening Falls?"

"We tumbled for a while, but the current let up and there was calm. I managed to angle us towards the shallows."

"I remember none of that," said Handir.

"You wouldn't. I thought you were dead when I pulled you out. I think you *were* dead."

Sontúr shuffled forwards, a deep frown on his brow. "You breathed him back?" asked the prince.

"Yes. Although I thought it was over. I was going to stop ... and then I remembered the Dohai, the effects of it on my wounds. Something happened, I ..." Fel'annár reached for his boots, pulled them on and struggled to his feet. He swayed for a moment and then turned to Pan'assár. "I'm going to check the camp."

They watched him leave and then turned back to the fire. Gor'sadén breathed deeply, his questions carefully stowed for later. Idernon made to stand, but a princely hand fell on his forearm.

"Let *me* go, Warrior."

Idernon arched an eyebrow at Handir, but bowed and settled back down beside Ramien and Galadan, watching the prince as he walked slowly after Fel'annár. Just behind him, Tensári followed.

Llyniel watched them leave the cave, a slow smile playing at the corners of her mouth.

"Well, then," began Galadan, "who would have thought?"

Pan'assár agreed. Something had happened between Handir and Fel'annár. Their trials on the river had brought about some fundamental change, something they were yet to see. But there was something that interested Pan'assár more. Something he wanted to know.

Why was Tensári here?

WATER BRUSHED REPETITIVELY over the pebbles and hissed as it retreated over the sands, the rhythm soothing. Fel'annár sat on a rock, hands on his thighs as he contemplated the wide expanse. He was surprised at who had followed him. He didn't turn when Handir spoke.

"I still remember the first time I saw the sea. I stood hand in hand with my father, my head somewhere around the pommel of his sword. I could not take my eyes off it, even though I knew my father watched me. I gawked." He smiled as he remembered. "My mouth hung open as my mind struggled to grasp the enormity of it. He warned me to close my mouth else I trapped a fly, or perhaps I would dribble." He huffed fondly. "Princes do not dribble, you see. So, I closed my mouth because the thought of swallowing an insect was horrifying, but still, I will never quite lose my sense of awe every time I stand upon the shores of Pelagia."

"A fond memory."

"Yes." Handir was struck by the fact that Fel'annár had no such memories of his father.

"What you did, Fel'annár. How you steered us down the river, kept me with you in spite of my useless flailing. You took the blows, turned me when a boulder blocked our way; you embraced me when we fell, conjured the tree and then you breathed me back to life. You kept me as safe as I could be."

"Duty, Prince."

The words were almost sad, thought Handir. They were, perhaps, Fel'annár's last attempt at fooling himself, an attempt even *he* knew would fail. "It was beyond duty. You protected your brother, not your prince. I felt that much."

Fel'annár turned from the sea to Handir's unwavering gaze. For a moment, Handir thought he would speak, but he did not. He simply sat there with his pale and bruised face gleaming under the half-moon. What would it take? he mused. What would it take to smash down that solid rock wall his brother held around himself?

"You know. Those terrible moments before the battle, when I stood upon the ramparts with Vorn'asté and Damiel, while you stood with The Company, alone before a horde of thousands. I suddenly wished we had known each other. I wanted to tell you how sorry I was. I wanted to tell you that I understood you. I wished I had called you *brother*, just once. And I wanted to tell you how proud I was."

Fel'annár's gaze was heavy with tears he would not allow to fall. Still, the emotion was there, that heavy silence almost too much for him to contain. Handir started when he did finally speak.

"When I saw you, lying beside me in the shallows, half floating on your back, I thought you were dead. I remembered my training, got you to shore and performed the techniques I had been shown, but you wouldn't come back. I breathed and I pumped and then breathed again. I pleaded with Aria, and the trees joined me, but they were grieving for *me*."

There. Fel'annár had told him that he cared, not directly, but in the only way he seemed able. Was this the consequence of growing up without parents? Terror at the prospect of loving and losing, because all you ever really wanted ... was the love of family.

Grief. Handir wanted to embrace him, but instead, he took a deep, deep breath. "I never thought I would say this, but I am glad you exist. Whatever the circumstances, the consequences it brought. I am glad to have found you. You have an elder brother, for whatever you may need."

Fel'annár turned back to him. Shock warred with his need for control, but love was vying for a way out, Handir could see it in his eyes, in the weight of them. He smiled.

"Stay for a while. I believe Llyniel is searching for an excuse to leave that cave."

Fel'annár raised an eyebrow, surprised at Handir's fine idea, relieved at the change of subject, yet only half-glad when his brother left. Minutes later, Llyniel stood beside him at his perch.

"Isn't it amazing?"

"Aye. But the absence of the forest is ... disturbing. I can't hear them."

"Well. Take advantage of the silence, Fel'annár."

"I can't. It's the wrong kind of silence. It's like failing to hear your own heartbeat."

"Then hear mine," she murmured, sitting beside him on the rock.

He turned to find her looking at him. She looked so strong, sitting there with the sea behind her.

"You must be happy, now that Handir and I are on better terms."

"I am, thank you very much. I told you, Fel'annár. He is a good elf, the best friend. A deeply passionate soul whose convictions are just as strong as yours."

His lips were upon hers almost before she had finished.

THAT NIGHT, while Idernon and Ramien guarded the camp and Fel'annár and Llyniel sat before the sea, Pan'assár looked around the cave. Galadan and Carodel were asleep against a far wall, Handir not far away. They were alone for now. No one would hear them so long as he kept his voice down.

He leaned in. "I found something. On Sulén's headless corpse."

Gor'sadén knew Pan'assár had hidden something, not because he had seen him do it, but because of the way his hand came up to his chest far too frequently. Gor'sadén frowned, watching as he slipped a hand under his cuirass and pulled out a journal. He set it on the rock that separated them.

"I found this. What it was doing on that traitor, I cannot fathom."

"It would help if you told me whose it is."

He breathed, chest expanding and then falling, faster. "This ... is Or'Talán's journal. His fourth and possibly last."

"What?"

"I know. I took it. Hid it. I said nothing to Handir but this, by rights, should pass to him, at least until we are back home and I can give it to Thargodén."

"Will Thargodén want it? I would think his memories of his father bitter, at the very least."

"He does not speak of his father. I think he finds it hard to hate him, and yet, hard to remember him fondly."

"And Handir. Will *he* want it?"

Pan'assár shook his head. "I don't know. Rinon would want to see it, but Handir ..."

"You should tell him, Pan, at least."

"No."

Gor'sadén stared back at him, saw the stubborn glint in his eye, knew he would not be moved. But he had to try. "You know that journals are handed down to the closest family members, friends if there are none. It would be Thargodén's right to dispose of it if he so wishes. You know this ... but you want to read it. And if the king finds out you held this back from him ..."

"I will not allow him to burn it, Gorsa. And it would be his right to do so."

Gor'sadén heaved a heavy breath. "Have you already started?"

"No. I'm not sure that I should, without Handir's permission."

Pan'assár's face was almost comical, but Gor'sadén didn't laugh. He understood. His brother had witnessed the most terrible of deaths. It was his last memory of their greatest friend but this journal ... it was, perhaps, the best thing that could have happened to Pan'assár. It was a chance to celebrate Or'Talán's life, stop replaying his horrific death.

"If I were you, I would tell Handir. He doesn't have to know the details. Just tell him you have found a diary and that you wish to read it. Make light of it. The chances are he will allow it."

Pan'assár looked down at the small book lying upon the rock. Robust and compact, unadorned. But what treasures lay inside? he wondered. What knowledge lay on those pages? All he wanted was to hear the voice of his brother one last time, for his voice to take away the screaming in his mind, the last memories of his greatest friend.

11

WHERE LOYALTIES LIE

"Treachery long coming, forged centuries before during the reign of Or'Talán. This was the day of its culmination."
The Silvan Chronicles, Book V. Marhené

King Thargodén cantered through the outer reaches of the city, into the still sparse forest where the trees were thin enough to ride at speed. For a moment, all that existed was him and his steed, the wind through his hair and the smell of spring in the air. Around him, his retinue kept apace with him, their faces straight, eyes watching the trees.

Just months ago, he had been sitting in his chambers, drinking and thinking, remembering the past and what he had lost; what had been taken from him. And then Lainon and Turion had found Fel'annár and given him a reason to wake up, to think of the future, rebuild his relationship with his children. He would meet the one he had never known, see Lássira in his face.

Band'orán be damned. He could burst his veins spreading his lies, but Thargodén would show his people that they were *his*, from the northernmost settlements of the Great Forest to the Evergreen Wood and beyond. He was strong, he sympathised with the Silvans, loved them as much as his father had, and even desired the return of the Warlord.

Not for the first time, Thargodén wondered if he could find the rebel Angon, speak with him. Huren would not be happy, and neither would Aradan, for that matter. But there was merit in the idea. If he could only show him that he wanted equity, he wanted the Warlord to return; if he could convince the elf that it was possible to live together. It was worth trying. There were few doubts in his mind that his dwindling army was at least partly due to Angon's encouragement.

Thargodén knew there were many who would no longer fight for him. Since the conclusion of the Forest Summit, hundreds of Silvan warriors had abandoned his army and made for the camp, or simply gone home to their villages, never to return. It was why he would visit the Outer City Barracks today. Captain Bendir was its commanding officer, and so it was *he* who lead the king's escort from the palace this morning.

A scout emerged from the trees ahead, and Bendir gave the order to stop. They spoke, and then Bendir turned his horse and approached the king. "Sire. I am dispatching four warriors to investigate suspicious movement to the west. We are being followed, perhaps by Silvan rebels. For now, the rest of us will escort you to Analei until the way is clear. There may still be time for you to visit the barracks, sire, once our scouts have returned and the way is deemed safe."

"And you think Analei is safe for me, Captain Bendir?" said Thargodén, moving closer to his captain, eyes narrowed. "How so?"

"Sire. Lord Band'orán will not openly allow others to harm you. We will be with you at all times."

The ground sped away from him, his stomach hurtling downwards. Bendir had taken him for an utter fool, and as his eyes travelled around the onlooking warriors, he realised there was no escape. He looked them in the eye, one by one, committing their faces to memory. He was glad at least that they could not look at him, that there was some semblance of shame. He closed his eyes and turned back to Bendir.

"What has he promised you, Captain? Riches? Lands? You, a founding lord, would follow a traitor and lose your honour, your very dignity?"

Bendir did return his gaze. There were no doubts in his mind about what he was doing. When he spoke, his voice was curt and confident. "Traitor is the king who promises a world and gives nothing but praise. Traitor is a king who promises nothing and gives no praise. It is time for a strong rule, my lord. It is time for *change*."

With a signal from Bendir, the guards moved in and ushered the king's horse forwards. Thargodén was a good swordsman, but Bendir was a Master, besides which he was outnumbered ten to one. No, fighting would be useless. There was no breaking free from the tight circle, and before long, he stood in the familiar courtyard before familiar stables.

Lord Band'orán stood upon the steps of Analei, watching as the horses were led away. At his side was Captain Dinor.

"Welcome, King Thargodén." Band'orán opened his arms, a peaceful sort of smile on his lips.

A hand appeared at the small of Thargodén's back, and the king murmured to Bendir behind him, "Unhand your king." But the hand did not disappear. It pushed harder.

How had he been so blind? How had he walked into this trap? It had been so simple, realised Thargodén. But then the answer came flooding towards him: Huren had organised the retinue. Huren had been searching for his son and his commander. Huren had been hunting for correspondence from Tar'eastór. *Huren* had been present when practically every tactical decision had been taken.

Huren had betrayed him.

His anger flared, at Huren and at himself. There would surely be little hope of escape from whatever awaited him now, but with the Gods as his witness, he would tell the traitor his mind.

"What now, Band'orán? Are you done with politics at last? Has all your scheming and manipulation been for nothing, then? By Aria, it must have cost you a fortune, only to be forced to these crude resorts. I thought you more elegant, more intelligent. You are quite a disappointment."

Band'orán stepped forward, pulled his arm back and then flung it sideways, slapping the king across the face with the back of his hand. The smack of skin against skin and then the clatter of metal, a rightful crown skidding over dark cobbles, landing upside down. The hand was back, pushing him forwards to the doors, and all Thargodén could do was pass through them. He took one last look at the sun, at the trees, and damned his stupidity. Then he sent a plea to whoever could hear.

I am here, at Forest's Edge.

The mighty doors of Analei slammed shut, but the king's last thoughts drifted over the high boughs, weaved a song of danger, a plea for help. It was a haunting tune that spoke of treachery and shame; of malice and greed. It marked the day, the place and the time, and the forest called to the only one powerful enough to hear.

Come, Forest Lord.

ANGON THUNDERED through the sparse forest, five of his best Silvans behind him. There was an Alpine patrol somewhere near. A scout had seen them and came to tell him. They had not ventured far into the forest. Indeed, they were still close to the city. Under any other circumstances, Angon would not have interfered. But they said the king was with them, bound for the Outer City Barracks. Angon would not forego the opportunity to tell him—tell him of the plight of his people, tell him that it had not been Silvans who had killed those merchants.

But that was not to be. The first body came into sight, an arrow through his heart. Angon frowned as he slipped from his horse, signalling for the others to remain.

He walked on to another body, another arrow, through the neck. And then another two.

All dead.

"Riders!" The voice of his second. He turned and came face to face with an incoming patrol. They skidded to a halt, its captain a flurry of leathers and fine wool.

"What have you done?" the captain growled, drawing the sword from his harness. "Where is the king?"

Angon had no time to speak, only enough to realise what had happened before the guards were dismounting and coming for them.

"Take them!" ordered the captain.

"Move!" shouted Angon. They were desperately outnumbered. He saw their hesitation, but he turned and shouted once more.

"Go! Tell them what has happened."

Angon's elves were torn. They wanted to fight, but their people needed to know, and five Silvans could not take on a patrol of twenty Alpine warriors. And so, with a last, anguished glance at their leader, they thundered away.

The next time Angon blinked, the captain was before him. "What have you done with our king?"

"I don't know what you're—" He staggered sideways, the force of the blow almost sending him to the floor.

"We found them like this," he shouted, indignant, holding his smarting face.

"Of course you did. Bind him! Truss him up like a hog for the spits! We drag this forest bastard home, to Huren and then the dungeons."

But Angon was not going quietly. He kicked out, swung his fists, landed a few punches, but he was overpowered in moments, and then there was the thump of fists and the smack of skin, boots in his face, in his chest. He knelt upon the ground, arms tied painfully behind him, face bleeding and swelling.

"Get him up. We ride home."

"Sir, the king?"

The captain shook his head, cast his eyes around the place, over the massacred bodies, and then turned back to his second. "Stay with them. I will send a contingent to bring our brothers home. They have taken our king, killed our warriors."

The lieutenant nodded and then watched as half their patrol galloped back to the city, Angon slung over their captain's horse like a prize stag at the hunt.

THE NEXT MORNING, with their camp packed away, the group assembled before Pan'assár, waiting for his briefing before the journey continued.

Fel'annár stood, somewhat crooked, feeling awkward that he had not been able to help with much of anything. It seemed that the more he rested, the worse he felt.

"Today, we arrive in Bulls Bay. The enemy may still follow, but even if they are all dead, there will surely be more lying in wait for us. We journey beneath the cliffs, out of sight and out of range until we reach the town. There, we must find the less-travelled route and find a safe place to spend the night, to rest and regain our strength. Tomorrow morning, we commission passage on a ship bound for Port Helia, and we do so anonymously. Hoods for all save Llyniel and the Silvans of The Company, except for Fel'annár of course."

Experienced eyes moved from one to the other, reading their strength, their fears, their understanding.

"No rank, no deference, no saluting. First names only and not even that for our princes or commanders. As for Tensári here, she is bound for Abiren'á but has joined our group for a part of her journey —and for all we know, that may be true." There was a significant pause before he continued the brief. "Now we are still in Tar'eastór, but just as Band'orán has his spies in Ea Uaré, so too may he have them here." His gaze landed on Gor'sadén. "Should we run into warriors, we must try not to be seen. We will need a meeting point should we be separated."

"If I may, Pan'assár?" said Llyniel. "I am familiar with these parts.

The Healing Halls would be a perfect place. I know Bredja and Hamon there. They will help us, find us a safe place to stay until we can board ship tomorrow. The Halls are easy to find, on the left side of the bay."

Pan'assár nodded slowly. "Alright. We make for the Halls, as Llyniel suggests."

"Heed me, all of you," said Gor'sadén from Pan'assár's side. "That town is not safe. Not for us. Yes, this is Tar'eastór, but it is close to the biggest sea port of Ea Uaré. Shadows will be lurking, checking the ports for any suspicious movement, and as my brother has said, some of them may be in the service of Band'orán, perhaps even Sulén. Stay alert. Stay as far away from everything and everyone as you can."

With the most physical part of the journey over, they set out towards Bulls Bay. Now, it was about stealth and wit, about hiding in the shadows until the time came to reveal themselves. It would be no less dangerous.

They walked along the shore, as close to the rock face as they could, while Idernon and Ramien walked along the water's edge, eyes on the cliffs above more than the path into Bulls Bay.

In the distance, boats and ships floated on the water, white sails curving in the wind. Such a foreign world, mused Fel'annár. Even the light seemed different. Still, that strange silence bothered him, for there were no trees at all. He felt detached. There would be no forewarning in these parts, should they run into danger.

Idernon left Ramien's side and trotted towards the cliff face where the rest walked. "There are three elves following our progress atop the cliffs."

In different circumstances, Fel'annár would have known that, but he hadn't, and it made him feel vulnerable. He winced as he stepped on a large pebble, watching Idernon run back to Ramien.

With the Glistening Falls behind them, the cliffs sloped downwards, softening into undulating hills that stretched towards the shore. Idernon and Ramien joined them, declaring that the three elves upon the cliff top had left.

Black dots upon the sandy shoreline ahead were now clearly visible. Bulls lay upon the beach as if simply enjoying the morning sun. Ramien turned to Idernon, brow high. He had never seen the like, and from his friend's silence, he rather thought none of them had. Bulls Bay, indeed.

The town was surrounded on three sides by hills and then rock, and then this expanse of sand that led out to the sea. On the shores, before the unlikely bulls, were small fishing vessels laden with nets and baskets. On the far side of the bay, a long pier stretched further out into the water, and two large merchant vessels floated, still too distant to make out any further details.

To their right, buildings crowded around the bay. There were small cottages and larger residences, surely those of lords and merchants. There were barns further afield, just before the onset of the mountains, but all was strangely close, hardly any distance between one house and another.

It was a new world for The Company but not so for Llyniel. She had lived on the larger of the two islands off the coast. A full day's navigation. Still, she had visited Bulls Bay often, knew it well.

They watched as a boat slid onto the beach and three elves jumped out, their nets full. Gulls flocked overhead diving and wheeling, squawking as they circled.

"I bet there are some good taverns there," said Carodel. "With good ale."

"And sausages," added Galdith.

"Sausages," murmured Ramien.

Sontúr smiled lopsidedly. "And sticky buns," he added.

Fel'annár almost laughed out loud as the memory of Sontúr spitting out his bun came to him. But he remained silent and schooled his wandering mind. He glanced at Pan'assár and Gor'sadén, saw the concentration on their faces and berated himself. Gods, but it was so quiet. The voice was gone, and Fel'annár felt lost.

The rocks to their right fell away, and they were finally in the open, upon the beach. They walked until they came to an incline of sand and rock, then climbed it. With their boots now walking over cobbled stones, they followed Pan'assár and Llyniel, who led them on.

With his face hidden under his ample hood, Fel'annár stared wide-eyed at the place. He'd never seen so many races and cultures together in one place, so tightly packed together. Grey, brown and blonde hair. Elves, humans, some of them bearded, walked this way and that, stood talking and laughing, while others carried boxes and chests, pushing their way through the crowds.

And then there were seafarers. Many of them wore strange breeches and smart hats. The smells, too, were unfamiliar and not all of them welcoming. There was a heaviness to the air, of meat and fish, salt and smoke, sweat and urine, stale alcohol. Looking up at the signs that protruded from the buildings, there were countless taverns with exotic names. 'The Last Ship', 'The Pirate's Finger', 'Paradise Hold'.

As they passed, a door was flung open with an accompanying blast of shouting patrons. A human sailed through the doors, landing flat on his face while two others stood on the threshold, pointing and laughing. A busty woman stood looking down on him, smiling as she offered him her hand.

A group of humans passed by, one of whom had wrinkles all over her face. Flesh saggy and eyes drooping, she laughed scandalously at some joke, jaw opening to reveal nothing but gums. No *teeth*. Fel'annár's eyes widened in horror.

There were children, too, scampering around the feet of their elders who seemed unconcerned that they should see such behaviour. Drunkards and prostitutes abounded, yet the mites were unafraid as they squealed and played their games.

He had heard of humans and their society, but he had never thought that elves would feel so at home amongst them. They did, for they were just as drunk, just as willing to share themselves for coin.

They turned a corner, walking upwards now, and the street was quieter. Even so, a man staggered into Pan'assár and slipped his hand into his pocket. The commander shoved him away, watching as he keened and almost fell. He was drunk, smelled of alcohol. Not a scout, then.

"How much further?" he mumbled to Llyniel at his side. There were too many potential dangers around them.

"Just up here."

They took a left turn into an even quieter street, at the end of which stood a large stone building. Soft light shone through a small window and Llyniel gestured with her head.

Pan'assár nodded. "You go first. Find your friends and explain what we need. We will wait around the corner for your signal."

"Alright."

"Llyniel? Have a care," he warned.

She turned, eyes steady and reassuring, and Pan'assár gestured with his chin. With that, she was gone, and the group melted into the shadows to wait.

Approaching the door, she took the heavy iron loop in her fingers and banged it against the wooden door three times. A small hatch opened at eye level, and two grey eyes landed on her. They widened, and the hatch was shut. With a deep groan, the door half-opened, and a figure bent around it.

"Llyniel! What the shite are you doing here?"

"Alright, me luvver?" she answered, easily slipping into the accent she had learned during her time in Pelagia. Bredja always laughed when she used it.

The chuckling from the other side of the door had Llyniel grinning even before it fully opened. There stood a short, round woman with smiling eyes, arms akimbo as her gaze travelled from Llyniel's fiery head to her booted toes. "Well, look at the everlass, will ya? Bugger me, but ya still look sixteen!"

"Bredja, you twat. Come here!"

They embraced, and Llyniel could smell the herbs and tinctures on her friend, the wholesome food and tobacco smoke. So many memories they evoked, and she squeezed tighter before stepping back, shocked at the passing of time on her human friend's face.

"I need a favour, Bredja, an important one. Can we talk inside?"

Bredja scowled, and then looked left and right. "You in trouble?"

"No."

Bredja's gaze lingered for a while before she stepped to one side. To the right was a small room where the healers assessed their patients. It was empty now, and they entered. Llyniel looked around. They were alone, save for one patient who lay in a bed at the far end of the long room.

She leaned forward, voice soft. "Bredja. I travel with ten merchants, bound for Ea Uaré and Thargodén's court."

"An intelligent way to travel, girlie. Keep yourself well guarded."

"What do you know of the goings-on in Ea Uaré?"

"Enough to stay well clear o' that place. They say the Silvans are turning wild, attackin' the Alpines and the merchants. They all go there with guards now, right armed."

"The people I travel with. Can you give us shelter for the night? Just until tomorrow?"

Shrewd eyes bored into Llyniel's unwavering gaze. "What 'ave *they* done?"

"Nothing. It's what *others* want to do, should they be recognised."

Bredja scowled. "I'll help you, if you tell me honestly who enters my house."

"Not a word, Bredja. Their lives—*my* life—depends on your silence. Will you keep it?"

"I trust ya." She nodded after a while. "There are three patients down the hall. I'll tell Hamon to open the back door. Meet us there in five minos."

Llyniel leaned forward and pecked Bredja on the brow. The human healer swayed backwards and batted at her. "Get off, ya dafty wazzock."

Llyniel smiled as she turned back to the others, but there was a hint of sadness in it. Bredja's hair was greyer and her eyes heavier, skin hanging about her jaw.

Five minutes later, the entire group of elves lined up at the back entrance to the Halls. Pan'assár surveyed the alleys around them, watching for unfriendly eyes, some movement in the dark, but found nothing.

Llyniel greeted a towering human who stepped aside to watch the cloaked elves as they filed through the door. Closing it behind them, he made his way to the fore and gestured for them to follow. Climbing a steep, narrow staircase, they emerged into a large room, dominated by a kitchen, and at the centre, a harvest table stood laden with fruit and vegetables. Behind, a large hearth with a healthy fire over which hung a steaming pot where Bredja stood stirring whatever it was that smelled so good.

"Now then," began the plump human. "You 'ave me silence, girl, in exchange for your honesty. Oo 'e these people you travel with?"

Llyniel turned to Pan'assár. "Commander?"

Both humans stiffened, turning to the one who reached for his hood and pushed it back.

"Ooz 'e, then?" asked Hamon, pointing in confusion and looking to Llyniel for answers.

"This is Commander General Pan'assár, leader of the military forces of Ea Uaré."

"What the shag's goin' on 'ere?" said Hamon, stepping forward, while Bredja gaped and scowled at the same time.

"Peace, man. We seek shelter for the night and will give you no strife. You have my word," assured Pan'assár.

Hamon looked lost as he turned to Bredja.

"So mister Pansa, oo 'e ye friends?"

Llyniel reigned in the chuckle that bubbled at the back of her throat, and she covered her mouth with one hand.

Gor'sadén stepped forward and shrugged out of his own hood. "I am Gor'sadén, Commander General of Tar'eastór. I am most grateful for your help."

"Gorseidn, as in ... like the king's ..."

"The same. Well met."

Bredja and Hamon shared a wary yet disbelieving stare. Bredja was the first to shake out of it. "Come on then the rest o' ye."

Sontúr stepped forward, revealing his grey hair. "Prince Sontúr of Tar'eastór."

Bredja's mouth formed a perfect circle, but she curtseyed to her prince all the same, holding her pinny up as she did so.

When Handir stepped towards her, hood down, Hamon gasped and then bowed. "Well if it isn't Maeneth's brother!"

"You know my sister?" asked Handir, wondering how they had guessed his identity.

"We do, Prince. Best elf-lass, save for Llyn 'ere. You're the spittin' image of her!"

Handir smiled and nodded.

"Two princes, two commander generals. Are there any other surprises for us, then?" asked Bredja with shining eyes.

"Just one more. Fel?"

Stepping forward and slipping back his hood, he smiled at the strange humans with whom Llyniel seemed so familiar. "I am Fel'annár."

They scowled, and Handir spoke. "Fel'annár Ar Thargodén. He is my brother."

Understanding, Bredja's tongue was loose before she could school it. "You're the bastard they're all going on about? The Warlord?"

"Bredja!" gasped Llyniel, no longer able to hold her mirth.

"Well, it is. Look at that," she said, stepping towards Fel'annár. "Eez a bootie and no mistake."

Fel'annár frowned in confusion, but Llyniel was chuckling once more. "She fancies you," she said, and Bredja smacked her on the arm.

"This here is Tensári, and then Idernon, Carodel, Galdith, Galadan. Finally, Ramien, our Wall of Stone," said Llyniel with a fond smile. Hamon stepped forward, gave a toothy smile.

"Well ain't it nice 'aving a fellow wall o' stone."

Ramien smiled back and then Bredja was ushering them to the table.

"Mister Pansa. Pull up those chairs and get yeselves around the table. Got some nice, wholesome stew an' man baps."

"Man baps?" asked Gor'sadén.

"Bread stuffed with leftovers from a haunch," explained Llyniel. Gor'sadén's eyes were instantly on the round pieces of bread and the meat that oozed out of one side. Hamon placed a heavy pot at the centre of the table, steam floating over the sides. The heavy pottery bowls clinked as they were placed before them. Bredja ladled broth into their bowls and then sat.

"Well, it's not every day that a simple 'ealer gets to share a table with princes and lords."

A loud slurp and then a gasp of delight was her only answer, and Llyniel laughed while Bredja elbowed her husband. "Mind ya manners, ya wazzock."

"Wazzock?" repeated Carodel, half-turning to Llyniel.

"Idiot," she said.

"It's just a question," said Carodel with a dark scowl.

"'Wazzock' means 'idiot', you twit."

Galdith laughed and then sunk his teeth into a man bap. Closing his eyes, he chewed slowly and almost seemed to growl.

"Oh 'e likes it." Bredja smiled, pointing to Galdith with her spoon.

Fel'annár watched the humans as he ate. He caught Llyniel's gaze as she chewed. He smiled, she mirrored it, and Bredja nudged her husband in secret delight.

THE FOLLOWING MORNING, there were fewer sitting at Bredja's table. Galadan had taken Galdith, Ramien and Carodel and made for the harbour in search of a ship to take them to Port Helia. Fel'annár had boldly sat next to Llyniel, well aware of Bredja's knowing eyes. There were so few moments for them to be together. His left hand stroked her thigh under the table while he ate. Llyniel smiled as she sipped on her tea.

Hamon was staring thoughtfully at Fel'annár while Bredja laid out their breakfast. And then, just like that, the morning's news tumbled from his mouth.

"The people talk of a great battle in Tar'eastór. A Deviant army led by some monster thing they're calling a Niwan," said Hamon excitedly, eyes glancing over the commanders, princes and then back to Thargodén's strange son. "They say it rode a Gas Lizard. I told you, Bredja. Jiman was right. He *did* see one, no mistake."

"Someone saw a Gas Lizard? When was this?" asked Gor'sadén, knife frozen before his mouth.

"Months ago. Reckons he saw one slippin' inte sea."

Fel'annár scowled, his rhythmic movements over Llyniel's thigh stopping. "Can Gas Lizards swim?" he asked.

"Apparently," muttered Pan'assár.

"Everyone thought 'e was bonkers. Anyways, this monster thing was attacked by the trees—"

"Oh, don't be a twat, Hamon," said Bredja, swiping her hand in the air. "Idle tittle-tattle. Trees can't move."

"That's not what they're sayin', Bredja. And they're sayin' 'e moved 'em." Hamon pointed with his finger at Fel'annár. "They reckon 'e stood with The Compny—six warriors, mind—before a massive 'orde o' rotters. They're callin' 'im *The Silvan*."

"'Rotters'?" asked Carodel.

"Deviants," whispered Llyniel.

"Oh ho hoo!" shouted Bredja in mirth. "Eez no wizzer, Hamon. Look at 'im, all bitty nice. No beard, no pointy 'at. What kinda wizzer do *that* make 'im?"

"I'm just sayin'," said Hamon, slow and a little pedantic, "that's what's out there on the streets." Hamon shook his head. "I'm not inventin' it. Anyways, Mista Pansa 'ere got gassed, din' 'e? And Mista Gorseidn got skewered in the leg. Tellem I'm right, commander sir," asked the wide-eyed human. Hamon knew he was right. Gor'sadén had a limp.

"He is right, Bredja," said Gor'sadén, unsure as to whether he should be alarmed or amused. Pan'assár was listening carefully.

"So then, 'e comes along and 'e only kills it, dun'ee?"

"What?" asked Bredja.

"The *Niwan*. They left it to rot in the trees."

"How did it get in the trees?"

"I dunno. I'm just repeating what they're sayin'."

"You believe anything that comes over the mountain. You're such a pim 'ed."

Carodel turned to Llyniel. "What's a 'pim 'ed'?"

"'Pim' means 'swollen'. Swollen head."

He snorted and then smothered it, but Hamon hadn't finished.

"So, they won the battle, right, then they all got medals. They're friggin' 'eroes, Bredja."

"You didn't tell anyone we're here, did you?" asked Pan'assár carefully.

"I did *not*, Mister Pansa."

Pan'assár nodded.

"I'll wait till yev gone."

The commander looked up at him with a scowl. He sighed. "Hamon. We are very grateful for your help, but there is a reason we have not revealed ourselves. The political situation in Ea Uaré is dangerous. There are those who scheme in the dark, elves who would do us harm should we be seen. They know we come for them and they will do anything to avoid that. We must get on that ship unnoticed, stay out of sight for as long as we can."

"There are some shifty ones out there and no mistake. It's only gettin' worse, but I haven't seen much of the Alpine warriors yet."

"And you won't for a while, Bredja," said Gor'sadén. "We are still recovering from the battle. There are priorities for Tar'eastór now."

She nodded, eyes glancing over Fel'annár. "I 'eard Milly talkin' about a new trade route, from Prairie to the Forest. She says there's lush money to be 'ad."

Pan'assár frowned. "There are no established trade routes between Prairie and Ea Uaré. We have all we need from the Great Forest and Tar'eastór."

"Gone for a while then, Commander? They say the Great Forest is closed. They say the natives won't let the Alpines pass, that they attack the merchants and confiscate their wares."

"Aria," muttered Pan'assár as he glanced Handir's way.

Handir's jaw twitched. He knew what that meant. The situation was far worse than they had imagined. It was no longer solely about Fel'annár and his appearance at the king's court. It was no longer about Band'orán and his move on the throne, or the evidence they carried that would discredit him for good. Their entire nation had been tossed into turmoil, pushed to the brink of chaos. The question was, what was the point of no return?

RINON STRODE across the courtyard before the Royal Palace, face a terrible sight. With one hand on his sword and uncontained wrath on his face, he ignored the bows and salutes. He wanted to punch Huren.

"When did this happen?"

"This morning, Prince. The king's retinue was ten strong. We found four dead and the king missing."

"Who was captain?"

"Bendir, Prince."

Rinon stopped, and Huren turned to him. "Why Bendir?" he demanded.

"Why not, Prince?"

"He is on the most *friendly* of terms with Dinor, with Band'orán. Why must I remind you of this, General?"

Huren straightened himself. "None of that affects his duty to the king, Prince."

"Doesn't it?" Rinon stepped close, too close for Huren's comfort. "That is quite the oversight, General. Had *I* been general, I would have made sure my king rode with captains that did not show their political inclinations. I would not have taken the slightest of risks with his welfare." Rinon's eyes glittered like diamonds under a moonlit river.

"I am sorry you see it as an oversight, Prince. It was not my intention to place my king at risk."

"I don't give a Deviant *piss* for your intentions, Huren. Only your deeds. You are my superior in the army, but as your prince, you will come to *me* for approval on royal deployment for the next month, until I can come to trust you again."

Huren bowed low, endured the prince's disdain, and then followed on his heels as he strode towards the guardhouse. Though fuming inside, he was not fool enough to defend himself, not to Rinon in his current state.

The news had spread. The king's guard had been attacked, most of them killed, with arrows from the trees. *Silvan* arrows.

But where was the king?

Rinon could hear his people, watched the Alpines as they glared at the Silvan citizens, muttered curses and murderous eyes. He watched the Silvans as they stared back, defiant and frustrated.

At the Inner Circle, guards snapped to attention as he passed, a whirlwind of anger and determination. He descended the stairs at a trot and then down again, along a dimly lit corridor and then right, right again. Dark stone, humid walls. There were never many elves down here, where chains hung from walls. Still, he could hear them rattle as he passed door after door, until the final cell where two guards stood to attention. Rinon nodded, and one unlocked the door. He ducked inside and allowed his eyes to adapt to the darker room.

Sat on the floor, knees tucked up against his chest, was Angon. His face was puffy and bruised, dried blood at the corner of his mouth, around his nostrils. Rinon stared down at him, at the rebel who had instigated violence against the Alpine merchants. This elf had disobeyed the mandates of his leader, Erthoron. He had terrorised citizens, threatened them, and then killed three Alpine merchants that they were aware of. And now this.

Rinon bent, perched on his heels. "Why?"

Angon's eyes were afire. All indignation and righteous anger. "Why *what*?"

"Why did you kill them? Where is the king?"

"Perhaps you should ask your own about that. The Silvans did nothing to your warriors."

"You were caught in the act."

"We were *not*. We came across them, already dead. Then your warriors came across us."

"They were killed from the trees, with Silvan arrows."

"That doesn't make the shooters Silvan."

"No. It does make it likely, though, doesn't it?"

"I can see how it looks. But for whatever it's worth, we didn't do it. My word. We have not killed a single Alpine, though Aria knows many deserve to die."

Rinon half-smiled and half-snarled. He stood slowly, towering over Angon, who could not rise to meet him, chained as he was to the floor.

"I don't know you. Your word means nothing to me." He turned, walked to the far wall and then followed it along. He ran his hand along the cool surface. "Where is the king?"

"I don't know."

"Of course you do. Wasn't this your dream? To be rid of the Alpines? Drive them from the forest?"

"I want to be free. I want a voice in my own lands. I want equality, to live in a country that recognises merit, not race."

"And how convenient, that our Alpine king is gone. Are you happy now?"

Angon wanted to answer, but Rinon shot forward, crouched before him and bunched the front of his tunic. He shook the elf hard. "Death awaits you, Angon. Does it not frighten you to die in dishonour? Are you not a warrior?"

"I have always served your father. And for that, I have received nothing but disdain. A sneer on an Alpine captain's face. A barked order for water, for food. In the king's army, I was a warrior and I was a *slave*. Now, I am a Silvan soldier, a fighter. I did not kill those warriors, and I don't know where your king is."

Rinon pushed him back. He rose in a flurry of fine cloth.

He stepped outside, gestured to Huren and the guard. "No more beatings. Feed him and treat him well, or you will answer to me. And I want to see the patrol captain who intercepted Angon, in my office and *now*."

That evening, as the sun sailed below the horizon, the Alpines of Ea Uaré took to the streets. The Silvans had killed four Alpine warriors, left their loved ones bereft. They marched through the markets, alleys and the artisan sector, torches held high, shouting curses as they searched for a Silvan to incriminate, a market stall or an establishment to destroy and burn. They smashed windows, kicked at doors. They threw stones at those who had not managed to escape the crowds. Some cowered down dark streets, covered their dark hair and tell-tale clothing, desperate for a place to hide, a way to the gates, to the Silvan encampment beyond.

On the topmost floor of the palace, Rinon stood looking down at it all. The fire had gone from his eyes but not his determination. Behind him, Aradan stood, joined him at the window. They watched the angry mobs chant their threats.

"Why don't you call for Huren, Prince? You need to stop this violence."

"I don't trust Huren."

Aradan said nothing, knew that Rinon would speak, that he was thinking.

"He chose Bendir as the king's captain. And Bendir is one of those who are missing. Convenient, wouldn't you say, Councillor?" Rinon turned, waiting for Aradan to face him. "Bendir has led the king away, either to kill him or to hold him to ransom. Perhaps to demand I renounce my birthright as heir to the throne."

"I have called an urgent council for tomorrow at first light. You must declare yourself regent and take your father's place before there are any further developments. The council has no legitimate reason to deny this, but that does not mean they will not later attempt to discredit you, threaten you perhaps with Thargodén's life."

"I have ordered Bendir's family questioned. I have sent a team of my personal choice to the scene of the attack. I have deployed Shadows to ascertain the whereabouts of Dinor, Band'orán, Draugolé and Barathon. They will follow and report to me daily. But there is no one I can trust to control the Inner Circle, Aradan. Turion is not here, but he needs to be. I need him here because anything I do now is susceptible to Huren's manipulation."

"You may be wrong about him."

"I may be. But that is not enough to trust him with my father's life. You know this."

"And the Silvan rebel? What will you do with him?"

"Once my team reports to me, I will speak to Angon again."

"Do you think he did it?"

"No. No, I do *not*. And neither do you." There was a challenge in Rinon's eye and Aradan, in spite of the dire circumstances, smiled in satisfaction.

Crown Prince Rinon would make a fine king, one day.

12

A SILVAN AT SEA

"It was one brief encounter. One glance at a Rainbow Jumper, and Ramien, Wall of Stone, knew that he would never forget it."
The History of The Company: Marhené

~

It was the day they would take ship from Bulls Bay to Port Helia. They would leave Tar'eastór behind and enter the realm of Ea Uaré, where Pan'assár was still commander general.

Galadan and Idernon had returned the previous evening and informed them they had acquired passages on the Pelagian Queen, scheduled to set sail at the eleventh hour. A merchant ship bound for Port Helia with wine and other produce to be sold at the auctions, it was the fastest vessel they had been able to find.

They had taken advantage of that last day at Bredja's Healing Halls to rest and take care of their many and varied injuries. Sontúr and Llyniel had stocked up with the supplies they would need for Handir and Fel'annár after their ordeal on the river, and Sontúr had listened carefully as the human woman told him of her special brew for submersion injuries.

The group stood just inside the Halls of Healing, waiting for Llyniel and Bredja to say their goodbyes, not for the first time but perhaps for the last.

"When you took ya book and left for Tar'eastór, I never thought I'd see ya again, Llyn. And now yer back, cavortin' with lords and flirtin' with that Felna boy."

"Green Sun. And I'm not flirting. It's more than that, Bredja."

"'Eez trouble, kiddie."

"He's worth it."

Bredja studied her eternal friend for a moment. "All that talk of moving trees and Warlords. What sorta life you gonna 'ave with one like 'im?"

"It won't be boring, no. But I have no choice in the matter."

"Ah. That's what I wanted to 'ere. 'Cos it's in 'iz crazy eyes for sure."

"There are many things in his eyes."

"Love. 'E loves ya, Bredja knows." She tapped a finger to her temple and smiled. "Ye my favourite ever-lass and I'll never forget that face o' yours."

"Are you saying goodbye again?" Llyniel smiled, but it faltered with Bredja's next words.

"I'm mortal, kiddie. We always say goodbye. Our end is a certainty, and I'm no spring bunny. I've seen many seasons, 'elped as many as I could in the Halls, 'ad me own babbers and lost friends to the north—to the rot. 'Ow long 'ave I got? 'Oo knows? 'Oo cares, so long as today is a good day?" She smiled.

"I'll return if I can."

"Live ya life, kiddie. And take me with ya, always."

They embraced, and Llyniel felt the rough cloth of her dress more acutely than she ever had. Bredja was right. What sort of a life would she lead beside Fel'annár? She didn't know and, in a sense, she was glad that it would not, at least, be predictable. But she meant what she had said. There was no choice. What was the point of fussing about it?

Bredja turned from Llyniel and walked back inside, smiling as she passed them all. Then Hamon circled his wife with his chunky arms as they climbed the stairs, back up into the kitchen. Back to their normal lives once more.

With a signal from Pan'assár, they left the building, hoods up and eyes on everything. Behind the commander, Fel'annár walked beside Tensári, trying and failing once more to listen to the distant trees. It was too quiet, a muted, muffled kind of silence. But then a weak voice brushed against his mind and his eyes strayed sideways, to a wheelbarrow parked to one side of the street that led into the town. Inside were plants, saplings and an array of tools. This was surely a gardener's barrow. He smiled at the collection, at their excited whispers, wondering where they would be placed, how much sun and water was to be had. But then he startled, turned and frowned.

"We're being watched. Back, left."

"How many?" asked Pan'assár without turning.

"Unsure."

The commander gestured to Gor'sadén. "Llyniel, Galadan. Go to the dock with Ramien, Galdith and that chest. Take off your hoods. Whoever is following us will not be interested in you. Look for the Pelagian Queen and board. We will join you shortly."

"And if you do not?" asked Galadan.

"Then wait for us in Port Helia."

Llyniel shared a wide-eyed look with Fel'annár, but Galadan was pulling her along. It wasn't until they had disappeared around the corner that Fel'annár knew they had not been followed, just as Pan'assár had predicted.

As they followed behind more slowly, Pan'assár kept Handir at his side while Sontúr walked beside Gor'sadén, Carodel and Idernon. Behind, Fel'annár and then Tensári at his back.

"Anything?" murmured Pan'assár as they turned into a busy street. Marketeers carried their goods to the town square, drunken mariners walked home on wobbly feet, and the smell of fresh fish inundated the place. But there were no trees here.

"Nothing. I hear nothing."

Pan'assár nodded from under his hood. "When they make their move, we split up and make for the ship separately. With multiple targets for them to chase, it will improve our chances of losing them."

The whoosh of an arrow, Tensári's yell for cover.

"Down!" She tackled Fel'annár sideways and to the ground, the wooden shaft skittering over the paving where Sontúr had been just a moment before.

"Run!" shouted Pan'assár.

Into the crowds, they scattered, Fel'annár and Tensári pushing through. Three mercenaries were coming towards them, hands on knives. They darted right, into a building, climbed the stairs three at a time. They heard the clatter of boots and swords below as they shot through a large room, full of rowdy humans smoking some foul-smelling weed. Fel'annár hacked as he ran, desperate for an exit, some way to get back down onto the floor below.

They scrambled through an open window at the far end of the room that led out onto a flat roof and ran to the very edge. There was another building in front of them. Too far to jump.

Fel'annár ran back. Tensári followed, but then Fel'annár stopped. She scowled in confusion as he turned back to the ledge. And then she realised.

"You can't ..."

But Fel'annár was running, sprinting, and then he launched himself off the ledge, arms high above him and reaching out to a balcony on the opposite building. He crashed into the metal bars, knocking the spittle out of himself. He clung to them, eyes scrunched up, chest on fire. Bending at the waist, he cocked one leg over the railings, straddled them and then turned to kick the window in. He turned back to the opposite building and Tensári.

"Come on!" he yelled, securing his hold on the bars with one hand and the other reaching far out over the distant street below.

"Sweet Aria!" she moaned. She glanced over her shoulder, saw the three mercenaries climbing through the window. She ran and then flew through the air—just in time as a mercenary behind her skidded and plummeted over the side. His two companions teetered on the edge of the divide and then watched helplessly as the Ari'atór collided with the balcony. Fel'annár's fist latched onto her pauldron, pulling, enough to get a hold on the fabric of her other shoulder. Her legs fought for leverage, found the ledge and stood on her own two feet. She blew out, cheeks puffing and then ducked into the room behind Fel'annár.

They came face to face with a naked, gaping elf. With no time for explanations, they wrenched the door open and sprinted down a corridor, coming out onto an inside balcony that ran the entire way around the building. Below were the cold marble floors of some inn. People screamed and scattered as they ran around the balcony in search of the stairs.

An arrow whooshed past Fel'annár's head. He swerved sideways and thumped into three men carrying bales of wool. They crashed to the ground, and Tensári skidded to a halt. She pulled Fel'annár up, turned and came face to face with a mercenary. He bore down on her with his sword but was no match for an Ari'atór Blade Master. They were soon running again, out of the house and down the crowded streets. They ducked into a dark alley and waited.

Nothing.

Fel'annár turned to Tensári. She frowned, straightened his cuirass and nodded. He let out a strangled breath that was more of a hiss and righted his crooked form. He smoothed down his cloak and pulled his hood back up over his head, aware of Tensári's persistent stare. Together, they merged into the crowds and walked towards the docks. Soon enough, they spotted the Pelagian Queen and continued towards the ship, ducking in between the bustling crowds.

Sailors ran up and down the quay in strange breeches and hats, under which a stretch of material was tied around their hair. There were ropes everywhere, some tense, some slack. Thick ropes, thin ropes, and Fel'annár looked up to the tall masts. He marvelled at the elves he saw sitting high above the decks, as comfortable as squirrels in a tree.

"We're surely being watched. Our pursuers may even be on board."

Tensári nodded, eyes searching as they advanced. Just ahead, they could see wide gangways breeching the gap between the quay and the ship. There were streams of elves coming and going, carrying sacks, crates and boxes, pushing barrows and carrying chests and caskets. One such group passed them by, and Fel'annár slipped behind a merchant with a tall bundle on his head. With Tensári behind him, they made it over the gangway and onto the ship, darting into a small gap between a cabin and the stairs that led to the upper deck.

Blowing out a breath, Fel'annár observed their surroundings, weighing their options. "We could slip into the cargo hold, hide amongst the crates. I can find the rest later, when night falls," whispered Tensári.

"And what if they don't open the hold?"

It was an unpalatable thought to them both, so they continued to observe. "The cabins on this deck are inside the ship, but see the lords? They take the stairs to the upper deck. That must be where the more expensive accommodation is."

"You think they will be up there?" asked Tensári.

"Well, there's no shortage of coin. That chest is full of it. Besides, we need to be together, and we need privacy. It makes sense."

"After you." She gestured to the stairs.

Fel'annár nodded. He waited for the next stream of passengers to board and fell into step with them, shielding his presence as best he could. On the upper deck, they crouched behind the railings. There were far fewer places to hide here, but what a sight it was. Fel'annár gaped at the open horizon; Bulls Bay on one side and on the other, the open sea.

"Aria," mumbled Tensári. She had never sailed the seas. She was accustomed to open spaces—Araria was sprawling and desertic in many places, and the moving sands were similar to the water—but here she felt detached, severed from some birthing cord she had never felt, until now.

Fel'annár turned to her. He wondered what she was thinking, whether she liked what she saw.

"It's like Araria, only blue," she said.

Fel'annár had never been there, but he had heard the stories of the Xeric Wood from Idernon. A sea of sand instead of water. Still, he was curious. "Don't you feel ... detached?"

She turned from him. "Yes, I do."

A whistle blew and a practised voice called out over the din of the crowds. "Fifteen minutes!"

"The others will be searching for us. The Company won't stay on board if they can't find us, despite Pan'assár's orders."

"Agreed," said Tensári. "I could reveal myself—"

"No. You are Ari'atór. There are humans here."

She nodded. Fel'annár was Ari, too, however much he didn't look like one. Still, he was right. The Ari'atór were scorned and feared by humans. Scorned because they killed mortals; feared because they were capable of killing children. No matter they were Incipient or Deviant, they were still children, they said.

"Then we join the crowds on the deck. They must be there somewhere, watching for us."

Standing slowly, they made for the side. There was no space left for a good view, and Fel'annár stood behind a shorter elf who was waving and shouting at someone on shore. Tensári's eyes were everywhere, hand on the pommel of her sword, hidden under her black cloak.

"Nice view."

Both heads whipped to the side and to Idernon's profile, sharp nose and high cheekbones. On his other side, Ramien and Carodel smiled into the soft, salty breeze. Now all that was left was to get away from the crowds and to their cabin, wherever that was. There was no telling if those mercenaries had followed them, whether they too, were on board. Idernon turned, cocked his head and led the way. Minutes later, they came to a simple wooden door. Idernon tapped on it, the call of a woodpecker, and the door opened.

"About time you turned up." The apparently disinterested voice of Pan'assár, but his blue eyes shone like fire.

As Fel'annár's eyes adjusted to the gloom, his muscles sagged at the sight of Llyniel, Gor'sadén, Handir and the rest of The Company. Galdith and Galadan were sopping wet, a story that would have to wait for later.

"Thank the Gods," said Gor'sadén, while Idernon turned to Fel'annár, eyes on a tuft of hay in his hair. He plucked it out and turned to Tensári, eyes on a white smudge down the side of her face. She reached up, rubbed at it and then brushed herself down. Fel'annár smirked at her, and could have sworn she returned it. There was an overdue conversation to be had, of why she had come, and whether she had forgiven him. But whatever her reasons were, he was simply glad she was here.

THEIR CABIN STOOD on the top deck. It was one of four that were equally distributed down the centre of the ship. There were windows on both sides, and through one, Bulls Bay covered their entire line of sight, extending back into the hills beyond and the mountains of Tar'eastór. When next they stepped foot on land, they would be in Thargodén's forest realm of Ea Uaré.

From the other window, the deep blue sea met with a hazy, light blue sky. There were ships, far far away, surely as big as the Pelagian Queen, perhaps even bigger. Other smaller vessels sailed closer, fishing or simply out for the fun of it. Two masses of land stood majestically in the distant waters, the island home of the Pelagian elves with their grey hair and their skill for music and art. Maeneth, princess of Ea Uaré, lived there.

The cabin consisted of a parlour which extended backwards and to a set of curtains that separated it from the sleeping area. There were no windows there, and the beds were stacked one on top of the other.

Ramien and Carodel dragged Handir's chest to the very back,

tying the buckles to iron loops fixed to the floorboards. With permission, Carodel had retrieved his lyre which now hung over his shoulder.

A rectangular table occupied the centre of the parlour. There, Handir sat together with the commanders and Sontúr, watching as the warriors and Llyniel placed their packs and cloaks on the beds further back.

Fel'annár set his weapons on a window seat to one side, ignoring the beds, for he was sure he wouldn't sleep with a slab of wood in front of his face. He wanted to, though; needed to. Now that he was free to relax, out of sight and well-guarded, the pain in his chest, back and feet had returned, pounding in his ears and stealing his breath. He would never take a running jump like that again. But in spite of his discomfort, he noticed his unusually quiet friend, standing before the window.

Ramien's eyes shone, were alive with some thrill the sea had awoken in him. He didn't move at all as the ship sailed further and further away from shore, the buildings becoming smaller. Fel'annár smiled and turned back to the table where Pan'assár began to brief them, taking a seat beside Gor'sadén.

"We must assume the worst, that one or a number of our pursuers followed us on board. If there are few of them, they may not attack but wait for us to dock at Port Helia. They may have back up there. But if there are more of them, they *will* attack before we arrive."

The warriors nodded, and Pan'assár continued. "I need The Company, save Fel'annár, to go on deck and watch. If you spot anyone suspicious, follow them. We also need to find out what is going on in the forest. Listen, ask questions and then report. We need to know what truth there may be to what Bredja and Hamon have said. Take as much time as you need, but remember, we are not safe here."

Galadan nodded, turned to Idernon, saw him watching Fel'annár worriedly. He did not want to leave, knew that he had to. Closer than friends, those two were brothers. Galadan had seen the evidence of it many times. "How is your arm, Idernon?"

"Well enough, lieutenant."

"Until later, Commander." He saluted, gestured for the rest to follow him and in his mind, a plan began to hatch. Idernon was well suited to command and he wondered if there would be time to speak to Pan'assár about it.

Outside, the sun was warm, the sky clear and a light breeze pushed against unfurling sails, ropes tensing. The many voices of the mariners sounded all around them. They shouted orders, multi-toned whistles from the now-distant quay. They were picking up speed, the breeze stronger, the salt tickling the back of Idernon's throat. He smiled in wonder of it all, and Carodel gasped as the wind caught the sails and pushed them away, faster. Galdith, though, seemed uneasy, while he thought Ramien bespelled.

Three days was all they had to find out whether they had been followed and garner information to prepare themselves for what awaited beyond Port Helia. Three days in which the princes, commanders and Fel'annár must remain hidden from view, away from prying eyes, wherever they might be.

By evening, Prince Handir had turned a sickly green, while Fel'annár sat hunched in one corner, a light sheen of sweat glistening on his upper lip. Llyniel and Galadan had gone in search of hot water and provisions, while Sontúr watched the two brothers, listening as the commanders paced while they spoke.

"From what we already know, some new trade route has opened between Ea Uaré and Prairie," said Pan'assár. "That is unusual, and I know Prince Torhén is in Prairie even now, negotiating such a deal for Tar'eastór. I had the impression his mission was delicate and somewhat difficult?"

Sontúr nodded. "It is. Humans are notoriously difficult to deal with. They have an abundance of wheat and grapes, which they know are coveted. Bread and wine! They make good use of that advantage to press for lucrative terms. They want exotic woods and gems, they want ore, and they want our weapons."

"It must be asked: what deal has been struck and how?" mused Handir. "No high-ranking dignitaries have before travelled on a formal visit from Ea Uaré as Torhén has done, at least as far as I am aware. And yet, trade is bustling. Look at the number of ships, of merchants and goods. Perhaps it is the humans that have travelled to my father's court. Or perhaps this is Band'orán's doing. He knows the power of the Merchant Guild." He just about managed to finish his sentence, his breath short, before he started coughing again.

"Buying votes?" asked Sontúr, watching Handir closely. He was still unwell from his near-drowning.

"Yes. Buying empathy. Giving the powerful a reason to follow him." He cleared his throat.

"They will not follow *him*?" asked Sontúr.

"No. Most are loyal to Or'Talán, to his memory, but some will be swayed if there is something to be gained. Band'orán surely knows this. He cannot escape Or'Talán's legacy unless he offers them something at least as great as that king."

"Money, power."

"Yes, exactly that."

Gor'sadén leaned forward. "It is certainly a good thing for business. I must wonder why Thargodén himself has not established these routes before."

"Trade routes can be lucrative and beneficial. But they can also enslave if the terms are unfair, Commander. If Ea Uaré has agreed to provide resin at a certain price, that price must be divided into production cost and benefits for all. If the price is too low, someone suffers, and you can be assured that *someone* will be the Silvan harvesters. The king will look at all these things and either agree or disagree to a price. All this," Handir gestured, "suggests that prices are low. This benefits no one save for the nobles at their tables and Band'orán himself."

"For now, it is all conjecture," said Pan'assár.

"Yes, well, politics often is, Commander," said Handir, and Sontúr nodded. The prince could keep his politics to himself. He had never wanted to get involved with all the machinations and the rhetoric.

A knock at the door and Pan'assár opened it. Llyniel and Galadan entered, laden with water and packages. Llyniel fell into a chair beside the window seat where Fel'annár still slouched. "Food and water for tonight, at least. It's a nightmare out there, albeit a jovial one." She reached up and placed her hand on Fel'annár's forehead.

"Did you see The Company?" he mumbled, trying and failing to escape her hand.

"I did. They are mingling, and Carodel is playing that lyre of his. Idernon is keeping them in check."

Fel'annár smiled, and Pan'assár caught Galadan's gaze, nodded. The boat lurched to one side, and Handir turned a darker shade of green. "Excuse me," he had time enough to say before he dashed to the windows on one side. Llyniel glanced at Gor'sadén, gestured to Fel'annár and then followed Handir with an exasperated sigh and a bucket.

Gor'sadén wandered over to his Disciple and crouched low. He observed him for a moment, then stood and held out his hand. Fel'annár looked at it with stubborn eyes, but the ones that looked back at him were like a freshly honed blade.

Sharp. Unyielding.

He reached out, pulling himself up with a partially stifled groan.

"Just a few hours. I will call you when there is work to be done," said Gor'sadén.

Fel'annár knew that he wouldn't, and that, should there be danger, there would be no warnings from the trees in this place. He felt vulnerable, and perhaps his mentor knew what he was thinking. Still, he would concede to that much.

"Just a few hours." He nodded and made his way to the sleeping area. With every step he took, his feet felt heavier and heavier. By the time his knees touched the back of the furthest bed, time seemed to still and the room filled with mist. It no longer bothered him that he was lying under a slab of dead wood. He lay back and tried to relax. He thought he saw Sontúr standing over him, but he couldn't be sure. The mist thickened, and Fel'annár slept.

∼

Fel'annár awoke in nothing but his breeches. He smelled of herbs and tried to remember. But there was nothing. He sat up on his elbows, wondering what time of day it was, but there were no windows here. He reached for his shirt and pulled it on. He stared at his boots, sitting neatly at the side of the bed.

He remembered a conversation he had once had about the convenience or otherwise of shedding one's boots while sleeping on patrol. It had been Angon who said he would never be caught in a fight in his bare feet. Fel'annár's lips twitched, and he pulled them on gingerly. There had been a tense start to their relationship. Angon had antagonised him until Fel'annár convinced him that he *was* Silvan, in spite of his looks. And then Fer'dán had lost his arm at the Battle of Sen'uár. Angon had turned bitter, and Fel'annár wondered where he was now, whether he still served in the army he had even then begun to loathe.

Standing, he realised that he felt better. He walked through the curtains and into the parlour. Sontúr momentarily looked up from where he sat playing a card game with Handir and Llyniel, while Tensári stared at him from where she sat cross-legged on the floor. The two commanders sat huddled together in the far corner. Gor'sadén caught his gaze, while Pan'assár continued to murmur. Fel'annár wanted to ask what they were doing but was interrupted by the arrival of The Company, Idernon at the fore. He looked relieved.

"You seem rested."

"How long did I sleep?" Fel'annár glanced out of the window. He couldn't see the sun but it was still light.

"Through the night and then some," drawled Sontúr.

"The whole ..." He ran a hand through his messy hair. "I must have been more tired than I thought," he muttered.

"Report," prompted Pan'assár from his corner, leaving his quiet discussion with Gor'sadén and standing.

"We have much to tell," Idernon started. "It seems Bredja and Hamon were right. The Silvan people have closed the Forest from trading with the Alpines. They say it's dangerous, that goods are confiscated and returned to their origins, traders left without wares or money to fend for themselves. There's no resin, no cork, no exotic timber and no confitures, amongst other things. Most won't go there anymore, preferring instead the steady sea trade that's all but crippling the authorities. It seems neither Tar'eastór nor Ea Uaré were sufficiently prepared for this. Strange. If this new trade route was the product of a Royal Council, you would think they would be better prepared."

Handir nodded thoughtfully. "Go on."

"They say King Thargodén is back, but that he cannot control the Silvan rebels. Others at court are clamouring for him to take action or step down. Some are frightened by this talk, but others are rubbing their hands at the wares an army would need, should it come to war."

Handir nodded again and Idernon continued.

"Of the vote, these people seem to be ignorant. All they know is that the Silvans are displeased with their Alpine rulers, that they in turn believe the Silvans want independence. They are unaware of Band'orán's scheming, of course, and I can see no judgement, only mild curiosity. It is the prospect of war that either terrifies or pleases, depending on who you ask."

"You have done well, Idernon," said Handir.

The Wise Warrior nodded, but he hadn't finished. "The crew are well-armed. It seems skirmishes are common and pirates abound."

"Pirates ..." said Handir, standing slowly.

"They say the military defend the ports as best they can but are hard-pressed to succour ships if they are boarded at sea."

"Are these pirates human?" asked Gor'sadén.

"They are both mortal and immortal. They work together, it seems."

"I assume the risk is minimal so long as we don't stop," said Pan'assár, but his brow was deeply furrowed.

"Many here have been attacked before. They say that sometimes captains simply surrender their wares so that their crew remain safe.

Others will fight for it, even fit their ships with safety measures to avoid being boarded."

"And what type is ours?" asked Pan'assár.

"The fighting type, it seems. I noticed barrels of pig fat hanging around the railings."

"Don't tell Handir that," muttered Sontúr and Llyniel snickered quietly.

"It's slippery stuff, stops unwanted visitors from climbing the sides. Mind you, the smell alone is enough to keep anyone away."

"Any sign of our pursuers?" asked Pan'assár.

"No, sir. Nothing for the moment. Most are merchants with their families. We have seen some artists, too, but no sign of warriors. Shall we take guard outside the cabin, sir?"

"See to it, Idernon," said Pan'assár, as if he spoke to Galadan. Fel'annár turned to his friend and saw the surprise on his face.

"Tomorrow evening, we will discuss our tactics for once we dock at Port Helia. Until then, Idernon, continue gathering intelligence."

Idernon nodded, glanced at Fel'annár and then was away again, with Ramien, Carodel, Galdith and Galadan behind him. Once they had gone, Llyniel joined Fel'annár, and together, they watched as the sun sank below the western horizon, mesmerised at how big it seemed out here on the sea.

Meanwhile, the commanders resumed their quiet whisperings. Always a distance away. Voices ever soft, too soft to hear.

Fel'annár was intrigued.

THAT AFTERNOON, the mariners were out on deck, swabbing them down and repairing spare sails. Some operated winches while others cleaned the hoops and chains. They scurried here and there, shimmying up the mast, pulling at ropes and other contraptions Idernon could only guess at.

Ramien stood beside him, twiddling a piece of rope in his hands, and the Wise Warrior spared a soft smile for his friend. He watched as Ramien tried and failed to recreate a knot someone had taught him. Carodel was close by, laughing and joking with another group, their eyes alight with mirth and perhaps even admiration. Idernon's smile turned wry as he faced Galadan and beside him, Galdith, leaning over the side railing, not sick but peering out at something he himself could not see.

Stepping up beside him, Idernon searched the waters for whatever it was that had caught his attention.

"There—there, see?" asked Galdith.

"See what?" asked Idernon, getting closer. Ramien and Carodel peered over his shoulder.

"There's something underneath the water. See how it swirls around? Oh!" he exclaimed loudly as spray broke the surface with a loud, hollow puff.

"Rainbow Jumpers!" laughed a mariner as she passed them, clapping Galdith on the shoulder.

"Rainbow Jumpers?" He scowled.

"An aquatic animal with translucent fins that shimmer in the sun," began Idernon. "I have read they can be—"

A roar of water became a mountain of grey and white, topped with froth and spray. The boat lurched upwards, and the seafarers shouted as they reached for ropes and poles. From the burgeoning silver tower of water, a black creature surged, almost as big as the ship itself. Turning mid-air, it splayed its fins, catching the early morning sun and casting a rainbow that arced around it in a perfect circle. It seemed to float, suspended in the air, then splashed back into the sea, its mighty tail the last to slap into the surface.

The boat lurched violently back down and then to one side as it rode the wave, and the mariners laughed and cheered. The Company, though, stood shocked and drenched, eyes shut as the ship rocked and heaved.

Ramien opened his eyes and roared, long and hard, then took his hands to his hair and screamed as he pulled, even as tears of excitement poured from his eyes. The others threw their heads back and laughed wildly. Carodel whooped and waved his hands in the air.

The passing mariners laughed and laughed again, shoving at each other and slapping their thighs as they doubled over, wheezing in mirth that would last the entire night.

Silvans at sea were just hysterical, they said.

"They can be *what,* you were saying?" asked Galdith, face shining in the afterglow of exhilaration.

"I was going to say, they can be quite *big.*"

It had been a quiet breakfast, after which The Company set out once more in search of news and mercenaries.

Not for the first time, Fel'annár wished he could leave the cabin and follow, experience life aboard a Pelagian merchant ship. But the truth was, he felt strangely bereft, like a squirrel in a cave. There were no trees for miles around. No greenery, no rough bark to lay his hands upon, no voice to listen to, speak to.

He rather thought Tensári agreed with him. She was Ari'atór, and though she couldn't, consciously, hear the voice, she felt the land deeply. She was probably just as anxious as he was to be back on dry land, continue their journey into the forest, rather than be here, floating on water, hidden away and utterly bored, in spite of Llyniel's steady presence beside him. Still, he had the Kalhámen'Ar, and Gor'sadén had promised to continue his training later. Then he turned to the commanders, who were once more engrossed in their secret discussion.

"What's that book that has you both so fascinated?"

Pan'assár turned to him, stared silently for a moment and then pursed his lips. It was Gor'sadén who answered, but not before sharing a silent nod with his brother. "It is a journal," he said carefully.

Before Fel'annár could ask more, Handir walked through the curtains from the bed chamber, his face a slightly lighter shade of green than it had been the day before.

Pan'assár paled. How much had the prince heard?

"I should have told you before, Prince. Still, it has been an eventful few days. There were priorities."

Handir's gaze was cool, calculating, and Pan'assár admired him for that.

"It is Or'Talán's journal, Prince."

Fel'annár turned from the window, Llyniel stirring beside him, while Handir continued to stare at his commander.

"I found it on Sulén's body. Why he would have this is beyond me." Pan'assár tried and failed to read Handir, and so he pressed on. "I would keep it for a while, until we are back home and I can give it to its rightful owner. If ... that is acceptable?"

Handir was thinking, unaware of just how daunting he seemed to Pan'assár at that moment. Indeed, the commander struggled with himself not to look away. He wanted this, as much as he had ever wanted anything.

"Do as you wish, Commander. My grandfather's business is not my concern."

Pan'assár wanted to soar on hot currents, only he had no wings. But then Handir's indifference grounded him. He wanted to tell the prince that it *should* be his concern, that he should be proud of who his grandfather had been. He wanted to tell him, shake him, make him see sense. But he could do none of those things, and so he bowed his head in thanks.

Fel'annár looked away, inexplicably glad that Handir agreed. Or'Talán was not his concern, never would be. He had all but killed his mother with his refusal to allow Thargodén to marry her; had all but killed his own son, breaking him inside, abandoning him to a life of grief.

Cruel king, heartless father, Or'Talán was a blight in his blood.

∽

LATER THAT MORNING, The Company was once more outside searching for news. In the parlour, Llyniel, Handir and Sontúr ate quietly, while Pan'assár read from Or'Talán's journal.

In the sleeping area, Fel'annár knelt on the floor in nothing but his breeches, Gor'sadén sitting in front of him. Fel'annár could not leave the cabin and although he was not fully recovered, he could, at least, continue with some aspects of his training.

"Do it again. Your mind must memorise the exact place. You do not want to hit bone; you want to sink between it."

Fel'annár had failed to execute the Enha'rei correctly when he had fought with Sorei for his Blade Master test. It had been enough to pass, but not sufficient for a future Kah Master.

He lifted both hands, palm up, turned one of them down over the other as if he held an orb. He pulled back his right arm, the left remaining. Hand now at his ear, he drove it forward once more, just as Gor'sadén had taught him. Left, then right, then left again. Confuse your opponent, and on the fourth beat—strike.

His fingertips touched Gor'sadén's shoulder bone. He closed his eyes in defeat.

"Do it again."

He did, failed once more.

"The Enha'rei is an advanced technique because it is not only about the precision of your hand. It is about allowing your mind to guide your eyes. You must not only see it. You must *feel* it."

The now-familiar knock came at their cabin door, and both rose to their feet, Fel'annár reaching for his shirt. Walking into the parlour, they watched The Company file through, wide-eyed and brimming with news.

"We are approaching Port Helia. It's ..." Idernon shook his head.

"*Massive*," continued Ramien. Fel'annár couldn't remember the last time he had seen Idernon speechless.

"It's an impressive sight from land. I can only imagine what it looks like from the sea," said Pan'assár. They had seen the increase in ships and smaller boats around them, knew they were getting close, but there was no view to the north from their cabin.

"There is, however, a problem. The crew believe the captain won't pull into port but will wait further out for the cargo to be transported to shore," said Idernon.

"Avoiding his taxes, is he?" asked Pan'assár. Handir bristled beside him but said nothing.

"I believe so. We, too, are to take one of the smaller boats into the port."

Pan'assár nodded. Under different circumstances, Fel'annár assumed he would speak to the captain and remind him that this was not their arrangement. However, their need for anonymity was more important.

"Listen carefully. Whether the enemy is onboard or not, we must avoid any contact with the authorities. Band'orán has many acquaintances here; distinguishing the loyal from the treacherous will be impossible. We stay out of sight and make for the stables to the north-west. I would get out of that town as soon as we can. Galadan, take Idernon and Ramien and get us that boat as quickly as possible. I would not have us wait around for longer than necessary."

Galadan nodded and gestured for the pair to follow him. With the three gone in search of transport to shore, Sontúr turned to Pan'assár.

"I wonder how long it will take your port officials to issue a warning to the captain. They have surely seen us."

"We are not the only ship angling at the entrance to port," said Pan'assár. "See there?" He pointed through the window to a vessel over to their right. "Flags upon the mast tell the port what they carry and what they require. They have wheat and bacons, and are requesting permission to dock."

Fel'annár followed Sontúr's line of sight to the two flags.

"We carry wine, and taxes are higher on luxury items," said Handir. "Still, it is no excuse for evading taxes. I wonder if this is common practice."

"If it is, I will see to it," said Pan'assár. "It is, perhaps, another consequence of this new trade route. Perhaps our magistrates are over-run, my warriors stretched too thinly. Huren may not know."

Soon after, the Pelagian Queen had, indeed, cast its anchor outside the port, and they collected their things, chest freed from its bindings and sitting at their feet. With their cloaks and hoods in place, weapons at the ready, and Or'Talán's diary safely stashed under Pan'assár's tunic, they watched as Galadan returned. He had had to pay for the privilege of using the first boat to shore. It hung from ropes on the other side of the vessel. Ramien and Carodel took up the chest between them while the rest surrounded Handir and Llyniel and set out to board it.

It was crowded on deck, each crew member busy preparing their goods for transport. With the cargo doors open, some tied ropes while others hoisted barrel after barrel of wine from the depths to the surface with a collective 'heave'. Others shouted instructions up the mast or further down the deck, and by the time the group arrived at the area where the rowboat awaited, other vessels were approaching, ready to receive the barrels and boxes and take them to the awaiting merchants on the quayside.

One such boat threw a line which was caught but not secured, and Fel'annár thought it strange that the mariners looked down on them yet did not tie off the ropes. He wondered what it was they saw, his own eyes travelling over the motley group of elves; and then he caught a peek of flesh between greasy strands of hair. Round ears.

Humans.

He only had a moment to wonder why there were so many of them in the boats when their purpose was to transport goods before …

"Du'an! Du'an!"

Ramien scowled. "What's 'du'an'?" he asked, turning to Galadan.

"Pelagian slang. It means *pirates!*"

Pan'assár and Gor'sadén were beside their princes and Llyniel in an instant, while Ramien and Carodel grabbed for the chest. Both Tensári's swords were in her hands. Their boat needed winching up, but the pirates would be upon them before they could board. Besides, who would be around to crank them down to water level?

"Back to the cabin, now! Run!" ordered Pan'assár. The nauseating smell of pig fat impregnated the air, and Handir's face turned green. Shouts exploded around them as the mariners drew their weapons. Those pirates who had boarded before the vats had been tipped were securing lines while others scrambled up the sides, skidding on the fat. Some fell, but others managed to swing over the sides and onto the deck.

They ran as fast as they could with the chest and against the tide of sailors and passengers, who either searched for a place to hide or made to join the fight. A large human barrelled into Gor'sadén. The commander staggered sideways but righted himself fast enough to turn and fight him off. Pan'assár himself was accosted from both sides. Dodging their blows, the commander was forced to stop and fight, but The Company continued to run, keeping Llyniel and Handir surrounded, the chest between them.

Their tight formation was shattered by a group of pirates who charged at them. Idernon and Ramien blocked them, pushing them back enough for Carodel and Galdith to continue their mad dash to the cabin. But Handir's chest was like a warm fire in the night, surely laden with jewels to the eyes of pirates, and another group came to confiscate it. Carodel and Galdith held them off but they, too, were forced to turn and fight. Carodel's lyre slipped from his shoulders and clattered to the deck. There was a crunch and a scrape of wood against wood. A large pirate shook his boot, once, again, until the ruined lyre skidded away.

"No!" moaned the Bard Warrior, but there was no time to truly feel his loss.

"Han, Llyn—take the chest. Take it! Run!" shouted Fel'annár while Tensári fought two just behind him.

With the prince on one side and the healer on the other, they dashed towards the cabin, struggling with the weight of the chest. They were so close, but still, the pirates came even as Fel'annár, Sontúr, Tensári and Carodel engaged them. Handir staggered and Llyniel shouted a warning, but he was soon steady on his feet and running surprisingly fast. Opening the door to their former cabin, they tumbled inside. The trunk crashed to the floor, Llyniel barely holding herself up over it and coughing at the dust it had raised.

"Block the door!" she cried, and Handir frantically searched for something heavy to wedge against it.

"It won't last. We're all but surrounded by windows," he said as he dragged the table to the door, just as it burst open, almost slamming into Llyniel who stood frozen before a towering pirate. He smiled, revealing almost nothing but gums, and there was no mistaking the gleam in his eyes.

"Duck!"

She did, and then looked up from where she crouched. Handir's fist smashed into the pirate's face, taking with it the last of his teeth. His shocked eyes went wide and he lifted his hand to his mouth. A sad frown and then the crash of pottery as Llyniel brought a water jug down on his head, just in case. His eyes rolled back in his head, and he fell with an almighty crash.

Llyniel turned disbelieving eyes to Handir who was cradling his hand, but there was no time to see to it. "He's blocking the door!" she shouted, grabbing a nearby water pitcher as she made for the other side of the unconscious pirate. They needed to drag him out, but she could hear another running towards the open door.

She stood and swung the pitcher madly before her. A yelp and then the body swerved and ducked under the arcing jug. Fel'annár's hood flew off, and Llyniel's eyes widened.

"Bugger!" she cried as she watched him drag the pirate away and close the door. With the table firmly wedged under the door handle, he turned to Handir and Llyniel, pulling his hood back up.

"Take the chest to the back—hide it and stay there, both of you!"

They weren't going to argue. They pushed it beyond the beds, into the furthest corner and then crouched in the shadows. They jumped at the sound of crashing glass, and Handir peered out from around the curtain.

"They're getting in!"

One pirate had driven the pommel of his sword through a window in the parlour and kicked what remained of the glass out of his way. Making to duck inside, he came face to face with Fel'annár, who brought his foot up and kicked him in the chest, sending him reeling. Another two charged at the now broken window, but there was something about them, in the set of their bodies, the way they held their blades.

Not pirates.

Fel'annár swung his shortsword upwards as he moved sideways, slicing through a leather harness. His opponent fought well, but Fel'annár pivoted, feigned left and ran his sword through his attacker's chest and then ducked under the arcing sword of his companion. Standing once more, they fought but Fel'annár was too quick. In three blows, the other warrior lay dead.

He turned, startled at how close Llyniel and Handir were to the window. Too close. Perhaps they had thought to help him.

"Back!" he shouted, and then reeled to one side as something smashed into his head. Llyniel screamed, and Fel'annár rolled over the floor, bringing his feet upwards and tripping his strapping opponent before he could skewer him. His attacker crashed to the floor beside him and Fel'annár sunk his knife through leather, into his heart.

Something shattered, and Fel'annár turned, saw the broken pottery in Llyniel's hands. A pirate's head was poking through the window, but he slowly sank to the ledge below, coming to hang over it, unconscious. Handir kicked him away.

"Shit," muttered Fel'annár, and staggered to one side to avoid the mad onslaught of another roaring pirate, desperate for the chest and the jewels he thought were inside. They turned to face each other. Fel'annár ducked a punch, blocked another with his forearm and smashed his fist into the face before him. Not hard enough, and before he could swing another, the pirate bunched his fists into his tunic, turning him and slamming him into the wall. Air rushed from his lungs, but still, he turned and smashed his forehead into the pirate's nose. The pressure was gone, and Fel'annár kicked him in the stomach, leaving him gasping for air on all fours. Then Handir brought a washbowl down onto his head with a hollow thunk.

Gor'sadén, Pan'assár and Tensári stumbled through the half-blocked door, skidding to a halt over shards of glass. The commanders' eyes flicked from Fel'annár to Llyniel to Handir, who stood with the half-ruined bowl still in his hands.

Fel'annár's head was smarting, hands stinging from cuts and

bruises, but Handir's face and Llyniel's gleaming eyes suddenly struck him as funny. Fel'annár chuckled. Llyniel snorted, and Handir smiled as he dropped the bowl and walked towards his brother. Fel'annár's chuckle turned into a full-blown laugh and Llyniel was off, her deep peels setting Handir off. Throwing back his head, the prince laughed as he had not done for decades, and one hand came up to Fel'annár's shoulder. He, in turn, laid his hand on Llyniel's. The circle of laughing elves stood amidst broken glass, splintered wood and groaning pirates.

And mercenaries.

Idernon barrelled into the room, the rest of The Company behind him, eyes wide until they frowned and raised their eyebrows at the unlikely scene. Idernon searched the dead and wounded bodies, straining his memory.

"I recognise this one. He was swabbing the decks, and yet now he wears vambraces." He wandered to another, a curved blade at his side. "And this one was cleaning the chains. A strange pastime for one who wields a scimitar."

"Mercenaries," declared Pan'assár.

Replacing his hood, Pan'assár bent and retrieved one of Fel'annár's throwing knives. Offering it to him hilt first, his heavy gaze lingered on Gor'sadén's Disciple. He nodded slowly, and then turned on his heels. "We leave. Now. Hoods up. Carodel, Galdith, get the chest. Galadan, lead us to the boats. There may be more where these came from. We need to get out of here. Fast."

MOMENTS LATER, they were striding past the mariners as they pushed dead pirates over the side and saw to their own. Llyniel's eyes lingered on the wounded, on those she knew would die if they were not treated soon. But Pan'assár was leading them on, oblivious to everything save the safety of their group, the integrity of Handir's chest and Or'Talán's diary.

They climbed down the rope ladders one by one, carefully

avoiding the areas where pig fat had smeared over the hull. As they rowed to shore, Fel'annár broke the tense silence.

"There must have been too few of them. They took advantage of the attack to try and finish the job. Do you think they were the same mercenaries that followed us along the cliffs?"

"It seems likely," said Pan'assár. "But they are surely not from the same group that attacked us on the river. That tells us there is more than one group after us. Port Helia will be riddled with them. A busy street, a crowded tavern, a drunkard with a knife ... we must find the quickest way around it. Still, perhaps those pirates were a blessing in disguise. Whatever danger awaits us at Port Helia, it will be before us, not behind. We can use that to our advantage."

AS NIGHT FELL, their small boat approached the torch-lit piers of Port Helia. This was Ea Uaré, and the soldiers they met would be under Pan'assár's command. He would be easily recognised, his presence a guarantee of Prince Handir's return, of Fel'annár's presence in the Forest. They had to keep their anonymity and find a safe place to rest, see to their wounds and trace out the path ahead. Find horses.

The commander threw a thick rope to a boy who stood on the pier. Grabbing it deftly, he made a knot and held out his hand. Once on shore, the commander placed a coin in his hand and watched as he ran to the next post to receive another boat that was coming to shore.

"Stay alert and silent," he murmured—but no sooner had they started on the path down the pier, than three warriors appeared before them.

"State your purpose and destination."

Ramien and Galdith carefully deposited the chest on the ground.

"We are merchants, seeking a place to stay," said Pan'assár.

"Where are you travelling?"

"Ea Uaré, to Oran'Dor in search of goods."

"You don't want to go there if you're Alpine. Lower your hoods. Reveal yourselves."

What choice did they have? Pan'assár couldn't disobey, or they risked being taken to the holding cells. A voice rang out behind him. Someone passed him and stood before the group. She inched closer to the guard.

"We are Ari'atór, Shirán on a mission of importance. We would not draw attention to ourselves, Warrior." She was close enough that he could see her dark skin and blazing blue eyes, the tattoos on her face.

After a moment of hesitation, the guard spoke. "You give your solemn oath?"

"We will cause you no strife, brother. You have my word."

He hesitated, but his eyes were transfixed on hers. "Very well. I accept your word, Shirán."

She nodded, then gestured to the others to follow. Five minutes later, they were off the pier and in the middle of a crowded street.

If Bulls Bay had been bawdy, Port Helia was outrageous. Exotic. Dangerous.

It was a far bigger place, and larger ships sat in the port and further out, dotted over the entire bay. The streets were wider, wilder even, and it seemed there was one inn for every two buildings. Pan'assár had wanted to avoid this, but with the intervention of the guards, they had had no choice but to walk into the city instead of hiding under the piers.

Outside an inn, three burly elves crashed into Galadan. Galdith held out his hand to steady his friend, but the lieutenant barely managed to keep his footing, and his hood slipped back.

"Alpine scum," growled one elf, spitting to one side and staring back at the group. Deciding there were too many for him to take on, he staggered away with his friends, and Pan'assár turned to the sign that hung over his head. Ramien followed his line of sight and smiled at the colourful painting of a Rainbow Giant arcing out of the water.

The temptation to enter the place and eat a hot meal, savour a glass of wine and sleep in a real bed was great, even for Pan'assár. He could feel Ramien's gaze upon him, but he turned and shook his head.

"We make for the shoreline and darkness. Circle round and find those stables." They half-skidded down the incline that led to the beach but kept close to it to better conceal themselves. They walked under the piers, around the fishing boats and bundles of netting, and after a while, Pan'assár gestured with one arm for them to follow him. They scrambled back up the incline, now on the far side of the beach.

"The stables are over to the left, behind the town; half an hour on foot. Come."

He led them behind the buildings, through dark alleys, and stopped at corners to check they were not being followed in the dark. They stopped and started until it was no longer stone underfoot but grass. They could still hear the noises of the city, see its lights, but it all grew dimmer and quieter as they travelled inland. Buildings were fewer and further between, and soon, there was nothing but open country, hills with a smattering of trees. In the distance stood a long, well-lit building and beside it, a small cottage. They had arrived at the stables, and with some luck, they could rest and eat. But by dawn, they knew they must be on their way.

Away from the sea, towards the forest, and whatever lay beyond.

AT PORT HELIA'S BARRACKS, the quay guard reported to his commanding officer. Shirán were afoot, he said. He had seen one and allowed the group to enter. He had expected a reprimand but received nothing more than a slow nod and permission to continue with the guard.

Once he had gone, the captain stood and covered his uniform with a long, hooded cloak, just as he had done every day for the past week. On a side table lay a neatly packed bag and beside it, a folded and sealed note he knew Pasán would read tomorrow morning when he saw his captain's pack gone.

It was a waiting game, a patience game, one he may even lose, because his quarry may not have taken the sea route—or perhaps they had but found trouble along the way.

Joining the clasps of his cloak at the neck, he slung his pack over his shoulder and snuffed out the candles on his desk. Time to join the heaving crowds on the streets of Port Helia.

One more night. One more chance.

13

KESTREL

"Bright boy, noble boy, brother of one destined to be a king. He was good at everything he did. Yet in his own mind, he was not good enough."
The Alpine Chronicles: Cor'hidén

It was dark here, on the outskirts of Port Helia, but the stables were well illuminated inside. Oil lamps burned steadily, emanating a soothing orange light and illuminating the path to the front entrance. The familiar smell of hay and manure jolted a memory in Idernon's mind, of the day he, Ramien and Fel'annár had left Lan Taria for their novice training.

Pan'assár stopped them in a quiet corner of the building. Crouching low, he unbuckled the chest, stuffed his hand inside and pulled out a fistful of coins. Closing it again he handed the money to Idernon. "A horse each and two spare. Have them ready for dawn."

Idernon nodded, then gestured for Galdith to join him. Ramien was too big for first meetings. He intimidated those who didn't know him—unless they happened to look at his face before his bulk. Then you would see his heart in his eyes, or perhaps lately, you would see the sea. Yet not for the first time, Idernon wondered why Pan'assár directed his orders at him and not Galadan.

They had found the stable master just inside the building and now, with the deal done, for half the coin Pan'assár had provided, the Silvan turned away from his customers. With a gleam in his eye, he limped to the end of the aisle, to where he knew he would find Raddy, the stable boy. Indeed, the lad sat with his back against the wall, knees high, chomping on pie as he watched his favourite mare fuss with the hay under well-cared-for hooves. Raddy looked up at his master, face rigid and pale.

"Not Willow."

"No. Fool boy. Go to the guardhouse. Find Turion. Tell him I sold *eleven*."

Raddy scowled but stood all the same, brushing flakes of pastry from his rough brown tunic.

"Don't speak to anyone else, mind," said Jarabon, tossing a coin and then fisting it, tempting the boy with the promise of money for treats.

"I won't!" He smiled, one tooth missing. He dashed away, clattered over the courtyard and then thudded across the field, towards the city he knew so well.

The Silvan stable master limped back to the entrance where his customers stood and held out his hand to them. "I'm Jarabon." He nodded, eyes moving from Idernon to Galdith. Idernon took the hand slowly and the Silvan smiled softly. "You don't have to worry about me, Warrior." He turned, allowed the light to catch on his patchy hair. "Used to be a soldier myself once, back when I could still fight. Got a spare aisle, if you're interested. Clean hay, warm enough."

"You're very kind, Jarabon. But we are camping close by. We would not put you out with our presence."

"It's no trouble, Warrior. But come, look." He gestured with one arm, turned inside without waiting for them to follow, though he knew they would. He limped to the very back, where four empty stalls lay open and clean. "Use them if you like, I'll not bother you." He nodded and then left them alone.

Once he had gone, Idernon turned to Galdith. "Make sure Jarabon lives alone here, that he won't raise the alarm. I will go and tell the commander."

Galdith nodded. Moments later, the rest of the group filed in, all of them except for Ramien and Galadan, whom Pan'assár had left outside to guard them. The commander inspected the stables himself, taking note of the doors and the windows, and then turned to Idernon.

"Alright. Where is this Jarabon?"

"Galdith watches him."

The commander nodded thoughtfully, eyes wandering for only a moment before they were back on Idernon. "Bring the others in."

Idernon nodded and before long, the four stalls were occupied. Pan'assár himself sat against the far wall, between the stalls and with a clear view of the main door, an escape route directly left of where he sat. He would allow them to sleep, but he himself would not. And so he sat and watched as the others settled down for a few hours of rest.

Inside one of the stalls, Idernon, Fel'annár, Llyniel and Tensári sat.

"What exactly do Shirán do?" asked Fel'annár.

They had heard the term before, but all anyone really knew was that they were the Ari equivalent of Shadows, in the service of the Supreme Commander. They were feared and yet strangely revered—strangely because even Idernon did not know what they actually did. Gor'sadén shared a knowing glance with Pan'assár from further away.

"Shirán are secret guards, Ari'atór with specific skills, sent on specific missions."

"And what missions are you referring to?" asked Idernon again.

"The ones that must be done. The ones no one wants to do."

Idernon wanted details. So did Fel'annár and so he continued to stare at her until she continued.

"The Shirán are charged with two things. The first is to stop human traders from bringing their unwitting brethren to Valley, charging them a fortune for their service, only to abandon them before the Last Markers. The Ari'atór kill them if they pass, even their children. That takes a toll, perhaps the greatest. The Shirán guard us as best they can so that we are spared such acts of necessary barbarity."

No one spoke. This was the very reason that Ari'atór were not only feared by humans; they were despised for what they considered acts of extreme cruelty. Even Tensári herself recognised it as *necessary barbarity*.

"And the second?" asked Fel'annár.

"The second is a search for knowledge. They search for the reasons why humans deteriorate past the Last Markers. They strive to understand why they become predators on the other side of the Veil."

Carodel swallowed thickly, while Idernon studied the palm of his hand. But Fel'annár stared back at her. He wanted more.

But Tensári was not offering, and with the fascinating story of the Shirán in his mind, Fel'annár turned to Llyniel. They were warm, sheltered from the elements, well-guarded and a hand slipped around her shoulders. Sleep came easily and they soon fell into a light sleep. Even Tensári dozed where she leaned back against the wooden stall.

From outside the stall, Pan'assár caught Gor'sadén's attention. He reached into his tunic and pulled out Or'Talán's journal. With his friend now sitting beside him, he lent it against his knees so that Gor'sadén could see it.

They had learned of Or'Talán's decaying relationship with Band'orán, or *Kes* as he would call him. Something had happened, something that turned the brothers against each other.

> *I have always wondered why Kes never asked for help. I knew there was conflict with the other boys, thought he could handle himself, but now I realise that he suffered, that he said nothing so that he wouldn't disappoint me, so that I wouldn't think him weak. Why would he do such a thing?*

"I can well see how Band'orán may have been hounded as a child, an adolescent," murmured Gor'sadén. "He was not quite as good at anything as his brother."

"But why would he turn against him? Orta tried to help him, loved him. We both know that. Why would he turn against him?"

"Strange as this may seem, perhaps it wasn't personal. Perhaps it was the mere fact that his brother was the root of his own suffering."

Pan'assár considered it. "Yet Or'Talán seems mystified. He didn't see it that way at the time, and this was written years after the colonisation."

"True, but it is often the case that we don't see our own blood in the same light as others do. We often brush things off. Perhaps Orta was denying the obvious." Their eyes turned back to the page.

Did it fester? Did it taint his mind, I wonder?

Pan'assár turned the page and took a deep breath. The sketch of Band'orán was beautiful, and yet there was something about it that made him sad. He turned to Gor'sadén, saw his own expression mirrored there.

"I wonder what he is thinking," murmured Gor'sadén. "I wonder how his life must have been, living it beside one such as Or'Talán. How do you live up to the expectations?"

Pan'assár shook his head. "You don't. You can't."

A click, the soft hoot of an owl. Pan'assár closed the journal, slid it beneath his tunic. He stood, pulling his hood over his head. Tensári, too, was on her feet, and then the rest, hoods up and weapons ready. Ramien and Galadan walked down the aisle and between them, a tall, cloaked figure, even steps. Not Jarabon.

"Who comes in the night?" murmured the commander, hand poised over the pommel of his sword.

The figure raised a hand and pulled down his hood. Alpine captain, a distant memory but no name. "I am Turion. I have come to take you home, by order of King Thargodén."

Pan'assár hesitated, then started when Fel'annár strode forwards, pulling his own hood away. He stopped just inches away from their visitor. "Turion!"

The captain smiled, shaking his head. He held out his hands, an offer for Fel'annár to take them, uncertain that he would accept the offer of a warrior's greeting. He had misled the boy, kept the truth from him back when he had led that fateful patrol into the Deep Forest. He wondered if Fel'annár had forgiven him, now that he knew the truth.

Fel'annár cocked his head to one side. He smiled and nodded, accepting Turion's greeting. Turion saw no anger in his eyes, no hesitation. Only joy. He turned back to the leader of the group. "Commander Pan'assár?"

Pan'assár stepped forwards, slid his hood back and then nodded at the rest. Turion saluted and then strode past him and to Handir. With a heavy breath, Turion dragged a hand over his mouth and then bowed. "Thank the Gods, Prince. Your father and brother need you urgently. You have commissioned horses?"

"We have," said Pan'assár. "How did you find us, Captain?"

"With difficulty, Commander." Turion's eyes lingered on the remaining elves and Pan'assár turned to them. "Allow me to introduce Prince Sontúr and Lord Gor'sadén."

Turion didn't know what to say, didn't understand. Two of the three were here, and a prince of the Motherland. He saluted, bowed low, and then he turned to Fel'annár, a sinking feeling in his gut and a question in his eyes. Where was Lainon?

"I lost Lainon, Turion. *We* ... lost Lainon." Fel'annár's gaze wandered to Tensári, and Turion followed, saw the marks on her face.

Connate. Widow.

Turion knew she was Lainon's Connate, and as the truth dawned on him, he turned away from them, from the truth. Lainon was dead, his closest and wisest friend. His best lieutenant was gone to Valley. He walked down the aisle, left the stable and stepped outside, stood under a sky full of stars and looked up. They blurred, colourful halos of blue and red. A hand on his shoulder, soft, and he half-turned to the cloaked figure he knew was Fel'annár.

"There's much I would tell you, Turion. The story deserves time and a safe place to tell it; wine and firelight so that it can be savoured. But he has found himself, returned and alive, across the Veil."

Turion's eyes flickered to the Ari'atór at Fel'annár's shoulder. He nodded, breathed deeply and then glanced back at the glittering sky. There were still a few hours before dawn, so he turned back to the stables, aware that Fel'annár and Tensári followed. Galadan, Ramien and Galdith would guard them, but sleep was slow to come and the silence was strange. There was so much to say that it would not come, and Lainon's loss still seemed impossible to Turion. So instead he leaned back and remembered his friend.

He was alive, they had said. He knew all Ari'atór found themselves, but how had it happened so quickly? It had surely only been a few scant months. Another question, one that would wait for dawn and perhaps beyond. For now, he would grieve for his friend, draw strength from the memory of his determination—to see Fel'annár reunited with his family, to save him from the wiles of the dangerous enemy that lay in wait.

Tomorrow, he would brief them all, make them understand what awaited them. But for these few dark hours that were left until dawn, he would watch them sleep.

THE NEXT MORNING, Pan'assár inspected the horses that were tied loosely to a long pole outside the stables. With his hood over his head, he turned to Gor'sadén at his approach. "Where's Turion?"

"He left before dawn. He has gone in search of provisions."

"Good man."

"A good captain, yes. Fel'annár was lucky to have him as his first commanding officer. He speaks fondly of him."

Gor'sadén's lips twitched under his hood. He didn't think he would ever get used to Pan'assár speaking so casually about Fel'annár, but he enjoyed it every time he did.

"Commander Pan'assár."

He whirled around, hood still up, and came face to face with Jarabon. The stable master had known who he was from the start, it seemed. He braced himself for rebuke.

"I served in your unit, lord, at the Battle. I was there that day, my own leg shattered and useless."

Pan'assár couldn't remember him at all, but then there had been two hundred in their patrol.

"It was the day I became useless. The last of my warrior days. After that, nothing made sense anymore." Jarabon shook his head. "Forgive my babbling, sir."

"It's not babbling, Jarabon. I understand, I think. I was fortunate enough to receive no incapacitating injury."

Jarabon stared back at him with Silvan eyes. "We were all scarred that day, sir. If you know what I mean."

Pan'assár nodded slowly. "You can't tell anyone about our presence, Jarabon." There was a warning in Pan'assár's eyes, one the veteran warrior would never think to disobey.

"It's him, isn't it?"

Pan'assár didn't answer for a while, but his eyes flickered towards Fel'annár.

"Why are you hiding him? You think they're out for him?"

Pan'assár leaned forwards, stared into the soldier's eyes. "We *know* they are."

Jarabon nodded, watched as trust softened his gaze.

"Why don't you come back, warrior? You can still serve in some capacity."

Jarabon shook his head slowly. "There is no return from warriorhood, sir. When you've stared into the black eyes of death, when you've charged at it all the same, accepted it ... there's no coming back from that. You go on, always a soldier, even when you're a stable master." Jarabon's eyes rested on Fel'annár, turned back to Pan'assár. "Perhaps one day, Commander. Just not this day."

In spite of his own words, Jarabon smiled, and Pan'assár thought this scarred veteran, this *Silvan* warrior ... magnificent. He held out his forearms and Jarabon clutched them.

"Turion!" called Fel'annár, striding towards the captain and young Raddy beside him, reaching out to help them with the bundles of provisions in their arms. Food, arrows, bows and receptacles, everything they may need for the remaining journey. There would surely be no other place to replenish their all but dwindled stocks. Between them, they portioned it all out, filled their quivers and slung the new bows over their shoulders.

Moments later, Raddy stood beside Jarabon, waving at the retreating warriors while Pan'assár's words echoed in the veteran's mind. Perhaps he would return, one day, when there was something to fight for once more.

"Filthy lies, all of it. He wouldn't do that, I swear it!" Captain Dalú paced backwards and forwards unevenly, and Erthoron rubbed at his temples. A sleepless night, just like the rest of them.

"And our people?"

"A score injured. Broken bones, bruises; stones, lord. They threw *stones* at us, by Aria." The captain was fuming, eyes overly bright.

"We must see this for what it is, captain," said Erthoron. "They are being lied to. They think we have crossed the line and taken the king hostage, killed those warriors."

"They didn't even consider that Angon had simply happened upon the scene, gave him no chance to explain. He sits in the king's dungeons, and the Gods know how they're treating him."

"Do you think they were killed by their *own*?" asked Lorthil.

"I say it is a possibility."

It was Amareth who next spoke. "If this *was* the work of Alpines, then Band'orán is making his final move. This is the beginning of the end."

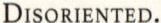

DISORIENTED.

He had been led into the palatial residence that had once been his father's, the one he no longer visited. First, because Band'orán had taken it as his own, and truth be told, Thargodén hadn't cared. And second, because there were too many memories of his days as a child when kingship was a distant, unlikely event. Memories of a father he had loved. A father who had then betrayed him, robbed him of his joy for life.

Bendir had tied his hands, albeit carefully, and a hood had been placed over his head. They had led him away, down into the basement, and then down again. He didn't remember two levels beneath the house. He thought perhaps he was in a cell but then he had heard the echo of water. And then someone had pulled the hood from his head, and his eyes had slowly adjusted to the new light.

Not a cell. This was an underworld.

He noticed the natural elements first. Stalactites, stalagmites, glittering ceilings and black pools of utterly still water; water and stone, entwined over time. But then he had seen the tables and candles. Sconces and chairs. He saw scrolls and books, jars sitting on natural stone ledges. There were life-sized figures, draped with armour and luscious fabrics. Someone seemed to live here, and he wondered if it was Band'orán himself.

These underground halls were below Analei.

Had Or'Talán known this place existed? He must have. And then truth sunk heavily into his bones. It would not be easy to find him down here.

He turned to the left. There was water further ahead, and before it stood a carved figure. He started. It was a woman, looking out over the still waters, but it was the crown upon her head that first gave away her identity.

Canusahéi. Alpine queen of Ea Uaré, mother of Rinon, Maeneth and Handir.

The world was slipping away from under him, as if he were

suspended in mid-air. Understanding was just beyond his reach, brushing against his mind. Head spinning, breath too fast, his eyes dared wander further left, to the farthest wall.

There she was again, her portrait hanging there, surrounded by the light of sconces and candles, heavy drips of old wax around them, falling down the walls, a river of it. It was a shrine, he realised.

When Or'Talán had told him he was to marry Canusahéi, he had not cared, had not cared for anything at all, not even food. Nothing mattered, not even the love he had seen in her eyes for *him*. He had never loved anyone except Lássira; never would.

"No way to treat a king, I say."

Band'orán.

"But then ... you are king no more, Thargodén." Band'orán stood a distance away from him and in his hands, the king's crown. He twirled it around in his hand as he spoke.

"Rinon will be angry. His anger will lead him astray. The council will see to that."

Thargodén knew he was right, but was unwilling to say it. Rinon's one weakness was controlling his temper, and kings could not be seen to be volatile.

"There's no point in your silence, Thargodén. Speak freely. You're not leaving this place."

"Is that your plan, then? Take me, force Rinon to take over, preempt his failure and then take the throne for yourself?"

"More or less. I must also deal with Handir. And with the bastard."

Dread, deep despair clawed at his insides. "I thought you a man of state, not a murderer."

"I am a ruler, Thargodén. Rulers do what they must for the good of their people, for the prosperity of the land."

"Save your drivel for your hounds, Band'orán. If I am not leaving this place as you say, then follow your own advice and tell me the truth. Why do you really want my throne? Riches? Power? You already have those things. What is it that drives you to this?"

"Your father was cruel, don't you think, nephew? How he made you suffer, for your love of her."

The claws were back, begging him to lash out, lose his temper and ...

"Don't fight it, Thargodén. There is no reason. No one will ever know. Will you not curse me? Damn me to the pits of torment? Ah, but you think yourself king, and kings do not lose control, do they? They must be strong, be *seen* to be strong. And you are; it's why I had to stop you."

"Spoiling your plans, was I?" Quiet voice, wistful almost.

"Indeed. But no worries. Everything is accounted for. Should Rinon pass the test and keep his cool, perhaps the Silvans will want to rid themselves of him—for the mistreatment, you see. They don't want Alpine lords. You should pray that he fails. There will be honour in his abdication to a stronger, better king."

Something snapped, and Thargodén whirled around. When he spoke, it was almost a roar. "If you kill him, Band'orán—if you kill any of my children I will damn you, curse you, find a way for vengeance. I will skin you alive, disembowel you and leave you to *watch!*"

"You'll be dead, you fool. Or will you come back a ghost? A house-less soul waving his phantom sword in the air. Then perhaps I won't kill you. Perhaps I will leave you here, in this new world. Underground and out of sight, my little secret. There are merits to the idea."

"If you want the throne, why not just take it? Be rid of me? Why kidnap me at all? Why didn't you just kill me?"

"I could have. We killed a part of your retinue. I could have killed you all, I suppose. But you see, Thargodén, this is personal."

"It's the throne you want ..."

"The throne is a *boon*, nephew. What I want is *retribution*."

"Retribution? For what?" asked Thargodén. The stone below him was cold and damp. With the shackle around his ankle, he could stand, but after two steps the chain would tense, hold him back and so he remained seated, despite his growing feeling that something important was about to be revealed.

"For a life in shadow." Band'orán said it almost wistfully, and Thargodén wondered if he even remembered that he was standing here in front of him.

"When you are born next to a sun, your own light is lost. Flooded, drowned. Nobody sees it. Nobody cares that you are there." Band'orán smiled fondly. "He was the only one who did—care, I mean."

"Who?" Thargodén was confused.

"Orta. He thought me weak, incapable of finding my own way. Wanted to help me, as if I couldn't help myself. Every time he tried, he would block my light even more. He just needed to step away."

"You loved your brother."

"Yes. Yes, I did. Everyone loved my brother, Thargodén. Except you, perhaps."

Thargodén held his breath. Band'orán was talking to him like a friend, reminiscing and smiling, and yet here they were, in some underground palace, prisoner and jailer. King and traitor.

"You did hate him, didn't you?" Band'orán stared at him, cocked his head to one side.

"For a time."

"Oh, come. You can do better than that, nephew. Tell me, did you ever want to *kill* him, for what he did to you? To her?"

"No," Thargodén shook his head, confused.

"He broke your heart, broke hers. You thought you could save her, though, didn't you? Thought you could keep her sane by creating a child."

Thargodén's face hardened, like freshly chiselled stone, sharp and cutting. "And what would you know about that?" he whispered. Dangerous voice. Warning eyes.

Band'orán smiled again, a smile that did not touch his eyes. "Everything. I know everything."

14

COMMUNION

"Lord of the forests, hear the mind of Aria, hear the voice of the world as it whispers its secrets to those who can hear."
Book of Disciples: Sebhat

The land was changing. It was still waterlogged and open, but now, the mountains hugged the rugged coastline, and the beaches were sandy and sprawling. Fel'annár spotted a brown bear lumbering through the shallow pools, off on some fishing mission. Cubs would be waiting in a nearby cave, wolves alert should the mother find some distraction along the way. Yet although it was all grey stone and jagged rock, toasted sands and clear pools of strange treasures, there was green, too. The forest was still some distance away, but even so, it was a sign that soon the land would change yet again. It was a transition, thought Fel'annár, from sea to forest, a mid-way place he thought quite beautiful, suggestive of the watery world that Ramien had loved so much, and the forest he himself yearned to return to.

Their camp that night was not so close to the water, not so open, and the evensong of the birds had changed. Only the occasional squawk and cackle of the gulls could be heard amidst the whistles and trills of the smaller forest birds. With the receding sea, the voice of Aria would return, and Fel'annár would be complete again.

With the camp set, Fel'annár sat beside Tensári at the fire and watched as Pan'assár pulled out Or'Talán's journal. He looked away, repressed a shudder and took up his own diary. He had neglected it, had hardly added anything to it on their journey back. Unsurprising, he mused, and almost wanted to laugh because it was a miracle it still even existed.

He opened it at a random page and then started. Lainon stared back at him, the hint of a smile on his face. He could not stop his gaze from wandering to Tensári. She had already seen it. Her brow furrowed as she looked down, said nothing. Her face was utterly still, but her eyes were as bright as he had ever seen them. She stood, grabbed her weapons harness and walked away.

Fel'annár turned back to his journal, took one last look at his sketch of Lainon and slowly closed it again. He turned his head to Pan'assár. "We won't be far, sir."

Pan'assár nodded. "Stay within the perimeter," he said distractedly, before adding, "and do not be long."

Nodding, he stood slowly. The pain in his chest and back was still there, but the deep weariness had gone, and his feet were not so sensitive. He found Tensári close by, sitting on a fallen log. He sat on the other end. He was surprised that it was her to initiate the conversation.

"Do they know?"

Fel'annár turned to her profile. "They know that I am Ari'atór."

"Commander Hobin told you," she deduced.

"Yes. But tell me. Did *you* know? Did Lainon?"

"Lainon knew. He never mentioned it directly, but he knew what *he* was and deduced the rest, however unlikely. I accepted that reality. And so yes; yes, I knew what you were. As for myself, after Lainon's death, I wanted to accompany Commander Hobin to Tar'eastór. However, he forbade it, and instead, he sent me into the wilderness of

Araria. He bid me meditate, think and accept Lainon's crossing. He knew I was angry. He knew I would confront you. And he knew something else, something I only recently came to understand." She turned to Fel'annár, a challenge in her eye.

"A Ber'ator is always an Ari'ator," said Fel'annár.

She nodded slowly, turned away again. "Hobin knew I had to purge myself of my negative feelings towards you. In my grief I blamed you, but as time tempered it and I began to feel Lainon's presence stronger in my mind, the warrior in me understood it was inevitable. You were not weak. You were simply outnumbered."

Fel'annár's eyes lost focus, his mind taking him back to the moment he thought he would die, the thud of an elven arrow in flesh that was not his own. "So many things have happened since then. The Battle ..."

"I have heard only rumour of what happened." She looked upwards to the dim stars above them and then back to Fel'annár. "Did you command the trees as they say? Did they fight?"

"To the death. They turned the tide."

"How did you know what to do?"

"I didn't. *They* did. They told me to touch, and I did."

Her gaze lingered on him. "You know what your purpose is?"

"Yes. I must help restore Ea Uaré. Become the Warlord the Silvans would have me be, if that is what it takes."

"A tall order. Where to start?"

"By returning, watching, listening."

"Only that?"

"We don't know what will happen once we're home. This Band'orán wants me dead. He won't be happy when he realises I'm alive."

She nodded. "You have not mentioned your family. The king, your mother."

"Amareth, her lies ..."

"She is Ara Zéndar, Fel'annár. Listen to her story before you condemn her."

They sat in silence for a moment until Fel'annár's curiosity got the better of him. "Do you have family?"

A frown, fleeting and quickly repressed, but Fel'annár had seen it. "I did once." She said no more, just as reluctant as he himself to speak of families, it seemed.

He thought he would try with another question. "What was Zéndar like?"

She turned back to him. "Zéndar was quiet and lethal. One of the best warriors I have ever seen."

Fel'annár nodded slowly. "Did he have siblings? Are they Ari?"

"He had a brother. Your great uncle is Silvan, I believe, but that is all I know."

"And Zéndar's wife?"

"I do not know her."

He turned away, felt awkward. The barrier between him and Handir had all but dissolved. The road before the two brothers was free to explore. But the wall between Fel'annár and Tensári was still there. There would surely be no better time to beat it down, if he could.

"I'm sorry, Tensári. Sorry I wasn't better. If I'd understood the nature of my gift sooner, I could have used it, just as I did at the Battle of Tar'eastór. Lainon would not have had to sacrifice himself for me."

"Then be sorry. But you cannot blame yourself for not understanding. Knowledge comes gradually. It is with the passage of time and the living of experiences that we learn. You are no different."

"But I should have known. I should have fought better, should have—"

"Stop. When you were a novice, *should* you have fought better then? And before you began to learn the ways of the Kal'hamén'Ar, *should* you have been a better warrior?"

Fel'annár shook his head while she took a deep breath, seemed to smell what he did. The forest, just half a day's trek away. "I'm glad you're here."

She nodded. "Lainon's presence is stronger when I am close to you."

"I think he's glad. Glad that you have come. Glad that we both understand now." He smiled at her, and a cloud of brilliant blue passed over his left eye. Tensári swayed backwards, startled when Fel'annár spoke.

"Don't get yourself killed for me, Tensári. Please."

She leaned forward, face cut in stone, but her eyes ... Fel'annár wondered if he would ever fathom the churning, swirling emotions he saw there.

"I must. I am Ber'ator, that is my purpose—just as it is yours to give your life for this cause, as Ber'anor. I do not question that sacrifice, and neither must you."

Fel'annár stood, and she followed. He held out his arms, and she clasped them tight. A life for a life, the ultimate sacrifice each would make for the other. To Fel'annár's mind, she had truly become a member of The Company that day, and for the first time since Lainon had died, Fel'annár felt no guilt in his heart.

LATER THAT NIGHT, after Fel'annár and Tensári had returned to camp, Turion watched the commanders discussing whatever it was they were reading in that journal Pan'assár always seemed to have in his hands or stuffed inside his tunic. It was obviously important to him, and Turion's curiosity was piqued.

"What *is* that?"

Pan'assár turned to him, glanced at Handir and Fel'annár, then answered him. "It is King Or'Talán's journal."

Turion was not sure he had heard right. He blinked. He turned to Handir and found him staring blankly back. Then he looked at Fel'annár who was scribbling something in his own diary, as indifferent as his half-brother.

Turion rose and sunk down beside the commander, only then asking permission. Pan'assár nodded. And Turion listened as they read. And as the story unravelled, he felt himself slowly falling into the fascinating story of Or'Talán's final days upon Bel'arán.

It was half an hour later, when the commander turned back to a page they seemed to have already seen, that Turion started. The sketch before him was beautiful; *she* – was beautiful. And then he heard her name. Lássira. This was Fel'annár's mother, but had he seen it? he wondered. He glanced back at him, didn't think that he had. But why would they hold this back from him? From what Turion knew, Fel'annár had not known his mother. He caught Gor'sadén's gaze, knew there was a special bond between him and Fel'annár. He had seen it during their short time together, indeed it reminded him of the friendship he had had with Lainon. And then perhaps they had not kept it from him at all, rather Fel'annár had been unwilling.

Flames lapped at wood. It snapped and crackled, sent incandescent specks into the air. Pan'assár read, as if in a daze.

I need to think, find a way to keep them together, and yet keep Band'orán away from them. I need to think. But the enemy encroaches on our northernmost lands. The fighting is well inside our borders and spreading southwards.

They must be stopped.

"This must have been the final weeks before the Battle. Before he rode out?" Turion leant forward, resisting the urge to fidget.

Pan'assár nodded. "He tried, and would have succeeded in bringing them together had fate not intervened."

"Someone needs to tell the king that," said Turion.

"He needs to know that his father did not betray him."

As Pan'assár, Gor'sadén and Turion continued their quiet discussion across the fire, Fel'annár chanced a glance at Handir. He wondered what he thought about his grandfather. Standing, he walked over to him and sat, aware of his brother's surprise.

"I was wondering. About Or'Talán. Are you curious? About what they're discussing?" He felt awkward, wondered how Handir would react to his somewhat forward question. Sontúr and Llyniel glanced at Fel'annár, trying not to listen.

Handir turned to look at the commanders and captain. "Not

really. I never met him, even though I am reminded of him constantly. His name everywhere. It is tiring—to be compared, I mean. You, though ... you have a mighty reason to hate him."

"He may as well have killed my mother. He may have been a great king, but he was a *monster,* nonetheless." He had spoken too loud, and Pan'assár's head whipped to Fel'annár. Gor'sadén held him back, shook his head.

"You should tell him, Pan. Tell him what we've learned."

"He's not interested."

"He *says* he's not interested," insisted Gor'sadén.

Pan'assár snatched his arm away, snapped the journal shut and stuffed it back into his tunic.

THE FOLLOWING MORNING, Fel'annár sat at the morning fire, sipping on tea. He was smiling like a child at a fair because he could hear the forest, as loud and as clear as he ever had. It was like wool being pulled out of his ears.

But as he glanced up at the lightening sky, a weight descended on him, tempered his smile. "Something has happened."

The quiet murmuring of his companions stopped, their eyes on Fel'annár, even Pan'assár's.

"The forest is tense. They fear something."

"Danger?"

"Not for us."

Pan'assár turned away and finished his tea.

"Sir. There is a farmstead not far to the west. It will be our last chance to stable the horses. Do we take them into the forest?" asked Galadan.

Pan'assár nodded slowly. "That depends on what awaits us. Sulén sent mercenaries from Senge, and most likely was also responsible for the attack at Bulls Bay and aboard the ship. We met no danger in Port Helia thanks to the fact that we did not stay in the town and were lucky enough to count on Jarabon's help. But that does not mean our pursuers were not there. Band'orán will surely do at least as good a job here in the forest."

"I can guarantee that," said Turion. "The king, prince and Aradan agree that Band'orán does not want Fel'annár in the forest and I concur, commander. Band'orán will do a far better job than Sulén at hunting for his prey."

Pan'assár nodded, turning back to Fel'annár, face sharp. He was still angry at him for calling Or'Talán a monster.

But he was, and Fel'annár was not sorry.

"Well, Lieutenant. Horseback or on foot?"

"I believe we should continue on foot. I understand the urgency of our return, but should we need to flee or hide, horses are not subtle creatures. They will give our presence away."

"Galadan?"

"Agreed, sir."

Pan'assár shot one last, cutting glare at Fel'annár, and then gave the order to make the detour towards the farmstead.

With their horses stabled, they slung their travel packs over their shoulders and continued on foot.

They followed the estuary mouth inland, watched as it became narrower. Hours later, it was no longer an estuary but a river, the Calro River. Fel'annár thought it a strange sort of half-way place. Neither sea nor forest. If you looked south, you would hear the sea, smell the salt, and if you looked north, you would hear the warblers, smell the loam and pine.

By evening, his feet were smarting, and although he would never admit it, he was glad when he could finally sit at the fire.

He had helped to bring water, collect wood, and even helped Galadan to fish. All the while, Pan'assár hovered, his orders curt. Still, if he expected an apology, he was not getting one. He briefly caught Llyniel's eye as he deposited a bucket of water by the fire and Galadan handed their catch to Carodel and Ramien.

With the watch set and the fish cut and skewered over their fire, the awkward silence was back. Pan'assár broke it. He leaned forward, staring at Fel'annár, waiting for him to acknowledge him.

"Or'Talán was *not* a monster."

"Pan." Gor'sadén's hand on his vambrace.

"No. He needs to know."

"He doesn't *want* to know." Turion stared back at the commander, disapproval in his eyes. But Fel'annár rose to the challenge.

"I would speak freely, sir."

"Granted."

"You will get no apology from me."

Pan'assár straightened, the lines of his face hardening, eyes glinting. "You think you know it all? That you can call an elf 'monster' because you *think* you know what happened?"

"What is there to know? Or'Talán kept his son from his soulmate. He broke their hearts. What was he, if not a monster?"

"You do not understand."

"No. No, I don't."

"And why do you not *want* to understand? This journal explains it all but you—you just sneer at it and condemn its author. You prefer ignorance."

"To acquire knowledge, you must first desire that knowledge—is that not so, Idernon?" It was not really a question, but the Wise Warrior nodded all the same. "And when your mother suffers the consequences of another's decision, you suggest I should *want* to understand the elf that brought her that torment? Is that your *suggestion*?"

"It is your *duty* to understand, as his grandson."

"It is my duty to *hate* him, as my mother's son!" Fel'annár stood and leaned over the fire, his eyes aflame with rising anger. He felt Idernon standing beside him, one hand on his arm. He snatched it away.

"Call him a liar if you will," said Pan'assár as he, too, stood to the challenge. "But he did not break his son's heart, nor your mother's. You have it *wrong* … we all did."

"Now you will tell me he must have done it for a good cause. That he did it for his land, for the good of his people. Duteous king, *sinful* father."

"For the love of Aria, I am telling you it is *here*, if you will just listen. If you still think he is a monster after then so be it. You and I will never be friends, but at least I will respect you for listening."

Fel'annár had nothing to say to that, and so he watched as Pan'assár shuffled through the journal.

"There is much to be said before we get to this moment—things you can learn of if you so desire. But for now, know that your grandfather was just as good as you with his sketches." Pan'assár circled the fire, stood in front of Fel'annár and held up the journal with both hands.

Wood hissed on the fire, flames flickering, bringing the image upon the parchment alive for a moment. There, before Fel'annár's very eyes, was his mother. The colour of her hair, the vibrance of her slanted green eyes. The utter beauty of that face. It was the face he had once seen in his dreams, the face he himself had sketched in his own journal. But there were details in this rendering, and in those details, a new truth was revealed.

She wasn't sad, didn't grieve, and in her hair, a double-threaded braid, tied at the end by the Seven Wheels. They had bonded.

He squeezed his eyes shut. He could not look at her, could not abide the pain. And yet curiosity opened them, and he stared, allowed his eyes to truly search.

She was smiling, seemed exuberant, and she was, undoubtedly, standing in the presence of Or'Talán, allowing him to draw her.

He shook his head. Didn't understand.

"You see what I mean, Fel'annár? See her expression, how he captured it. He not only met her; he *knew* her. He accepted their bond."

"And then he ruined her life," he whispered. "He knew they were inseparable."

"No. He did none of that. He tried to help," explained Gor'sadén as he came to stand beside Pan'assár. "As we read this journal, Fel'annár, the truth came to light. I once told you that if Or'Talán had forbidden his son to marry Lássira, there was a good reason for it. Now, we know what happened. All you need do, in your own words, is to desire that knowledge. Do you? Do you want to know why?"

Fel'annár had always been angry about what Or'Talán had done, and his anger was a sure sign that he cared. He caught Gor'sadén's steady gaze, and then he nodded curtly. He would listen, at least, and then he would come to his own conclusions, Pan'assár be damned.

He sat back down and Pan'assár returned to his place at the fire, the journal sitting in his lap.

"So far, we have learned of how and why the two brothers became distant. And we know of Band'orán's journey from loving brother to scheming would-be king. But what most concerns us now is that Band'orán demanded that his brother disallow the marriage of Thargodén and Lássira. Whether Band'orán knew that his nephew had already bonded, we do not know. Whichever is the case, Or'Talán didn't understand, wouldn't do it, but Band'orán threatened him. He told his brother that if he should allow their union, he would destroy her, *kill* her. With Lássira's death, Thargodén would be all but dead himself. Or'Talán knew his son had already bonded. Yet, to the Alpines, he was still unwed. Or'Talán was left with two choices: forbid the union and give Band'orán what he wanted, or allow it and risk his unsettled brother persecuting her, killing her. He chose neither."

"What do you mean?" asked Handir.

"He played Band'orán for a fool," continued Pan'assár. "He told him he would forbid it. And then he went in search of Lássira and told her of his plan. He told her to trust him, that he would find a way to bring them together. He was aware that perhaps he would need to take drastic action against his brother, but he needed to do so carefully. Band'orán had his own following, a shared doctrine of racial hatred. He had to show his brother was guilty of conspiracy, to exile him to Valley and beyond."

Handir was staring at Pan'assár as if he had gone mad. He turned to Fel'annár when he spoke.

"He told my mother, but not the king?"

"Band'orán is insightful, skilled to the extreme in reading others.

Or'Talán knew his brother's strengths, and so he told his son he could not marry Lássira. It was the only way to show Band'orán that he had agreed to his terms. But it was always in his mind to undo that wrong. It broke his heart, but he says it was just days later that he was called urgently into the field. We have yet to read the rest."

"And then he died in battle," murmured Fel'annár. "But why didn't he tell Thargodén before he left? Why leave him in agony like that?"

"We do not know, Fel'annár. But should we read of it, do you want to know? Would you listen?"

He lifted his head, met Pan'assár's gaze. It was no longer hard and challenging, but open and honest. Before he could answer, Handir spoke, and Fel'annár was grateful, wondered if he did it to help him. "I would hear it, Pan'assár."

The commander bowed at the prince, glanced at Fel'annár, acknowledging his curt nod.

Pan'assár tucked the journal away, glad, at least, that Fel'annár had listened, that his anger seemed to have ebbed. He was stubborn, as much as he himself, but he couldn't blame the boy. None of them had imagined what Or'Talán had planned, how that plan was fatefully interrupted by war. And then he wondered, apart from the Silvan people, who else had known that Lássira and Thargodén were bonded? Only now did Pan'assár truly understand why that first rent between their people had opened. It had started with the banning of Thargodén's love for a Silvan woman, with the death of Or'Talán.

That day, the Silvans lost not only a king. They lost a rightful *queen*.

THE VEGETATION WAS BECOMING DENSER, the rocks less prominent, and the air was no longer tangy but ripe with the smell of pine. Even the fire smelled different, more fragrant and heady. From the edge of the camp, Fel'annár inhaled it, half-closing his eyes, the memory of cold Sunday mornings and hot pea soup momentarily taking his mind off the night's revelations. It didn't last long before his mind was back on the conundrum. Why had Or'Talán not told Thargodén of his plan before he left for the Xeric Wood?

He caught sight of Handir, picking up a small travel pack that Turion had given him. They crossed gazes. What was Handir thinking? he wondered. Was his curiosity piqued like his? He could ask, of course. But Handir turned away, made for the chest that sat close to the fire.

Turion watched Fel'annár from afar, then turned to his companion at the morning fire. "Llyniel Ara'Aradan." He smiled. "I have struck up a singular friendship with your father these past months. He is a great man."

Llyniel stared back at the captain. She seemed shocked as she nodded at him, her Bonding Braid sliding forwards. Turion had spoken the truth. His friendship with Aradan had become close. The Royal Councillor had opened his heart to him, enough for him to know that Llyniel was the grief Turion could often see lurking behind his clever words and rhetoric. Llyniel was the yearning in the councillor's eyes when the younger courtiers passed him by. But it wasn't his place to tell her that, and he glanced at Fel'annár once more.

"He will be happy for you," he prompted.

Llyniel's lips twitched. "I would think he would be shocked, and my mother ... well, you surely know her, too."

Turion smiled. He did, indeed, know Miren. How the woman could talk! Still, he had a soft spot for her. She loved Aradan so much that she could not help fussing over him constantly. His friend was used to it, would simply smile and bat his hand at her when she would not stop.

"I would say your mother would be proud. In a sense, you have become royalty."

"What do you mean?"

"Well, last night we learned that Lássira and Thargodén were married in the eyes of the Silvans. By their laws, that makes Fel'annár a prince and therefore you, a princess."

She raised both eyebrows at the captain. There, Turion could see the same expressive face her mother had. She had not thought of it at all, and Turion was glad of it. He liked Llyniel, her natural ways, how her feelings danced over her lovely face, her deep-seated empathy.

His gaze drifted back to Fel'annár. His finest novice had become a warrior, a lieutenant, and the love in his eyes for Aradan's daughter was plain to see. He smiled again, for in the midst of the hard times that would surely escalate into the worst times the forest had ever seen, there was beauty in the love they shared. It made Thargodén and Lássira's plight all the more significant, strangely central to the conflict they were walking into.

Fel'annár returned to the fire, nodded at Turion and sat for a moment. He watched Ramien, eyes lost to the now distant sea. He knew his friend would miss it, would never forget the Rainbow Jumper he could not stop talking about. Fel'annár had imagined it in his mind as Carodel had explained to him. Ramien standing open-mouthed upon the decks of the Pelagian Queen, watching as the beast leapt out of its liquid garden and splayed its multi-coloured fins, a proud display, a graceful glide through air, fleeting and utterly beautiful. Carodel had shone in his description, and how Fel'annár had wanted to see it. But he hadn't. Instead, he would remember the sound of waves breaking over shingle, the incessant hiss of an ever-advancing blanket of water, foam frothing and fizzing out. He would remember its smell, and the strange things he had seen inside, the shell creatures and the slimy spiders. He understood Ramien's obsession with the sea, his sadness because it was fading away.

But there was no voice in the water.

Fel'annár turned to where the forest would soon appear. The song of the trees was incessant now, and he wondered if Tensári could hear it. The warning was there, too, intertwined with the greetings.

He turned to the Ber'ator, watching as she whittled away at a piece of wood with her boot knife, cross-legged before the fire. Whatever it was she was carving, it was small enough to be concealed by one hand as she worked.

He shuffled closer to the fire, accepting a mug of tea with both hands and crossing his legs at the ankles, studiously avoiding Pan'assár. He felt better today, he realised, for although there was a lingering ache in his lower back and his feet still hurt at the end of the day, thanks to the rest he had gotten on the ship, the pain had mostly gone.

Idernon nudged Ramien. "We're going home, brother. But we'll come back here one day, you'll see."

Ramien turned to his friend, studied his face for a moment, and then nodded, mustering a weak smile.

"Here," said a deep, whispery voice, a dark hand held out towards him, palm up.

Ramien looked at the small object in Tensári's rough palm, eyes roving over the exquisite curves and lines. The arch of a body in flight, the splayed fins and the open, beak-like mouth. A Rainbow Jumper. His eyes darted up to the Ari'atór. She didn't smile, but her eyes were bright and soft, and Ramien reached out and took it slowly, reverently. He held it up to his eyes and marvelled at the detail. The scales along its back, the expression on its face. His fingers curled over it protectively, and a true smile blossomed on his face. Beside him, the rest of The Company watched. Fel'annár approached him, kneeling behind him and placing one hand on each shoulder.

"We'll all come back when the Restoration is complete and we have earned our rest. We will come here to swim and dive and drink in the taverns Carodel so wanted to visit. We will sail the seas once more and watch the Rainbow Jumpers. Am I right, brothers?"

"Aye!" they shouted—even Tensári, who Galdith would later swear had smiled a little.

"And I think that after this strange show of emotion from our dark warrior, it is time we declare her one with The Company, would you not say?"

"Aye!" they shouted again as Tensári turned to Fel'annár, a dreadful scowl on her face, one Fel'annár pointedly ignored.

"Have you thought of a name?" asked Sontúr.

"I have. She is the Guarding Warrior."

The Company knew exactly what he meant, as did Llyniel and Gor'sadén. But all Turion, Handir and Pan'assár could do was wonder why he had chosen such a name.

GENERAL HUREN STRODE across the courtyard towards the Royal Palace. It was busy that morning, and Huren returned only a few of the salutes he received. Others he simply missed, his mind on the messages that had arrived in the night, personal messages from the sea. The small square of paper all but burned in his inside cloak pocket. It gave speed to his legs, long strides covering the last few steps upwards and to the main doors.

"General."

He stopped, faced Prince Rinon, returned his salute.

"Is there news?"

"Of the king? No. We remain ignorant of his whereabouts."

Rinon's glacial eyes lingered for too long. Still angry, then. "And Prince Handir? Pan'assár? *Still* no news?"

There was sarcasm lurking beneath the apparently innocent words—if anything about Rinon could be called *innocent*. The paper in his pocket was heavy, seemed almost to pulse. "Nothing. I will inform you immediately, of course."

"Of course." Rinon nodded.

Huren saluted and continued on his path towards the palace. He knew that the prince was watching. He thanked the Gods once more that it was a busy day, and he was soon lost in the crowds. He could not let Rinon see where he was headed, to Band'orán's office to deliver the news.

Sulén had failed once more, and now it fell to him to see the bastard dead. Sulén was not a military man, but Huren was. He knew how to organise covert operations. It was part of his job, and he was good at it. So was Bendir.

No sooner the message had arrived, he had sought out the captain who, in turn, had moved his Shadows. Huren had done likewise with his own mercenaries, oiled the pockets of those in Band'orán's favour. Everything was in place. All that was left to do was tell his lord that it was Huren who now took over from Sulén, and assure him that he would not fail.

But where was Sulén? He should already have arrived, and Huren was sure that he had. He was hiding, fearing that his stolen missives would be used against him. He surely feared Band'orán for what may have been written there, for having failed his duty.

It was Huren's time to prove himself to his new lord. Time for him to shine, for the rewards would be sweet indeed.

THERE WERE STILL a few hours before the light failed them, and they must stop once more. Fel'annár's gaze was anchored on the space between two hills where the forest would appear any minute now. However much it was beautiful here, this watery world could never compare to the green sea of leaves under which he had contemplated the world for the first time.

They crested a hill, and a gull screamed its farewell, sharp and piercing in his ear, arcing and wheeling in the sky, testing the currents, bold and daring.

Whether Fel'annár realised it or not, existence slanted in that moment. Lifting his gaze to the watchful gull, it hovered for a while, expectant, and then with one, final squawk, it flapped its wings and flew away to the salty, briny air of its home. Turning away, Fel'annár looked forward, over the crest of the hill and homewards.

Humid moss and ripe bark, the earthy aroma of the forest floor, home to the sustaining roots of the trees. Trees whose voice was that of Aria, playing in the air amidst the Silvan fragrance he had been born to. It called to him now, not playful or naïve, but urgent and demanding. A deep wooden musk that whispered words of belonging, of inseparable minds, of a danger lurking in the depths.

You are ours.

His feet tingled in his boots, a warmth transcending the thick soles and climbing up his wool-clad legs. It snaked around his waist and writhed upwards, a heated embrace, strong and uncompromising.

I am changing.

The bitter milk, life force, white blood hung around him. He breathed it, felt it mix with his own red blood, and he was hotter, ears ringing, eyes stinging.

I am changed.

A rook cawed, a squirrel scurried. A rabbit sat up on its haunches, terror in gleaming eyes, or perhaps it was excitement for the tales it would tell. It darted into the ferns, for the forest lord was coming at last and others must be told.

They must be warned.

A haze was before him as he moved and it carried with it all those sights and smells, sounds and emotions. It spoke of sureties that could not be reasoned.

But he wasn't frightened. Not anymore. He was changed, and this land recognised him, beckoned him into its bosom as an ancient thing, beyond the years of his life; beyond the wisdom of his youth.

Lord of the forests, hearing the mind of Aria, hearing the voice of the world as it whispered its secrets to those who could hear. And Fel'annár could. He knew that it heard him, too, not from outside but from itself—himself. The forest was him, and he was hers.

If he breathed, he did not feel the rush of air into his lungs nor the steady rise and fall of his chest. And if he was walking, he did not feel the ground beneath him, the thud of boots over loam.

The song of ancient trees rose from the quiet, deep and hollow, like the giant trumpets of Araria, a fanfare to a mighty king, a crownless king. This was the voice of the sentinels, he knew. They stirred the Silvan blood in his veins, watched the Alpine flavour, bowed to the Ari in him.

Fel'annár.

He entered a tunnel only he could see, a rent in the fabric of the world. It was a world that spoke to him and he to it.

And he felt ...

Pain and sorrow; grief and anger. He felt a past of pride and joy, of honour and dignity. He heard the ancient drums and the percussions. The dances of old that he was too young to remember. There was laughter, and there was justice in this place. There was harmony under the rule of a different king. It was the past and it was the future. What had been and what the Restoration would bring.

He felt the ground beneath him and the rush of air in his lungs. He blinked, twigs and leaves under his nose, dancing on the trail of his breath. Hands splayed over moist soil, fingers curled inside, hair pooling around him. He closed his eyes and allowed his forehead to cover the short distance to the ground, touching lightly. For a while, he simply knelt there.

Something shifted around him, and he sat up on his heels, soil-stained hands resting on thighs. A presence beside him, familiar and yet not so. He looked up into the dark face of Tensári, felt Lainon's presence. They were the only two who could truly understand him in that moment.

To stand in the presence of Aria. To feel her touch on his very heart, velvet soft and good. Two hands entwined, brown and white, bound by love. It was all that mattered.

She pulled, and he stood. Tensári smiled for the first time he could remember. And Fel'annár would never forget.

But then an afterthought, an echo, a fleeting, collective thought, not from this forest but from another, further afield.

Fear. Fear for a king. A warning to the forest lord.

15
THE REBEL AND THE REGENT

"Prince Rinon trusted no one at the Inner Circle, save for Turion. But he was in Port Helia. And then the rebel Angon provided him with a singular opportunity."
The Alpine Chronicles, Book IV. Marhené

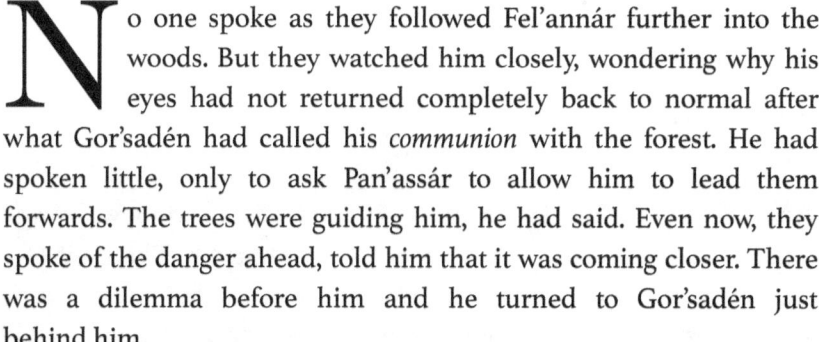

No one spoke as they followed Fel'annár further into the woods. But they watched him closely, wondering why his eyes had not returned completely back to normal after what Gor'sadén had called his *communion* with the forest. He had spoken little, only to ask Pan'assár to allow him to lead them forwards. The trees were guiding him, he had said. Even now, they spoke of the danger ahead, told him that it was coming closer. There was a dilemma before him and he turned to Gor'sadén just behind him.

"There are different groups of mercenaries, each at different distances. I could recruit the help of the trees to neutralise them when I know exactly where a given group is. But it would not be subtle. They would give away our presence and could present a danger to us if we are too close. Trees are not precise in their movements."

Gor'sadén turned to Pan'assár behind him. "Perhaps their help must only be mustered in the case of dire need," said the commander quietly.

Fel'annár held up a hand. They stopped. He listened and then lowered it, urging them onwards once more. They daren't speak and risk breaking Fel'annár's concentration, and thus the morning wore on.

Stop. Start. Stop. Continue.

By nightfall, Pan'assár called to Fel'annár and spoke quietly with him and Galadan. He knew a cave system not far to the west. They would scout first and then spend the night there. It was too dangerous to camp outside. But Fel'annár asked that they scout the caves together and Pan'assár agreed.

They sat now in near darkness before a small fire at the very back of the cave. And still, Fel'annár's eyes shone softly. Carodel repressed a shudder, wondering if it burned, but he didn't ask, daren't speak at all.

There were quiet whispers that did not touch Fel'annár at all. He sat and he listened, and from time to time his head would turn to the cave mouth. The whispers would stop, only to return timidly when his eyes were back on the fire.

No one slept.

RINON'S SHARP, chiselled features reflected off the window, beyond which the Evergreen Wood stretched to the horizon. The sight of it was calming, and Rinon needed that now, as his heart slowly returned to its natural rhythm. His anger cooled from a rigorous boil to a slow simmer.

He had ridden to Analei himself, ordered Band'orán step aside and allow him and his contingent to search the property. Band'orán had smiled softly, been so very gracious, and Rinon had searched. He had opened every door, moved every rug, every piece of furniture. He had ordered his warriors to look behind every work of art, run their hands over every statue, every bookcase.

Nothing.

Aradan watched him as he poured wine. He stepped up beside his still dusty prince and held out the goblet, watching, assessing. Rinon turned and looked at the lovely container, but Aradan knew he didn't really see it. He gestured that he should take it and drink. A strong hand wrapped around it, steered it to parched lips and drank.

"What have they done with him? Why have they not just killed him?"

"Because they need him, Rinon. Whatever their plan, they mean to use him as leverage."

Rinon drank again, then turned and slammed the goblet onto the table where a map lay flat, thanks to stones and other objects that had been placed around its edges. Cutting blue eyes roved over it, his mind visualising the places that were marked there.

"Do they need Handir, too? Is that why he is not here? Do they already have him?"

Aradan shook his head. He opened his mouth to speak, but Rinon was circling the table like a caged puma.

"Where are they?"

Aradan thought that if pumas could speak, they would sound just like that: deep and gravelly, words and sounds spilling into each other. The prince's temper was rising again, and Aradan had work to do. He stepped up to the table, watched Rinon go over things as he pointed.

"We have deployed warriors here, here and here. We know they come from Port Helia and there are only a limited number of routes they could have taken. Still, there has yet to be any sign of them," said Rinon, slamming his hand down on the map over an area not two days' travel away from the fortress.

"Perhaps it was a ploy," said Aradan. "Perhaps King Vorn'asté purposefully misled us to protect them. Perhaps they took the mountain route after all."

"I doubt that. Had they come over the mountains, they would be here." He poked at the map, hard enough to crease the parchment. "And if they are not here, they ventured into the woods. But they surely would not do that, not with Pan'assár and Handir in their midst."

"But what if they are unaware of the situation? We know our missives have not reached them. What if they are ignorant of the hostility of the forest towards Alpines?"

"It is possible. But I don't think they took the obvious route ..." Rinon's voice trailed off.

"You don't trust Huren, and I am starting to wonder if you are right, Prince."

"It makes sense, doesn't it?" Rinon turned to Aradan, riding gear crumpled, hair tangled. "All our discussions, our thoughts and our plans—he has been present for most of them. He knew exactly what was going on. We ordered patrols to every single entrance point. No word. No bodies. Nothing. He knew of the king's outings, arranged his retinue, and suddenly he is gone. Failure after failure. Week after week."

He smoothed a hand over his tousled hair, took a breath. "According to Vorn'asté, they should have been here already. If they are not, it is because they met with some hindrance. But then, is it not true that if they were dead, we would all know of it? It suits Band'orán just fine. He would be spewing it to the Alpines, blaming the Silvans the moment the word got out. Instead he spreads lies about Fel'annár being dead, about how he does not care enough about his people to return. No. They're not dead, and neither is my father."

"Agreed. And now, Huren has supposedly deployed contingents to search for the king." Aradan turned from Rinon, his own mind working in spite of himself.

"We cannot trust to that," Rinon said. "I must continue to search for him myself, Aradan. You must stay here, do what you did for my father for so many years."

"Just be sure that you are not captured in the process, Prince.

Keep your head cool, reason your decisions, and I will help you. But if they caught the king himself, they can do the same with you."

Rinon nodded. "I will ride to the Silvan encampment."

"It is too dangerous."

"It is what the people expect. Many of them believe the Silvans have him. They do not understand why we have not already searched it."

"That has Band'orán's mark all over it, Rinon. It is what he wants you to do, provoke them beyond their limits."

"And yet it has to be done. I do not believe he is there, but we must be sure, and the people must see that we are sure. To their eyes, the Silvans have motive enough to abduct the king, demand the fulfilment of their *requests*. Tension is close to snapping, Aradan. The Alpine people want the head of whoever is behind this, and I must show them it is not the Silvans. If I can stage this, perhaps even recruit Erthoron's help ..."

"Erthoron has motive, aye, but so too is it in his interest for Thargodén to remain on the throne. The Silvans know the consequences, should Band'orán succeed. I see the merit in your plan. But have a care, Prince. This may be exactly what Band'orán wants you to do. You are the only person in his way now, and that makes you vulnerable. Don't let them get to you, Rinon, because that will be the end of this rule, of the line of Or'Talán."

Rinon let out a breath. "Our army is sorely depleted. Not more than three hundred at the City Barracks. I would call on the Outer City Barracks, but damn it all, that was Bendir's command. He is conveniently missing, Aradan. Too many coincidences. Captain Sar'pen has taken over in Bendir's absence. I will speak with him and arrange for the transfer of two hundred more."

"If you are decided on the matter, Prince, you must take adequate numbers with you to that camp."

"There are a handful of those I trust implicitly, and then ..." he paused, hesitated, turned to Aradan. "And then there is Angon."

"Rinon ..."

"Think about it. He is being blamed for this. It is in his interest to find the king. And he is not exactly going to sympathise with anything Band'orán may say."

"He is being held for serious crimes; you cannot just take him out of the cells."

"I can."

"He is proclaiming Silvan independence."

"Is he? That is not what he said to me. He said he wanted to be free. He said he wanted a voice in his own lands, to live where merit is recognised, not race. Isn't that what these votes are about?"

"Yes. Still, I think you take unnecessary risks."

"Turion is not here. I don't know who to trust, Aradan. But I have many reasons to trust *him*."

Aradan said nothing and Rinon turned back to the map. The Calro River, almost home. Handir, Turion, even Pan'assár. He needed them all if he was ever going to keep the kingdom together, find the king and preserve his throne.

Tomorrow, he would rally those he trusted the most, and then he would speak to Angon, test his own theory. If he was right, if he *could* trust Angon, then he would free him and ride in his company to the Silvan encampment. A favour for a favour. Rinon would stage the search and satisfy the demands of the Alpines, while Angon would rally enough Silvan warriors to search for the king, to show their Alpine brethren that they cared. He could counter Band'orán's campaign of lies.

Over the years, Rinon had antagonised his father at every opportunity. And yet, after so many rebukes, angry words and hurtful comments, Rinon realised that the wrathful youth who missed his mother and pitied his siblings had gone and, in his place, stood a better elf, a better prince. Thus, the truth was bared to Rinon's conscious mind at last.

He had always loved his father.

∽

The sun had just reached the zenith of its upward journey, over the horizon, but Fel'annár's shadowed hand in the air was clear enough to them all. They had only been walking for a few minutes, and already, there was danger. The hand motioned skywards, a signal to climb into the trees.

Now.

Carodel and Ramien vaulted onto the lower branches, reaching down for the chest and taking it from Galdith and Galadan. Pan'assár held his hand out to Handir. The prince reached out, latched on to strong arms and was hoisted aloft. Llyniel needed no such help, and before long, they were all sitting in the trees, peering down through the canopy.

A sudden breeze, light yet sufficient to set the trees to rustling softly, masking their breathing and the inevitable creak of leather or clank of metal. The wind covered their tracks, low-lying bushes scraping over the forest floor. Below, a line of cloaked figures passed, their quivers and harnesses full to brimming with metal and wood. They walked single file and disciplined, and the commanders had little doubt as to what they were.

Shadows.

Many minutes passed before Fel'annár signalled to Idernon, who repeated Fel'annár's movements to the rest of The Company. Thudding to the ground, Ramien steadied the prince. Handir brushed himself down and then looked to Fel'annár. Eyes still bright, he ushered them along with a plea for silence.

Slowly and carefully, they pressed on. They rested in the trees, long enough only for dried meat and water. Then they continued, straight through the afternoon until twilight. One more day, just a few more hours, and they would be before the gates to the city. But they couldn't make camp, not yet.

The hairs on the back of Fel'annár's neck stiffened, ears ringing.

Move. Move now.

He turned, eyes wide. Pan'assár mirrored the expression. There was no need for silence, no need for hoods.

They had been found.

Handir ran to the chest, fumbled with the buckles and threw

open the top. He grabbed at the papers and stuffed them messily into his tunic. His crown and his clothes were inside, but damn them. They needed to get out of here. Fel'annár flipped the lid closed and dragged the trunk to the base of a tree. He knelt and Handir watched. And as surely as he had seen it one moment, the next it had disappeared under a carpet of leaves. Handir turned to Llyniel, his own surprise mirrored on her face.

"Handir, Llyniel. Up!" Llyn was away into the trees, reaching down for Handir. He was too heavy, but Idernon was at her side, helping her to pull the prince up. Idernon nodded at the healer and scurried back down to the forest floor.

"How many?" murmured Pan'assár on Fel'annár's left.

"Fifteen, maybe twenty." Even as he said it, his heart seemed to flop over. He had never killed an elf in battle.

Pan'assár signalled for Turion and The Company to take to the trees. They would cover the Sword Masters with their bows until they were needed on the ground. Tensári hesitated. She wanted to stay and yet, if these three were to dance the Kal'hamén'Ar, she would hinder more than help them with her proximity. Reluctantly, she climbed into the foremost tree, almost above where Fel'annár stood.

"Shadows are not Kah Warriors, Fel'annár, but they are the next best thing." Gor'sadén clapped him on the shoulder.

Fel'annár nodded, unable to avoid a glance over his shoulder at where he knew Turion and Galadan sat in the boughs. He wondered if they had ever killed an elf.

No time. Grey Shadows emerged from the trees before them, bows strung and notched, pointing forward. They searched the boughs as they advanced.

The creak of wood as bows tensed and Fel'annár and the two commanders darted sideways, taking cover behind the nearest trees.

It wasn't necessary, for no sooner had the arrows been released than the soft breeze became a gust of wind, strong enough to make them all stagger sideways, their bolts flying haphazardly into the surrounding bushes. The Shadows discarded their bows and drew their swords, striding forwards, braids flying about their faces, eyes wide but jaws clenched.

Fel'annár steadied himself. He drew both his swords, almost in unison with Gor'sadén and Pan'assár, and bound forwards. The wind was not so strong around them.

Fel'annár repeated words in his mind, words that would allow him to fight, push back his fears, so that he could kill.

They are the enemy. They are elves. But they are the enemy.

The three Kah Warriors turned, moving sideways in their attacks, blades arcing around them. The Shadows jumped backwards, staring at the strange movements. Their pause didn't last long, and they closed in, only to stagger back as the three moved again. Circles, overlapping but not touching; a strange steely machine that moved rhythmically, identically.

The Kah Warriors attacked, and one by one, their enemies began to fall. Shouts, elven shouts. Screams, not the wail of Deviants, not the shriek of Sand Lords. Fel'annár closed his mind—he had to. They were the enemy. They would kill Handir, kill Llyniel.

They were *elves*.

His sword sliced through flesh. He turned and brought his sword down, again. Again.

Behind him sounded the thwack of arrows, and before him, the thud of bolts piercing flesh. More screams, immortal screams. And then there was the overly loud crash of a dead weight upon the forest floor. Leaves danced on the ebbing wind, lingering over the ground as if afraid to land there. Fel'annár looked down. He looked away and then down again, glowing eyes as cold as iron as they landed upon a dead elven face.

He turned, wiping his blades with the hem of his cloak, and slid them into his harness. He looked at nothing except from the corner of his eyes. He saw Pan'assár peer at the dead faces, pulling their hoods back, while Gor'sadén watched as Handir and Llyniel were helped down from the trees.

Fel'annár looked at none of them, rebellious eyes returning to the dead elves.

Did I do this? he wondered.

He startled as a hand rested on his shoulder. It was not soft, not comforting. It was an anchor, heavy and grounding. Gor'sadén.

"You killed the enemy, Fel'annár. As hateful as any Deviant, as dangerous as any Sand Lord. You killed the *enemy*." A fierce whisper, a last, powerful squeeze that almost hurt, and then his Master was gone. "We leave now. Fel'annár, at the fore."

THAT NIGHT, they sat in nothing but moonlight at the centre of a natural stone circle. Pan'assár, Turion, Gor'sadén, Fel'annár and Galadan debated in fierce whispers.

"The Silvan encampment lies before the main gates," said Turion. "We cannot go that way, not with Pan'assár and the prince in our midst. And should they see Fel'annár, our hopes of entering the city in secret will be dashed. I say our only hope is to approach the fortress from the east. The stables are close to the secondary entrance that warriors often use, guarded but not overly so. There is a stairway up to the main foyer of the palace itself, the route lords take to the springs. We wait for nightfall, enter the gates and make straight for that entrance. Llyniel and I can go to Aradan's quarters and explain. From there, we must get ourselves from the foyer to the penultimate floor unseen."

"It sounds risky," murmured Gor'sadén.

"To a point," said Pan'assár. "The king instructed us to take the Dark Road. But that is not going to happen if we cannot reach the entry point." Gor'sadén stared at him in realisation, but Turion was confused.

"Fel'annár. Can we travel south-west?"

"No. That road is too dangerous."

Turion was still confused, and Pan'assár clarified. "The Dark Road is a safety mechanism, a route of escape should our king find danger outside the gates and inside. You must not speak of it." Turion nodded, and Pan'assár continued. "We must go with Turion's plan. It is the only path left open to us. We need to rest, move at first light. There has been enough fighting for one—"

Fel'annár stood abruptly. Llyniel and The Company followed. "We move now," said Fel'annár quietly, buckling his harness tight.

Within minutes they had left no trace of their passing and slipped quietly into the night, following Fel'annár, who walked with his right hand splayed, as if he reached for something they could not see. Below his hood, a green light illuminated the material on the inside.

They changed route three times that night and did not sleep at all. Still, they had moved closer to the fortress, even caught glimpses of distant lights. But come the dawn, Fel'annár stopped and turned, head moving from side to side.

"We are surrounded. There is no longer a safe route on the ground. The Silvan camp is close by, over to the right. Commander, I can show my face, make for the camp with The Company and draw the enemy to me. You must climb, navigate the trees towards the fortress, deliver our prince," said Fel'annár, eyes moving from Handir to Llyniel.

"We can't—"

"We are surrounded. The only way is up, Commander. Get into the trees, get our prince up there, out of the way. *They* will help you."

For the first time, Pan'assár stood unsure. Fel'annár asked him for blind faith.

Handir could not even climb up a tree on his own, let alone navigate a forest as the Silvans could. He would plummet to his death. This wouldn't work.

"The Company and I will be safe at the Silvan encampment." Fel'annár's eyes were blazing yet clear enough for Pan'assár to see the urgency, the conviction in them.

"Don't let them see you, Fel'annár. You must not proclaim your return, not yet." Handir's urgent voice.

"I will reveal myself to the enemy so that they follow us. I will hide from our allies and wait for your instructions."

Handir nodded, pale-faced, almost petrified at the prospect of jumping through the trees.

"You won't fall. I promise."

Handir started, met his brother's unnatural eyes. He felt the breeze as it picked up, heard the boughs swaying to and fro.

"Fel'annár?" called Pan'assár.

"Commander. They are coming."

One last nod and Fel'annár pushed his hood back, revealing his gently undulating hair, baring his face, his identity, a magnet for the assassins.

"Climb." He gestured with his head.

Gor'sadén turned, eyes reluctant to leave the figure of his Disciple, but now, even he could hear the enemy's feet trampling over the forest ground. The breeze became a wind, and he held out his hand for Sontúr. But the prince shook his head.

It was Gor'sadén's job to see his prince safe, yet on this journey, Sontúr rode as one of The Company. The king had acceded to it, and against his instincts, he nodded, eyes full of words. Stay safe, keep *him* safe.

"Step up, reach for the branches."

It was ridiculous. Handir knew he would never be able to reach that far. It was impossible.

"Step up!" shouted Pan'assár once more, and Handir did, knowing he would fall. He placed a boot in the commander's clasped hands, felt the upward impulse from strong arms. Not enough, too slow. His hands reached for the lowest branch. Too far.

A creak of wood, a groan and the branch was suddenly before him. He encircled it with his arms, and his feet were free, kicking nothing but air. He really tried to remain silent, but all he achieved was a long, long scream as Prince Handir of Ea Uaré disappeared into the dense boughs of the Great Forest Belt.

"RAMIEN!" warned Carodel as his feet sped over the forest floor. An arrow flew past his ear, and he swerved sideways. They were running again, Shadows and mercenaries moving in from behind, left and right. Only the fore was open to them. Galdith fired to the left, then reached for another arrow whilst Galadan, Sontúr and Fel'annár fired their own bows, again and again, but still they came.

Fel'annár waited until The Company passed his position, heard the enemy crashing through the foliage and he was firing again. The Silvan camp was so close, so far.

Too far.

Their attackers closed in, came together, and The Company turned, slowed to a walk backwards, inching away from their pursuers, knowing it would come to blades. They could see their faces now, see their shock, their hesitation when their eyes rested on Fel'annár, glowing eyes and dancing hair. A forest mage, or was it the great king's spirit, come for vengeance? They stared at him, both fascinated and horrified. They moved in, and The Company engaged.

Fel'annár's longsword shrieked down his opponent's shorter blade. A Shadow, one of the leaders, he knew. In his left hand, his shortsword angled this way and that. Testing, gauging, every move was countered, anticipated. He was good.

Steel moved towards his face. He lurched sideways, swung around, and thrust his sword through his opponent's side. He fell, but another came.

A glint to his left. He blocked a strike from the side, felt a blade graze over his right cheek. His own elbow drove into a face, with the crunch of bone and the thud of a body falling to the ground. He stepped forwards, found another, killed him.

He saw Tensári beside him, wielding her sword with both hands. A terrible sight, all in black as she bore down on them and Fel'annár strode towards his next opponent. There was another behind him. He crouched low, brought his blades around and felt a frozen sting across his arm. He ignored it, stood and lunged. His sword was blocked, so he twisted sideways, shortsword stuck on a scimitar. His longsword took off a hand, blood spurting everywhere. He moved back and kicked the flailing body away.

Everywhere he turned, there were Alpines. It was only a question of time before one of The Company took a serious injury. They needed help, but he couldn't risk unleashing everything. It was too dangerous. Trees were not precise in their movements. It would be too easy to be caught in the maelstrom.

Topple them. Hinder them. Distract.

The energy inside him pulsed, his hand splayed, and the breeze became a whirlwind. Hair and braids flew this way and that, while Shadows fell to the floor and others crouched low, clutching at the foliage. Beneath their feet, roots swirled and coiled. The Company knew what it was, but not so the shocked and horrified enemy. Tensári thrust her sword through the chest of one who had been struggling to rise, while Ramien cut another's throat. But the enemy were soon on their feet once more, distracted but not defeated.

Something brushed against Fel'annár's mind, no time to think and he saw a Silvan figure he did not recognise beside him, and then another. Not the enemy, surely, for they were engaging the mercenaries.

Thrust and kill. Dodge, kick out. A strangled moan.

Get up.

Turn, slash and slash again, a rhythm found.

One, two, three—*strike*.

Lights, green and purple, made colourful trails behind each movement of sword, arm, leg, head. They danced around his face as his arms moved, swords arcing left, right.

He ducked, though not quickly enough. Something pierced his shoulder. Not deep. He felt a hot rush beneath the leather as he brought his blade up and sliced open his enemy's throat. A wet gurgle. He stepped back, watched the remaining attackers run. They would surely regroup and try again.

His chest heaved, and the wind died. A dark, familiar presence at his side and then another before him. He stared, smudged face and messy hair, brown eyes afire. The figures sharpened before him, and the elf spoke.

"There are still ten left. We must follow."

"Wait," said Fel'annár.

"They'll get away, you fool."

"They won't. They can't."

No one spoke, not even the Silvan warriors who had joined the fight. As The Company came to stand beside Fel'annár, a sound rent the air, ripped through it and chilled their blood. A trumpet blast, the deep groan of some giant monster. They stood, too petrified to move. From beyond the trees, they heard screams and shouts, a call for retreat cut short. The boughs swayed violently, and wood creaked and cracked.

The Silvan warriors watched with eyes too full. They stepped backwards, simple clothes blowing in the wind that did not come from above. One of the Silvan warriors chanted over and over as he watched, panic tinging his voice.

"Aria lady of light and wind.
Aria spirit of earth and wood ..."

It stopped as suddenly as it had begun, boughs still, the wind gone, but when the Silvan leader turned back to Fel'annár, his hair was snaking around his head, eyes glowing like liquid glass under water.

"What the *hell*?" hissed the Silvan leader, scowling, even as he stepped away from the mage.

The Company arranged themselves behind Fel'annár, Tensári and Idernon at his side. They were exhausted, wounded, hungry, but if they had to face another battle, even with their own people, none of them would falter.

Fel'annár had not been able to hide his features from these warriors, and now, as the forest calmed, the danger gone for now, his hair settled around him and the glow dimmed but did not die. The Silvan fighters who had aided them dared a step forward, eyes wide with curiosity. And hope.

"You're Ar Lássira, aren't you?" asked the leader.

Fel'annár nodded, pulled his hood back over his hair.

"What we just saw ..."

Fel'annár stepped forward, a stubborn lock still teasing his peripheral vision. "What's your name?"

"Farón."

Fel'annár hesitated, recalled a teasing conversation between Lainon and Turion back when he was still a novice. They spoke of who had found the better warrior, of the bet they had placed on whether it would be Fel'annár or Farón to be promoted first. "You were Lainon's pupil?"

Farón swayed backwards. "Did you read my mind?"

Fel'annár resisted the urge to chuckle. Instead, he shook his head. "A distant memory. I, too, was Lainon's pupil." He smiled at the unlikely coincidence, inexplicably glad that a little part of Lainon's legacy had come to aid them. "Will you take us to Lord Erthoron, Farón?"

The warrior stared back at the figure of Or'Talán returned, the one he knew was Green Sun. And then he nodded, confused thoughts waring in his mind, unsure of what to think, of how he felt. He gestured with his arm that they should follow him. As they walked, Fel'annár drew abreast with Farón.

"My presence must not be announced. The future of this forest depends on my anonymity."

"Good luck with that. They said you were dead. Many believe that. When they learn that you are alive, and here at the camp, there will be no stopping them. They have placed their hopes in you, and whether that is justified, I cannot say."

Fel'annár nodded. "All I need is two days."

"What's going on?"

"Take us to Erthoron and hear it for yourself. But help me pass through your camp a simple warrior, come to join the cause."

"A simple warrior," echoed Farón. "What *are* you? I thought you were a Listener."

"I am." He turned to look at the warrior, held his gaze and said no more. The warrior turned away, clenched his jaw.

"Hide those Alpine features, then. I would hear what you have to say."

The truth was that Farón had believed Band'orán's lies. Many of them had. It was why Angon was so popular with the warriors. Popular aye, but foolhardy, rash, unsuited to command. Indeed did he not sit now in the city dungeons? Farón huffed. No, Angon was not the leader they needed.

HANDIR KNELT upon the forest floor, unsure whether he could stand on his own two feet. He daren't look at the others. His throat was raw, had made sounds he had not thought himself capable of.

He reached up, shaking fingers glancing over his sore cheek, the only evidence of his journey through the boughs—that and his knotted hair and ripped clothing.

He would have given anything to see what had happened from a different perspective. A bird or perhaps a squirrel. All he knew was that he had been tossed from tree to tree, held aloft when he would have fallen. He had swung between trees, had even fallen and been caught. He remembered his fevered dreams in the cave after their flight over the Horizon Falls. He remembered falling fast and then floating. He remembered the strange bruises around Fel'annár's body.

This was what had happened at Horizon Falls. They had been saved by a tree.

He looked up, saw Llyniel adjusting her tunic, pulling her cloak straight. Her hair was a sight, but it somehow made her prettier, he thought. He wondered if she was mad enough to have actually *enjoyed* what had just happened to them. She turned, caught his eye, and he knew that she had.

"In all my years," began Turion.

"In all *my* years," added Gor'sadén, rolling his shoulders and stretching his neck.

"Later. We need to get inside," warned Pan'assár.

"If Fel'annár has reached the encampment, it is a matter of hours before the Silvans give us away. They won't be quieted after waiting so long for his return. I wonder what Band'orán will do," said Turion.

"He will assume we are with him," said Handir, standing on

wobbly legs. "And don't be so sure they will give Fel'annár away. Did they not hide him for fifty-two years?"

"The circumstances are not the same."

Handir said nothing, and Pan'assár spoke instead. "Your plan, Turion. Once we are inside the gates, go with Llyniel to Aradan, warn him of our coming. No one will think anything of your presence. We will make our way to the springs on the lower level and hide ourselves away."

Turion nodded, and the group began the trek into the city.

It was almost comical, mused Handir. Sulén had tried to kill them, time and again. On the river, after the river, in Bulls Bay and aboard the Pelagian Queen. He had chased them here, to the very gates of the city, and now they would simply walk in, just another group of anonymous, travel-weary elves in search of food and shelter.

Turion lowered his hood, and nodded at the guards. They saluted, stepped aside for the Alpine captain and his hooded companions. Unknown to them, their prince was home at last.

Handir turned his head to Llyniel beside him. "Is he well?"

She smiled fleetingly. "I believe he is."

BAND'ORÁN SAT in the gardens at the rear of the palace. Here, the view into the Evergreen Wood was stunning to look upon, like a wall of brown and green, every shade, every texture the mind could conjure. Inside, nothing but trees and plants, animals and birds.

No elves.

Not that Band'orán cared about that. The forest was not his home, never had been. In that, Or'Talán had it right. Still, it would be his to rule over. This Evergreen Wood was a symbol, and when he was king —soon now—he would show them. This was his land, his forest, to walk in if he so desired.

For now, though, he was not allowed to pass the closed and guarded gates.

Careful steps behind him. He waited for Draugolé to sit on the bench beside him and report. "Bendir's Shadows have yet to return. They are surely on to them."

Band'orán turned to Draugolé. "That bastard is key to our success, even more so than the king himself. You have seen the Silvans, heard what they say about him, how they talk. I know how dangerous his kind can be. I lived with one for many years. They burn anyone in their path, draw others to them, beguile them. Everyone else is a worm, a worthless shell at his side."

Draugolé listened and bolstered his courage. He had heard this before, recognised the tone and the choice of words for what it was. It was Band'orán's driving force, the reason for his deeds, deeds he himself subscribed to. Only in his case, it was for gain, for coin and power. But not so his lord. For him, it was personal. It wasn't a choice, not really. It was days like these when Draugolé knew he would need all his acumen.

"If Huren fails, I will send my personal guard to do the job." There was a frigid sort of calm to his lord, a mood he knew could turn dangerous with a single wrong word. He was suddenly glad he had bid Barathon wait outside the gardens. The boy would surely have questioned his father, would have been confronted for it, treated like a 'worthless shell'.

"With that rebel in the dungeons, it seems the indecisive have come to realise how dangerous it is to allow the Silvans a say in our military strategies. The violence has convinced them this is no simple plea for justice. It is a crude demand to yield or die. It was a stroke of genius, lord." Band'orán nodded, but he said nothing, and so Draugolé pressed on. "With the Warlord banned, presumed dead, and Angon's pending trial and execution, it should be enough to keep the Silvans at bay. The Council will vote in our favour, especially now with the king gone. It has created a sense of unease, unrest, which only an experienced statesman can handle. They will allow Rinon the regency, of course, but it is surely a matter of time, little time, before our prince shows his shortcomings as a ruler. I assume that is the plan?"

Band'orán stood a little too abruptly and walked towards a rose bush. There were no buds on it in spite of the season. A strong hand reached for a stem, finger brushing over a green leaf. "Then, the Inner Circle and the Royal Council is ours. The king has been dealt with. Only Rinon and Handir stand in my way now."

"And Maeneth?"

Band'orán's slips quirked. "She's a *botanist*, Draugolé. A would-be fighter turned academic. She is no threat to us. So much like her mother ..." He stroked the rose once more, wondering if it would ever bloom, whether he would ever see those extraordinary yellow flowers *she* had loved so much. "We will deal with her when the time comes."

Band'orán turned to Draugolé, gaze wandering over his dark robes and dark eyes. He smiled, watched him leave, and briefly wondered where Barathon would be. He turned back to the plant. It hadn't bloomed since she had left, hadn't bared itself to the light in all that time. Truth be told, although he stood under the warm spring sun, neither had he.

A WEEK OF FRUITLESS SEARCHING, but still, the king was missing.

Huren had patrols raking the forest—or so he said—from the Calro River as far as Sen Garay. Rinon had ridden out himself, overseeing those patrols nearer to home but he daren't venture further, not when he couldn't trust Huren; not when Turion was away. Every time he considered it, a sinking feeling assailed him, one thought hounding him: what if that was what Band'orán wanted him to do? What if he was walking into a trap, as Aradan had suggested?

Huren had wanted to dismantle the Silvan encampment, disperse its people and be done with the damned place once and for all. It was what Band'orán wanted because he knew that it would bring violence, just as he knew framing Angon would enflame the Alpine people against the Silvans. Rinon had forbidden it, told Huren that he would deal with that place in good time.

Still, freeing Angon now would be a death sentence without proper escort out of the city. And even if he did make it to the encampment, the Alpine people would hunt him, demand his return for trial, or perhaps even attack the Silvans themselves. Angon was a catalyst, one that could trigger chaos or initiate change.

That was Rinon's objective.

"Open the door!"

With a click and a heavy bang, Rinon entered the half-gloom. He spotted the Silvan sitting in just the same place he had found him the first time they had spoken.

"Angon."

The rustle of cloth, only a slight movement.

Rinon stepped closer, crossed his ankles and sank to the floor, hands clasped in his lap. "Your word, Angon. You offered it the other day. I would hear it again, see your eyes. Tell me you did not kill those warriors, that you did not abduct the king."

Angon's eyes anchored on Rinon, tired and steady, with only a glimmer of the anger he had seen previously. "I swear it. But your people will never believe that."

"No. Not unless I show them."

Angon lifted his head, scowled at the prince. "How?"

"I could take you back to your people, show the Alpines that the king is not at the encampment, as many believe. I could show them that the Silvan warriors want to find the king; that you ride with the army once more, for the common good. We could show the Alpines that you are still loyal, that the army that sits on their doorstep is not hostile, that you will not turn against them. Do you see what I mean, Angon?"

"You presume much. The Silvan people will not be contained much longer."

"Perhaps you, too, are being lied to. Perhaps you think all Alpines are Purists. Is that it?"

"It's not a *lie* we believe, Prince. It is a perception, born from years of discrimination. I am not a politician, Prince, and the Gods deliver me, I never want to be. I am a warrior, a protector of my people, and bless their souls, but they are hurting. It is my duty to help them."

Rinon observed his prisoner. He was tired and hungry, bereft of sunlight and the forest, Silvan elf that he was.

Elbows on knees, Rinon leant forwards. "Help me to bring our people together, Angon. Help me show them their assumptions are wrong, that your people care. We show them that the king is not there, that I trust your leaders and your warriors. You must help me stage the play, and then you must play your part. Rally your fighters. Ride with us and find our king."

"The Silvan warriors will no longer tolerate Alpine commanders unless they are ordered to by their leader."

"And Lord Erthoron will not order it?"

Angon leant forward, shook his head as he spoke. "He doesn't move them."

"And you?"

Angon straightened, considered the question. "I have my followers, Prince. But ... the truth is that I do not inspire them as *he* does. I am a voice they respect. I stir their anger, but ... I am not the Warlord they seek to reinstate. They have placed their faith in a figure, a dream they do not even know for the most part. They have placed their hopes in a young warrior from Lan Taria with no experience in battle or politics. If he ever does come back, if he's not dead, I fear their disappointment—what it may drive them to do. I know I am not alone in this."

Rinon breathed deeply, his mind made up. "It makes sense, Angon. The crown wants Lord Band'orán gone," he murmured, just loud enough for Angon to hear. "He is the enemy that spreads lies, watches as they sink in and spread like a plague. The crown wants the return of your Warlord, and it wants equity on the Council. On that, you have my word. But for that to happen, Band'orán must be cast from these lands, one way or another."

"And his legion of Purists? The commanders of our army?"

"All that will change. With the return of the Warlord, our army will be restructured; the Inner Circle rebuilt from the ground upwards."

"Outposts?"

"As many as your Warlord deems necessary."

Angon did not speak for a while and Rinon watched his struggle. The elf wanted simple things, basic things, all of them meant to defend his people. Rinon admired him, even liked him.

"I'll trust you. I must. It is, perhaps, our last chance for peace."

Rinon nodded slowly. "How are they treating you here?"

"The beatings have stopped. The food is bat shit."

"I need a little more time before I can get you out of here. There are few I can trust, especially with Turion abroad."

"Captain Turion is a good captain."

Rinon started, but then he remembered Turion telling him he had commanded Angon once, said he was a good warrior. "Yes. Yes, he is."

"Another day, then."

"Enough for me to plan this."

"You are bold, Prince. I'll give you that. Walking into our camp in these days of conflict. Your warriors will be all too ready to fight us, for what they think we did."

"And we must show them they are wrong."

"It's a gamble."

"And I love a bet," said Rinon, upper lip curling.

Angon almost mirrored the expression. "So do *I*."

16

THE RETURN

"From the high plains of Tar'eastór to the trees of the Great Forest Belt, Prince Handir and his host had returned, at last."
The Silvan Chronicles, Book IV. Marhené

Farón and his elves strode through a sea of tents. Warriors honed their weapons, bakers kneaded their dough and smiths hammered at their anvils. But when Farón passed, they raised their fists and cheered. It wasn't a joyous cheer but a rebellious yell. Angon had been taken, arrested and surely beaten, but Farón was here and that was the next best thing.

Fel'annár watched them from under his cloak. The camp was larger than any of them had imagined, and far more complex. It was more of a makeshift village, capable of sustaining itself. There were stables, training rings, collective dining areas, even a forge. Fel'annár wondered if they had water pumps.

It struck him that there were so many warriors here. Had they deserted? They stared back at Farón and The Company, whittled arrows and sharpened blades. Their uniforms were worn, oftentimes incomplete. Some had replaced their standard-issue cloaks with a brighter green version, while others wore only the leather skirts but not the customary black breeches below. There must have been hundreds, mused Fel'annár.

Just beyond the sea of tents was a plain, and a fifteen-minute canter to the city. He was so close now to meeting his father, his other brother. He realised that, where before he had felt nervous and somewhat ambiguous, now curiosity was winning over everything else. He knew his father wanted to meet him, and Fel'annár had always known that he was duty-bound to agree. But it was no longer about obligation. He *wanted* to meet his father, wanted to see his face. He wanted to know what kind of elf he was. Was he strong and resolute, like Gor'sadén? Was he introspective and academic, like Handir? Or was he like the Great King, powerful and beguiling?

He had hated Or'Talán from the moment Lainon had told him who he was. Yet now, there was a burning question in his mind. From Pan'assár's account, he had discovered that Or'Talán had cared, had known that his mother and father were bonded in the ways of the Silvan people. He hadn't purposefully broken his heart but tried to help his son. But things didn't go to plan, and the question remained: why hadn't Or'Talán told his son before he left for war?

Not for the first time, Fel'annár tried to imagine his life without Llyniel. He breathed deeply, revelled in her presence in his mind. She was safe; they all were.

His mind sharpened, focussed on the present. The voice of the trees was so strong in his mind. Even now, behind their reassurances that his friends were safe, an underlying warning was becoming clearer. They spoke of his father. They spoke of ...

He placed a hand on Idernon's forearm, careful not to disturb his hood. "Something has happened in the city," he whispered.

"What is it?"

"The trees speak of a deposed king."

Idernon's step faltered. He picked it up lest he draw attention to their group. They still weren't safe.

They came to a stop before a large, circular tent. Farón spoke with the guard at its entrance, and then he turned to the warriors who had accompanied him, to those who had seen the strange lights in Fel'annár's eyes, seen his face. "Not a word. On your oath."

They nodded, and with a lingering stare at Fel'annár's hooded form, they disappeared into the surrounding crowds. Farón nodded, then ducked inside, The Company behind him.

It was dark inside, save for the fire at the centre, and the candles which stood on a table to one side. But the warm glow was enough to tell a surprised Fel'annár that it was Amareth who stared at him from one side of the table, a curious Erthoron at her side, and further back, the dark features of an Ari'atór, familiar beads gleaming and winking as he stepped forward. Narosén—and if he was here, Lorthil surely was, too.

He heard the rustle of cloth, the fall of heavy, oiled weave behind him and the crackle of the fire. He stared at the four elves before him, standing utterly still, like a life-sized tapestry. But then Amareth stepped forward, and the illusion was gone.

"I knew you would come. That you would return. Even though I feared it."

Erthoron's head snapped to Amareth, and then to the foremost hooded figure. "Fel'annár?"

A bloodied hand reached up and slid back the hood. Fel'annár stared at Amareth, saw her wide, shining eyes, intense as they wandered over him. They paused at the Bonding Braid, the honour stone and the barely recognisable Heliaré. Gods, but he wanted to hug her, and yet reproaches clamoured for release. His eyes travelled to a wide-eyed Erthoron, a shocked Lorthil and a satisfied Narosén.

"I need your reassurance that my identity will not be disclosed."

"You have it. Although I confess, I don't understand. Surely it is in our favour to tell our people. Many thought you dead or simply indifferent to our cause." Erthoron stepped closer.

"Until word comes from our allies in the city, we must stay out of sight."

Erthoron nodded, turned to Farón. "Find Captain Dalú. We need to reinforce the perimeter guard and provide protection for our guests. His identity is to remain a secret."

"I have sworn my elves to secrecy, lord."

Erthoron turned back to Fel'annár. "Will you not introduce your companions?"

Fel'annár half-turned to The Company behind him. They, in turn, pulled their hoods down and waited. "This is The Company. My brothers and sister. They go where I go."

A female Ari'atór, although uncommon, was not unheard of. But it was Galadan's blond locks that Lorthil stared at.

"And the Alpine?" he asked, pointing with his finger at Galadan.

Fel'annár's features sharpened as he took a step forward. "The *Alpine* is a trusted lieutenant, a loyal and brave warrior. He would die for you."

Lorthil started, looked away.

"As would I," said Sontúr, stepping forward. "I am Prince Sontúr Ar Vorn'asté of Tar'eastór." He watched them for a moment, and then he bowed, aware that they returned the gesture. Fel'annár could see their shock, their questions. A prince of the Motherland stood before them, more Alpine than Alpine, despite his grey hair.

"We have many questions, lords, and I am sure you have your own," said Erthoron with a heavy sigh. "Farón, have a tent set up as close as you can to this one."

Farón nodded and then turned to Or'Talán incarnate. He stood there for a moment, eyes unreadable even to Fel'annár. There was mistrust in his eyes, some confusion, or perhaps scepticism. It mattered little to him, for his shoulder twinged and reminded him of the blade he had taken there. He felt Tensári's hand at the small of his back, and then Idernon stepped forward.

"Lord. Can you provide food and clothing? Our journey has been long and eventful."

"Of course. I will send for a healer."

"No need, lord. We have our own," said Fel'annár, watching as Sontúr arched his eyebrow at the Silvans and stepped to his side.

Erthoron returned the gesture, watched as they turned to leave.

Narosén caught Fel'annár's line of sight. He smiled that same mischievous smile Fel'annár remembered from back in Sen'oléi, the one that said he knew more than he should. But the smile faltered as he regarded Tensári. He bowed to her, to Lorthil's visible surprise, and then he left, staff thudding over the ground beside him.

But Amareth had eyes only for her son, the one that would not return her gaze. He was angry, and she had expected no less. But her ruse was over. She was free at last to answer his questions, and she would, as soon as he had rested. After that, she had her own questions, about his journeys, about his Bond.

Minutes later, the new tent was erected and The Company, hooded once more, were led away.

"Well?" Erthoron smiled and Amareth returned it, but it faltered too soon. She had missed nothing of his childhood, and yet, it seemed she had missed every day of his adulthood.

"Did you see his eyes, Erthoron?"

"I did. They are not the eyes of a child."

"No. No, they're not."

LLYNIEL HEAVED a deep breath as she rounded the final corner. One last corridor and she would be home, ten years on.

Turion had said he had become friends with her father, but she couldn't help but wonder at the unlikely friendship. Turion was a hardened, resolute captain, while her father was ... an academic. A philosopher. He was cautious, wary of change.

If everything had gone to plan, the others would be in the bowels of the palace, in the caves and natural springs below, waiting for the right moment to make it inside, unseen. There was no way of telling who was loyal and who was not. All it would take was for a disloyal guard to see them, and Band'orán would have the upper hand. And so, to the eyes of others, Captain Turion made for the king's quarters as he so often did, returning from a mission in Port Helia. Beside him, Aradan's rebellious daughter, making for her own family quarters on the level below. No one would think anything of it.

On the second-to-last floor of the palace, where the king's closest advisors dwelled, Llyniel stopped. She turned and faced the ornately carved double doors that opened into Aradan's suite of rooms. She had been born and raised here.

She remembered her mother's face, looking down on her and laughing, that scandalous cackle Miren was famous for—that and her incessant babbling. She saw her own pleading face, still podgy and rosy. She wanted to go to the forest, wanted to play in the trees. She saw the sadness in her mother's eyes—duty or heart? And what did it matter? It had all been sacrifice, one Llyniel hadn't understood at the time. She saw her father's quiet laugh, herself as she swiped at his arms, scolded him as she laughed. She remembered his voice as he read to her, his pride when she excelled. She remembered the hurt in his eyes when she told him she was leaving. It was because of *them*. Because they would not make a stand, defend the Silvan people. She hadn't understood. Still didn't.

Her hand hovered over the wood, eyes glancing at the round knob. All she had to do was knock, and Bala would surely answer. She heard it, then, as if it had not been her own hand to rap sharply over the ornately carved wood. Too late to change her mind. She waited, heard a click, saw a Silvan elf in a black robe, his face blank. He scowled, but then his eyes bulged and his mouth opened wide. He gasped, smiled and stepped back.

"Bala? What is it, you fool?" A woman approached from behind the shocked servant, peering around him until her eyes locked with Llyniel's. One hand rose to cover her mouth.

"Mother." Llyniel stepped over the threshold, heard Turion behind her, and then the door as it closed.

"My child," said the woman, stepping towards Llyniel and embracing her, squeezing the breath from her chest. Her own arms rose, unsure and tentative, slowly returning the embrace. But it was stilted, and the woman stepped back, holding her daughter at arms' length as tears rolled lazily from her hazel eyes. "You are travel-worn.

Here, come sit and eat. Your father will be back shortly." Miren nodded at Turion behind.

Llyniel allowed her mother to pull on her hand and lead her to the kitchen. Turion followed slowly. Water bubbled over the open fire, two pots hanging above it. The smells of home. Bala set about preparing tea, unnaturally quiet.

"Mother. Listen carefully to what I am about to tell you, and please, keep your questions for later." Miren stepped back, the familiar shadow of hurt or perhaps grief lingering in her forest eyes. Llyniel hadn't meant to be curt. "We need to speak with father. It's urgent."

Miren nodded. "He will be upstairs with Rinon." She answered Llyniel but her eyes were on Bala.

The servant nodded and hurried away, while Miren gestured for Turion to sit.

"I *will* answer your questions," said Llyniel as she sat at the long table.

Miren pursed her lips, nodded, eyes moving between Llyniel's Bonding Braid and the tea she was preparing. "You have other more important tasks to see to. I understand that."

Llyniel recognised the phrase. Miren had said that to her father many times. It must have taxed their relationship, yet still, they had remained together, and she respected that.

Those five minutes of silence were the most awkward Llyniel could remember. She had crossed great plateaus, navigated a raging river, descended the Glistening Falls and sailed the Pelagian gulf. Now she sat, watching her mother make tea, not knowing what to say.

The door clicked open, and Llyniel flinched, turned to the door. A tall Alpine lord stood before them, breath a little too quick. He didn't acknowledge Turion but strode straight to the now standing Llyniel, all but crashing into her, taking her utterly by surprise. This time, though, Llyniel's answering embrace was not so tentative, not so cold.

"The Gods have blessed this day, child." A smile lit up the dour face, but it faltered when she spoke.

"Father. Sit. I know you both have questions and I will answer them, but there are priorities. I need urgent help. *We* need urgent help."

Aradan's eyes rested on Turion, eyes widening. "Tell me you have found them, Turion."

The captain answered with a soft smile. "They are waiting below, for a safe passage inside."

Aradan swayed backwards. "You *found* them!"

Turion nodded, and Aradan closed his eyes in relief. He turned back to Llyniel. "But how? How is it that *you* are here, daughter?"

What to say? It was all so unlikely. Still, she knew her father had heard some things in his time and so, as she often did, she opted for the simplest explanation.

"I travelled to Tar'eastór from Pelagia. I met Handir and decided to come back with him."

Aradan was still processing her words, his eyes on her Bonding Braid, but Turion bent forwards. "Aradan. We need to get the others here so that we can report to the king. We have news, vital information that can help. Tell me the votes have not yet taken place."

"They have not, but ..." Aradan sighed, and Turion frowned. "Turion. There was an ambush. The king is missing, and Rinon rules in his stead."

"*What?*" Turion stepped forward and Aradan raised his hands for silence.

"Band'orán is blaming it on the Silvans, and the Alpine people are turning on them. This is the beginning of his final move for the throne. He is pitting Alpine against Silvan, creating chaos so as to tax Rinon beyond his experience and control, so that he can step in and deliver the nation, take the crown."

"When did this happen?"

"Over a week ago."

"And Huren has nothing? Some clue, some trail ..."

"The prince doesn't trust Huren. He has not called for him since the ambush."

"What? Why? And *you*?"

"I have my suspicions."

Turion's eyes were stuck on Aradan, mind racing. "I must speak with Rinon. Aria forbid, but from the outside, this sounds like ..."

"A coup. Yes."

Turion turned, put a hand to his head and walked around the table. He strode back to his friend's heavy eyes. "There are dangerous times ahead, Aradan. Perhaps even more dangerous than our journey from Port Helia. But I will be at your side, see the king returned, whatever it takes. There is no time to lose. Take me to Rinon."

The councillor turned to Llyniel, sorry eyes searching her face, lingering on the Bonding Braid. This was the story of his relationship with Llyniel, exemplified to perfection. Duty to king, before duty to family. But where once she would have stared at him with rebellious eyes, now she smiled.

Aradan frowned. Did she understand at last? That he loved her more than life? He startled when next she spoke.

"Father. I am coming with you."

Aradan raised his eyebrows, but Turion nodded. He had accompanied the group from Port Helia, but only she could tell them what had transpired in Tar'eastór.

∼

R<small>INON SAT</small> at his father's desk, hunched over a map of the area outside the gates, towards the eastern foothills. He didn't look up at the knock on the doors. "Come," he called absently.

"Prince."

"Aradan," he murmured, only half-aware that the advisor had company. He sat back, drew a hand over his weary eyes and turned.

He shot out of his chair and in two strides he was before Turion. Tangled blond hair, dirty clothes and tired, but the captain had returned and hope blazed in Rinon's eyes for the first time in days—hope and confusion, because Llyniel was beside the captain.

"I found them."

Two strong hands clapped him on the shoulders. "I knew it. Knew you wouldn't fail me. And you ..."

"Nut head," said Llyniel, a sly smile ever so fleeting.

Rinon pursed his lips, resisting the temptation to reply to the odious childhood name. And then his eyes rested on her braid. "It's not Handir, is it?" he murmured, only for her. She shook her head minutely. Rinon turned to the side table, relieved, and then poured a generous goblet of wine for them all. "Has Aradan told you, Turion?"

"Of the king, yes." Turion took his goblet from the prince and drank deeply. Only then did he sit as Rinon gestured to the chairs before the hearth.

"Where are the others?"

"Waiting in the springs. We thought it best they not be seen."

"Handir's idea," guessed Rinon. "And he's right. It works in our favour. Who has come?"

"Handir, Pan'assár and Gor'sadén are at the springs."

"Lord Gor'sadén? Of The Three?" He sat up, leaned towards Turion.

"An emissary from King Vorn'asté, and Fel'annár's Kah Master, I believe."

"How did he achieve that?" he muttered, sitting back. "And where is the Silvan?"

"We were set upon, not a day from the city. We were cornered, and he led the enemy away so that Pan'assár could get us to the gates. We believe he is at the Silvan encampment."

"What? Gods, no. That is not what we need." Rinon was on his feet again, thinking and drinking, listening to Turion.

"He knows to try to keep his identity a secret until we can coordinate our efforts. I believe he will achieve that."

"I am not so sure. With Angon locked away, the Silvans are angry, just as angry as the Alpines towards them for supposedly killing our warriors and abducting the king. The people clamour for justice. They want the Silvan leaders in our dungeons, Turion."

"We need to get the others up here. Handir has urgent news—good news—but if we cannot find the king, it will all have been for nothing."

Rinon banged his goblet on the low table. He turned to Turion and then Llyniel. "We will find him. Never doubt that, captain."

"He may be dead, prince." Turion said it carefully, slowly rising from his chair.

It was Aradan who answered. "If it had been Band'orán's intention to kill the king, he would have made it known. Why draw this out? With the king gone and no evidence to incriminate him, he would move to the next stage of his plan: try Rinon's inexperience."

"And none of us thought he would be so bold as to abduct the king himself," continued Rinon. "We know Band'orán has to have him. What we don't know is where and why he has not killed him."

Turion placed his own goblet on the table, straightening his crumpled tunic. "I will bring Prince Handir. Can the guards be trusted?"

"Who can say in these times?" Rinon stepped up to the captain, smiled curtly. "Turion."

"Prince."

"You have served well. When this is over and my father restored on his throne, I would have you by our side. I would have you as our general."

Turion didn't smile, despite the honour Rinon bestowed upon him. Instead, he felt grief, deep sorrow for how it had come to this. He wondered, then, if any of this mess could be mended; whether anything could return to what it had once been. But then he caught Rinon's fiery gaze. His doubts dissolved, something tightened in his chest and his mind focussed.

He saluted his fellow captain, bowed to his prince and in his eyes, a pledge to the future king of Ea Uaré.

PAIN SHOT through Fel'annár's shoulder, and he held back a gasp behind shaking lips. Water sloshed in a bowl. Sontúr's hand squeezed the herb-laced cloth and cleaned the wound that bled sluggishly.

His tattered shirt lay in a heap beside him where he sat upon a stool in nothing but his breeches and boots. A fire had been lit at the centre of the tent, and around it, The Company sat, seeing to their own cuts and bruises. Farón's closest had come and gone with clean linen shirts for them, but for now, the prince worked in silence on the injury. It was nothing in comparison to what he had had to mend before.

With his shoulder finally wrapped in bandages, Fel'annár stood slowly. The ache of barely healed bones and bruising became deeper now that he could rest. Reaching for the clean shirt, he slung it over his back, too late to hide his scars from Farón, who stood in the doorway.

"The Council would speak with you."

Fel'annár nodded. He turned to The Company, eyes landing on Idernon and Sontúr, beckoning them to follow. Tensári slid her blades into the harness on her back, adjusting the bandage around her right hand, and joined them.

With their hoods once more in place, Farón ducked out of the tent and led the four elves to where Erthoron and his closest advisors waited in the next tent, holding the flap open for them to enter.

Inside, Narosén, Lorthil, Erthoron and Amareth stood talking quietly amongst themselves while Captain Dalú stood at a table, staring down at a map. Fel'annár slid his hood back and waited.

The Silvan captain looked up, gasped, and then turned away as if blinded by the sun. Breathing deeply, he stepped closer, slowed when Tensári's hand moved to the pommel of her dagger.

"My king?"

Fel'annár thought the warrior's voice would crack, but still, he moved closer to the fire, more carefully now and with one eye on Tensári.

"I ... I saw you fall," he murmured, head shaking in denial. "I mourned your passing, lost my will to serve. I saw you *fall*." He scowled into Fel'annár's face and flinched when he spoke.

"I am not Or'Talán, Captain. I am Fel'annár."

Dalú nodded, stepped back. His brown eyes travelled from Fel'annár's scuffed boots to his mass of silver hair and then shook his head. "They said you were dead, or perhaps that you didn't care …"

"I am alive. And I care. They have *lied* to you."

Dalú's eyes flitted from one side of Fel'annár's face to the other. "It all started with Or'Talán. And now, perhaps, it will end with him, too. With his blood. Gods, but surely *he* was unique." Dalú's eyes flickered wide as they inspected the face, so familiar, even after all this time. "Welcome, then, Aren Or'Talán." He dared take a step closer. "See if you can make sense of this mess. See if you can sort it, lad." Dalú stared a while longer and then straightened his crooked form as best he could.

The Silvan leader stepped forward. "Fel'annár."

"Erthoron," he replied, purposefully omitting his title.

Lorthil cocked a brow at the overly familiar address, but he said nothing.

"Will you tell us what is going on. Who you travelled with? Where they are?"

"And what happened in the forest?" added Narosén.

Erthoron held up a hand for silence. "Fel'annár. The warlord vote is imminent. The Royal Council convenes the day after, and Angon, one of our best warriors, is in the dungeons, falsely accused of killing four warriors and abducting the king. We have sent messengers into the city, have told Prince Rinon that it was not us."

"It's true, then. The king has been abducted." He didn't seem surprised.

"Four killed. Conveniently close to our camp. The Alpines are raking the forest for any signs of him, and they blame us."

"Has the prince not answered your messages?"

"He has, but all he says is that he will see justice done. He tells us to wait. But wait for what? We have been waiting for days!"

"Lord," said Idernon, glancing at Fel'annár as he stepped forward. "I would suggest it is related to the expectations of his people. They must be angry. We must, perhaps, assume that he is waiting for the best time, either to investigate or release Angon. This may seem callous, but with the king missing, he surely has priorities."

Fel'annár nodded at the logic of it, impressed at how Idernon's words seemed to calm Erthoron. With Pan'assár back, he would surely lead the search parties himself, and Gor'sadén would accompany him. They would surely come here.

"Are our people searching for the king?" asked Fel'annár.

"Not actively. Besides, it's clear to us that this was done by his own people. Wherever he is, he is not in the forest."

Fel'annár stared hard at Erthoron, not sure that he liked the tone of his voice. "You can't know that," he said, watching for a reaction to his words, and finding it. "Still, you happen to be right about him not being in the forest. I would know."

He felt Erthoron's eyes on him, following him. "But then perhaps none of this will matter soon. Prince Handir has something that may help us be rid of Band'orán. He may be able to accuse him of high treason."

"What are you talking about? How could you possibly know ...?"

"I travelled here with Prince Handir, Prince Sontúr here present, and Commanders Pan'assár and Gor'sadén." Fel'annár ignored the sharp intakes of breath and pushed forward, as succinctly as he could. "We have written evidence that Lord Sulén conspired to kill me, apparently at the behest of Band'orán. Prince Handir will strive to discredit him before the council, enough for the vote to swing in our favour. However, before we move on him in earnest, we must find the king. If we push him too hard, he may do the unthinkable."

"If the king is not already dead," said Amareth.

Fel'annár nodded, but closed his mind to the consequences, to his own feelings on the matter.

"Even if we had a chance with the Royal Council vote, Pan'assár will never agree to a Warlord," said Erthoron.

"He will."

Erthoron shared a confused glance with his Silvan companions. "How? He is ..."

"He is a Purist. Doesn't give a damn for his Silvan fighters," said Dalú.

"All that has changed, Captain. Believe me. Things have changed."

Dalú didn't believe him. Fel'annár could see it in his eyes. But it was Lorthil who spoke. "What are the prince and commander of Tar'eastór doing here?"

It was a fair question, but he wasn't going to explain the more personal nature of his Master's task. It was Sontúr who stepped forward and answered.

"I travel at my father's behest, as his emissary. Our commander general must share vital intelligence with your king. I am here to show your people that King Vorn'asté stands beside King Thargodén."

Erthoron stared back at him, mind working furiously. "Your father's support for the king works in our favour, and this evidence you speak of ... perhaps there is at least a chance, although it may be too late for Thargodén. For now, we will make our plans for the investiture tomorrow morning."

"What investiture, lord?" asked Idernon.

The Silvan council stared at Fel'annár, at the prince on his left and the warriors on his right and behind. "Did you think we would wait for the Alpines to vote against the Warlord?" said Amareth. "We have our own Council, representatives of the noble houses of old. It is decided. They will it or no, you will be our Warlord. Tomorrow."

Whether they will it or no. *And what of me?* thought Fel'annár. They had not asked him, as he knew they wouldn't. Anger surged from the depths. They didn't care about what happened in the city. They didn't care about the king, whether he lived or died. But then, why should they? he asked himself. Why should *he*? But he *did*.

"I won't be here."

"You must be," Erthoron stated back at him.

"I know it is a lot to take in," began Amareth.

"Don't." Fel'annár tried once more to quell his mounting anger. It wasn't the moment for reproach.

"Fel'annár," said Erthoron, stepping forward.

"*Lord* Fel'annár. We are not sitting together under the eaves of the schoolhouse or standing at the baker's ovens. We are not a child and an elf I looked up to. We are strangers who have changed. I am a lieutenant and you ... are a *liar*."

Amareth stepped towards him. "We are *all* liars. Every one of us lied to you. We kept the truth from you, confiscated the books you could not read, begged your family to stay away. And I justify those lies, cruel though they were. You see, death is crueller, Fel'annár."

Fel'annár stared long at the elf he had always called 'mother'. He believed her, but there were other reasons for their deception. "You were protecting me, yes. So that they would not kill me. So that you could have your Warlord. You never asked me. You never considered me in all this."

Erthoron glanced at Amareth, but she did not acknowledge it. "It was always your destiny, Fel'annár."

"I know that now," he murmured as he walked towards her slowly. He did know, had understood his dreams, had heard Hobin's words. "The question is, how did *you* know?"

He had left her at a loss for words. She still had secrets, and he wondered if she would ever tell them. Her next words surprised him. "I *will* answer your questions. There is no longer any reason to remain silent. But bear with us. Tomorrow, when you are Warlord, and while the realm searches for its king, I will tell you everything I know."

"I told you. I won't be here, Amareth. As a warrior of this realm, it is my sworn duty to protect the king. The Company and I will be out searching. Only then can there be closure. When the king is found, and Handir exposes Band'orán, only then can we have our own representatives on the Council, have our Warlord. Those are *my* priorities, and once that is done, I will thank you kindly for telling me why you did not tell me all this before I left for novice training. Why you threw me into the Deviant horde without warning me that I would be recognised, that others would know who I was before I *myself* did. So you can save your clever words of what is cruel and what is crueller. There are many forms of cruelty."

Amareth stood shocked, but Fel'annár was angry. Even now, she could not admit her fault. "Postpone what you must. The king must be found. We leave tomorrow morning."

Dalú stepped forward. "You must take more warriors with you. Eight is not enough to confront whatever Band'orán has standing between the king and you."

"We will move quicker this way. We can scout, bring back news."

"So can others."

"Not like us."

Dalú hesitated, then spoke again. "You mustn't engage, lord. You don't have the numbers."

Fel'annár stared at the captain, wondered if he was remembering the Battle Under the Sun and how the king had been outnumbered. "It is not my intention to engage, Captain."

The Silvan leaders stood silent. With their plans dashed and their hopes doused, all they could do was watch as Fel'annár nodded, turned and left with a Silvan warrior, an Alpine prince and the Ari'atór who always seemed to be behind him.

Farón held the tent flap open for them and then stepped inside. Narosén turned to him. "Farón. About what happened in the forest …"

He shook his head. "I don't know."

"Your best guess?" prompted Amareth.

Farón straightened. He knew they wouldn't believe him. "Magic." He saw their eyes flicker, saw the crease on one side of Narosén's mouth. Farón left.

There was something important he had to do.

HANDIR WALKED down the corridors that wound along the top floor of the palace, his home since birth. But he had never seen it like this. Dark, deserted. Turion told him what had happened, yet still, his mind had not come to terms with the implications, not entirely. Gods, but they had endured so much, only to arrive a week too late for the king. His father was in the hands of a madman, and panic welled in his chest.

Turion walked ahead, opened the double doors and there, before the wall of shutters, where the king should have been, was Rinon: strong, still crowned a prince, a fire in his eyes that was entirely his mercurial brother. Handir was filthy, dusty, must have looked like some refugee from the northern wastelands, but he didn't care.

Rinon held out his arms and Handir stepped into them. He felt them, strong around his back, squeezing, and his own aching limbs answered. He had made it—down a river and across the sea to the cliffs; through the woods, quite literally. He had not embraced his brother like this for many years.

"Come," was all Rinon said. The two brothers led the way, followed by Pan'assár, Gor'sadén and Turion. Behind them all, Aradan stared as he closed the doors, eyes trained on the legendary Lord Gor'sadén of The Three.

Handir made for Llyniel, held her at arm's length and then embraced her. No words, only relief. Aradan watched them carefully, wondering if they had finally come together as he always thought they would—as he had always wanted them to. But there was something brotherly in that embrace, and there was no Bonding Braid in the prince's hair – not that he was Silvan. No, she had not bonded with Handir.

Rinon tugged on a cord beside the hearth that led all the way down to the lower floor and the kitchens, while Aradan poured wine and handed a goblet to Handir, concerned eyes roving over his tattered clothes and matted hair. The prince reached for it and drank, the smell and taste of wood and spices bringing memories of family in this very room. He watched as Gor'sadén was introduced, his brother's curious eyes that turned cautious and wary when they landed on Pan'assár. The commander bowed low.

"I have questions, Commander. Questions which must wait until the king is returned." Rinon's eyes lingered on Pan'assár, then drifted to Gor'sadén, only to meet Handir's tired eyes.

Handir reached into his filthy tunic and pulled out what used to be scrolls, now folded, creased and stained. "These were left in my chambers in Tar'eastór. Missives from home that never arrived, that kept us in the dark about what was happening here. Amongst them is an unfinished letter from Lord Sulén Ar Ileian to an unknown lord we are sure is Band'orán. This missive led us to search Sulén's residence. There, we found further evidence that shows Sulén was sworn to this lord in return for the lands of Oran'Dor."

Rinon listened. He made to ask his first question, but Handir had not finished.

"It is possible that Sulén may have said something to Band'orán about his missing correspondence, sent some such message after the event, telling him of his failure to kill Fel'annár. Whichever the case, he fled Tar'eastór, coming here, or so we thought. But we cannot ask him. He is dead, slaughtered by Deviants." Handir did not say how the bodies had been beheaded and hung from the trees. It was something they would need to discuss later when the king had been found.

Rinon paced as he listened to Handir, while Aradan watched his apprentice carefully, observed his hands and the way he moved, registered his words and his tone of voice.

"I believe Sulén prepared for our return, that he foresaw our route back. Mercenaries and shadows hounded our journey, from Senge and to the town of Bulls Bay. But that was only the beginning. Whether at Sulén's continued behest or Band'orán's, the persecution became inescapable as we entered the forest. We were separated, but still, Fel'annár lives and Band'orán may already know that."

Aradan stepped forward, let out a heavy breath. They needed to trace a plan. He faltered when Handir continued to speak.

"This is what I think we should do. I propose that we continue with the votes, which gives us two days. The Inner Circle will impede the return of the Warlord, but this can be proclaimed null later when the truth is out. But the Royal Council must be balanced. A skewed government will be tantamount to a coup. Our king will have no power to rule, even if he can return, and for that matter, neither will you, brother. I must call Band'orán out at that council and pray that you find the king before that happens. If I succeed and Band'orán is stopped, there is no telling whether he will cooperate and tell us where the king is. Perhaps the promise of a kinder sentence will loosen his tongue."

"And if we don't find him?" asked Rinon. "What then?"

"Then you will be our king, Rinon."

The two brothers looked at each other, aware of the implications. Rinon's eyes rebellious, Handir's heavy. "And what of the bas—of Fel'annár."

Llyniel bristled from where she stood at the fire. "*Fel'annár* is well, safe at the Silvan encampment."

Aradan arched an eyebrow and then turned back to Rinon as he spoke. "I will ride out again tomorrow. Commander, you will accompany me to the Silvan camp with Angon, speak with Erthoron, garner his cooperation if we can. Our Alpine people expect us to take drastic action against the Silvans, but in all conscience, we cannot do that. I do not believe they killed those warriors or abducted the king, but our Alpine people *do*. Our Alpine *warriors* do. I hope the boy has the sense to stay out of sight."

"He will. The Silvans will see to that," said Handir. "But who is this Angon?"

"Angon has been causing trouble for months, harassing our merchants, turning them away from the forest. He is accused of abducting the king, killing his guards."

"And did he?"

"No. No, this is Band'orán's work, I am sure of it. I have investigated the case. The arrows used to kill his retinue were unlikely to have been Angon's. I have spoken to him, struck a bargain of sorts. He will help us to search for the king and in return, his freedom, and my promise of equality, of the return of the Warlord."

"If he is a simple warrior, what makes you so sure Erthoron will listen to him? Agree to join the search?"

"Angon has a following. The Silvans are furious with us for withholding him, just as Band'orán knew that they would be."

Handir turned for a moment, processing the information.

"Prince. What of General Huren? Is he coordinating the search?" asked Pan'assár.

"No, Commander. I have told him to steer clear of it. We had a ... confrontation. He knows I am displeased with him."

Pan'assár scowled. "Surely you do not question him? His integrity?"

Rinon narrowed his eyes. "Oh, I question it, Commander. And I wonder what you would say to that. You, who confided in him, made him general."

Pan'assár's nostrils flared, upper lip twitching. "You *wonder*, Prince? You dare question *my* loyalty?"

"I am curious that you did not notice anything out of the ordinary. I told you I have questions, Commander. But they must wait. For now, I am placing my tentative trust in you."

Pan'assár lifted his head and looked down his nose at the prince. Then his eyes strayed to Gor'sadén, looked away.

"But you *are* searching for him?" asked the commander, quieter now.

"Yes. I am seeing to it myself. I have searched Analei, Band'orán's residence. Better, perhaps, to say I all but ripped it apart. The king is not there. We have searched everywhere. Still, if I can convince Erthoron, with Angon's help, it is one more chance. Perhaps the last." Rinon's eyes rested coolly on Pan'assár. "I *am* glad you are here, Commander, in spite of my concerns."

Pan'assár nodded at Rinon, turned back to Handir.

"Then we have a plan. At first light, Prince Rinon leaves with Commander Pan'assár and Angon. They make for the Silvan camp and recruit Lord Erthoron's cooperation. You must also ensure that they do not proclaim the Warlord. Fel'annár's presence must remain a secret until those votes, or at least until the king is found. We must keep Band'orán guessing. Once we have Erthoron's help, we proclaim that Fel'annár stayed in Tar'eastór, under the protection of King Vorn'asté.

"Meanwhile, I need to take stock of Band'orán himself—where he is, what he is doing, who he speaks with. Turion, I would have you here. I need your eyes at the Inner Circle while Prince Rinon is away." He breathed deeply, turned full circle. "We have come this far, so far. We cannot fail now, however dire the odds may seem. We go on with our plan firmly in mind. We find the king, we expose Band'orán, and we rebuild this land."

Rinon stood tall, hopeful eyes turning to Aradan, seeing his own feelings reflected there. The chief advisor stared, wide-eyed and open-mouthed. But his gaze was misty, and his nostrils flared, not in anger but pride—pride for the quiet prince who had ventured to the motherland and returned a statesman.

A leader.

BAND'ORÁN HAD BROUGHT with him a tray of food and drink, fit for kings. It stood upon the cool stone floor between them. Thargodén watched as his uncle's steady hand poured the wine into two goblets. He gestured with his other hand.

"You choose. It's not poisoned."

He picked one up, watched as Band'orán picked up the other and toasted. Ignoring it, he drank, waiting for the story to continue, praying that it would. He needed to know, had always needed to understand that his father had loved him, had not sacrificed him for the greater good.

"Ah, but it hurts, doesn't it, Thargodén? All that wondering why your own father would do such a terrible thing. Why he broke your heart..."

Thargodén watched as the once sharp, intelligent eyes of Band'orán turned hazy, lost their focus. He was in the past once more. "He broke mine, too."

Thargodén didn't understand, wondered if he should shake Band'orán from the past with questions. He waited and he drank.

"There is strength in identity. You can move worlds with the power of pride, of land and king, the pride of culture and homeland. I created my own culture, one in which Alpines would be great again."

"The Glory Days."

"Yes. Or'Talán reigned during those years, was loved for it, and then died. But before he did, I made sure it would be *me* to sit on his throne in the years to come. Not you."

Thargodén stared at his uncle. He placed his goblet on the floor beside his knee, dared not speak lest Band'orán leave again, leave him yearning for the full story. If he was to die down here—and he was sure that he would—then he would at least do so knowing why, perhaps knowing that his father had loved him.

"You are quiet, nephew. No questions?"

"I'm listening."

"Yes, of course." Band'orán smiled and stood. Thargodén resisted the urge to pull him back. "Eat up. It's good. I have matters to attend to. A Silvan to kill." The words slipped from his mouth so smoothly as if he spoke of cooking the midday meal.

"Band'orán ..."

"Why the worry? You have never even met him."

"He's my son." Thargodén couldn't help the pleading in his eyes. Nothing mattered at that moment. Everything Band'orán had done, his own pride, it didn't mean anything. All he wanted was for his uncle to heed him, not kill Fel'annár.

"How can you love him, Thargodén? Tell me. This boy, this symbol of your lost love. What if he is unworthy? He may not live up to your expectations. You should be glad I am getting rid of him for you before he can disappoint you."

"No." Thargodén smiled, shook his head. "He reminds me of what I had. I was bonded with Lássira, still am. In the eyes of the Silvans he is no bastard. He is the legitimate son of a king."

"Yes, yes. I do know that. And you search for Lássira in him. A little piece of your love in his eyes." Band'orán turned to the lady on the shore. "Just as I sought *her* in my own son, but never found her ..."

Thargodén was confused again. Band'orán was talking to Canusahéi ... and then everything fell into place. "You loved her, didn't you?" asked Thargodén. "You loved the woman that Father chose as my queen. You wish that Barathon had been *her* son."

Band'orán spun around, clothes and hair fanning around him, and his face spoke of murder. He strode towards Thargodén who still sat, looking up into that thunderous face. But then he stood slowly to face him.

"Why did Or'Talán not want Lássira as the future queen?"

"Because I told him to disallow it. I warned him, told him what would happen if he did."

A heavy cloak descended on Thargodén, as if some terrible doom awaited him at the end of Band'orán's words. "What ... would have happened if he had allowed it?"

"You would have been strong, too powerful with her at your side, and I would never have been king. I waited for Or'Talán's passing, knew I could never overthrow him, but you —with your broken heart and a queen you did not love. I had a chance. I *have* a chance."

"Why did he accept?"

Band'orán smiled. He cocked his head, anger sliding away, replaced by pride. "Because he was afraid that I would kill her." He stepped towards Thargodén, leaned into his face. "It was retribution that led your father to choose Canusahéi as your queen. She was the only one I ever loved, could ever love. Your father broke your heart to save her from death, and in return, broke mine. And so you see, in time, I had to kill Lássira."

Tears pooled in Thargodén's eyes. He had always suspected Band'orán's hand in her death, but he had never understood why. Through his crushing grief, a question wiled its way out of his mouth. "Why didn't you kill the child?"

It was a good question. Band'orán remembered how his envoy had reported the events. He said he had killed the mother, and the babe in her arms. His eyes sharpened, turned back to his captive. "That was the plan. Someone lied to me, but I did not come to realise until fifty-two years later. He paid the price for his cowardice."

"Until a boy with the face of Or'Talán joined our armed forces as a novice. How it must irk you, Band'orán, that he should look like your brother."

Band'orán straightened, stared for a while and almost seemed to nod to himself. "You know, perhaps I will allow you to see him before the end. Despite what you may think, this is not personal. I do not wish for your death, do not enjoy your suffering. It is simply necessary. As for the boy, though. He is proof of my failure and bears the face of one I both loved and hated. Yes, I may allow you to see him, but I do not vouch for my actions."

The gaze lingered, slid into a smile, and then he turned, composed once more.

Thargodén felt cold from the stone beneath him and the mounting dread in his heart, in his mind. The Gods forbid Band'orán ever got his hands on Fel'annár. The Gods forbid they meet here, in this place, where a madman ruled. A madman who would be king of Ea Uaré.

17

UNBEARABLE BURDEN

"The things we do to protect. Whether for love or duty, perhaps both. Amareth broke her dwindling family, shattered the trust that had once bound them together. All that was left was the fading hope that they would understand. She had done it for her people. She had done it for love. She had not done it for Fel'annár."
The Silvan Chronicles, Book IV. Marhené

∽

"How did it go?" asked Ramien, handing Fel'annár a plate of cheese and freshly baked bread. A goblet of wine followed.

"We've told them what they need to know, about the evidence and Handir's intentions. But it seems the trees were right; the king has been abducted."

"*What?*" Galadan was on his feet.

"He and his retinue were ambushed. The Alpines are searching for him day and night. I would join them."

"When do we leave?"

"Tomorrow."

"I am coming with you." Farón stood in the doorway, and Fel'annár invited him in with a tilt of his head. "Lord. I am aware of the circumstances, know the land well."

"It's not necessary, Farón."

"But how will you know where to search? I know every cave, every hidden glade, every corner of these parts. I can help."

So did the trees, mused Fel'annár. He didn't need Farón, but the warrior was adamant. "I am a good scout, a good warrior, one of Lainon's pupils," he tried, faltering when he saw Fel'annár's eyes flicker, saw Tensári's head turn. "What is it?" asked Farón.

"Lainon crossed the Veil. He has found himself in Valley."

Farón stared back at Fel'annár, then nodded slowly and breathed deeply. "I will miss him. I have fond memories."

"We all do."

It was a while before anyone spoke.

"Farón. We will need horses, basic provisions, arrows. Can you provide them?"

"I can. I have been assigned to your safety, lord, but I will ensure those things are ready for us at first light." He nodded and left the tent.

Galadan turned to Fel'annár. "So, what's the plan?"

"We find the place where the king was taken. The trees may tell us something. If they do and we have some clue as to his whereabouts, then we come back and plan our way forward. Take some of these warriors, perhaps."

"What of the Elders? What do they think of this plan?" asked Galdith.

"They meant to make me Warlord in spite of the Inner Circle."

"What did you say?" asked Ramien.

"I said no. They wanted to do it tomorrow morning, while the king is still out there."

"You disobeyed the Council?" asked Galdith, quite unnecessarily.

"They weren't pleased," said Idernon from behind them. "They've been waiting for this since the start of the Forest Summit."

"Then they can wait a few more days, Idernon. There are priorities."

"Perhaps. But unifying our people is one of them. We need a military leader to keep us all together. Angon is locked away, and his followers are surely planning something that Erthoron won't like. We need unity, and we don't have it. And once the Warlord vote is made known ... I don't believe these people will stay quiet about that. Erthoron will have his hands full."

Galdith nodded. "He's right."

"I know. Still, it will have to wait. The king must be found and delivered safely. If Band'orán kills him, there will be war, whether I am Warlord or not. Besides, this is a scouting mission. I just need to find where the king was taken, listen to the trees. Once the king is found, I won't object."

He turned away from them, in part so that he could order his own thoughts. But it was also so that Idernon would not see his eyes. He hadn't lied. There were priorities, and a ceremony now meant revealing himself to the entire camp. Band'orán would find out soon after, and Fel'annár had promised Handir to wait for instructions. And then, of course, there was the nagging voice in his mind.

They never once thought of me.

THE COUNCIL OF ELDERS sat at the fire, flames dancing in their eyes. Narosén threw his tokens on the ground once more, finger hovering over them.

"Whatever I expected, it was not this," murmured Erthoron.

"He is not the same elf, that is for sure," confirmed Lorthil. "Aye, we knew he was a Listener, but what Farón said today ... there is something we do not know. Did you not notice anything when he was a child, Amareth? Did you never suspect he had powers?"

The flames flickered over her face, eyes unblinking. "I did not suspect," she said quietly. "I *knew*. I always knew."

Narosén straightened, shrewd eyes moving between Amareth and Erthoron, the two elves who knew Fel'annár the best as a child.

"*How* did you know?" asked Lorthil carefully. Narosén twirled a token between his fingers.

She breathed deeply and pulled her gaze away from the comforting fire. It landed for a moment on Narosén and then fell on Lorthil. "His eyes shone from the inside for the first seven days of his life. He was Ari, in spite of his appearance. Lássira took him away, into the Deep Forest, to protect him."

Her words were met with silence until Erthoron broke it. "We knew then that by some strange quirk of nature, Fel'annár was Ari'atór. It seemed to us that if Aria had made him pale, it was to hide that fact."

"And if Aria wished to hide it, there was a purpose, a reason." Narosén nodded in understanding.

"Did you see him, Erthoron? Did you see the lord? The leader? Our Warlord—the one who will unite this broken forest?" Amareth's eyes were alive, burning with pride.

"He doesn't want that. He may never accept it."

"He will. He understands the need for unity. But he doesn't understand why I did the things I did."

"Then go to him. Explain," Lorthil began. "Our people will not be held back for much longer, not by us. We need to show them that Fel'annár is here, that he will lead our warriors and stand for what the Silvan Council rules."

"He won't change his mind, Lorthil. But I will speak with him. And when he's back from this scouting mission of his, I believe he will agree."

Something clicked and thudded onto the ground. Narosén leaned forward. Pieces of carved bone were strewn over the floor around him. He looked up, to Amareth and then to Erthoron. "There is a Guiding Light in Tensári. She is Divine Protector, Ber'ator."

It was half the truth, enough to startle Amareth and raise her suspicions. She had known some destiny awaited her sister's child, but surely Narosén was not implying what he seemed to be. "Are you sure?" Her voice wavered.

The Ari turned to her, studied her face for a moment. "As sure as I am that there is guilt in your heart. As sure as I am that you never meant to hurt him."

She nodded, and started when Narosén spoke once more. "But you did."

Amareth pursed her lips, turning away. She had spent a lifetime justifying what she had done, to her family in Abiren'á, to Fel'annár ... to herself. But perhaps it was time to admit that she had not always been right, admit that she had underestimated those who would have helped, family that would have shared the almost unbearable burden of lying to a child.

Lorthil breathed after what seemed too long, even for an immortal. "Beloved Aria."

Erthoron smiled quietly, watching Amareth as she struggled with herself. When Fel'annár had been fifteen, he, too, had pleaded with her to tell the boy of his family. Not of the king, but his family in Abiren'á. Alei and Bulan. But Amareth had never wavered in her beliefs, and Erthoron had supported her all that time. She was Aren Zéndar. He trusted her as much as he had come to love her.

"I wonder, though. Does Fel'annár know? Does he know that he is Ber'anor?" asked Lorthil.

"He knows," said Narosén, sorting through his tokens with his index finger. One was carved with a sun, the other with an oak tree. "He knows."

THAT AFTERNOON, Llyniel sat perched upon a window seat, eyes fixed on the Silvan camp beyond the city walls. Her mother was behind her, sitting at a table and nursing a cup of steaming tea.

"I still remember how you would beg me to take you to Sen Garay to visit with your cousins." She stopped, eyes on the wood grain of the table, worn yet well-polished. "We hardly ever did. Your father needed us, needed our presence to anchor him. He has all but ruled these lands in the latter years of Thargodén's rule. The responsibility, the weight of it ..."

Llyniel listened. For the first time, she truly listened to what lay beneath her mother's words.

"It broke my heart, that pleading face of yours. So Silvan, and yet I kept you away from what you most loved. The forest, the trees. Your heritage. The Silver Wolf."

"You did it for love." Her voice was a soft murmur, a simple echo of the thoughts in her mind.

"Yes. But in doing so, I pushed you away, didn't I?"

"I didn't understand."

"And now? What has changed, Llyniel?"

She turned to her mother, but words wouldn't come. It was Fel'annár, her love for him that had changed, that allowed her to understand her mother's words.

"Come with me to the camp. Now. Let's go to the Silvan side." Miren didn't wait for her daughter's response, thought that perhaps she wouldn't answer. But she was accustomed to that. Whatever Llyniel decided, Miren needed to speak with Erthoron, warn him about tomorrow's visit.

"Now?" Llyniel frowned, pulled from her thoughts.

Miren shrugged. "It's still light, and the streets are quiet enough. Come with me, as we should have so many times in the past and never did. Aradan doesn't need me now. It's Rinon that needs him, and he will not be back this night."

Llyniel nodded, smiled tentatively, even though curiosity gnawed at her. Miren, meek wife of Aradan, would walk into the Silvan encampment just a few hours before sunset. She had been told of the riots, of the vandalism and the hatred that was growing by the day. What was she thinking?

Moments later, three cloaked figures left the palace, two bearing baskets and the other with a larger pack on his back.

"It's possible we are being followed," said Miren. "They do follow me sometimes, but they stay away from the camp."

"Why do they follow you?" asked Llyniel, eyes darting around.

"I am the Royal Councillor's wife."

Llyniel didn't understand why that would draw the enemy's attention, but Miren said nothing more and Bala turned, chanced a glance at Llyniel and remained silent.

They passed the gates. They would close at sundown and, should they wish to return, they would be forced to identify themselves. But Llyniel had no intention of returning tonight, so they pressed on until the first Silvan guards came into sight. Llyniel stiffened, realising they would be stopped. Indeed, Miren stood still, and Llyniel watched as she pulled her hood away just a little. The guard nodded and stepped aside. Llyniel realised her mother knew exactly where she was going. She scowled.

"You've been here before."

"Many times, yes."

She wanted to ask more, but the camp was too much of a distraction. This was nothing short of a forest town. The familiar smells of yeast and cheese, of resins and honey cakes, filled the air. Her Silvan blood pulsed in her veins. She wanted to reach out to these people, embrace them, but above all else, she wanted to see Fel'annár.

"You've missed this. However much I tried to make of you a lady in an Alpine court, you were never that. You are Llyniel, Lady of the Silver Wolf of Sen Garay."

Llyniel smiled. She liked that a lot better.

They came to a large, circular tent. Bala stepped forward and whispered to the guard who stood at its entrance. He disappeared, and soon returned to hold open the flap. They stepped inside.

"Lady Miren. You come on the dawn of decision. What news?" Lord Erthoron stepped out of the gloom and nodded respectfully at Miren, turning then to Llyniel. He cocked his head to one side.

"This is Lady Llyniel. My daughter."

Erthoron smiled. "A pleasure, lady. Your mother has been of great assistance to the Silvan cause these past months. Is there news, Miren?"

"Oh, yes. There is news." She smiled, nodded, and accepted Erthoron's invitation to sit.

Her mother was a spy.

Llyniel stood and listened as Miren told Erthoron about how Rinon didn't believe that Angon was responsible for the deaths or for the king's disappearance. She told him how he planned to visit tomorrow, bringing Angon with him. He would search for the king himself, she said, and Handir hoped young Fel'annár would stay in the shadows.

Erthoron asked questions, which she answered, telling them of the missives Prince Handir meant to use to discredit Band'orán. As they spoke, Llyniel's eyes wandered to the elf beside Erthoron. A distant memory of a village far north. This was Lorthil, she realised, and so the Ari'atór was Narosén. But the woman in the corner she did not recognise until Miren turned to her and smiled.

"You must be overjoyed at the return of your son, lady."

Amareth's smile was sparing. "I am. There hasn't been much time to talk. Their journey has been a difficult one."

"Well, yes, judging by the state Llyniel here was in when they arrived. She journeyed with them, you see."

Amareth nodded slowly, and Llyniel couldn't find it within herself to be cross with Miren.

"You must have many adventures to tell," said Amareth, curious eyes resting on Llyniel, on her Bonding Braid.

"I do. Your son is an extraordinary elf, lady."

Amareth's smile was wider now, but Llyniel had seen the conflict in her gaze, knew a little of Fel'annár's upbringing. And the Gods knew she had her own family issues to resolve. The thought of her mother as a coward suddenly seemed absurd to her now as she looked about the tent. The maps and the plans, all hanging on her words. And then she realised that her father must surely know about it. Miren loved Aradan far too much to deceive him like this. How long had they been helping the Silvan people this way?

Miren finished her report, and Amareth extended an invitation for them to stay for the evening meal. Miren accepted, but Llyniel politely declined, much to the surprise of her mother. She just wanted to see Fel'annár, be with The Company again. She had become one of them, had shared so many events with them.

She missed them, even Pan'assár.

Erthoron directed her to the tent beside theirs, and with a humble bow, she left with Miren on her heels.

"Will you not dine with our leaders?"

"I have friends here, Mother."

"Oh," she said, following Llyniel to the tent. She watched as her daughter spoke with the guard.

"I want to see The Company."

The Silvan guard looked down at her. "Who?"

A head appeared through the half-open flap. "Us. The Company. Llyniel!"

"Ramien!"

It felt like a decade since she had last seen the Wall of Stone, and Miren watched keenly as Llyniel disappeared, wrapped in a mountain of muscle. Ramien stepped back, nodded and pulled her in. He spared a calculating glance at Miren as he disappeared inside.

She followed.

And then she faltered, mid-step, mid-thought. There, before her, standing tall, was Or'Talán, returned from battle victorious, not dead. The mighty king held out his arms, drew Llyniel to him and kissed her fiercely, arms entwined, hands roving.

She backed away, out of the tent, and returned to the command tent. She opened her mouth to speak but couldn't. Miren was speechless for the first time in her immortal life.

"What is it?" asked Amareth.

"Your son and my daughter ..."

"What about them?"

"They ... they know each other."

"Of course they ... do." Understanding hit just before finishing her sentence. Erthoron's eyebrows rose to his hairline, and Narosén's mouth was a perfect circle.

Fel'annár slept like a bear in winter. Turning onto his back, he realised he couldn't feel one arm, having slept with it over his head for so long. He lowered it to his side with the other, waiting for the pins and needles to pass. Sitting up with a groan, he found Tensári staring back at him, cross-legged on the floor.

"Have you slept at all?" he asked.

"Yes."

"Are you hungry?"

"Yes."

"Have you seen Llyniel?"

"Yes."

He scowled, frustrated at her monosyllabic responses. "Is that it?"

"Yes."

He rolled his eyes and got up, stretching and wincing. He pulled on his shirt and tunic, then collected two twisted locks from either side of his crown and tied off the rest in a high tail. They stuck up on either side, making him look more like an Ari than he ever had. Lainon would like that, he grinned to himself as he undid the clip Gor'sadén had gifted him with and fumbled with his Heliaré. He startled when Tensári smiled. It was, perhaps, the second time he had seen the gesture. He shook his head, in case he had imagined it. "I need to speak to Llyniel before we leave."

Slipping out of the tent, they passed Farón and three others who sat around a fire. They nodded as the two passed, watched as they made for Lady Amareth's tent where he knew Llyniel and Miren had spent the night.

Inside, Amareth sat cross-legged before the fire, a mug of steaming tea between her hands. She stood and walked over to Fel'annár. "Would you like some?"

"No, thank you."

"Will you walk with me?"

He glanced at Llyniel, who approached. "Can it wait?"

"It is important, Fel'annár."

He pursed his lips and glanced once more at Llyniel. She nodded, and he turned back to Amareth. "Of course."

"I will wait for you with The Company," said Llyniel. Fel'annár smiled at her and then left with Amareth.

They made for the tree line, past the last tents until they were alone. Tensári stood a respectful distance behind. Fel'annár felt the presence of another, too. It was Farón, charged with his security, and he did not mind, so long as he stayed far enough away. He gestured to the base of an oak, and they sat side by side, shoulder to shoulder. Fel'annár bent his knees, rested his elbows on them while Amareth's simple brown boots peeked out from under the hem of her dress.

"My father was Ari'atór. Perhaps he still is, across the veil." Amareth only half turned to Fel'annár, enough to know that he was not shocked as she thought he would be.

"Zéndar is alive, yes."

She shifted, faced him, eyes wide, brows furrowed.

"I spoke to Commander Hobin. I know what he was, who he served and how he died," explained Fel'annár.

She pursed her lips, tried to relax her shoulders. "I would have told you, that you have a grandmother and an uncle in Abiren'á."

"But you didn't. Not even when I was old enough to understand."

"No." She breathed deeply, collected her thoughts. "You were always a warrior. I always knew you were Ari, like your grandfather. But you see, it was clear to me that Aria wished to hide it. It made sense to assume there was a reason for that. I believe that, had I made it known, you would have been forced to travel to Araria with the other Ari children. That is their destiny. But it was never yours, Fel'annár."

"But you could have told me."

"I could have, but then you would have accepted that destiny. You would have gone to Araria. Tell me I'm wrong." Her honey eyes stared hard at him, challenged him to contradict her.

He said nothing.

"My mother, your grandmother, Alei, and her son —your uncle Bulan— had much to say of my decision. It has cost me their regard.

But Lássira charged *me* with your life, Fel'annár, not them. It was my decision to make. *I*, not *they*, had seen Band'orán's malice. I watched as the face of a child slowly changed into the face of a king. It was too dangerous. Band'orán would have found you."

"You have lived in fear of Band'orán all my life."

She frowned. "You make it sound frivolous, cowardly. But there was nothing cowardly about what I did. It broke my heart every time you asked me where your mother was, who your father was. Every time you pleaded, I ..."

She turned away, and Fel'annár watched her. He still didn't understand. If it wasn't cowardice, then what was it? "Did you think I couldn't keep that secret? That I wouldn't understand?"

"Yes. That is what I thought. You always wanted to know about your family, Fel'annár. It was your one wish, to know about your mother, about your father. I knew that, had I told you of them, you would have insisted on meeting them, and I couldn't allow that. You may think me overly careful, but Band'orán has many eyes in the forest, always has. He found Lássira. He would have found you."

"Even in Abiren'á? Or in Ea Nanú amongst the Giants? Would he have found me there?"

"That is what I thought. What I still think."

Fel'annár turned away from her. He breathed deeply and looked up into the boughs. "Am I a total stranger to them?"

"No. I managed to keep them away with the promise that I would speak to you of them when the time was right, and that I would keep them informed of your life. Our relationship suffered for it. My mother didn't agree with my silence, thought it unnecessary. She said the Ari of Abiren'á would protect you. I disagreed."

"And Bulan?"

"My brother is a warrior, was a captain who refused Pan'assár's call to duty. He serves in Abiren'á as a weapons master."

Fel'annár nodded slowly. "Master of what?"

Amareth smiled, turned back to the forest. "You and your weapons. I saw your bands, Fel'annár. Swords and the bow. And I see a Heliaré ... messy, though."

Fel'annár's lips twitched, but he held her gaze, wanted to know about Bulan.

"He is a Spears Master, not that he has many pupils now. It is a dying skill."

"Spears!" He turned away from her, mind reeling at the possibilities. "It runs in both sides of my family then," he murmured.

"So many things. My father's line is graced with many Ari'atór, while my mother's line is of the House of the White Oak. You are a great warrior, just like Zéndar and Bulan. Your eyes are your mother's, but your face ..." She huffed, shook her head. "It kindles love, garners hatred. It inspires *loyalty*." She smiled, but in her eyes was a plea. "Band'orán would have found you, and then he would have killed you, just as he did Lássira."

Fel'annár heard the words, let them settle. "How do you know that?"

She tried to comfort him with a look before she spoke the words, words she knew would unsettle him. "What do you know of Or'Talán? How much do you know of what happened?"

"Until recently, I thought him a monster. I thought he had forbidden my mother and father to wed, that he had broken their hearts because he was more concerned with the Alpine Purists than he was with his own son. But then, we found something. I am not sure of the details, but it seems that Or'Talán met Lássira at some point." He watched Amareth, searched for the signs that it was indeed so. He found them.

"He did. They met many times. He told her that Band'orán had threatened to kill her if she continued to see Thargodén. He told her that his prohibition was nothing more than a lie to a madman. He told her that he could not tell Thargodén this because Band'orán would realise. He knew it would cost his relationship with his son for a short time, but his life was more important. And then he told her to wait, to have faith. That he would fix it."

"But he was called to war."

"Yes.

"Dear Gods. I don't understand why he didn't tell his son the truth. He believes that his father betrayed him."

"He does. But until Band'orán is gone, he cannot know."

"He would kill him."

"Yes. Yes, he would, whatever the consequences, perhaps even his own execution."

"I spent so many nights damning my grandfather. Hating my own face because it was his. I hated it every time I was called Aren Or'Talán in Tar'eastór."

"He was a good king, Fel'annár. A good father and a great friend to Lássira. I hope that one day you will be proud to bear that name."

Fel'annár said nothing. Whatever he had thought to discover from Amareth, it was not this. His gaze drifted upwards, to the slowly lightening sky. "And now, his son is sitting in some prison, captive of that madman who killed my mother."

"You must bear this knowledge carefully, Fel'annár. This story, your story, will soon play out. No more secrets, no more hiding. Perhaps it is your purpose—to save the king, save our forest from war."

Was that all he was to her? A child she had promised to protect? An elf with a purpose, a duty to others?

"My purpose ..." He turned to her, *looked* at her. "Did you ever love me, Amareth? As a mother does a son? Or was it all for duty?"

Her eyes filled, but the tears would not come. He saw the hurt, and he saw resolve. He saw her steely defences and the spark of doubt in her eyes. But there was love there, too.

"When Lássira died, and I held you in my arms as your mother for the first time, I knew there was something special about you. Something I could not grasp. Just yesterday, a powerful Ari'atór revealed to me just what it was that I had always sensed, something just beyond my grasp. You see, I felt something, something I could never explain. Erthoron said it was because I was the daughter of an Ari'atór, the daughter of a Ber'ator ... that it made me more sensitive to the ways of Aria."

"What ... did Narosén say?" asked Fel'annár, head turned to her, watching.

"He says you are Ber'anor."

A breeze rustled the leaves, a sigh of relief.

"Do you believe that?"

"It makes sense, yes. You once told me you dreamt of a lady in the trees. You asked me if she was your mother. I knew that she wasn't because you said her eyes were blue. That was your Dream of Revelation, Fel'annár."

"Dream of Revelation?"

"For Zéndar, she was always upon the riverbank, hands raking through the sand. When he was old enough to travel to Araria for training, he met Hobin."

"His Ber'anor."

She startled. "Yes." She turned away, pursed her lips. "Tensári is your Ber'ator?"

"Yes."

"Does anyone know about this?"

"The Company, Gor'sadén, my Connate."

"Llyniel?" She chanced a smile, latched onto the brief twitch of his lips.

"But no one else, Amareth. That is for me to reveal, if I ever do. I must be seen to be doing this for the forest, not for Aria. They need to trust me, not fear or revere me."

"I understand that. But Narosén knows and so does the rest of the Council."

"Narosén will say nothing, but tell the others to keep it to themselves. I will not have my nature used for political leverage." His eyes were hard, a warning all too clear to see.

"Alright. You have my word." She shifted on the ground until she was kneeling before Fel'annár. "You are still angry with me, aren't you?"

"I can understand that much of what you did was for the good of our people, but even if you were right – and I am not sure that you were – I will never understand why you didn't tell me before I left for novice training. What did you think would happen, once I was recognised? If your goal was to protect me, why did you not warn me?"

She looked away, up to the trees. "I wondered whether you would rush into the city and demand answers. I thought you might put yourself into even more danger by pursuing the truth. I underestimated you, thought you were still a child. I look at you now and wonder how I could ever have thought that."

Fel'annár frowned, turned away from her. "It was a wrong decision. It was wrong of you."

"Aria knows Erthoron tried to persuade me, but I refused. I couldn't see past my own stubbornness, past my own heart that told me that you would hate me if I told you."

He nodded, said nothing, still not sure that he believed her claims to have been protecting him.

"Can you at least forgive me for those fears, at least?"

A deep sigh, the rustle of cloth as he shifted where he sat. "I forgive you for that, Amareth. But it takes time to accept. Then, perhaps, we can move on. When the trust is rebuilt. When understanding runs deeper. We can try to mend the damage that was done."

She nodded, still troubled, the plea in her eye still there, dampened.

The sound of warriors and horses was louder now and Fel'annár looked at the sky. The Company would be waiting for him. He stood.

"You're leaving to scout? Will you not wait for Prince Rinon's visit?"

"No. What for? I want to search alone with The Company. You go on. I won't be long."

She nodded, made her way back, eyes lingering on Tensári as she passed.

With Amareth gone, Tensári stepped noisily towards Fel'annár lest she surprise him. She watched as he spared one last glance at the canopy above.

"Did you find your answers, at last?" she asked.

After all these years, he had, indeed, found most of his answers—

and in his mind, his purpose flared, his resolve stronger than it ever had been because now, he was no longer ashamed. Now, he knew who had killed his mother, knew that it would not be Thargodén to bring Band'orán to his knees.

He would do it himself.

"Yes. For the most part, yes, I did."

His remaining question had no easy answer. It was an answer that could only come with the passing of time. But he would know, one day – know if his aunt had ever loved him, loved the boy and not his destiny.

Tensári nodded, and together, they began the short walk back to camp.

They met Farón on the way. "No need to guard me, Farón. I have Tensári."

Farón nodded, approached. "Captain Dalú ordered it. I must at least make the effort, I suppose." He smiled and fell into step between the two. He raised both hands, rested them on their shoulders and Tensári scowled at the brotherly gesture. And then she faltered, opened her mouth to speak, but nothing came out. Alarmed eyes locked with Fel'annár's. And then he felt it. A lance of pain in his neck, and his legs felt weak. He tried to call out, but couldn't. And then the forest lay sideways, dimmed. Legs before him, brown eyes bending over him.

"It's nothing personal, Warlord."

18

ONE DAY

"In one cycle of the sun, the future of a nation would be revealed. It began the day Fel'annár was betrayed. The day he saw his father's face."
The Silvan Chronicles, Book V. Marhené

Prince Regent Rinon led fifty Alpine warriors through the city gates, towards the Silvan encampment. Beside him, two of The Three sat proud in the saddle. Just like the glory days of old, said the warriors. Only it wasn't Or'Talán who accompanied them. It was his grandson.

The arguments and debates, the scheming and bribery, it meant nothing to them at that moment. They knew some had turned, that many more had deserted. But whether they were loyal to Thargodén or not, they would always carry Or'Talán in their hearts. They rode for him today.

And then Pan'assár was back. And if he was back, then so was Prince Handir. No one had seen him yet. Nor had they seen the bastard. But Turion was back, and they reckoned it had been him to find the wayward retinue.

The people smiled in spite of their worry and apprehension. They held out their hands, a proud farewell, a silent wish for them to find the missing king where others had failed. It was, perhaps, their last and only hope. If *they* couldn't find Thargodén, surely nobody could.

Angon rode behind, brown hair and beaten face, the face of a kinslayer. Their smiles froze, features tight. They turned their backs as he passed, swearing and cursing under their breaths. Angon had killed those brave fighters, they said, and how the Alpine people loved their warriors.

Rinon was sure that, had he not been riding with Angon, they would have stoned him. They did not understand why he was being set free. They did not understand why Rinon had not searched the Silvan encampment before. It was obvious, they said. The king was there, surrounded by an army of deserters. And then the rumour spread that Rinon would offer Angon's life, in exchange for the king's. They were indignant ... and they were hopeful.

Rinon half-turned his head to the commanders. Their Heliaré and purple sashes waved in the breeze as they cantered towards the Silvan encampment. They were like a greeting from the past, last of the Kah Masters—perhaps even the last Kah Warriors.

Soon, they approached their destination, but they did not receive the welcome they had expected. Rinon held up a hand for the warriors to stop and Pan'assár mirrored the movement. They could go no further, for before them, stretching along the entire width of the encampment, was a line of mounted Silvan warriors, warriors who had once been a part of their own army and yet to look at them, no one would say it was so.

Brown horses, white and dappled horses, tack adorned with symbols and etchings. Their standard-issue uniforms had been modified. Gone were the breeches beneath the knee-length leather skirt, and no shirts lay beneath their jerkins. Bare arms were adorned with leather bands, symbols of skill and weapons of choice. Vambraces, exquisitely embroidered with green and blue thread, hair braided and twisted, laden with stones, tokens of thanks. Honour stones for honourable service. Blades, bows, daggers and ropes hung from belts, shoulders, harnesses. It was a sea of brown, green and blue, of glinting blades and curved bows; brown hair and honey eyes burning bright, their warning clear.

Stop.

Rinon could almost feel the hatred from behind. Had he given the order, his retinue would surely have charged straight into the Silvan lines, cut them down and slaughtered the people beyond. He caught Gor'sadén's gaze, Pan'assár's eyes, and felt their loyalty. Now, all he had to do was show his warriors that the king was not here, show them that these Silvans were still loyal, that they would join the search. Angon had said it was a gamble, and for the first time, doubt stirred in Rinon's mind.

"We search for our king."

"He's not here!" Another voice, equally strong but worn and scratched. Dalú.

"I require the promises of your leader, Lord Erthoron."

Dalú turned in the saddle, watching as Erthoron strode through the lines until he stood beside his captain's horse.

"You have my promise. King Thargodén is not here."

"We must see it for ourselves."

"Would you allow us to march into your city with our army? Search for our Warlord, if we had need?"

Rinon waited, knowing that Pan'assár and Gor'sadén were looking at him. They all knew Fel'annár was here, that they wouldn't need to march into the city in search of him. But Erthoron's question was nothing but an example, one more part of the play so that the warriors could hear for themselves.

"We have brought Angon. Tell us, lord. Did he kill our warriors? Did he abduct our king?"

"He did *not*!" Voices shouted out from the lines, angry words, and Dalú straightened in the saddle.

"*Silence!*"

"Prince Rinon. Did you check the arrows that were used to kill your warriors?"

He had, but he allowed Erthoron to spell things out for his people.

"If you did, you would see that those assassins killed your warriors with standard-issue arrows. Angon never uses them. He makes his own, all his elves do. Arrows, to the Silvan warrior, are a very personal thing, Prince. You may know this, but perhaps you don't. You have locked away an innocent elf, condemned him before he ever had a chance of defending himself."

There was a roar of anger from the mounted Silvan warriors, horses stirring beneath them, agitated and ready.

"I spoke to Angon myself. He told me this, and I can confirm what you say, Lord Erthoron. I have brought him here, as a token of my goodwill. In return, I need your assurances that there will be no violence between our warriors. I have come to ask you to help us search for the king."

"Then we must talk, Prince. Until the votes are cast, our future is uncertain. We do not know if you are friend or foe."

The Alpine warriors stirred behind their prince. Pan'assár glared at them.

"Show us that the king is not here, as your own token of good will."

Erthoron nodded, murmured something up at Dalú.

Rinon, Angon and Pan'assár dismounted, and Gor'sadén turned to the troops, steering his horse down the line, a warning in his eyes.

You answer to me now.

With a signal from Dalú, the Silvan line opened, enough only for the three elves to pass. It was an act of utter faith. The Crown Prince of Ea Uaré walked willingly into the Silvan camp, outnumbered, at their mercy.

It was a risk, one Pan'assár would have preferred not to take. But then he himself was probably in the most danger. He had mistreated these warriors for years. He could feel their hatred, feel their resentment stretching the air around him, pulling it tight. He kept his eyes open and his mouth shut, not for the first time wishing Galadan were beside him. This was what Angon must have felt like when they left the city.

Every tent they passed, its owners came to stand outside, held open the tent flaps so that Rinon could see inside. Nothing, just as they knew would be the case. They passed the farrier's huts and the blacksmith's anvils. They passed the ovens and the pens, the training pits and the supply areas. Smaller tents, warriors' tents, and then they came to the two largest tents at the centre of the settlement. At the entrance to one of them, a warrior stood, as tall as he was broad. Rinon approached, ducked inside. There, to his shock, was Llyniel, sitting together with a group of warriors. They stood, bowed, and Rinon searched them, for any signs of a bonding braid. But there was none. He caught her gaze, all stubborn and rebellious as she had always been with him. He arched a brow, tucked away his questions for later.

The very last tent was Erthoron's. Indeed he stood there together with a group of elves, one of them an Ari'atór.

"We must talk," said Rinon, and Erthoron nodded, held out his arm to the entrance of their command centre. Rinon turned to Pan'assár.

"Stay here."

The commander nodded, bolstered his courage and stood at the now-closed flap. Before him, the entire Silvan camp watched. Amongst them, the faces of warriors who had once served in the army he himself commanded. He had belittled them, ignored their courage, allowed others to all but enslave them. He had done them wrong, and all he could do was stand there and endure their silent judgement.

Gods but he wished Galadan were here.

INSIDE THE TENT, Narosén managed to stare at Rinon while he bowed. Erthoron's lips were pursed while Amareth was once more struck by the similarities this elf shared with Fel'annár.

"That was well done," murmured Erthoron.

Angon turned to Rinon, and then back to Erthoron. "You knew?"

"Of course we did, Angon. You have my thanks, Prince, for seeing justice done."

"It was my duty, but I will not pretend that was the only reason. We have a unique opportunity, Lord Erthoron. One last chance to bring our warriors together. The king is nowhere to be found, but if our warriors can search for him together, if the Alpines can see that you care, that you are still loyal, we can stop this descent into rupture. Help me find him. Help me to show them that you did not abduct the king. You did not kill those warriors. Rise above those lies and *show* them."

"We shouldn't have to."

"No. But we are fighting Band'orán. This is *his* game, not mine. Not the king's. He plays on loyalties, on past injustices. He creates conflict where there is dissent. He makes a war from a disagreement. If he is to rule, he must separate us. So far, he is succeeding."

An elf offered wine from a tray of goblets, and Rinon took one, admired the craftsmanship.

"The votes are imminent. As it stands, the Inner Circle will vote against the Warlord, and the Council will vote against the inclusion of new Silvan advisors. Our only hope now is to find the king, prove Band'orán's treachery."

"There is no time, Prince. It has been many days since the king was taken, and only one more day for the votes to take place. And what then? There will be no more reason for us to stay here. No more reason to trust your people. There will be no more justification for peace, Prince. I certainly cannot guarantee it."

Rinon drank from his goblet, studied the liquid inside it for a moment. "Then one day it is, lord. You have Angon to help with the warriors, to rally them and organise patrols. If it is the Silvans who find the king, then that would be a mighty triumph, Erthoron. It would say so much to my people, show how Band'orán is wrong about you."

"It is a pity that should be the only way."

"In an ideal world, Lord Erthoron. In an ideal world, we all judge a person by the merit of their actions. Many Alpines have not done that. Many Silvans have not done that. It falls to their leaders to carry them forwards, would you not say?"

Erthoron straightened. Amareth's lips flickered and Angon nodded firmly.

IDERNON TIGHTENED his harness and left the tent, The Company and Llyniel behind him. "This is taking too long."

Galdith shrugged. "They had a lot to talk about."

"And is she back?" asked Idernon, not waiting for an answer and making for Pan'assár outside the command tent.

"Commander. Have you seen Fel'annár?"

"No. Why?"

"Is Amareth inside with the Elders?"

"If you are referring to the councillor, she arrived some time ago."

"We were supposed to be leaving on a scouting mission. I must speak with her. I don't like this, commander."

Pan'assár cocked his head and Idernon entered the tent. "Lord Erthoron," he nodded, turned and bowed once more to the prince. "Please excuse the interruption. Lady Amareth, have you seen Fel'annár?"

"We parted ways a while ago. He was with Tensári." She frowned. "He said he was leaving on a scouting mission."

Idernon's mind was desperately searching for a reason why Fel'annár would not have returned. "Where did you last see him?"

"I'll show you." Amareth rushed past Rinon, Angon, and then she was outside, jogged past The Company and Llyniel. She led them into the trees where she had talked with Fel'annár earlier that morning. Not twenty paces away, they saw Tensári, struggling to stand.

Idernon and the rest sprinted towards her, but there was no sign of Fel'annár. He watched Sontúr help Tensári stand and check her eyes. Then he turned to a wide-eyed Amareth as she spoke. "It's not possible. There are guards everywhere ..."

"They used a toxin," began Sontúr.

"Some ... something stuck in ... in my throat ..."

Sontúr peered at her neck, reached out with one hand. "Stay still." He pulled out a splinter, and then another. By the time he had finished, there were six black thorns in his hand. "What the ...?"

"Dream Vine," said Llyniel. "If you step on the whole thing, your heart stops within minutes. But just one of those thorns is enough to render you unconscious and delirious for hours." Llyniel was staring at the splinters, gaze moving up to Tensári's foggy eyes. "You should be dead."

"How long ago did this happen?" asked Galadan, handing his water flask to Tensári, watching as she drank.

Amareth stepped forwards. "Half an hour, perhaps. Gods, after all this time, just when he is guarded the most ... Wait. I passed Farón on the way back to camp. How could he not have seen ...?"

"Farón," said Idernon, lip curling.

"No. Not Farón. He was Lainon's pupil, one of our best warriors, he wouldn't ..."

"It was ... Farón," confirmed Tensári. Amareth buried her face in her hands while Sontúr steadied Tensári. A strange silence settled over them as they waited for Galdith and Carodel to return from a wider inspection of the area.

"They have not even bothered to cover their tracks," said Galdith. "They lead north-east."

Idernon grit his teeth. "Meet me at the stables in ten minutes."

He strode back towards the command tent in search of Erthoron, unaware of Galadan's lingering gaze behind him. They had let their guard down, thought they were safe here with Dalú and Farón, but now, Idernon trusted nobody.

Nobody except The Company.

∾

Rinon had shared tea with the Silvan leaders, had spoken of Handir's return, and of course Pan'assár's, who remained outside the tent. Rinon almost felt sorry for him. But there was still one important question to address. "What are Fel'annár's intentions?"

"His plan is to ride out, a scouting mission to gather intelligence as to the king's whereabouts."

Rinon stared at Erthoron, wondering why the boy would do such a thing. Rinon had come to do precisely that himself, had brought the power to take on those who may be holding the king hostage. He shared a glance with Angon.

"And the rest of your warriors—will they join him, then?"

"They may. But we must give Fel'annár, Angon and Farón the time they need to convince our warriors." said Erthoron. "Pan'assár's command has taken a great toll on the king's army."

"Pan'assár can no longer lead our Silvan warriors," said Angon. "They won't accept him. Our only chance at reuniting the army, slim though it is, is for Pan'assár to be gone."

"Pan'assár won't leave, Warrior. Pan'assár is *back*."

Angon turned to the prince, lip curled with unashamed hatred. He opened his mouth to speak, but Erthoron held up his hand for silence. "Angon. Leave it. You are here, and Pan'assár is just outside. He obviously believes that you are not responsible for what happened. Give him a chance. We can speak of the commander later."

Angon held his tongue, and Rinon waited, wondering if they would return with the Silvan. If they did, he told himself he shouldn't care what the boy looked like, how he spoke, how he carried himself or the things he would say. And then he heard it: distant shouting, rising voices, sounds of alarm. Rinon strode outside, passed Pan'assár, hand on the hilt of his sword. Standing before him was the same Silvan warrior who had interrupted them previously, but he was no longer worried. He was seething. He felt Pan'assár's hand on his forearm and then watched him step forward. He did not expect Pan'assár to address him, let alone know his name.

"Idernon. What has happened?"

"They've taken him. Here in the camp. Farón has betrayed us."

There was a shocked near-silence around them, and then the gritty voice of Dalú as he approached from behind Erthoron. "Farón is no traitor, Warrior."

Idernon was livid. "Then let's *ask* him, shall we, Captain? Tell me, where is he?"

Dalú signalled to the guard at the tent, eyes back on Idernon. "What happened?"

"Fel'annár and Tensári were poisoned by Dream Vine. Farón meant to kill her but failed. The tracks lead north-east, and I wager he is being taken to wherever the king is held." Idernon turned to Pan'assár. "Commander, Dalú won't find Farón, and every minute we waste is a minute further away from Fel'annár, perhaps even the king. The Company leaves now."

"You will ride with us," said Rinon, turning to leave. He stopped mid-stride and turned back when he realised Idernon had not moved.

"The Company rides alone."

Rinon's nostrils flared, eyes narrowed. "That was an order." His eyes flickered to Galadan further behind, knew he was a lieutenant.

"We answer to the Warlord, Prince, as do these Silvan warriors around you."

"What Warlord? That vote has yet to be taken."

"Not by them. They have not invested him, but it hardly matters. He is their leader, whatever you wish to call him."

"As your *prince*, I could command it."

Idernon straightened himself. "And will you?"

Rinon watched the warrior with glittering eyes, steely and unyielding. "No. But it makes sense to ride together. Scout ahead if you will but stay within ten minutes of the main group."

"We ride for the foothills."

"We have already searched that area."

"We will search it again, Prince."

"You won't find him. But do what you wish." He waved a hand in the air between them. Over the past week, they had searched every cave, every cottage and every flet in the trees. They had searched Analei and found nothing.

The guard was back, breathless and too pale. "Captain. Farón is not at the camp."

"He was on duty," said Dalú, almost a whisper, studiously avoided Idernon's hard glare.

Rinon turned to Erthoron. "Remember, Lord Erthoron. Work with me, and we can pull this nation back together. Trust me, for a while longer at least. For one more day. *We* search the eastern mid-flank." He stared, waiting for his answer. It came in the form of a curt nod.

"We search the western flank and northwards. We will find our Warlord, and the king if he is with him," said Dalú, fierce face driving home his message, and Rinon understood exactly where the captain's loyalties lay.

Rinon bowed to Erthoron and nodded curtly. With a last lingering stare at Angon and Dalú, he strode away.

Pan'assár made to follow, but he paused, turned back to Idernon, Galadan at his side. "Find him, Wise One." He nodded, almost bowed, glanced at Galadan and then left with his prince.

Idernon turned, ran back to the stables where Llyniel and The Company would be waiting. The Silvan warriors shouted their warnings ahead to the stable hands and by the time Idernon arrived, The Company was mounted. He quickly climbed into the saddle and as he wheeled his skittish mount around to face them, another came cantering towards them. The Silvans warriors on foot made way for him, eyes on his cuirass and the purple sash around his waist. Gor'sadén stopped before Idernon.

"Where to?"

Idernon looked at the others, then back to the commander. "We believe he is being held somewhere in the foothills, to the east."

"They have already searched there."

"We think they missed something."

"He lies under rock, in the foothills to the east," said Tensári.

Idernon nodded at the Ber'atór, glanced at Llyniel on the ground, looking up at him. Idernon remembered his moment of weakness on the river. He had given up hope that Fel'annár had survived the river. He would not make the same mistake twice.

"He's alive, Idernon," she said, eyes wide and steady.

He nodded resolutely. "Then we ride north for as long as the light lasts, then circle back, along the base of the mountain. The votes are tomorrow, but we have no need to be there. We search until we find them." Idernon caught Gor'sadén's gaze, saw the minute nod of his head. Wheeling his horse around, The Company and Gor'sadén kicked their mounts into a canter.

Llyniel raised a hand to The Company, her mind reaching out, searching for a glimmer of her bond with Fel'annár, but as yet, there was nothing more she could tell them. A little further off, Amareth too, watched them leave, slowly losing her battle against her rising panic. Her shawl fell away from her shoulders, arms lax, breath too fast. She felt Erthoron's steadying hand at her back. "Gods. All this time we have kept him safe, only for one of our own to take him."

Dalú turned to her, his face a terrible sight. He had trusted Farón, loved him even. What had Band'orán offered him that his own people could not provide?

Their best warrior turned traitor, and it was all his fault.

THAT MORNING, while Rinon was at the Silvan camp, Prince Handir reappeared before the court. It was the last regular Council session before the votes would take place, and throughout the proceedings, all eyes had been upon Handir and Turion. Of course, they had also seen Commander Pan'assár riding out with the crown prince just that morning.

But where was the bastard?

As the councillors spoke and discussed the upcoming votes, Turion turned to the prince. "Band'orán seems calm, unconcerned. If he has the king, he does an admirable job of fooling me."

"He has him."

Turion started at the conviction in those words. No doubt at all. Turion thought himself insightful when it came to judging character, but how could Handir be so sure?

"He is not worried, Turion. He is not worried because he knows where the king is. He is in control, at the helm, watching us with something akin to pity. They are not sorry. They are not concerned for his plight. They are glad of it."

Turion thought it a long shot to assume so much on so little. Still, he continued to watch Band'orán as he spoke with the other councillors. The king's uncle smiled and nodded. He listened, patted shoulders. For him, it was a normal day in the council chambers. But for Turion, it was the day in which war may come to Ea Uaré. Silvan warriors against Alpine warriors and the Gods forbid that Rinon lose his infamous temper at the Silvan encampment. All he could do was thank Aria that Pan'assár was with him.

As Turion watched Band'orán and wondered what the day would bring, Handir began to realise that his father must surely be dead. Common sense dictated that he was. There was no reason for Band'orán to keep him alive, save the memories of the past.

His heart felt leaden. Despite his father's years of aimless wandering, the near indifference he had shown his sons, Handir loved his father. He always had but never told him that.

"Excuse me." Barathon approached, saluted Turion, bowed to Handir. "I was hoping to see Captain Rinon before he left. He has freed the Silvan rebel."

"He has. Evidence was uncovered. He rides to investigate." Handir stared at his cousin.

"Of course. And of the king? No news then?"

"No news, Captain. Your father will be ecstatic." Handir's eyes were hard, voice soft. Turion didn't recognise him at all, could have sworn it was Rinon, not Handir, standing beside him.

"He's not." Barathon frowned. "He is concerned. Don't let his demeanour fool you. He is difficult to read, but King Thargodén is his nephew, his blood."

"You think that blood would stop him from achieving his goals?"

"It must." The frown was back.

Turion watched the captain. Wondered if he truly believed what he said. If he didn't, he was good, too. Good at fooling himself that his father cared about Thargodén; that he cared about anyone.

"It should, yes. As for me, I will wait and see for myself whether you are right. But I hope that you are, Barathon. For your sake."

"I am right, Prince. He means to serve this land. His motives are good." Barathon smiled, and Turion was struck once more by the boy. He could have been good. He could have been kind and honourable. Instead, he stood here, defending a traitor, a kinslayer.

"Will you return to Analei tonight?" asked Handir.

"I believe so. The Council is tomorrow evening."

"The road may be dangerous."

"We will be careful then, Prince." Barathon smiled.

Handir nodded slowly. "Captain. If there is ever anything you wish to discuss ... you can come to me in confidence."

Barathon paled, his smile gone. He saluted, and Turion watched him return to his father's side.

THARGODÉN SAT upon the cold stone floor, his ankle still shackled to the ground. He jumped as something banged in the distance, echoed off the walls. Scuffling boots, a cry of pain. Muttered words and a yelp.

"Hold him, for the Gods' sakes!"

A hiss of pain, the thump of a boot against something solid.

Two warriors dragged a struggling elf towards him. Hooded and with his hands tied, the figure pulled and kicked, lurched this way and that, but he was held fast. They threw him forwards, and Thargodén watched as the body crashed to the ground and then rolled. On his side, he sat up slowly, breath harsh through the hood over his head.

Too fast for Thargodén to truly appreciate, two legs rose and caught one of the warriors in a vice, pulling him to the ground, wrenching from him a strangled cry. The warrior hit the ground with a crack, and his companion was there. He kicked the hooded figure in the head and dragged his companion away, as far as he could from their prisoner.

One sat, the other stood, both turned to the sound of confident strides.

"Secure him."

The standing warrior approached the hooded figure, lying still on his side and Thargodén watched him, wondering how Band'orán had recruited a Silvan to do his bidding. The warrior pulled at the chains attached to the wall behind Thargodén and snapped a shackle around one ankle as fast as he could before scurrying backwards, wiping at the trickle of blood that ran down his face.

Band'orán watched him. "You have served well. You will soon be rewarded, Warlord."

Farón bowed to his future lord, acknowledging his reward for having brought in the bastard. He had betrayed his people by bringing Fel'annár to Band'orán. Still, it was the best he could do by them. They had set their hearts on this boy, because of who he was, because of his father. It was a dream they had created, a delusion that would end in disaster for the Silvan people. Fel'annár would demand loyalty to the king – to his father. And Farón could not condone that. It was Band'orán they should bow to, not Thargodén the weak, Thargodén the lesser son of a great king. Had he not given Pan'assár free rein in the forest? Had he not condoned his careless tactics that had led to the slaughter of his people? It wouldn't be like that with Huren as Commander General. He had promised outposts, a new way of facing the enemy that would protect the Silvan way of life.

Band'orán gestured at him to leave and Farón turned, back to the entrance. As soon as Farón had learned all he could of the Kalhámen'Ar from Band'orán, he would train his own people in the ways of the Kah. He would make the Silvan warriors of Ea Uaré the mightiest of them all - when he was Master and Warlord. It was a pity that Fel'annár had to die. He liked the boy, admired his skill and his loyalty to the Silvans. But he was his father's son, he willed it or no. His was a necessary sacrifice.

Alone now with his two shackled hostages, Band'orán approached. One was sitting up, trying to make sense of what he had just heard, while the other lay on his side, only now beginning to stir.

"You fight well. You would be a welcome addition to my personal guard. Pity you are who you are. Tell me, though, who is your Master?"

There was no answer, and Band'orán stepped closer. Thargodén watched his gleaming eyes. He saw curiosity and his own was piqued. The hooded figure sat up, a noisy breath through the thick hessian over his head. Band'orán knelt, close enough to touch.

"Gor'sadén of Tar'eastór." It was the voice of a Silvan, he realised. Thargodén knew that accent, knew it intimately—the coloured 'r', the music in it.

Band'orán's face changed so suddenly a cold wave washed over Thargodén.

"One of The *Three*. Mighty warriors, the best we have seen, will ever see. There was no one as skilled as they. Gor'sadén, Pan'assár, Or'Talán. No one as good as Or'Talán."

Band'orán reached out, touched the wool, pinched it between thumb and forefinger. He pulled back slowly, eyes steady. He saw silver strands, braids and twists, a mass of hair. He cocked his head. With his other hand, he reached out and smoothed back the hair that hid his prisoner's features.

Band'orán inhaled, unable to stop the sound that accompanied it, long and deep. He swayed backwards, pushing himself upright, holding out a splayed hand. His mouth opened but he said nothing and, in his eyes, Thargodén saw horror—horror and grief, guilt and wrath.

He staggered backwards and then whirled away, his back to Thargodén. He left in wavering strides, banging a door closed, and Thargodén turned to the seated figure with the strangest silver hair. It was a colour he had only ever seen once, on the head of his father. The figure turned, and Thargodén sat breathless, boneless, utterly confused. Or'Talán with the eyes of his love.

Fel'annár. Green Sun.

Dear Gods, but he was beautiful. He was hideous. The beautiful face of the father he had loved, the father he had hated. The father he thought had betrayed him. But then, Band'orán had told him the truth and the question that still haunted Thargodén now was why? Why had Or'Talán cowed before Band'orán's threats? Why had he not arrested him for high treason?

But the elf beside him was not his father. It was his son. He was Lássira's son, the son he had dreamed of meeting since that fateful day when Aradan had told him he had been found. He had only half-believed the resemblance they said he shared with his father.

All he could do was wonder at the humour of the Gods. His son was identical to his father in everything except the texture of his hair and the colour of his eyes. And of all the places he could have conjured in his mind for their first meeting, of all the circumstances ... he had never considered this. Shackled to a wall, prisoners of a damaged mind that wanted them both dead.

Fel'annár's chain was long enough for him to shift his position, stretch out both legs before him and straighten his aching back. His head throbbed, chest ached. He'd twisted a finger, been punched in the back. But he had landed a cracking blow to Farón's face, and he had frightened the spittle out of Band'orán, if that was who it had been. He had yet to turn to his fellow captive, his silent spectator.

He knew who he was, though.

He turned sideways, saw the other through his own tangled hair. There, in the gloom beside him, was the king of Ea Uaré. His father.

He didn't know what to say, whether he even needed to say anything. He scooted backwards, testing the length of the chain again. He felt the wall behind him, leant back against it, allowed his head to rest there against the cool stone.

"Fel'annár."

He only half-turned. "My king." His voice had been surprisingly steady, he thought, as his eyes wandered over the room, or rather the hall, that they sat in. He couldn't remember half of his journey here, had no idea where he actually was. He listened, but all he could hear was the whisper of still waters, the drip of humid rock and his own mind chanting the obvious.

He was sitting beside his father, the one he had yearned to know as a child. The one he had hated as an adolescent. He had later accepted his heritage, even agreed to meet him, but now that he was here, albeit under circumstances he had never imagined, he was lost for words.

He allowed his eyes to wander for a while. He wanted to know where they were, but that would start a conversation, and still, he would be speechless.

"This is Analei—or rather, under it. It used to be my family residence in the summer. When my father died, Band'orán took it for himself. I never knew this was what lay beneath it."

Fel'annár nodded. He had not wanted to face his father, but the king had most definitely been watching him and understood his expression. He had known exactly what he was thinking, and it irked him. He tried and failed to school his face, and still, he didn't turn to the king because that would start a conversation. Anger warred with reason. Reason warred with reproach. But it was his curiosity that was begging him to look, to open his mouth and speak to his father.

"Analei is about an hour's steady ride from the city. It's Band'orán who uses this place now. You know of whom I speak?"

And there it was. A question he was bound to answer. He opened his mouth, feeling stupid. The tension between them was all but tangible, a thick aura of discomfort, of wanting but not knowing what to say to cut through it. Break the barrier.

"Are you well?"

Was he? He shifted, jostled his finger. It was bent awkwardly to the left. Holding it against the stone behind him, he pushed down, heard a crack, a muffled groan he had tried to hold back.

"Better now," he murmured. "Band'orán, yes?" He willed himself to turn, to just look at the elf beside him, see the face that had been denied him for so many years. He found the king staring back at him, eyes wide, full of questions. Those eyes wandered to his Bonding Braid and then back to his eyes. Did his face look like that? he wondered. He could see himself in the set of the king's jaw, the hairline and the nose. "That was him, wasn't it? Band'orán?"

"Yes. He means to kill me, take the throne and subdue the Silvan people by taking you. My only question is why he has not killed us. What use are we to him alive?"

Fel'annár could hear Handir in the king's tone as he toiled to understand Band'orán's motives. He knew the answer. Pan'assár had told them as he read Or'Talán's journal. But Thargodén had no idea. Could he tell him? Could he recount to the king how Band'orán had tried to coerce the king, threaten him? Could he tell him that his father had played along, that he had tried to help?

It didn't feel right. It was such a personal conversation to have. The king needed to hear it from someone close, someone who could explain and empathise with him. Fel'annár couldn't do that, could he? And yet he couldn't leave him wondering. He leaned back against the cool stone wall and only half turned to the expectant king.

"Commander Pan'assár believes it is personal, sire."

Thargodén's brow twitched. "Pan'assár?"

Damn it all. Here was the conversation he did not want to have, the feelings he did not want to feel. He reminded himself that he sat beside the king, not his father. He was a soldier, reporting to his commanding officer.

"How do you know that?" prompted the king.

"I don't. Commander Pan'assár ... found King Or'Talán's journal. He has read it. He says his motives are related to his childhood."

Thargodén stared at him as if willing him to continue and feelings were starting to break past Fel'annár's defences.

Pity. He felt pity because Thargodén had once had a father he had loved, a father he believed had betrayed him. He could see the need in the king's eyes—in his father's eyes. But then the intensity was gone. His features smoothed over and the king looked away.

"Rest for a while, Warrior. We will need our strength for what is to come."

Fel'annár blessed those words. He had felt himself slipping into a place where he could not identify his own feelings. Even now, as his eyes wandered over this dark place, he grappled with them. Everything he thought he knew about his feelings for his father had dissipated, like snow upon an open palm. Fluffy and soft, then liquid escaping through fingers.

He wasn't angry. He wasn't resentful. He was overwhelmingly curious, but not brave enough to admit it.

19

THE BONDING BRAID

"Marriage to the Silvans is a voluntary act, a union of minds, declared by a single braid, tied by the Seven Wheels. Once the braid is woven, the bond can be broken by no one save by the bonded themselves."
The Silvan Chronicles, Book I. Marhené

The king had remained silent, had surely noted his discomfort, and that was just fine with Fel'annár. He preferred the heavy silence to probing questions, to his own dithering answers and confused emotions. His eyes wandered to the carved figure that stood before the almost empty lake beyond.

"Who is she?" He blurted it out as if he had spoken to himself. He could have punched himself.

Thargodén was silent for a while. Fel'annár hoped he wouldn't answer, but he did.

"That is Canusahéi. She is the elf I was encouraged to marry. She was Queen of Ea Uaré."

Canusahéi. Handir's mother. The woman Thargodén had married instead of his own mother. He had not loved her, and her suffering and subsequent departure to Valley was the reason Handir had hated Fel'annár, just as his own mother's suffering had led him to reject Handir. And yet now, after everything that had happened between them—now that Handir had told him he had a brother he could count on—it no longer seemed to matter. Not to the sons, at least.

"It seems strange that there should be a carving of my queen down here."

Fel'annár snapped out of his musings and turned back to the king. He knew why. Or'Talán had written of it. Band'orán had loved her. But he couldn't tell the king that, and instead, a question bubbled out of his mouth. No sooner had he said it than he felt himself cringing on the inside.

"Did you know that King Or'Talán had met with my mother without your knowledge?"

Thargodén's head whipped to face him, expression stern, demanding. "No."

"He sketched her in that journal he kept, the one Commander Pan'assár found on Lord Sulén's body."

Thargodén stared, confused. "Why would Sulén have my father's journal? Why didn't my father tell me he had met with her? Why did *she* keep it from me?" The king shook his head, eyes pleading with Fel'annár to continue, filled with a deep-seated need to understand.

Fel'annár couldn't keep it from him, father or no. It would have been cruel. "When I saw the drawing—when *we* saw it—we realised that Or'Talán must have known my mother quite well. I don't think it was one casual meeting. More a friendship, perhaps. She was smiling and, she wore a Bonding Braid."

The frown on the king's face was deep, almost disturbing. One hand reached up to a smooth lock of hair, and Fel'annár wondered: had Thargodén ever worn his? He looked away, wished he hadn't asked his stupid question.

"Band'orán has told me many things since I've been here, everything except one. I wonder if the answer lies in that journal—and if it does, would you tell me, Fel'annár?"

Would he? He turned to the king once more. And then he faltered. For a moment, he saw himself all those years ago ...

What happened to my mother? Who was my father? Why won't you speak ...?

"Do you know why King Or'Talán agreed to Band'orán's demand, Fel'annár?" A careful question, not softly spoken, yet neither was it an order.

And there it was. It was the question Fel'annár knew must have tormented the king all this time. Thargodén had always known his father, loved him. And then he had hated him for what he had done.

Yes, he knew the answer to that question.

"He didn't agree. He *lied*."

Thargodén flinched, searched Fel'annár's face.

"He told my mother of his plan, to find a way to stop Band'orán, but he couldn't tell you. You had to believe it, so that Band'orán would believe it. But then—"

"The Battle Under the Sun. He died. He didn't betray me. He didn't ..." The king stood, turned away and walked as far as his chain allowed. Fel'annár watched as the truth that had eluded Thargodén slowly sank in, taking with it years of suffering and grief, and although one stood and the other sat in some underground palace, chained to a wall, when Thargodén turned back to his son, he was smiling.

And with the Gods as his witness, Fel'annár tried not to feel. But he did.

LATE MORNING, and The Company sat in a small cave. They drank water and chewed half-heartedly on strips of dried meat.

"Tensári?"

She turned to Idernon, eyes shining almost as bright as Fel'annár's. He scowled, and Sontúr leant forward. "Is this what we saw in Tar'eastór, when Lainon fell? Is this your Guiding Light?"

She nodded. "It is Aria's gift to a Ber'ator. She guides me to him.

He is alive, and I know he is under rock. But this is new to me. I am trying to fathom his direction."

"Further north?" asked Gor'sadén.

She shook her head. "I do not know, but it feels right to be at the foot of the mountains. But whether he is further north or south towards the city, I cannot tell."

"Then we continue north until twilight and then circle back. The patrols surely missed something. But they didn't have Tensári. We are counting on you, Ari'atór." He saw her careful nod, and as they mounted to resume their search, Gor'sadén repeated those words in his mind.

I am counting on you.

AT SUNDOWN, Pan'assár, Rinon and his warriors rode towards the city. Another day of fruitless searching. Still, the Silvans had indeed ridden out, though they made it clear they did it for their Warlord.

Rinon turned his head to the camp, a ways over to their right. A small group of warriors was galloping towards them, and Rinon slowed their own pace.

It was Angon himself and a small group of strangely decked elves.

"What news, Angon?"

"We have searched everywhere, short of reaching Sen Garay. That will be our next step. From there, we pan left and right. We will find our Warlord, Prince."

Rinon knew what he meant; they all did. Wherever Fel'annár was, the king was surely there, too. "You have my thanks, Angon." He steered his horse as close as he could to the Silvan, spoke quietly so that the troops would not hear him. "The votes are tomorrow afternoon. Past that point, it is unlikely we will find them alive." He stared at Angon, saw his resolve. He had not been wrong. Angon was an honourable warrior, one he trusted.

"We will not stop, Prince. Even once those votes are cast, we will not stop."

Rinon offered him a respectful nod. "Until tomorrow, then."

"Safe hunting, Prince."

Angon wheeled his horse around and galloped back to the camp. Even as he returned, Rinon could see other smaller groups leaving. A surge of pride rolled over him, for how he had believed in Angon and not been wrong, for how he had dared believe the Silvans would still help him, even after everything that had happened.

He turned back to Pan'assár, who was watching him through narrowed eyes. "How much did you hear back at the camp?"

"Everything," admitted Pan'assár. "You did well. And you were right about Angon, I think. He holds more sway over the warriors than Erthoron."

This was surely not the same bigoted, racist commander who had left for Tar'eastór with his brother all those months ago. Was it the battle that had changed him? Or was it something else that had happened along the way? Something he had yet to speak of? Whatever it was, Rinon was grateful. Pan'assár had stood outside that tent and endured the stares and the whispered insults for almost an hour, and not one word of disdain had left his lips.

The situation was as dire as it had been that morning, but Rinon's resolve was bolstered. On their way once more, Rinon spoke. "Who were those elves who raised the alarm about Fel'annár being taken?"

"The Company, Prince. That was The Company; warriors loyal to the Silvan. The boy takes after his grandfather, as do you, although in a different way."

Rinon said nothing for a while, but Pan'assár seemed to know he was curious about something else.

"I am surprised you have taken so well to him, given your *animosity* towards Silvans," said Rinon.

"So am *I*." One side of Pan'assár's mouth quirked upwards. Grim humour. Rinon smirked, but he kept his questions to himself for now, and he rather thought Pan'assár was grateful for that.

He needed to speak with Handir, coordinate their security for tomorrow's events. Rinon could not shake the idea that Band'orán may not even wait until the Council tomorrow. Perhaps he would make his move tonight, while the king was lost and the people in turmoil. He needed extra security for Handir, needed Turion to ensure that their guards were loyal. It would be a tense night, an even tenser day tomorrow at court and in the field where the search for king and warlord would continue. But it would continue without Rinon, without Pan'assár, for tomorrow at least. They were needed at the palace, with Handir. After the revelations he would make, there was no telling how Band'orán would react. Ea Uaré needed its regent present, needed its commander to protect the line of Or'Talán, rally their army behind the ruling house, if such a thing were still possible.

"I doubted you."

Pan'assár started, turned to Rinon. He knew it, and had been angry with Rinon for saying as much in front of others. "I know."

"I do not regret it, because it was your own actions in the past that led me to question your loyalty. Now, I see a commander general, a defender of my grandfather's line. I see your anguish because my father is still out there somewhere. I know what you are thinking—the same thing I am thinking. When Band'orán makes his move, tonight or tomorrow at the vote, the king's life will be forfeit, and yet, there is nothing further you nor I can do. We must see tomorrow through and ensure the safety of our people. Only then can we resume the search for my father, even if it is only to honour him in death."

Pan'assár watched the prince turn away. His words were the words of a king, of an elf who would sacrifice the most sacred of all things for the land he ruled over. He would sacrifice his own blood. Here was a worthy cause indeed, and Pan'assár steeled his nerve. The prince was right. Soon, there would be no reason for Band'orán to keep the king alive.

A memory rose in his mind. Six warriors standing under a dome of coloured light. Six warriors standing between the citadel of Tar'eastór and the black host of Deviants that meant to overrun it. The Company. Only now there were seven, searching for the eighth, their leader. There was still hope for Thargodén, hope for Fel'annár, and he smiled fleetingly, remembered Gor'sadén's words from just days ago.

Kah Warriors do not die easily.

And neither do they despair, thought Pan'assár. He turned to Rinon.

"There is still hope, Prince. Gor'sadén rides with The Company, even as we return to protect this realm. And let me tell you, that is a mighty host of eight. So let us pass this last night together, with stories of Tar'eastór, stories of hope, and then come tomorrow, it will be Handir's time to shine."

Rinon's eyes were wide, searching. He had surely never seen this side of Pan'assár. Indeed, he smiled, despite his fierce mien. "Your words are a balm, Commander."

Pan'assár nodded, cast his gaze to the slowly closing gates and the distant Silvan fires now behind them.

Do not fail me, brother. Idernon, Galadan, Ramien and Galdith, Carodel, Sontúr and Tensári. Find them. Bring them home.

The mighty gates of Ea Uaré banged shut, but the prayer in his mind did not end.

FROM A WINDOW HALF-WAY up the royal palace, Barathon watched Pan'assár and Rinon return from their search, without the king. They would never find him, and after tonight, he knew it would no longer matter. He just hoped that his father would be gracious with the king. He deserved to be treated with respect, deserved a noble death at least.

Barathon's doubts had returned. He had backed his father in everything, but this ... his plan to kill Thargodén weighed on his soul. It was wrong. Surely there was some other way?

And then he remembered Handir's words.

"If there is anything you wish to tell me ..."

But how could he? Band'orán was his father. All he had ever wanted was his recognition, some approval of his worth—a word of praise, a proud smile. But there had never been any of that. It was why he had been close with Silor.

His friends were ambitious, kept his company for what it might mean for them. Silor had been no exception, but there was a deeper understanding between them. Sulén had been much the same with his son. Only Draugolé seemed to understand him, had helped him on those occasions when his father had turned volatile, when his temper would sometimes lead him to do questionable things. Barathon had always tried not to see those moments, not with his own eyes, because somewhere inside himself, he knew that he would not like it, could not condone it. Even now, with the king sitting under the mountain, where he himself never ventured.

He could not condone it.

But he loved his father. No, he *wanted* to love his father.

He turned from the window, mind awash with confusion. It was why he had sought out Draugolé that evening, to iron it all out in his mind and decide what he should do. Draugolé had protected him before. Liked him, even.

The door clicked shut quietly. Barathon turned to his father, dressed in riding clothes. "Any news, father?"

Band'orán nodded, unlaced his cloak and draped it over the back of a chair. "Most things are running according to plan. Rinon is stirring the Silvans, but thankfully, he is too late." He smiled, stared at his son for a while.

"Home then?"

"Aye. The meetings are over. A moment. There is something I need from my desk."

Barathon nodded and went to his adjacent room. He picked up his cloak, strapped on his harness and pulled on his gloves. With one more look around his rooms, he turned. Together, father and son walked to the stables, bound for home. Tonight, he would sleep above the king and his estranged son, as estranged as he was from his own father, the one he had known all his life.

Ten of his father's personal guard awaited. All cloaked in black, they merged with the night save for the odd glint of their blades. He knew what they were, and it unnerved him. Still, there was, perhaps, no safer place to be than in their company, and so they mounted and cantered away.

Fires glowed to the west. There was the thump of many drums, but they, decked in black, could hardly be seen and soon, their path turned eastwards to Analei, perhaps for the last time.

Or so Barathon thought.

RINON HAD RETURNED to the king's quarters while Pan'assár met with Turion and arranged for added security. Band'orán himself had ridden out to Analei with Barathon, but still, there was no telling what might happen in the night. It would not do be taken by surprise.

With the princes and the Inner Circle sufficiently watched and guarded, commander and captain walked down the corridor that led to the king's suite of rooms. They would join the princes and Aradan for a nightcap, and perhaps share stories of their time abroad, things that Rinon and Aradan still didn't know about the battle, about the Nim'uán.

"Pan'assár. Would you lend me the journal?"

The commander turned to him, surprised.

"I won't go past the day of the battle. I would prefer you to read that first."

Pan'assár was glad of that. He would not hear of those final hours from any other than Or'Talán himself, and he appreciated Turion's integrity in the matter, his inbred sense of honour. "Alright."

His tone must have reflected his worry and Turion was quick to assure him. "It will be safe in my hands, Pan'assár."

"I know."

Turion nodded and together they walked through the guarded doors. Inside, they found Rinon sitting with Handir, Aradan, Miren and Llyniel.

"When did you arrive, Llyniel?" asked Rinon, joining the others before the hearth. He sank heavily into a stuffed chair, allowing himself a groan.

"A few hours ago. The camp is in an uproar. There are warriors coming and going all the time."

"You have done well, brother," said Handir.

"I have done as much as I could. We were lucky to count on Angon's cooperation."

"It was your idea to recruit him," added Aradan, and Rinon nodded, accepting a goblet from Pan'assár.

"You have heard the news, of course?" asked Rinon, eyes on Handir.

"Llyniel and Miren have told us. He let his guard down," murmured Handir.

"Betrayed by Farón, of all people," said Llyniel. "Farón was Lainon's pupil, deep in the trust of the Silvan Elders."

"I spoke with Farón many times," admitted Miren. "Never in all my years would I have said he would turn on his people."

"We must brace ourselves for what may happen tomorrow. Once those votes are taken, Band'orán will waste no time. There will be little point in keeping our father alive," said Rinon.

"And our brother," added Handir. Rinon turned and stared, a question in his eyes. But Handir did not answer. Instead, he turned to Llyniel. "Is he well?"

"He is *alive*," she rectified.

Rinon's eyes were wide, his questions answered but Aradan turned to his daughter, even though his words were meant for Handir. "How would she know?" He turned back to Handir, and then Miren. He found a soft smile on her lips and caught his daughter's rebellious eyes; saw the Bonding Braid in her hair. "No ..." But he knew it was true, and as the news sunk in and his mind began to process it, he realised that he was happy—happier than he could say. He had always hoped his daughter would marry Handir, or Rinon even. But this ... the king's Silvan son ... His elation was short-lived. His daughter's bonded was surely sitting beside the king in some dungeon, passing his last night in this life. "Gods ..."

"They have dealt us a complex hand, for sure," said Handir. "But tomorrow is the end of that game. Tomorrow, everything unfolds, and we must be ready."

"We are ready, brother. As ready as we can be," said Rinon, himself still shocked that his childhood friend, Handir's closest friend, was bonded to his own half-brother, the brother he had yet to meet.

"When will Erthoron arrive?" asked Aradan, turning to his wife.

"At midday tomorrow. I told him we would send an escort." Miren's eyes drifted to Pan'assár.

"I will arrange it." He nodded.

"Will Amareth come?" asked Aradan.

"No." Miren shook her head. "She rules in Erthoron and Lorthil's absence."

"A pity. We are family now," he mused and caught his wife's proud, satisfied expression. Aradan nodded at her, smiled sparingly as he turned to Llyniel. But she was asleep, head resting on the shoulder of an equally slumbering Handir.

Rinon turned to the commander, voice softer. "Well then, Pan'assár. Will you tell us of this Nim'uán?"

The Council of Elders had spoken to them all, issued its orders to Dalú and Angon.

One more day, they said. One more chance for the Alpines. But should the votes turn against equality, should their Warlord never return, then Erthoron's hopes for peace would be dashed, and chaos would surely give strength to Angon's call for independence. Many would answer it, others would not condone the violence. It would be the end of Silvan unity.

Dalú and Angon walked through the encampment, their orders still lingering in their minds. Their people sang songs of hope, rebellion, peace and war. Others sounded the drums and evoked the Gods in the face of a new enemy, the Alpine enemy.

Aria, Spirit of the Trees, of the Land, Divine Guardian.

Duria, Spirit of Light and Warmth.

Galomú, Spirit of Evil, of all things Cruel and Dark. They asked her to take the Purists.

But so too did they sing of love, of unity, of the inherent goodness of the immortals. They prepared their weapons, mixed dyes and painted their bodies with symbols of protection and loyalty. They chanted as they braided their hair, showing their origins, their rank, their ruling houses.

"I have spent weeks justifying rebellion, Dalú. I have avenged my people by turning away Alpine merchants, showing them the cost of their disdain, and yet now, on the eve of those votes, I cannot say I desire independence."

Dalú turned to the warrior he considered a son. Angon still bore the marks of his mistreatment at the hands of the Alpines. "If we can find Fel'annár. If he is with the king, then there will be no need. But if they are lost, things can never go back to the way they were. War will be inevitable if Band'orán wins, and no, I do not desire that either. But I desire slavery even less."

Angon turned to his mentor, offered him a sorry smile and watched as he heaved a deep breath. "I trusted him, Angon. I trusted Farón and I was a fool."

"No. We all trusted Farón. He was Lainon's pupil, how could we not? Farón was good once. I still think he loves his people. Whatever his motives, I think he believes in them. I don't think he does this for wealth, Dalú."

"What does it matter? He betrayed us, turned his back on us, the warriors who loved him, looked to him for an example. What could have moved him more than that regard, Angon?"

The Silvan rebel had no answer. All he could do was shake his head.

"If it comes to battle, Angon; if we lose those votes and our people can no longer be detained ... if it comes to killing those we once fought beside, will your hand falter?"

Angon turned to the scarred captain. "It will. But I will fight beside you nonetheless."

Dalú looked away. An honest answer, his own answer, and Aria forbid that prospect become real. Aria guide Prince Handir, help him win his battle of words in the Council Hall so that it would not need to be fought with swords.

∽

BARATHON STOPPED AND DISMOUNTED SLOWLY, as he looked around for any signs of what his father had seen, what had made him dismount and step into the forest in the dead of night. The ten mounted guards sat silently by, almost invisible on a moonless night.

"Father?"

"Here."

There he was, a little further on, standing with his back toward the group, looking at something Barathon could not see. All black save for his silver hair that almost seemed blue in the moonlight.

"What is it, Father?"

"Yes. That is the question, is it not? What is it, when a son turns on his own father?"

Barathon closed his eyes. Draugolé had betrayed him, told his father what he had said. "I have not turned on you."

Band'orán approached him, and although his face was harsh and unyielding, Barathon thought him magnificent. He was frightened of the father he had always tried, and failed, to impress.

"He tried to defend you, but you see, although he has always had a soft spot for you, he fears me. You made a grave error of judgement, Barathon. Once more, you fail to understand. You fail to see what I am doing ... why I am doing it."

"I would have followed you, whatever your motives, Father. But you have abducted a king, conspire to murder him. He is family, in spite of whatever separated you in the past. I cannot condone it. I will leave. Change my name, my life. You will never see me again if that is your wish."

Band'orán stepped closer still. "It is. How can I look at you after this? How can I see your face and not remember that you turned on me?" Deep lines of some ancient hurt scored between his brows, blue eyes swimming with a pain he had never voiced because to do so would drive him to this. "You were always weak, Barathon. You were never enough. Whatever you did, however well you did it, it was never better. You never impressed anyone."

Barathon stepped backwards, up against a silver birch. His father's hand came out from under his cloak, fingers wide, covered his throat and held him in place. With bulging eyes, Barathon brought his own hand up to grasp at his father's steely grip.

"Second, never first," said Band'orán. "Good but never better. Wise but not the wisest. Second to one, second always to Or'Talán. You were not good enough, Band'orán."

Barathon was starting to panic, but still, the slip registered. Who was his father? Who did he think he was talking to?

"Father ... stop!"

"It never stops, son. You are a failure. Mediocre warrior, mediocre statesman, better than most, but always second."

"I ... I tried."

The hand around his throat tightened, and Barathon's hands pushed back. But both his arms were not enough to loosen his father's chokehold. He could feel his windpipe narrowing, could hardly speak. "Please..."

"Don't beg. Accept it. Your life means nothing. Not when you walk beside *him*."

He couldn't breathe, couldn't move his head. He was held in place, forced to watch as his father's madness was given free rein. He felt dizzy, panicked, grappled with the hand but another came up. Band'orán pried his son's hands away and pushed until something scraped against the back of Barathon's neck. His eyes bulged, sagged, closed, heart shuddering in his chest.

Band'orán watched as he squeezed, face shaking with the effort, tears unchecked. Then he gasped, staggering backwards. He watched the body crumple to the ground, first into an awkward sitting position, only to slowly keel sideways, inert.

"Band'orán?" He stepped forwards. "Barathon?" He knelt down, took in the chin and the face. "Barathon."

A gasp. He covered his mouth with his other hand, a tear splashing onto his son's still chest. "Your life had no meaning, child." A hoarse whisper. "It's better this way. No suffering. No pretending. You're free now." He smiled, lips quivered. "See? See how peaceful it is?"

He turned away, despair and grief were only fleeting. Ire was building in his chest. He knew who was responsible. He knew how it had all started: with the one that could not be beaten. With the one who had always been better, had never failed his father. Even now, he was sitting in his underground realm, alive and at his mercy at last. Now, even when there were no witnesses to it, *Band'orán* would be better. *Band'orán* would be cleverer, more skilled. He would outwit them all and then be a king, better than *him*. Better than Or'Talán.

He stood, walked back to his silent guards and mounted, leaving his son lying dead in the forest, all but forgotten. He had killed Band'orán—Barathon—and now he would kill Or'Talán, at last.

THE COMPANY CONTINUED THEIR SEARCH, Tensári at the fore, eyes burning bright, and Gor'sadén at her shoulder. They rode through the forest, up hills, along ridges. They searched every cave, crossed every glade. But there was still no sign of Fel'annár or the king. Rinon had, indeed, searched these lands well.

Gor'sadén startled when Tensári turned to him. "Rock. Rock and water. There is water, Commander."

He frowned, turned to Idernon. "Are there any water sources here? Lakes, streams, some tributary of the Calro?"

"No. But these are the foothills of the Median Mountains. There are bound to be underground rivers, although where I cannot say.

However," he continued, more slowly, "it would make sense that they were close to the Calro ..."

"Further south? Back towards the city?"

"It is but a guess, Commander."

"It is all we have. Tensári?"

"Agreed."

"Then we ride!" He wheeled his horse around, back in the direction they had come from. They would ride slowly, carefully, search everything, even the ground beneath their feet.

"Do you remember your mother, Fel'annár?"

He turned where he sat, knees bent, arms resting on them. "No."

"Did you ever see her in a picture?"

"I saw her in a dream."

"Then you know that she was beyond beauty. Gods, but those eyes of hers. Like emeralds under a forest brook, under a hot summer's day."

Fel'annár's eyes strayed to the rough-cut emerald that sat on the king's index finger. It was an odd piece, he mused, as if it had been split unintentionally by an axe, part of a once whole gem. He turned away again, listening as the king continued to remember his love.

"But it was her heart. Her heart was so big, so open. A Silvan heart, giving and caring. How the people loved her, and how she returned that love. I saw her, just once from a distance, as she handed a loaf of bread to a soldier. She didn't look at me." He smiled, almost a grin. "She thought me a pompous prince come to parade himself, *swagger and flirt* as she later told me. She could be so brash at times, had a tongue on her that would not be stilled even in the face of royalty."

Fel'annár's mind strayed to Llyniel, wondered if she was still at the camp.

"I returned the next day. I was supposed to stay with the tents, but the village was safe enough. I stole away and watched her as she worked, sat amongst the trees and watched her hands as they weaved a basket, as they tucked her hair behind her ear."

"Fond memories. I am glad you have some." Fel'annár knew the king was watching him, but he kept his own eyes on the now dry lake beyond.

"Amareth cared well for you." Careful words, spoken softly.

"She is not my mother."

The silence seemed to deepen, stretched on until something banged loudly, glass smashing on stone. Thargodén and Fel'annár stood slowly, trying the chains once more. They watched as Band'orán came striding towards them, and to Fel'annár's utter shock, he wore the purple sash of a Kah Master. Behind him were four others wearing grey sashes, and one of them was Farón, nose still puffy from where he had broken it. Fel'annár caught his eye, curled his lip at the traitor. But there was no time for questions.

A hand streaked past his peripheral vision, striking him across the cheek and sending him reeling sideways, barely keeping both feet beneath him. Thargodén steadied him and Fel'annár straightened, looking the Kah Master in the eye. He saw the glint, the strange emotions, and wondered whether it was madness.

Band'orán half-turned, kicked him in the chest, then moved in and swiped the legs out from under him. Fel'annár crashed to the floor, could hardly roll. A kick to the side, and another. All he could see were Band'orán's black boots, his sash settling around his knees. He drew in a painful breath and gasped.

"Fel'annár." A whisper from his other side.

"You disgust me. Half-Silvan spawn of a whore. You should have died in her arms. What was Aria thinking?" A hand in his hair, pulling his face up and back. Band'orán peered closely at him in fascination and confusion. "You don't deserve that face."

The hand pushed back, and Fel'annár rolled as best he could, standing slowly. Band'orán's words echoed in his mind.

"You should have died in her arms."

"You don't deserve that sash." Fel'annár's voice was nothing but a breathless whisper.

"And what would you know? You're nothing but a warrior, barely out of novice training. Not good enough for me, Silvan. Not good enough."

There was a pattern, thought Fel'annár, and he remembered those nights on the road when Pan'assár had told them the story inside Or'Talán's diary; the story he had tried to ignore but which had stuck in his mind.

"A true Master would not have missed my head with that kick. You're not fast enough."

Band'orán's mind flashed silver-white, and he rushed forwards, reaching out with both hands for Fel'annár's throat. He thought to throttle the boy as he had done Barathon, but a head smashed into his forehead, a boot in the knee, in the gut. Band'orán staggered backwards, almost fell as he gasped for air.

Not a novice. No simple warrior.

The four disciples behind him rushed forwards and this time, they were prepared, would use all their Kah training in hand-to-hand combat. Outnumbered, one leg shackled to the wall and his hands tied, all Fel'annár could do was prepare for the beating that would surely ensue.

Thargodén watched, and on his face, Band'orán saw horror, dread. It fuelled him, surged through him and fed his muscles, his desire to hurt, as others had hurt him. "It is hard to watch the demise of a son, isn't it, nephew?" The voice was whimsical, far away and the king braced himself, watched Band'orán face his captive son. He stared for a moment, and then his fist flew, again and again. He struck the face, the chest, pummelled into him, eyes on nothing at all.

"Stop! *Stop!*" But Thargodén's pleas were like oil for the fires in Band'orán's eyes.

All Thargodén could do was watch as his son was beaten, as Band'orán threw him against the wall, against the floor, like a child's rag doll, almost as limp, and when he had finished, he stood breathless over the crumpled form of Fel'annár, of Or'Talán.

"It all started with you, brother. You and your little birds. But I never belonged in the trees ..." Nothing but half-whispers echoing off water-eroded walls, but Thargodén was piecing together the story, bringing together the fragments of the past.

'You should have died in her arms.'

Band'orán flexed his hand. "She left because of *you*. She would have stayed, if only you had never existed." He turned to Thargodén, walked towards him, and the king watched as Band'orán—the mad brother, the killer brother—changed before his very eyes. The madness was quelled in an instant. Gone were the strange glints in his eyes, the tremble of lips, the muttered and disjointed phrases. Band'orán was a lord once more, royal brother, councillor.

"I must leave for tomorrow's proceedings. I will vote against the Silvans, as you already know. And perhaps you can guess what lies in store for your heirs. I am in no rush, Thargodén. But sooner or later, this realm will be mine. I will rule, and Or'Talán will be dead at last. Enjoy these last few hours, nephew. It is all you will ever have with *him*." He smiled. "You will never see me again. You will both stay here, in the past. I walk to a new future, free at last."

Thargodén watched him leave. But the Kah Disciples stayed. Unlocking the father and son's shackles, they dragged Fel'annár away, pushing him along just behind. They descended, into the heart of the rock and at the very bottom, one guard opened a door which led into a shaft. Or perhaps it was a well, thought Thargodén. At the very top was a door, too high to climb. There were no footholds, just chiselled rock.

With their shackles back in place, the door banged shut. Thargodén gave thanks that Fel'annár could not see what he could.

Bones. Bones and chains, strips of wool and broken skulls.

"Fel'annár." An echo. Another.

And then he heard it. Water, trickling, running, whispering over rock. He startled, felt the frigid water beneath him, soaking his clothes. He frowned, wondering where it was coming from. And then he realised. The dry lake above, the smooth rock below. This was an underground tidal lake, and the tide was rising.

∽

SALO HELD up his hand to the patrol behind him. Dismounting, he walked into the small glade that had caught the Silvan lieutenant's attention.

Further inside, at the base of a silver birch, was a body half-sat half-laid upon the ground. An Alpine captain.

Salo frowned as he knelt before him, inspecting the body. He reached out and tilted the head backwards.

"He has been strangled. Dead for two hours, perhaps. Search the area," he ordered. "Henú, wrap him in something. We'll take him back to camp. His identity may tell us something."

Henú nodded. "Sir, there are tracks. Some ten riders heading north and south."

"They split up, then," deduced Salo. He glanced at the now black sky. Had they gone in only one direction, he would have followed, but his patrol was too small to cover both ways. "We ride home."

With Barathon's body wrapped in a blanket and slung over the back of Salo's mount, they made for the encampment to report their grim finding to Lord Erthoron.

～

"GALDITH?" Galadan peered into the trough they had come across, the light from Galdith's torch illuminating the dirt on the walls. "Nothing," he called back up. "Just a hunter's trap. No exit except up. No blood, no tracks."

Ramien threw a rope down to him and braced as he pulled Galdith back up. Standing, he dusted himself down and then mounted.

"We move," said Gor'sadén, Galadan's torch flickering wildly amongst The Company as they rode. At this rate, they would be back at the city in three hours. This was well-searched terrain, Gor'sadén knew. Still, Tensári's eyes were still bright. Fel'annár was alive somewhere near, and frustration was beginning to gnaw at him. There would be no rest for any of them, no place left unsearched, not until he found his son.

20

TO ARM A SILVAN WARLORD

"That day marked the return of the noble houses of the Silvan people. The Silver Wolf, the Grey Bear, the White Oak and the Fire Fox. They danced upon the standards, shone proudly in the eyes of warriors no longer enslaved but free to serve and to die with honour."
The Silvan Chronicles, Book IV. Marhené.

As a new day dawned, the first day of his new life, Lord Band'orán stood before the doors of Analei. It had been his home for many years, a home he would now leave behind, never to return.

He was the epitome of a noble Alpine councillor, honourable member of the Royal Council. His black robes of office draped perfectly over his equally black tunic, the purple sash of a Kah Master carefully concealed below.

Around his neck was the symbol of his office, of what he had sworn to uphold. It was a beautiful collar, a solid silver semi-circle, reaching from one shoulder to the other, held around his neck by three chains fastened at the back. Lines of gems, blue for the mountain, green for the forest, diamonds for the strength of his loyalty to the crown. At the very centre, dripping from the precious metal was the acorn and emerald of Ea Uaré, gold and emerald, symbol of the house of Or'Talán. Many would fight for the honour of wearing this, even just to touch such an exquisite thing. Yet more than the worth of its materials, it was the honour and prestige it bestowed upon its bearer.

Today, it would not be the venerable Lord Councillor Aradan to lead the proceedings, but Prince Handir. The prince regent had decreed it, and Band'orán had no objections. Indeed, Handir's inexperience could well work in his favour.

He accommodated himself in his saddle and turned to Barathon.

But he wasn't there. And then he remembered what he had done. He frowned, schooled his face, and turned to the large elf who stood to attention before him. "Muster the Shadow Kah. Wait for my summons."

The guard bowed low, and Band'orán and his company left for the palace, his new home. Behind him, ever smaller, was Analei and the past, its ghosts free to roam where they would. As for him, tomorrow would mark the first day of his victory. He would dwell in the king's quarters, feast on his ascension to the throne. He smiled, looked over his shoulder, saw a guard.

Not Barathon.

GOR'SADÉN and The Company crouched behind the trees directly before the courtyard, the stately manor of Analei in the distance.

"Prince Rinon already searched it," whispered Galdith.

"But he did not have the Ber'ator, Galdith. She has led us this way, and I say everything this way must be searched." Gor'sadén watched as a group of black-clad warriors mounted, hooves clattering over the cobbled stones as they approached another who sat waiting, silver catching on the early morning light.

"That is Band'orán," whispered Galadan.

Gor'sadén nodded, watched as the foremost warrior drew a blade and saluted. He sucked in a noisy breath.

"What is it?" asked Idernon on his other side.

"That was no ordinary salute. It was the Kal'hai, the oath of loyalty, from a Kah Warrior to his Master."

"*Kah Warriors!*" Galdith gasped.

"Illicit ones. Band'orán is no *Master*."

Once Band'orán and his warriors had left, Gor'sadén bid The Company mount. They rode down the hill and to the doors of a now apparently abandoned forest manor. It was a beautiful place, sat with the mountains at its back and the forest before it. But the trees were not close. There would be no help from them, not to Fel'annár if he was inside. And Gor'sadén thought that he was.

Through the open main doors, Galdith looked about the lordly place. "There's no one about. Not even serving staff."

"He's here." Tensári's lip curled, eyes slanted, body as rigid as rock. Gor'sadén wondered how much of her anger was directed at herself for having lost the Ber'anor in the first place. He didn't know the story, but he wanted to.

"Under stone, you say. Then we descend."

The Company nodded and followed the commander down the stone steps. They came to a landing. More doors and passageways, and Gor'sadén turned to Tensári for guidance. She shook her head, and Gor'sadén led them further down. As he did so, he remembered those anguished moments in which they had searched the banks of the Cor'hidén, wading through the reeds and wondering if they would find Handir or Fel'annár's body floating there. They hadn't, but would luck accompany them one more time?

But then, what had luck to do with any of this? Nothing, he decided.

I am coming, my son.

WATER POOLED AROUND THEM, cold and pure. It soaked their clothes, rising quickly. Fel'annár rubbed his bruised forehead, scraping a chain over the raised stone behind him, again and again. He had been doing it for a long while with no success, and Thargodén watched him, wondering that Fel'annár thought he could break his shackle this way. It was the king's shackle that he worked on, not his own.

"It will not come loose, Fel'annár."

"It will."

The boy was desperate. He had started on the chain no sooner than he had come round, battered and bruised, the shirt barely still on his back. He had rubbed his own bonds against a sharp rock and freed his hands and then set to work. Just when Thargodén was about to dissuade him again, Fel'annár took the chain in his hands and began to twist and turn. Did he think he could break it with his bare hands? He was strong, admittedly, but not that strong. He breathed deeply, looked up to the small circle in the roof, and then down at the water that now covered the floor. It would be over their heads in minutes. Of all the ways he thought he would die, he had not contemplated drowning.

Dread stirred in him. He tried not to think that he would be forced to watch his son drown. After all this time, they had had but hours to speak. Thargodén had discovered that his father had not betrayed him, Fel'annár had learned that Band'orán had ordered his mother's death and that he, too, should have died with her. Thargodén had told his orphan son of his mother and the boy had listened, had surely reproached him in silence for having no memory of her.

But Fel'annár had not forgiven him.

How could he? Thargodén had obeyed the dictates of his father. He could have disobeyed, but he had put duty before his heart. He had obeyed his father and betrayed his love. Then Or'Talán sought out Lássira, traced a plan. The plan that failed and yet Fel'annár was here, and she was dead. He wanted to laugh, wanted to cry, wanted to hug the boy. And all Fel'annár did was scrape at his chains, twist them in his bruised and bloody hands, pull and then start again.

And then, to his utter shock, the chain broke, and the king was free. He stared wide-eyed, shook his head.

Wordlessly, they both took up Fel'annár's chain and repeated the process. But in Thargodén's heart, a new reality became clear. It had taken Fel'annár far more time to break the chains than it would for the water to cover his head. It would soon be submerged in water, there would be no friction. No footholds. Thargodén was free of his shackle, could float upwards and to the door in the roof, but Fel'annár was chained to the ground. He would drown first and Thargodén would surely join him minutes later.

And he had not told his son that he was sorry. So very sorry.

DOWNWARDS THEY CLIMBED, and Sontúr trailed his fingers over the stone walls. They were cold and oddly wet, and he told Idernon as much. "Perhaps you were right about the underground rivers, Idernon. It's humid down here."

Idernon nodded. With their curiosity piqued, they continued down into the basement. They turned right, right again, opening every door only to find nothing. And then Tensári's urgent voice.

"Commander."

"What is it?" The group stopped, turned to her.

"He's here. I am certain."

"There are no doors here. We've searched them all." Galdith didn't understand—none of them did. Idernon's eyes were searching —the walls, the ceiling, the floor—for the slightest hint of a crack, some trap door. Nothing. Similarly, Sontúr turned and raked his eyes over every single detail, every ridge and every chip of rock. Nothing. They were at the end of a corridor with nowhere else to go except back, and so they turned—all of them except for Tensári.

See.

See what?

The word had popped into her mind, unconnected with her own thoughts. Not hers.

She turned, concentrated. Eyes burning, itching.

See.

Gods, what was she supposed to see? She turned back to the very end of the corridor, saw the torch in the sconce flickering in a draft. But there were no windows here. One hand reached up to touch the cold stone, at the very top where it met with the ceiling. She smoothed her fingers downwards to the floor, and then back up, further right and to the very top. Fingertips felt the uneven surface, worn with time and this confounded water. Up and down, further right; up and then down.

She froze.

Her fingertips retracted over the odd etching. Half a circle. She peered closer.

See.

C.

"Commander!"

She felt him at her side, even as she dug her finger into the etching, felt it give.

There was a deep groan, some mechanism clicking and creaking, the rumble of heavy stone moving.

"What the *Hell*?"

Before them, a gaping hole, a black stain on the rock. A frigid breeze blew into their faces, blowing out all but the furthest torches. Almost dark, they waited for the mechanism to grind to a halt.

"We've found them."

Carodel ran back down the passageway, grabbed two torches still alight and hurried to rejoin the rest. He threw one to Idernon and then followed behind Gor'sadén and Tensári, into the near dark. Idernon placed a hand on her shoulder, squeezed, and then left her side to lend more light to Gor'sadén.

It was a slow incline, but in the distance, lights were shining. As the tunnel became wider and their eyes adjusted to the gloom, Band'orán's underground world opened up before their disbelieving eyes.

Idernon held his torch high, in case his eyes were deceiving him.

But with more light came the surety that someone lived down here, had done for many years. And whoever it was, had been here recently.

They saw weapons of old, shields and standards, sigils and portraits. It was a place of magnificence in its own dark way. Colourful rocks rose and fell, and water reflected light off the chiselled walls, made it all glitter. It was a wonderland, dark and light, multi-hued and at times shadowed. Was this where Band'orán had hatched his plans? wondered Idernon as his eyes drifted over the paintings, and then stopped before one of them. He reached out with his free hand, leaned closer. "Queen Canusahéi."

"Surely not." Galadan turned, and then faltered, eyes wide. Idernon was right.

But Tensári saw none of the wonders which decorated such an unlikely place. Her senses were reaching out, eyes hot as she turned full circle. Water, water ... Something pressed on her chest.

They crossed the room, waving their torches here and there, lighting up the corners and the walls as they passed. High above them, a sigil swayed from a chain and Galadan stared up as they walked beneath it.

"What does that sigil mean to you, Galadan?" ventured Idernon.

"It is the queen's arms."

Idernon frowned. C upon the wall, the portrait, the queen's arms ...

There was no time to ponder the question because Gor'sadén had stopped. He peered down at something, and then crouched. The sound of jangling metal and Idernon glanced over his shoulder, lending more light. There, in the commander's hand was a shackle, attached to a chain in the wall. He closed his eyes, dread mounting, and yet Tensári's eyes still shone. Fel'annár was here, he was sure of it, sure that he was not dead.

"Commander?"

Galadan's voice jolted them all and as one, they turned to the lieutenant. Held reverently in both hands, the most exquisite work of art sat winking and glinting in the flickering light of their torches. Craftsmanship from centuries past, never bested.

The crown of the house of Or'Talán.

"Guard it well, Galadan. Guard it well."

IT WAS A BEAUTIFUL MORNING. Too beautiful for a day such as this.

Pan'assár had been careful with his attire, ceremonial cuirass already glowing in the late spring light. He wound the purple sash of the Kah Master around his waist, tied it, wondered briefly how he had discarded it for so many years. He adjusted his belt and longsword, checked his shortsword just above it. He was ready—ready to face the Inner Circle, to stop the inevitable from happening if he could.

Leaving his suite of rooms on the second-to-last floor of the palace, he climbed the stairs that led to the king's chambers, returning the various bows and salutes as he passed by. Turion had seen to the duty rosters the night before. These were the guards he most trusted. He had also ensured that those who would guard the doors in the Council Chamber were also loyal, at least as far as he could possibly know. It was a gamble, their best bet.

The doors were open but guarded, and Pan'assár waited for the warriors to present arms and step aside. Turion sat in one corner, candle burning low and the palm of his hand about to slip off his face.

"You should get ready, Captain."

"I am ready, Commander." He carefully closed Or'Talán's diary, stood and placed it on a side table. He was, indeed, ready, decked in his own finery. He had obviously dressed a long time ago and returned to his reading.

"You are engrossed." Pan'assár gestured with his head to the journal.

"It paints a very different picture of Band'orán. I had never guessed at the vulnerability Or'Talán writes of. Not a word I would ever associate with him. But there is something, Pan'assár, something that does not sit right with me. I have read the same twenty pages over and over. My mind has latched on to something I have yet to understand, about who was deployed where just before the battle."

Pan'assár frowned, moving closer, and Turion pointed at the passage he was referring to.

We have stopped, had to because there are too few of us. We will run headfirst into the Sand Lords, and we need reinforcements. I have sent riders to Sen'uár, with a message for Captain Dinor.

Pan'assár stared at the page, turned away and then looked once more, thinking perhaps he had it wrong.

Dinor.

"*Harahon* was in charge of Sen'uár, not Dinor. I checked the registers, looked at every command. This doesn't make sense," said Pan'assár. "Unless Dinor replaced Harahon for some reason I was unaware of. These things happen, but then why were the registers not amended?"

"I have a distant memory of Dinor telling me of his part at the battle. He said he was close to Sen'oléi, not Sen'uár," said Turion. "If there had been a change, Dinor would surely have told you."

Pan'assár said nothing for a moment, at least not to Turion. The captain was right. Dinor *would* have told him. He reached for the journal but hesitated. "Do you want to keep it for a while?"

Turion considered it, shook his head. "No. You keep it safe, Pan'assár. When all this is over, perhaps we can read through to the end. Make some sense of it."

Pan'assár took it, felt the comforting leather in his hands, and then turned to Prince Handir as he entered the room.

"Good morning Commander, Captain."

Here was a prince, indeed. He wore the black robes of a Royal Councillor, and underneath, a deep blue tunic that separated him from the rest. He was the king's son. Rinon's ceremonial uniform was different in the same way, the same deep blue denoting him as a royal scion. Around Handir's neck sat the heavy collar of gem-encrusted gold and silver that marked him as chosen by the king to sit on the Council, the ruling body of Ea Uaré, over which the king himself presided. His hair told the story of his nobility and station, too. Gold thread entwined in his braids, dotted with jewels. Ar Thargodén, Prince of Ea Uaré.

The two warriors bowed. Handir nodded and then sat at a small table beside the wall of windows that looked out over the Evergreen Wood. "My father's favourite spot. He hears them sometimes—these trees," he clarified. "Not like Fel'annár can, but he does feel them: their unease, their joy."

"And you, Prince? Do you feel them at all?" Pan'assár wondered if it was something that ran in the family, although he had never heard Or'Talán mention any talent in that respect.

"I feel unease, but not from them. It is the entire kingdom, Pan'assár, perched precariously upon the ledge of a chasm. I have a good case against Band'orán, but with the king gone, the councillors may well vote on the side of strength, on the side of experience."

"This is a vote to decide on equality amongst our councillors."

"No, Turion. This is a vote of *confidence*. This is a vote on who the Council will heed. Band'orán wants that power, the power to wield the Council like a weapon. It is a first, giant step towards the throne."

"There is still a chance we will find him."

They turned to Rinon, bowed. "Any news, Prince?"

"None, Pan'assár. Our patrols return empty-handed and this *Company* of yours, they have not returned at all."

"They may not come back to the city, might think it is too dangerous."

"And they would be right, Turion. Still, once that council begins, that is where the danger will be, I think." Rinon shook his head. "There is some urgency in the air this morning. The Inner Circle was thick with it earlier. Some captains are nervous and overly curt, while others are far too quiet. Even the few warriors still at the barracks are on edge. They wait for their brothers from the Outer City Barracks, but there is still no sign of them."

"How many are being sent?"

"I asked for two hundred."

"Added to our 150 ..."

"The Silvans will not attack us, Commander." Handir stared at Pan'assár from where he still sat at the window. "They promised us until the votes."

"Prince, without Fel'annár to convince them—"

"They won't attack, not today."

Pan'assár turned his sceptical eyes away, to Turion.

"And time will tell if our own warriors are with us, or against us," said the captain.

"Has anyone seen Huren?" asked Rinon.

"He left his quarters early, made for the Inner Circle where I assume he remains." Turion knew this because he had ordered him watched. He well knew Rinon's distrust of the general. He stepped towards Pan'assár, holding out a folded and sealed parchment. "My vote, Commander."

Pan'assár took it and then turned to Rinon. The prince opened a drawer in the desk and extracted a similar note, handing it to Pan'assár. Slipping both of them into a small pocket inside his cloak, he bowed to the princes.

"It is time to face the Inner Circle. Once we have the vote on the Warlord, I will bring it to the Council Hall."

His gaze lingered on Turion. He offered a slow nod, an order to protect, his own vote of confidence and the promise of aid at the Council, once the Inner Circle had concluded. Pan'assár needed to be there when Handir made his final move on Band'orán.

He strode down the corridor, Or'Talán's journal in his hand and Harahon and Dinor on his mind. Only one of them was still alive to tell the tale. Who had really been commanding officer at Sen'uár? Harahon, as the records showed? Or had it been Dinor, as Or'Talán claimed?

The underground well that Band'orán intended as a royal mausoleum was filling with water.

Thargodén broke the surface, spluttering and heaving for breath. "Damn it, just—"

"It's held fast," gasped Fel'annár as he broke the surface beside the king. We're not strong enough. We have no weapons, no loose rocks ..."

"I will never stop—*never!*" And he wouldn't. He had turned away from Lássira because his father had asked it of him. His king had demanded it. He had turned his back on his soul, duty over love, but this was a chance to right that wrong.

He ducked under the water once more. He pulled, boots pushing off the stone, arms straining, desperate. A muffled shriek, bubbles everywhere, but no air. The chain attached to Fel'annár's shackle would not break.

Thargodén surfaced, yelled, veins bulging, voice echoing off the walls. The chain was too thick. He was not strong enough, never had been. Chains of duty, hatred, power, taking everything he loved. Lássira, Fel'annár ...

"There's nothing more you can do, my king."

Thargodén was trembling with the effort it took to stand there, stand in the water and watch it rise, faster and faster. Just a few more moments and Fel'annár would be beneath the surface. Lássira's son, the child they had conceived in hope. Wrath, ire, the injustice that his life had been, culminating in this travesty, the unthinkable moment of a father watching his son die.

"I'm sorry. Child, I am so ... so ..." Thargodén squeezed his eyes shut, tears spilling through his lashes. In that moment, when the water was at Fel'annár's chin as he stood chained to the ground, he truly searched those eyes that had beguiled him from a distance, that had stolen his breath, claimed his heart. He had never forgotten them, never would. There was acceptance in them. Fear, too. And then he saw it: a spark of something else. Panic, because there was no time left, no hope left. There was surely no more time for reproaches, no time for anger or rejection.

"Don't be sorry."

How could he not be? And then he could no longer stand, the water around him heavier than he was. He watched every breath his son took, deep and fast, anticipating the moment in which the last would come, and his heart would stop and it would be too late.

So brave. So young.

Love and pain surged through Thargodén's blood. Love for a stranger,...

A harsh breath and he knew the chain had tensed. Water bubbled at his son's mouth, his last word barely audible. Thargodén felt his face crack and quiver but he couldn't look away.

"Father ..."

Thargodén surged forward, arms out. He encircled the rigid, panting body, holding his head. "Aria *don't!* Stop! *Stop it!*"

He looked down, watching in despair as the water swirled over his lovely face. The emeralds blazing brightly, slowly dimming.

He cried out, loud and raw, until there was no more breath in him, no more breath in his child. His own heart sped out of control, even as he felt the body he held jerk, once and then again. It slackened.

"Damn you, Band'orán! Curse you to the pits of torment! Burn in eternal agony! *Fel'annár!*"

~

Fel'annár.

Tensári shot up, turned, wide eyes blazing.

"*Here!*" Tensári's call from beside the bronze statue which stood before a dry river bed.

The others ran to her. Idernon brushed his hands over it, admiring the detail on her dress.

"That's Handir's mother," said Galadan.

"C. The key to this place." Tensári was thinking, piecing it all together. "C for Canusahéi, the road to the queen." Tensári bent, ran her hands over the smooth stone to the base. The feet, naked and perfect, and below them, one word.

Eternal.

Tensári's eyes travelled past the statue, to the ground, along it. Her skin flared as if it had caught fire and been doused with frigid water. Ears ringing, heart hammering against her heaving chest, she reached down and felt the bed of this natural river. It was cold. It was wet. A crack. No ... a line, another, and another.

"Quiet! All of you, *quiet!*"

Her words echoed around them, and she was kneeling, Sontúr at her side, ear to the ground, eyes blazing blue.

A grating sound. No, a *grinding* sound.

"There's someone down there." Her voice was desperate, full of dread. Her eyes searched for a mechanism, a way to open what looked like a hatch, to whatever lay below.

Gor'sadén's hands roved over the riverbed, Galdith and Galadan doing the same while Carodel and Ramien searched further into the dry bed but it was Idernon's voice that called out.

"Here!" He pressed his finger into the indentation he had found, identical to the one on the outer wall. A rumble. Something shifted at Canusahéi's feet. A slab of rock had moved sideways. A shout, of fright and then panic, a hoarse voice and a white hand that reached from the crack. A head, heaving and spluttering for air, a voice hoarse and desperate.

"He's drowning!"

Sontúr and Galadan held onto the king, held his head above the water while Idernon, Gor'sadén, Carodel and Ramien pushed the stone all the way to the side. Water oozed from what looked like a well, spilling over and rising. Galdith and Tensári knelt, peering into the darkness that was slowly opening before them.

Thargodén coughed, couldn't speak for a moment as he struggled for breath. He cleared his throat. "He's drowning! His foot is chained to the floor!" It was almost a scream from an elf on the brink of panic.

"Move it. *Move!*"shouted Gor'sadén.

Ramien roared and pushed with all his might and then Sontúr and Galadan pulled the king out. Tensári dived in, Idernon right behind.

Below the surface, a body floated, arms out to the side like a bird soaring upon hot currents. Silver tendrils undulated in the current, surrounding a face frozen in time. Eyes open, mouth open.

Tensári was at his feet, one of them shackled to a chain. She tugged on it, looked up at Idernon and shook her head desperately. Idernon surfaced.

"Ramien!"

The Wall of Stone jumped in, water sloshing over the sides. He sunk straight to the bottom, ignored the bones and chains that littered the place. He followed the loops, one by one, knowing what Fel'annár would have tried to do. And then he found it, a rougher link, and then another.

He pulled, Idernon and Tensári helping.

Idernon surfaced, gasped for air, then ducked back in. Tensári did likewise, rolled back in. With a sudden jerk, the chain floated apart. The body rose, free at last and Ramien was under him, pushing him up, and then he was out. Hands grappled with sodden clothes, pulled the inert body to the shores of the rising lake. Fel'annár was free of the water.

And he was dead.

Sontúr threw himself to his knees beside the body, eyes registering the slack, grey face, dull eyes half open.

The king coughed again, sat up. "Gods, no. Bring him back. Bring him *back!*" He was angry, frantic, could hardly move. He coughed again, eyes wide as he watched Sontúr dig the heel of his palm down, the other hand on top, pumping at Fel'annár's chest. The prince leaned forward as he worked—didn't think, couldn't think. Technique. Pump, breathe, check pulse.

No pulse. He breathed into his friend's mouth, again and again. Started pumping again.

He stopped and leaned back on his heels, watching the chest for any signs of movement. Checked the pulse at his neck again.

"Don't stop! *Don't!*"

Sontúr ignored the king. Ignored Gor'sadén and Idernon. He didn't look at any of them, only at Fel'annár's chest. Inert. He'd brought him back on the battlefield after the bite of the Nim'uán. He could do it again.

He could.

He unbuckled the chest protection, pulled at it. Idernon helped. He started again, pumped hard, breathed into Fel'annár's mouth.

He sat back, watching the bare chest.

Nothing.

"Damn it, brother!" Sontúr started again, trying not to panic. "So cold ..."

Tensári stepped backwards, horrified because she had lost him, because the Ber'anor would die. But then her head shot sideways as Gor'sadén lurched forward.

"I can help." Ignoring the startled looks from the rest of The Company, he knelt and took a cold and lifeless hand into his own. The memory of Fel'annár's words played in his mind.

'I swear, there is something about the Dohai that is mending it ...'

As Sontúr continued to pump and breathe into Fel'annár, Gor'sadén searched for his reserves of energy—energy created by the Dohai. Reaching deep inside himself, he beckoned it forth. Energy pulsed through his body, but he did not know what to do with it.

'... I can almost see it in my mind, like a cauterising fire. Like a soothing balm.'

Gor'sadén let his senses take over. He felt warm and then hot, felt the rush of energy through his veins, transcending skin. A soft translucence seemed to rise from Fel'annár's body, and The Company watched, speechless and breathless, as they willed his still chest to rise.

And it did, awkward and uneven.

Sontúr lurched forward, ignoring the shouts behind him. He took Fel'annár's head and turned it to the side, allowing himself the smallest of desperate smiles. It faltered as he watched water run from Fel'annár's mouth. And then the smile was back as his friend retched, coughing up more water and groaning.

Fel'annár rolled on his side, got a hand under himself, his other hand falling away from Gor'sadén's. He coughed again, drops of water flying. He cleared his throat and rasped out, "That hurt."

Sontúr barked out, laughed hard even as he took his cloak off and began to dry his friend. He wanted to weep in utter relief, but instead, he laughed and wiped his face with his shoulder as he worked, briefly catching Gor'sadén's gaze.

"You bloody fool. What next?" mumbled the healer prince.

It was a rhetorical question, and while Fel'annár coughed again and the king stared in disbelief, Tensári took a tentative step forwards. She felt Idernon's hand on her shoulder, Ramien's on the other. She turned, to The Company, to the commander.

"Aria bless you, Ber'ator," said Gor'sadén.

A smile so fleeting pulled at her lips. She stood there, clothes sopping wet, Ari twists plastered down the side of her face and neck. King Thargodén looked up at her from where he still knelt upon the ground. He had heard what Gor'sadén had said, but couldn't seem to find words to formulate a question, couldn't even stand on his own two legs. Still, he bowed to her from where he sat, knowing that she wouldn't see it.

He turned back, watched Gor'sadén kneel before Fel'annár and place both hands on his still heaving shoulders. He shook him gently. Curious eyes watched as his son's hands rose, covered those of the commander. Gor'sadén stood, helped Fel'annár up, and with only a brief hesitation, he pulled him into a hug.

Strange emotions assailed Thargodén. Gor'sadén's simple gesture - the way Fel'annár returned it - it brought with it a yearning, a need to feel that same regard as Green Sun had shown the commander. Gods, but he was proud of his brave warrior child. And perhaps he could tell him, one day. If he would listen.

Sontúr touched the commander's arm. "We need to get above ground. Set up camp and get him warm."

Gor'sadén nodded. "Up. Stay alert. We found no one coming in, but that does not mean they are not there. Sontúr, Tensári, with Fel'annár. Galadan, Galdith, to the king."

Retracing their path, they were soon climbing the stairs, upwards through the deserted passageways of Analei, Fel'annár half-walking, half-carried.

Galdith turned to Idernon. "Will the water continue to rise?"

"No. The lake below is tidal. With high tide, the chambers below are flooded as water fills the basin. A cyclic phenomenon."

Galdith nodded, though he hadn't understood half of it.

They shielded their eyes as they emerged from the house, and Thargodén turned to Fel'annár, held up by Idernon and Ramien. Sopping hair and beaten face but still, there was fire in those eyes, even more here, near the trees. It was hard to look away.

They sat Fel'annár down against a tree and Thargodén watched as a sluggish hand reached out to the grass below him. He started when Fel'annár took a blade of grass between his fingers and rubbed. The flicker of a smile ghosted over his lips, at the habit they unwittingly shared, that inborn impulse to touch nature, draw strength from it.

While Galadan and Ramien left to retrieve their horses, the others sat, watching as Sontúr made a fire, big enough to boil water. Rummaging inside his pack, he retrieved a small paper wrapping. Opening it carefully, he poked about with his index finger and then emptied the entire contents into the now boiling water. The smell of mint and eucalyptus infused the air, and Carodel leant forward, breathed it in with relish. "What is that?"

"Something I picked up at Bredja's halls. I knew of the cleansing properties of mint and euca, but the Pelagians add lobelia and osha to treat water inhalation. After Prince Handir's experiences on the river, I thought I should carry some. I didn't think I would need it again on this journey. I was wrong."

"Insightful as always, Prince," said Gor'sadén.

Sontúr stared back at him. "And you are full of surprises, Commander. That was quite the trick you performed back there. Would you care to share your methods?"

"I wouldn't know how." He turned away, to Thargodén who sat silently beside him. "I am glad to see you once more, Thargodén, although not in these circumstances."

Thargodén smiled sparingly, but his eyes were on Fel'annár as he drank Sontúr's brew. The stilted tension was back, the same discomfort between them that had lifted only in those final moments when death had been a certainty.

"Will you tell me what happened?" asked Gor'sadén.

"I was lured into a trap by Bendir and brought here. Band'orán has ... lost his mind, Gor'sadén. Fel'annár has told me of the journal, told me that my father did not betray me, although I still have questions. And then they brought Fel'annár in." He smiled, watched his son and his friends around him. "He gave them a good fight."

Gor'sadén nodded. "I expected no less. What then?"

"He slammed us in that well, chained us to the ground. I do not know how he did it but he freed me. There was no time to work on his own chain before the water ..."

Gor'sadén closed his eyes, the image all too vivid in his mind. He could only guess at the anguish they had suffered. "He is alive, Thargodén. You both survived."

Thargodén nodded. "I can see you are close to him. I am glad that he has you, at least."

Gor'sadén smiled. "He will always have me."

Thargodén's eyes were back on Fel'annár. He seemed to have recovered a little. He would give him a few more minutes. But Band'orán had a head start. He needed to get back, stop Band'orán if he could.

"Perhaps you could introduce me to these brave warriors, Commander." Thargodén's voice was stronger now and Gor'sadén gladly obliged.

If the king was surprised that an Ari'ator and a prince of Tar'eastór were part of this *Company* that followed Fel'annár, he did not show it. And then Gor'sadén had called the Ari'atór Ber'ator and he wondered, who did she guard?

It was one of many questions, not least of which was what Sontúr had referred to by *'Handir's experiences on the river.'* Still, there was no time for questions now, and Thargodén looked over his shoulder, to Analei, perhaps for the last time. "When all this is over, I will tear that place down. There are too many memories here. Too many crimes haunt those walls. Barathon will fight me on that, but my mind is set. I wonder if he knows what his father is, the extent of his treachery."

With a nod from Sontúr, Gor'sadén held out a hand and waited for Thargodén to take it. He pulled the bedraggled king up and led him to a horse which Idernon held steady for him. Galadan stepped forward and reached to his belt. Unbuckling it, he freed the king's crown and held it out reverently. Thargodén stepped forward, nodded his thanks at the Alpine lieutenant. He hesitated, wondering if he deserved to place it back on his head. But there was nowhere else to put it and so he sat it carefully over his wet hair. Mounting his horse, he waited until Fel'annár sat in the saddle behind the Ari'atór. They were ready to return and Gor'sadén spoke to them all.

"With the king and the Warlord back, Band'orán is lost, whether Handir proves his guilt or not," said Gor'sadén. "Pan'assár knows that the captains may turn to Band'orán, betray their king and the troops may or may not follow. We must assume the worst: that the army will be against us. Our only hope is backup from the Outer City Barracks. Still, there will not be many, and there are only nine of us."

"The Silvans, Gor'sadén. The Silvans will ride in the name of the king."

"Fel'annár ..."

"They will." He coughed, cleared his throat. "And those who do not wish to *will* ride in the name of the *Warlord*." He coughed again, rubbed his chest.

"They will look to you to command them," said Gor'sadén, a challenge.

"And I will command them, with The Company at my side."

Galadan stood straighter, head held high, and in his eyes, satisfaction. This was Fel'annár's final test. He had always commanded his band of brothers, but could he command an entire army?

Thargodén smiled at the gravelly voice and determined eyes of his Silvan son, while The Company raised their fists, shouted as one.

They wheeled their horses around, south-westwards, and galloped away towards the Silvan encampment.

With the wind in his wet hair, Thargodén raised his crowned head and felt the calming peace of the trees. In that one cycle of the sun, he had seen Fel'annár's heart, knew that he loved him. Yet so, too, did Thargodén love his own father once more, despite the one last question that eluded him, the reason why he had not told him of his plan before riding to war.

He had learned something else, too. Lássira had been happy, lived in hope of their reunion, a Bonding Braid in her hair.

He felt free, and he felt alive. All that was left to do was be rid of Band'orán.

And then he would live—again.

Can you see him, Lássira? Can you see the son we share?

~

Captain Dalú stood at the makeshift stables at the back of the Silvan camp, Angon at his side. They hardly moved, hardly breathed.

Before them stood a wet and bedraggled King Thargodén, and beside him, the Warlord. It did not register that Gor'sadén and The Company were gathered behind.

The captain and lieutenant bowed. Dalú's eyes landed on Fel'annár. Wet hair, beaten face, half-naked.

"Farón fooled you. He is an illicit Kah Disciple, loyal to Band'orán."

Dalú lifted his gaze slowly. "I am sorry. We all trusted him, loved Lainon. But it was my responsibility. I will relinquish my command ..."

"No. I don't want that. He fooled us *all*. I trusted him, too. But I would know his motives."

Dalú bowed reverently, and Fel'annár turned to Angon. He smiled, then pursed his lips. "I am Silvan." He waited, wondered if Angon would remember those first words they had shared, back on his first patrol, when he had still been a Novice.

"You don't *look* Silvan."

Fel'annár's smile widened, and then he felt Gor'sadén's hand, discreet at the small of his back. It was time, and he stepped forward, aware of the people that had gathered around them, most of whom were seeing Fel'annár for the first time. They stared, mostly silent save for the whispers and murmurs from those further behind.

"Captain. Who do you follow?"

Dalú seemed taken aback. He glanced at Angon. "I obey the Warlord."

Fel'annár nodded slowly, took another step. "And the Warlord obeys the king. Who do you obey, Captain?"

Dalú faltered, looked down and then back to the Warlord. "I will ... obey King Thargodén ... for as long as you do."

"Then rally all our troops, Captain. I want them armed and ready to march in one hour. We must show the city that we are with the king. We must show them our strength, that they cannot rule without the consent of the Silvan people. It may not come to open war, but if it does, we must be ready to strike down those we have served with if that is what it takes. Band'orán cannot be allowed to rule. He and his Alpine Purists must be banished from our forest. He has committed high treason and would make slaves of us all. We must stop him, banish those warriors who protect him."

Dalú straightened his uneven frame, narrowed his eyes as he glanced at Thargodén and then back to Fel'annár. "I will do it for the Warlord. I will do it for the House of the White Oak and for Zéndar's folk."

Fel'annár nodded. It was enough, as much as he could hope for.

The Silvan captain turned to the king. "Sire, last night we found the body of Captain Barathon. He had been strangled that very same evening."

"Strangled?" Thargodén half-turned, eyes searching, focussing on nothing. His cousin was dead, murdered, and he did not think it had been the Silvans. Indeed he remembered Band'orán's words to him.

"It is hard to watch the demise of a son ..."

Thargodén closed his eyes. "Very well. I will send someone for him when there is time. For now, I must return to the city. As we speak, the Council decides the future of this land. They must be told of Band'orán's treachery, not with words but with my very presence."

"Not alone, Sire. It will be dangerous. We do not know what Band'orán has planned for this day, nor how he intends to achieve it," said Gor'sadén.

"I can enter undetected, Commander. But if I wait until that council is over, it may be too late. As you say, we do not know the circumstances. I will secret in and make for the Council."

Gor'sadén's eyes were on Fel'annár, but his words were for the king. "I will accompany you, Sire."

Fel'annár stared back at him. The task before him suddenly seemed unsurmountable, because Gor'sadén would not be there to guide him. His Master's eyes drifted to Galadan and Fel'annár followed. And then he remembered the lieutenant's words to him, on the night before everything had gone wrong.

'If you can achieve this, then you will know that you are a commander.'

Galadan nodded at him.

Angon stepped forward. In his hands, a horn. He held it out to the Warlord. Fel'annár admired it for a moment, recalled a passage from the War Tomes he had read many years ago.

'The Ashorn, symbol of the Silvan warriors of old. It is a call to aid, from one ally to another.'

Fel'annár turned to Angon, nodded, thinking that he understood the gesture, and turned to the king.

"Take it, my King. Call on the Silvans if you need aid."

Thargodén reached out, took it in his hands, watched his son. He wondered if he could read his mind, if he could see the gratitude in his eyes. "Thank you, Green Sun – for my life; for a chance to unite this land, return it to what it once was, under the rule of my father. When all is done, I wonder if we can talk, speak of things that have brought us to this moment. Know each other, if you wish."

"I would listen, my king."

Thargodén held his gaze, recognised the words for what they

were. Caution. He turned away and waited for the commander to say goodbye.

Gor'sadén turned to Fel'annár, a soft smile on his lips. There was a light in his eyes, the light of pride, a light he had struggled to rekindle all these years. It was a light that had returned with the appearance of Or'Talán's grandchild, the son he had not wanted but would never forsake. Their hands clasped upon each other's forearms.

"You must call on all your strength. Use the Dohai if you can."

Fel'annár nodded. "We will gather at the gates and wait for your call."

King and commander mounted. Thargodén spoke to the Silvans once more, but his eyes were fixed on Fel'annár.

"May this day mark a new dawn. May there be justice and the return of a Warlord."

King and commander galloped away amidst the cheers and cries of the Silvan people. Soon, they would be back, interrupt the Royal Council and arrest Band'orán.

All Gor'sadén could do was pray that they were not too late.

THE PRINCES WALKED along the corridor, down the stairs. In Handir's hands were the scrolls they had brought with them from Tar'eastór. Over rock, across water and through the trees, and still, they had survived that journey—they all had.

Turion watched the guards as they passed. He had supervised the rosters himself, but still, he could not be sure whether they were loyal or if they had been swayed. All he could do was stay alert and hope that Pan'assár would finish quickly.

On the ground floor, they made their way to the Council Hall, and the princes smiled and nodded to the people who stopped to watch. Handir was indeed back, side by side with the prince regent. There were smiles, but they were fleeting, and Turion realised there were no children about the place.

They were afraid, he realised. And they were right to be.

The grand doors were open and guarded, and a steady stream of councillors and invited dignitaries filed in. At the very doors, a group of angry protesters shouted out to the councillors. They would not accept Silvan rule, they said. They had slain their warriors, taken their king. Why had Prince Rinon released the rebel? He was a murderer, they shouted. Bring him back and try him! Guards stood before them, arms out to the sides lest they rush inside the Hall where they had not been invited. Worse still, they would perhaps confront the few Silvan councillors as they passed.

Turion caught sight of Lords Erthoron and Lorthil. Beside them, as ever, was Narosén. The Ari turned to the yelling mob. They quieted, noise ebbing to almost nothing. When it was silent at last, he turned away, to Lady Miren and Llyniel, greeted them and then entered the Hall together.

The princes were next to pass the crowd, Rinon's rebellious eyes daring them to admonish him. None of them did.

Inside the Council Hall, Erthoron and Lorthil stood talking quietly, while Aradan rose from his chair and greeted his family. Turion approached. "Lady Llyniel," he greeted, nodding at Miren and Aradan.

"What news, Turion?"

"I have none, Llyniel, but you ...?"

"I can't be sure, but I don't think he's dead." She looked up at him, so close he could see the golden flecks in her eyes, her determination, her strength. She was a warrior, too.

"You must be ready, Llyniel. Ready for anything. Stay away from Band'orán. Stay away from the guards."

Her eyes darted around the Hall. She nodded, and then caught his forearm. "Take care, captain. I have come to trust you."

He smiled and bowed, moved by her words, then left to rejoin Aradan and the princes.

The floor-to-ceiling doors were closing, the noise without and within slowly receding. At the front of the Hall, on a slightly raised stage, were four thrones. The highest of them was empty. In the one to its right, Rinon sat, crown prince, and high above him, the sigil of the House of Or'Talán, the sword and emerald. Across from him, in one of the two remaining thrones, sat Handir.

Before the stage, a semi-circle of high-backed chairs where the Royal Councillors would sit, where Aradan now sat. Today, it would be Handir to conduct the session, for the first time.

Behind the councillors was an auditorium, holding tiers of cushioned benches where dignitaries and guests were still standing and talking amongst themselves. Lords, ladies, and representatives of the Merchant Guild, the Academics Guild. Most were Alpine, save for the odd smattering of darker hair. In one such group, Llyniel, Miren and Narosén sat and watched the spectacle in silence.

The councillors sat with their backs to the audience, the symbols of their noble families emblazoned on the lush fabrics that covered their chairs. Amongst them, the Silver Wolf of Sen'Garay, the White Oak of Lan Taria and the Grey Bear of Sen'oléi.

Llyniel's gaze crossed with Handir's. He smiled at her. She returned it, pride warring with concern. A small table sat close to him, and upon it, the scrolls, neatly placed between two oil lamps. How insignificant they must look to the councillors and guests. But to Llyniel and Handir, they were the embodiment of everything they had suffered in the last weeks. The persecution, the fighting, their battle with nature, with Hounds, with mercenaries and Shadows. Now was the time to show that it had all been worth it.

Llyniel's gaze drifted to Turion, who stood beside Rinon's throne, and then upwards to the oversized standard of Or'Talán. For the first time, she felt proud of the Alpine side of herself and prayed that she would not be disappointed in it when the Council was over.

Handir, too, was observing the Hall, just as Aradan had taught him many years ago. Lord Draugolé was speaking with two councillors while Erthoron and Lorthil spoke with Lady Vardú. Only then did he realise that Barathon was missing. He turned to Band'orán, who was nodding and smiling at a fellow councillor. Unconcerned.

Interesting.

Behind the circle of councillors, Handir's eyes swept over the dignitaries. He had already seen Llyniel and his gaze drifted sideways and to Melu'sán of the Merchant guild. His public smile slipped as his eyes drifted over her ridiculously opulent attire, the would-be matches that flitted about her, so very engaged with the yet unwed woman. Handir couldn't stand her.

He turned away, eyes coming to rest on Lerita of the Academics Guild. Finally, he glanced at Turion. But the captain was staring at something at the very back of the hall. Handir frowned at his expression, watched as he leant in to Rinon and murmured something in his ear. He saw Rinon's scowl, and started when his brother turned towards him. Then Turion was approaching his throne.

"What is it?" murmured Handir.

"I chose the guards for this event, Prince, duly recorded at the Inner Circle. Those are not the guards I chose." Turion's face seemed cut from rock, and his eyes glinted oddly. "That bastard has tampered with my orders."

"Huren?"

"Yes. Rinon was right. Huren is a traitor."

With the great doors now shut, the guards presented arms before it. Too late. The Council would begin. It was Handir's time to bring Band'orán to his knees. All he could do was trust that Turion would protect them, that Pan'assár would return from the Inner Circle to help them.

FEL'ANNÁR MADE for the command tent. He stood as straight as he could before Dalú, Angon, Salo and Henu, The Company behind him.

"How many warriors do we have, Captain?" he asked, clearing his throat.

"Just over four hundred. Many left for the villages, while others never wanted to come this close to the Alpine city."

"How many in the forest?"

"A thousand more at least, too far to help."

"Abilities?"

"One hundred archers, the rest blades."

Fel'annár nodded, tilted his head back for a moment.

No one spoke, but everyone watched the play of light in his eyes.

"Idernon," said Fel'annár at last, "did you see any Kah Warriors at Analei?"

"Gor'sadén said he recognised one at least."

"And then Farón. Not enough for what they say …"

"Who? Who says what?" Dalú stepped forward.

"The trees, Captain. They speak of a *host* of Kah Warriors."

"That's not possible."

"It is. We know the Alpine warriors at the Inner City Barracks are not Kah Warriors. This host is something new, something Band'orán thought he could hide from me."

"I don't understand," said Dalú, shaking his head.

"I know, Dalú. Now listen carefully. This host of Kah Warriors is not out here on the plain. Wherever they are, they are hidden out of sight, yet they *are* near. And if they are hidden, we must assume that they have no horses. The question is, where could such a host hide itself?"

"The Dark Road!" said Sontúr. "The Dark Road which Commander Pan'assár spoke of."

"Yes, you're right. But he didn't say where it was," said Idernon.

"No, he would be under oath not to. Still, it is most certainly a tunnel of some sort, with more than one entry and *exit* point," said Sontúr.

"But that could mean that they are already inside the walls," said Dalú.

A stunned sort of silence ensued, until Fel'annár broke it. "They won't have horses if they're in a tunnel, but presumably they will have archers, possibly short bows. Captain, we need long bows, arrows—plenty of them—and we need shields. Do we have them?"

"We do, lord."

"We ride to the gates and wait for a sign, or perhaps the call of the Ashorn. Until we know what is happening inside, we must not intervene. Dalú, make us ready for arrows, for the charge on foot, for defence at the gates. If they do not have horses, then we will not sacrifice our own. And if it does come to battle inside the gates, they will be more of a danger than an asset. But heed me: if those warriors are Kah, they will be hard to bring down. I suggest units of two to three warriors for each of them."

"How many are there?"

Fel'annár shook his head. "I don't know."

"Do you think they are below ground, then? If you can't sense them?"

He turned to Idernon, nodding slowly. "It makes sense, yes."

"Sontúr, you have something similar in Tar'eastór?"

"We do."

Idernon's eyes raked the land around them, settled on the only building outside the gates that he could see, almost shielded by the trees.

"How long could those tunnels be? Long enough to connect them say with that building there?"

"Easily."

"That is the Outer City Barracks ..." said Dalú.

"If they are underground, there is little other explanation for it, save for what lies behind the city," said Idernon.

"That is the Evergreen Wood. No buildings, Idernon," said Dalú.

"It is a supposition," began Fel'annár, "but it is a likely one. This host I sense may be at the Outer City Barracks, entering the city from there, undetected. Which means that there will be no help, no back up, and there are far more traitors than we had ever anticipated."

"And the king? If it was his intention to enter the city that way ..." said Idernon.

"We must trust to hope that they will realise. Dark Roads have many doors, Idernon," explained Sontúr.

"Lord, your armour awaits, and we would offer appropriate attire for The Company," said Dalú.

Sontúr's eyes lingered on the Silvan warriors, their strange attire.

He leaned forward and whispered in Fel'annár's ear. "I am not wearing a skirt."

Fel'annár smothered his grin, then stifled a cough as he turned back to Dalú. "You have our thanks, Captain. We must be ready in less than an hour. These are your lieutenants?"

"They are, Lord. Angon you already know. These here are Salo and Henu."

Fel'annár nodded. "Alright. But know that The Company answers to me."

Dalú and the lieutenants nodded their understanding and left the tent, Fel'annár and The Company behind. Angon gestured to them to follow him, while Amareth stood close by, beckoning to him. Idernon caught Tensári's gaze. She nodded back at him. She would not be caught unawares a second time and she followed Fel'annár, to wherever Amareth led them.

She had heard little of what happened during his captivity, after Farón's treachery, but her vision and imagination filled at least some of the gaps. This would be his life now, she mused. A life of service and hardship, one she had helped prepare him for, sometimes ruthlessly. Emotion welled in her chest, but she quelled it, as she had so many times before.

"Come, Warlord."

~

AS THE ROYAL COUNCIL was about to begin, Pan'assár sat in the largest chair at the Inner Circle.

One hundred and one captains, eight of which were Silvan. But they were not present. Some had been deployed into the forest, while others had simply gone to the Silvan encampment, wagered Pan'assár. He had seen Dalú there.

Turion and Rinon were at the Council, had delegated their votes to Pan'assár. He had presented their letters to the clerks, who had duly noted the fact. Everything was recorded at the Inner Circle. Every order, every death, every commendation. He watched as they registered the document, gave it a number, assigned a drawer, a room where it would be stored.

Harahon or Dinor? No. Or'Talán had not been wrong. He had always known where his captains were.

Pan'assár pursed his lips. Turion's concerns were distracting him from the proceedings that would commence in just minutes. Not that the outcome was a mystery to him. But he would have his say, at least. After today, Huren would surely flaunt his own candidature for Commander General, and Pan'assár would not be shoved aside easily. Huren was under suspicion, and a plan began to form in his mind.

He nodded, saluted, played the part as the other captains sat and settled. But all the while, his mind was digging deeper, making connections, understanding consequences.

His eyes drifted to Dinor, watched as he spoke to a fellow captain. Cold and conceited, unconcerned with the outcome of the vote, confident in its result.

Dinor was, perhaps, the only one who could clarify Or'Talán's words, and Pan'assár wondered if he should just ask him.

Sometimes, things were much simpler than they seemed.

FEL'ANNÁR HAD WASHED QUICKLY, and then eaten the food that had been left for him. In nothing but underwear, Fel'annár wandered to the table that occupied the centre of Amareth's tent. His eyes were first drawn to the grey sash of a Kah Warrior. He frowned, and then he realised. They must have found the chest he had concealed in the forest, the day they had been forced to separate. His journal would be somewhere, and Handir's crown, he mused.

His gaze drifted to the magnificent pauldron of leather and brass, the matching bracers, reinforced with the same brass over the forearm. How long had it taken to carve this? To etch those symbols? To capture the forest and emblazon the White Oak, symbol of Lan Taria? *He* would wear it, he told himself. It was what the Silvan people wanted; what Aria wanted.

"Fel'annár?"

He turned to Amareth, as she walked towards him, a bundle in her arms, eyes upon the scar the Nim'uán had left him with.

"We should start, else you'll not be ready." She watched as he nodded, knowing he was unsure of where to start.

"This was made by Cala, master seamstress of Sen'uár before its destruction. She survived, remembers you. The colour comes from Scaly Moss and Brack Leaves." Amareth held up the tunic, voice distant, as if she envisioned the woman as she worked, stitching the robe and dying it until it became this vibrant green garment, silver worked into the hem and waist. Sleeveless, it fell down to his calves, soft and warm, meant only to protect his skin from chafing. The fabric embraced his trim waist and then fell away, flaring only slightly on its journey downward. Amareth's hand smoothed down his back, admiring the fit. She reached for the war skirt and wrapped it around his middle, fastening, pulling, adjusting.

She had done this before, for her father.

"This was hunted, fleshed and prepared by Boru of Ea Nanú, our best tanner. He passed it on to Doran of Sen'tár, who spent six months etching and dying the leather. She worked with Paronar, also of Sen'tár, who made the brass elements."

Fel'annár listened as she told the story of his garments, felt her hands as she pulled and tested, adjusted again. He had arrived in Tar'eastór several months ago, while his people were already working towards this day, crafting armour for an unwitting Warlord.

She held out the cuirass and slipped it over his arms. It sat heavy and yet as she began to fasten the buckles under his arms, down his sides, it did not feel cumbersome. Not that he understood much about leather armour, but he did know that the more he wore this, the more it would mould to his body, become uniquely his.

Next came the pauldron over his right shoulder, bracers over forearms. "This armour is our finest work, Fel'annár, fit only for the Warlord, even for a Ber'anor."

The words rang in his ears. All this workmanship, the skill and craft, the knowledge and the love that had gone into these his garments, his armour. He was theirs. He understood now.

You are ours.

"This cloak is of the same fabric as your robe, only it is combined with silk from the western regions of Ea Nanu, close to the borders of Abiren'á. See its sheen, Fel'annár? It reminds me of your eyes as a child." She tied it in place and then took the boots and placed them before his feet. "Enad of Oran'Dor made these. The silverwork took her months to complete, but she said she had known Fer'dán, that he had patrolled with you."

So many memories, mused Fel'annár. So many people had touched him during his time as a Novice. That he had touched them in some way was a driving force for his Ari soul. Once, he would have baulked at all this, felt sorry for himself for not having a say in any of it. But time and circumstance had changed all that. Did anyone get to choose the paths their lives would take?

A mother's hand glided over his strong arms, bare from bicep to elbow. "There is only one more thing left for me to do; one more thing I can do for you before I give you to my people." Her hand moved up to his slowly drying hair. "Do you remember? You were always clumsy with this. I used to braid it in the style of Lan Taria, simple and practical for an active boy. But now, I will weave for you the story I could never reveal before now."

Fel'annár sat on a stool by the fire and Amareth began to work. "I will show the Silvan blood of your mother, the Alpine blood of your father and the Ari blood of your grandfather. I will show them the warrior, the bonded lover, the divine servant. I will honour the white oak, symbol of our house, and I will remind the son of my love for him." She fell silent after that, and as she twisted and tied, pulled and straightened, Fel'annár remembered.

Crumbs on a hungry boy's face, tears on an angry boy's face. Pride for a perfect shot, frustration for questions unanswered. He remembered sad eyes, grieving eyes, sorry eyes and proud eyes. He remembered her braiding his hair, and he remembered how he had hated her; how he loved her.

Pea soup on a cold winter morning.

WITH THE PREPARATIONS OVER, Fel'annár stood outside his tent with Tensári behind. They had honoured her, too. Her customary black and silver attire was now clean, hair intricately braided.

The Heliaré sat heavily on one side of Fel'annár's head, the honour stone and Bonding Braid on the other, and down the centre of his head, the most intricate braid of them all. Those well enough versed in lore recognised it as the mark of a Ber'anor. Around his waist, the grey sash of a Kah Disciple.

Before Fel'annár and Tensári, the entire camp stood in silence. The warriors amongst them bore the symbols of their ancient houses upon their skin. Silver Wolf, Grey Bear, White Oak and Fire Fox. They murmured that he was Or'Talán returned, said he was Lássira's son, their Warlord. This was the elf they had protected, their prince in the shadows. They had been told once that a warrior would emerge from the depths of the forest and mark the second era of the Silvan people. But none of them had understood Aria's part in their scheme.

As Amareth watched him mount, her mind took her back. She had shielded him for fifty-two years, lied to him for fifty-two years. With this last act, she had armed him for war, for a future without her. She had given him all that she could, protected him in all the ways that she could—some of them dubious.

It was time to give him away.

A strange sense of peace and finality descended upon her as she watched him face the crowds, the very image of Or'Talán.

And she knew, beyond all doubt, that just like that great king, they would follow Fel'annár, wherever he would lead.

21

THE VOTES

"It was a day marked by history. A day of treachery and loyalty. A day of bravery and cowardice. A day of returns."
The Silvan Chronicles, Book V. Marhené

∽

Lord Band'orán walked like a king. Crownless, queenless, but a king nonetheless. It was a simple matter of time, always had been, ever since he had made his choice. He had chosen the crown over his heart, over Canusahéi. Radiant Aura.

Or'Talán had been a good king, one Band'orán had loved. But there was something inside him, something that told him he, too, was a king. He had thought to wait until Or'Talán died upon the battlefield. He was a Kah Warrior, after all. But then his brother had wed, had an heir ...

"King Thargodén is broken." He did not speak again until the echo had completed itself. "King Thargodén is a good king, but fate took away that which he loved the most. His soulmate is gone, and his heart went with her. I will not condemn him for that. But we must ask ourselves: where is he? Has he finally stepped upon the Long Road?

"Prince Regent Rinon has taken his father's mantle, doing what any duteous son would. But Prince Rinon is a captain—a good one. He is a warrior we are all proud to boast as our prince. But he is not a man of state. He knows little of our dealings with humans or the Merchant Guild. We have Silvans massing at our doors, clamouring for equality and threatening our very way of life should we not give it. And then we have Prince Handir, our king's youngest royal scion. A brilliant mind, a tactician—but not a warrior, not an elf of action. Likewise, Princess Maeneth chose the road of learning. She has not resided in Ea Uaré for many years.

"We have a dilemma. Our land is at war with Sand Lords and Deviants. Our king is failing - missing. We need a unifying factor, and that factor is this Royal Council. We must guide our young regent so that he makes the best decisions possible, guide our inexperienced royal councillor so that he comes to understand what ruling a land truly entails. Together, we can put this nation back in its rightful place. We need a strong king to rule us, and if we cannot have that, then we need a strong Council to defend these lands, bring prosperity and vanquish the common foe.

"But if we bring in new councillors, Silvan or Alpine, we are leaving ourselves open to distraction. We must think of the enemy now. We must be strong once more. This is not the time for experiments. It is the time for action. Let us concentrate on pulling our great nation back from the brink and *rule*, as Or'Talán once did!"

A mighty cheer filled the hall; inspired Alpines and despairing Silvans. Miren saw her husband's back as he sat at the end of the semi-circle of councillors. Too tense. Llyniel watched Handir, fire in her eyes, waiting for the moment he would stand and answer, but from time to time, her gaze shifted to her father.

Band'orán held out his hands, waited for the noise to abate. "I do not condemn my king, nor do I take merit from his noble sons and daughter. I simply state the obvious. I do not hate the Silvans. But I do not wish for Silvan rule—it is not the Alpine way. And yet, we *can* live together, respect one another's strengths and use them accordingly. But to do that, we must be strong. I say nay to any changes proposed for this Council."

Band'orán's eyes swept over the councillors. Then he faced the front, caught Handir's gaze, and in the lord's eyes, the hint of a smile behind his practised façade.

Satisfaction.

Pan'assár had still not returned from the Inner Circle and Handir could see the apprehension in Turion's eyes. Still, he could not delay his intervention. Every minute that passed favoured Band'orán's speech, allowed it to be savoured. He steeled his nerves and walked forwards until he was directly in front of the Royal Council.

WHILE BAND'ORÁN SPOKE in the Council Hall, the captains of the Inner Circle were completing their short speeches and casting their votes. Even now, Pan'assár's mind was working. Harahon ... there was something about him that had struck some chord in his mind, and it resounded, again and again. There was something he should know and didn't—or perhaps he had forgotten.

Harahon had died, but when? How? Who had even told him that it was so?

And then he realised. Dinor himself had told him. In the haze of the aftermath, Dinor had taken charge of Sen'uár.

But *when* had Harahon died?

According to Dinor, it would have been during the battle, because he himself was at Sen'oléi. But Or'Talán's words implied it had been before. Pan'assár himself had been gravely injured, carried home for most of the way, leaving Huren in charge of their forces.

But why was he dwelling on this? Why was it so important? There was a key to something bigger in that simple sentence they had read in Or'Talán's journal, the one he had found on Sulén's headless corpse ...

'... We need reinforcements. I have sent riders to Sen'uár, with a message for Captain Dinor.'

Sulén. Pan'assár frowned. He looked down and to the side, as if he was listening to something. And he was. It was his own voice in his mind, a memory of reading the missives Handir had found on his desk.

'*I have it, Ras'dán. I will bring it with us, for although it burns all those who touch it, it is our guarantee, should our new lord find fault in our deeds.*'

Had he been referring to the journal? Sulén had kept it in his tunic. It was an item he guarded well. Why would it burn? It was something Sulén could use against Band'orán, should he find himself in trouble. There was something inside that would incriminate Band'orán. Pan'assár had not finished the journal, had still to read of the final battle, and then circumstances had not given him the peace he needed to continue.

If only he could check the records once more, see the date and circumstances of Harahon's death.

Three more votes had been cast, all of them against the Warlord. Now, it was Dinor's turn.

Pan'assár looked up and watched him move, powerful and confident. He was the only one who could answer the question. And then he hesitated, for a passing, fleeting thought teased at the frontier of his consciousness ... and then brushed passed the lowered defences of a mind that had guarded itself from those tragic events, protected Pan'assár from the terrible pain of those memories.

"*Harahon was a good captain. I need someone to replace him ...*"

A voice from the past, sitting on the ground, heat and thirst ... Or'Talán, his brother. Or'Talán *himself* had told him that. Pan'assár's skin flared, felt like fire sweeping over brush.

"I second my fellow captains' words, for the most part. Should we allow the figure of the Warlord, the Silvans will use him to pressure our king into yielding lands and power. It would be the beginning of a larger revolt, one they have been planning for months, their own army amassing at our very doors. I say it is dangerous. I vote—"

"Captain Dinor!"

Dinor started. He turned to the commander general across the circle. "Commander?"

"I beg pardon for my interruption. But a question, if you will." Pan'assár stood slowly, watched Dinor nod curtly.

"I remember you telling me – and many of us – of your experiences at the Battle Under the Sun—how you fought almost to the death, just north of Sen'olei, the very day our late king fell."

Dinor frowned and shook his head, but answered. "That is correct, Commander."

Pan'assár nodded. He stepped away from his own chair and then stopped. He could feel eyes upon him, frowns and shifty gazes, but he wouldn't look at the rest of them, not yet. He wanted to see Dinor's eyes.

"You wondered why Harahon had not given the order to send backup to our king—we all did. You said it was inconceivable, an oversight or perhaps some error in the chain of command, some ambiguous order."

"I believe that, Commander. Our king died. Many of us here almost died."

"Commander Pan'assár, this is highly irregular." The ceremony master held his arms open.

"A moment, Esta'hen." He held up a palm, stepped forward again.

Huren sought Dinor with his eyes but daren't move his head, daren't draw attention to himself or any of the others. Pan'assár would see it.

"Harahon, too, died. Didn't he?" Pan'assár took another step forward, into the inner circle and towards Dinor. Just close enough to see the lines and creases of his face, his pupils and the set of his brow.

"Yes, I believe he did."

Even now, as he moved closer, the pieces were coming together in his mind. He saw emotion pushing through Dinor's defences. Not confusion. *Realisation.*

And then Pan'assár had it. Or'Talán had told him of Harahon's death. That captain had died before the final battle, had been replaced by Dinor, and that substitution had not been recorded. But

Dinor had always said he had been at Sen'olei. No, Or'Talán had not been wrong.

"Indeed, he died. Strangely, I would say, he died *before* the Battle Under the Sun. And the dead do not give orders, Captain Dinor."

"Then some mistake—"

"Ah, mistake you say. *You* said it was Harahon. How did you know? Who told you that? He was dead before King Or'Talán sent out his summons for more warriors. Come, Captain Dinor. Who told you it was Harahon who had erred?"

Dinor was shaking his head, trying his very best to seem confused, but Pan'assár could see his deception, the flicker of his gaze to the right where Huren stood. He had him, had them both. Rinon was right. Huren had betrayed him *all this time*. He moved in.

Standing now at the very centre, his captains around him, loyal and traitorous, he held out his right hand, and in it, the unassuming leather journal of Or'Talán. "You do not answer, and perhaps that is because it was long ago. Perhaps you don't remember who told you. But there is someone here who knows. Someone here." He shook the journal in front of him.

With his eyes on Dinor, he opened the journal. Looking down, he flicked to the page, close to the end. And then he raised his voice, slow and powerful.

'*We need reinforcements. I have sent riders to Sen'uár, with a message for Captain Dinor.*'

"You lied to your commander general. You *knew* Harahon had died before the battle began. It was *you* who received our king's call for reinforcements."

Gasps around the circle, from those still loyal, from those swayed only by the threat of civil war.

"I wasn't there. I was at Sen'oléi."

A wave of rage and ire took Pan'assár, so powerful it wrenched from the others another gasp. Huren's hand was on the pommel of his sword.

"This is the fourth and final journal of King Or'Talán. He wrote this as he sat under the unyielding sun, defending his people. He knew he would die if those warriors were not sent. *You* received that order. *You* ignored it. You left our greatest king to *die!*"

That last word echoed off the walls, slamming into the shocked captains again and again until it died, and Pan'assár stood trembling in rage before Dinor, who could not look at him. He cowered, half-turned away from the terrible sight of an enraged Kah Master.

"Tell me he was wrong, Dinor." But the captain said nothing, couldn't, and then Pan'assár slowly covered the few short steps towards his general. "Or'Talán was never wrong about where his soldiers were. And that brings me to the root of all this." He faced General Huren, stepped closer. "Were you not responsible for deployment, General? Was it not you who would have seen the register of Harahon's death, you who replaced him with Dinor?"

"No."

"Then who? It was your job. You delegated it to someone else. Who?"

Huren looked to Esta'hen, saw his thunderous face. He looked at Sar'pén and Era'mor, then back to Pan'assár.

The commander's lips stretched into a smile, but his eyes ... his eyes were fire and ice, grief and wrath. "What happened, Huren? Did he find out? Did Harahon threaten to spoil your plans?"

"What plans? I don't—"

"Did you kill him yourself? Put Dinor in his place? Tell me, Huren. Were you playing me? Even then? Even before I had made you my highest-ranking general?"

"I did not play you, Pan'a—"

"Look at me!" Pan'assár's thunderous voice sent the hall into silence. He continued, softer now. "Tell me it was *you* who gave Dinor the order to withhold our forces. Tell me you left our king to *die.*"

Pan'assár couldn't give a damn that his captains were stirring around him, that he could hear buckles rattling, the whisper of steel through leather. His eyes remained on Huren. And then he saw it, the moment his denial fled and in its place, hatred.

"You were always a fool, Pan'assár. You just let everyone else get on with it, didn't you? You couldn't be bothered with anything or anyone, but you took the praise, didn't you?"

"I trusted you."

"Like I said. You're a fool. You followed the wrong leader."

"You were loyal."

"For a time. Or'Talán was a great king, but he was not generous with his lords. I soon came to understand that I would never shine under his command, or under yours." Huren looked around him, to Dinor, to Sar'pén, to Era'mor and to Bora'sen, all those who stood to gain from the vote against the Warlord.

And now, the ultimate test of these captains' loyalty to the new and generous king. There was no other way out for Huren now. "Seize him!" he ordered, pointing at the commander. Dinor moved forward but the others just stood there, eyes on Pan'assár. Huren had always known that their support hinged on keeping Or'Talán's memory sacred, and Pan'assár had shattered that illusion. He tried one more time.

"Seize him! Dinor ..."

The other captains turned accusing eyes on Dinor. Lurching forward, they took him by the arms, and Huren drew his blade, waved it before him, a warning to any who thought to do the same to him.

Pan'assár drew his two swords. He crossed them before his twisted face and then held them for a moment over his head. With a mighty whoosh they descended, and Huren met them, staggering sideways under the force of them.

"You know how it goes, Huren. You know what will happen now. Traitor. Kinslayer. *Kingslayer*." Pan'assár's longsword clashed against Huren's once more, and the general struggled to keep his grasp on it, the panic in his eyes growing. Eyes Pan'assár had once trusted.

"Pan'assár! This is not necessary. I have my reasons."

"I know. You want power. You want glory. You want it all, and I was in your way. *Or'Talán* was in your way, wasn't he?"

"I would have served you, served Or'Talán, had you simply recognised me, had some such words of praise, some *boon*, Pan'assár."

"A warrior needs no boons, Huren. He serves. That is his recompense. You never understood that, did you? The Warrior Code means nothing to you." He lunged forward, a testing stroke, easily countered.

"You're no saint, Pan'assár. Have you forgotten how you treated our Silvan warriors? I always respected them at least, but you? You treated them like slaves. Where is *that* written in the Warrior Code?" Huren sneered, countered another mocking attack.

"I'm not perfect, no. I have much to atone for where the Silvans are concerned. I have done much already to show them I am sorry. But what have *you* done? Deployed them away from the city? Or are they in the dungeons, waiting to have their throats cut? Will you do that at *Band'orán's* behest?"

Huren laughed, a hint of despair in it, for Pan'assár's strikes came heavier, harder, quicker. "There is nothing you can do. The Silvans despise you."

"The Silvan Warlord doesn't."

"What, Farón? What did you promise him? Office in exchange for a good word with the Silvans?"

"Not Farón the Betrayer. Fel'annár Ar Thargodén, Aren Or'Talán."

Pan'assár could hear harsh breaths around him, surprise that he would even mention the *bastard*, that he thought him alive.

"He's dead." Huren closed his mouth, startled at his own words, words that had been heard by all.

"What makes you say that? The assassins you sent to kill him? In Tar'eastór? In Port Helia? The southern forest? Did they tell you they had killed him?"

Huren was lost. He knew that now. It was Band'orán who had told him that just last night. "Pan'assár. You don't know the power of Band'orán."

"He has no power over me. No power over my worthy captains."

"He killed Or'Talán. *Band'orán* killed him." It was the only thing Huren had, his only offering. A half-truth in exchange for his life.

A wave of breathy gasps, but Pan'assár managed a word.

"What?" It was almost a whisper, and yet loud enough for those closest to hear.

"*He* ordered it. Band'orán had Harahon killed, and messed with the reports so that the backup *I ordered* would not arrive."

Pan'assár tried to control his breathing, but his heart sped, beat out of rhythm. "*He* left us there, under the desert sun, a sacrifice in exchange for power ..."

"I didn't know."

"You are lying. You had to know where Dinor was. Whether Band'orán messed with the reports or not, you *knew*. Seize him! Bring Dinor!" Pan'assár eyes glittered with the promise of retribution should they not obey. "Arrest them on the charge of high treason."

"I didn't *know*."

They were upon Huren, dragged Dinor to his side, jostling for a chance to bind their hands, but especially Huren's. His blade clattered to the floor and Pan'assár watched, merciless as they tied the ropes far tighter than was necessary. He enjoyed their fear, rejoiced as he watched his captains shear through their hair, braids of office, watched it fall to the floor around him. They pushed at the traitors, jostled them, shook them and spat on them—and Pan'assár let them. When it was done, he stood over the kneeling, panting elves.

"I won't kill you. But you will tell the truth. You will tell everyone what you have just told me, or so help me, Aria, I will execute you in public, as is my right. You killed my brother. You killed a *king*. The greatest we have ever seen."

His eyes welled yet glittered, teeth clenched together, but still, he sheathed his sword and stepped back, turned to the others. "You all have much to answer for. There are matters that must be discussed before I can fully trust any of you again. But you can atone. As I have."

One captain ripped his eyes away from Huren, turned to Pan'assár and saluted. "I will atone, Commander. So help me, Aria."

Then another stepped forward, swore his loyalty, and soon, every single captain had stepped up, saluted and given their oath while Huren and Dinor struggled only half-heartedly.

"The Inner Circle must never again turn its back on the Warrior Code, betray its king. This vote is a mockery. Huren and his dark lord killed our great king, surely abducted King Thargodén, Lord Fel'annár, and perhaps even killed them. We are Alpine warriors, holders of the Code. We cannot allow treachery to rise victorious. We must fight it, to whatever end. Protect what is left of Or'Talán's line and make it great once more.

"Who fights for Thargodén Ar Or'Talán?"

The Inner Circle shook with their answering cry.

So many months of frustration, of confusion, of dark machinations and philosophical debates. So many subtle prompts, promises of land and wealth. So many lies and veiled threats. It had all brimmed over, oozed now, like the crumbling banks of a river, falling away, widening its course with unstoppable conviction.

The captains turned their eyes to the main doors, to the palace beyond, wondering now how they could undo what they themselves had conspired to bring about.

"Bring them. We march on the Council."

FEL'ANNÁR LOOKED DOWN at his bandaged hands. He buried the memories of frenzied moments, of panic as he realised his own chains would not come free and he would drown. He tried not to think of the arms that had embraced him in those final moments, the word that had escaped him.

Smoke from the campfires settled over the ground, and an eerie sort of near-silence accompanied it. There was the occasional murmur, the odd nicker of a horse, the clank of metal against metal, the rush of blood in his ears.

Fel'annár nudged his horse forward. He turned to the warriors who would follow him into battle if he so ordered it. He felt too light, as if he floated in some dreamscape. But the moment was real. He felt the charger beneath him, the weight of his armour, the beat of his heart and the Ashorn at his belt, the twin of the one Angon had gifted to the king.

His skin prickled and tightened, gaze turned inwards to the lady in the trees. He saw her blue eyes, arms holding out the acorn and the emerald, hands coming together until they were one.

Unite this land.

He saw the green eyes of Lássira smiling down on him, Amareth's solemn nod. He saw Aria and the symbols in her hands. This was the moment he was always meant to live. He breathed and ushered his horse forward.

"It is time."

The soft murmurs disappeared.

"It is time for justice to return to our forest. It is time to serve our king, one more time. One more chance for him to return to us what was taken. *I* will ride in his name, so that he may show us the nature of his rule. Let him show us that he loves this forest, as much as his father before him did; as much as she who holds his heart, the one who should have ruled at his side.

"I don't know what awaits us beyond those gates. I don't know if we will kill our Alpine brethren this day. It will be hard to tell friend from foe, the loyal from the treacherous. But heed me, warriors of Ea Uaré. Don't let your hatred rule your swords and your bows. There are many who have been misled, who do not deserve to die by our hand. But if the Alpine warriors we once served with should turn their backs on us, draw their steel against us, then we cannot falter. Now, with our leathers of old, our ancient symbols, our hearts beating to the ancestral drums once more, perhaps they will *run* at the sight of us!"

"Aye!" Some chuckled.

"Or perhaps they will cower behind their mothers and fathers!"

"Aye!" they shouted louder, smiling.

"To stand in the presence of an armed Silvan warrior is not for the *meek!*"

"Aye!" they roared into the smoky air that swirled and coiled around them.

"So come. Let us scare the Alpines, if we can, and not kill them ... if we can. We ride to the gates, and then fate will show us the way. For King Thargodén!"

"Aye!"

"For Lássira of the White Oak!"

"*Aye!*"

"For the return of the Deep Forest!"

"*Aye!*"

The chorus echoed across the plains, and in their wake, the drums began. It was a rhythm of war, a marching rhythm, the sound of a people united. And then the chanting began, the singing and the clapping, and Captain Dalú caught Idernon's gaze as he approached the first line. Angon was with him, the same fire and determination in his eyes.

Fel'annár had asked if the Silvans would ride in the king's name, and Dalú had once hesitated. Now, though, he had his answer.

They would, because at last the day had come. The day they would be set free.

The Warlord had returned.

"Well now, who would have said. Lord Band'orán is not against the Silvan people. You sit, and you stare, unconcerned, confident that the Council will not vote against your wishes." Handir walked to the centre of the floor, pointed at Band'orán. "There is the hint of a challenge in your eyes. I can see it. You say, *stop me if you can*. You think that I can't."

Aradan's brow twitched from further along the semi-circle. This approach that Handir was taking was bold, a trait previously unrecognisable in his pupil.

"Since you ask, let us see if I can't. As you all know, I have spent the last six months in Tar'eastór, under the tutelage of Lord Damiel, by the grace of King Vorn'asté Ar Carenar. Lord Fel'annár Ar *Thargodén*," he emphasised before continuing, "was serving as a warrior in my retinue. We spoke. I conveyed the king's wishes that he be a lord and that he come to his father on his return." Handir turned back to Band'orán's chair. "And then, someone tried to *kill* him."

There were murmurs amongst the crowd, but the councillors sat and listened, amongst them, Erthoron and Lorthil.

"He escaped, but then it happened again with hired assassins, and the question is, *who* hired them? Remember my question, councillors."

Draugolé tried not to turn to Band'orán at his side. Handir was attacking with everything he had, and Draugolé braced himself for what he would say, and perhaps more importantly, how Band'orán himself would react. Not for the first time, he wondered where Barathon was, whether he had said too much last night.

"'Who hired them?' we asked. But then battle came to the Motherland. That is a mighty story that will one day be told, one of extreme bravery by the hands of Lord Fel'annár and The Company, warriors all, loyal to King Thargodén—but today is not the day. Commander General Gor'sadén and Prince Sontúr Ar Vorn'asté came with us, to thank our king personally, bring tidings and commendations, King Vorn'asté's unconditional support for Lord Fel'annár and for his ally, King *Thargodén*. The *Motherland*, councillors. The Motherland is with King *Thargodén*."

There were whispered comments amongst the crowds behind, but the councillors sat in silence, listened to the challenge Prince Handir was answering. Aradan thought it shrewd, indeed. None of these Alpine lords wanted to become an enemy of the Motherland. He was reminding them of the consequences of turning against Thargodén.

"After that war, we uncovered missives, messages, correspondence that had been intercepted on its way from Ea Uaré to Tar'eastór. Messages from my king, important missives for Commander Pan'assár. We even found a map with scribbles in the margin, giving thanks to Lord Band'orán. Oran Dor had been crossed out, and in its place, *Sulén* Dor."

There were shouts of outrage from Erthoron, Lorthil and Vardú, from the smattering of Silvans amongst the dignitaries behind the councillors.

"It is almost comical, except that the security of this realm was placed in danger. And suddenly, we knew." Arms out, Handir turned full circle. He stopped and stared at Band'orán, returned that knowing gaze. He was rewarded with a flicker of concern, one Band'orán tried to hide.

"The person charged with all these vile deeds is here. He sits with a challenge in his eye and the threat of a satisfied smile. But those scrolls are here, for any who wish to read them. The map is here, for your perusal. And as we speak, our security forces are searching for Lord Sulén, a holding order from the Motherland in their hands. He will be questioned and then charged with high treason. I wonder what he will say."

The shouts from behind the councillors were almost too loud for Handir's voice to be heard above them, but he pushed forwards, over the din.

"How many more will be charged with high treason after today?"

"Order! *Order!*" The bang of the Council Master's staff upon the stone floor, voice powerful. The noise subsided and finally petered out.

Rinon watched, wide-eyed and engrossed, shocked at his brother's skill. Before him was a master councillor, and his eyes strayed to the rest of the Royal Council, where Aradan stood watching his pupil. He recognised the shine in his eyes.

Pride.

"But it doesn't stop there. Our journey back was similarly fraught with persecution, and I myself was placed in danger many times. I thank Lord Fel'annár and Lord Pan'assár for my life. But the question is, who was responsible for all these events? Remember this question, councillors. Remember it well."

Handir glanced at the door, but still no Pan'assár. Something had happened to him, Handir was sure of it.

"You rallied your followers and succeeded in instilling fear in the indecisive. The Silvans will attack us, you said. They are already beating at our doors, ready to expel the Alpines. You said Lord Fel'annár was dead! Said it to wrest hope from the Silvan people. You had it all worked out, didn't you, Lord Band'orán? But there was one thing, one person who eluded your web of treachery. Lord Fel'annár had to die because you knew that he was the unifying factor. You knew that he would lead the natives of this land and make them strong. He was in your way. That is why you tried to kill him, why you still try."

Band'orán's eyes had changed from clear blue to icy cold grey, the pupils strangely dilated, as if he stood in the dark. A shiver ran the length of Handir's spine, but he was almost there, had to push on.

"Remember my question, councillors. Who is responsible for all these events? Consider, if you will, the common factor. No, not Lord Band'orán." He looked beyond the Royal Councillors, to the audience behind. "King Or'Talán."

Gasps, frantic murmuring, but Handir pressed on, faced Band'orán – not too close. "Or'Talán was your undoing, wasn't he, *Kes*?" He watched in satisfaction as his enemy wavered, shocked that Handir should know that term of endearment.

"He was the sun that drowned your light, and now his grandson shines just as brightly. *He* marks your ending, Lord Band'orán and we both say, you cannot have this throne. It was never yours. It is over."

No one moved. Not the councillors, not the dignitaries outside the circle. Miren watched her husband, while pride shone in Llyniel's eyes for the one her mother had always thought she would marry.

Draugolé's fingers curled over the arm of his chair, but his face remained utterly still. Waiting.

Band'orán stood and walked towards the prince. He suddenly seemed taller, darker, stranger. Handir wanted to step backwards, wanted to turn to the door in search of Pan'assár. Turion stepped forward, his mind willing Handir to move aside, but he would not.

A distant hail, then another shout, coming closer—a crowd from afar. Voices were rising amongst the dignitaries and councillors. Something was happening in the courtyard outside, and it was coming closer. Even Band'orán looked to the two guards nearest him.

A mighty crash tore into the air as something collided with the main doors from the outside. They could hear voices. Someone was trying to get in.

Handir backed away, to Turion and Rinon's relief, and then the doors burst open, smashing against the stone walls on either side with a mighty crack. Candles flickered, and the sigil banners swayed high above them. Screams and falling chairs from behind, and then silence.

The councillors gasped and looked at each other, wide-eyed. Band'orán stared blankly at Gor'sadén, Thargodén and Pan'assár, and behind them, what seemed like the entire Inner Circle.

"My king!" shouted Turion.

"Father!" Handir's smile was wide and desperate, and Aradan's eyes shone as they had not done in decades. But Rinon's gaze was on the guards at the doors, on the strange set of their hands, their eyes that did not look straight ahead but at Band'orán. But *he* was staring at the king, eyes wide, brows furrowed.

Thargodén and Gor'sadén stepped aside, and Pan'assár dragged a still struggling Huren forwards. "Behold your general, Band'orán. Your loyal traitor, even before the Battle Under the Sun. Behold the face of *shame*, treason and murder!"

Huren tried to pull away, but he was trussed up and shorn, held fast. Pan'assár pushed him forward, watched him stagger then crash to the floor, unable to break his fall. Behind, Dinor was held fast by the other captains. He tried to look away but they held him by the chin, forced him to watch.

"Our *king*." Pan'assár faltered, started again, softer. "Our king, Or'Talán, was purposefully left to fight an impossible host, his orders wantonly altered. Tell them, Huren. Tell them *who* ordered it."

The dignitaries and councillors were murmuring, voices slowly escalating, but someone called for quiet, again and again until the silence was back, barely contained.

Huren struggled, made a low moan of utter dread as he angled himself into a sitting position as best he could with his arms tied to his body.

"Your life, Huren." A warning from Pan'assár, glinting metal poised in expert hands.

"Lord Band'orán. He ordered it—I didn't *know*."

"Traitor!" shouted a captain from behind, a lord from beside Llyniel.

"Murderer!" shouted another. And then the shouting became a churning, raging sea of reproach, a wave of outraged threats and shaking fists from behind Pan'assár, from the very councillors who had conspired against the king. They had wanted power and wealth, but their collective memory of Or'Talán was stronger. Band'orán had always known that. He watched as those who had promised their loyalty to him now shouted at him in outrage.

Miren and Llyniel were on their feet. Narosén stared at Band'orán, reading him while the crowds around him yelled and cursed.

And then Handir gestured for silence.

Pan'assár watched Huren, knew what he was thinking. He couldn't crawl to Band'orán for fear of death, but neither could he return to Pan'assár and the captains, for fear of slaughter. The princes, the council and the audience watched in pity and disgust at the fall of General Huren, Alpine veteran, decorated hero, as he grovelled upon the floor, his dignity and his hair gone.

"You killed my brother, Band'orán." Pan'assár held out his arm, pointed at the elf he wanted to dismember, just as the Sand Lords had done to Or'Talán. "You killed him, and Huren and Dinor helped you do it. Aria help me, but I made him my *general*."

"You were not hard to fool, Pan'assár," said Band'orán, his eyes moving from Pan'assár to Huren, and then to the captains behind, where Dinor stood pale, face full of dread. His gaze wandered over his own guard who now surrounded the entire room. Behind his back, he signalled to them.

Pan'assár looked down at Huren. "You will never serve again." And with those words, he surged forwards. With one expert strike, he drew his blade over the back of Huren's legs, severing tendons he knew could never be fixed.

Huren screamed, rolled and tried to crawl away from Pan'assár, who towered over him. It wasn't enough. He considered skewering him through the chest, but Thargodén's hand was on his shoulder. He moved away, a warning to the king in his eyes: do not approach Band'orán.

But he did.

"Well then, Band'orán. You have sentenced yourself, have you not? You conspired to kill my father, you conspired to kill Lássira of the White Oak, tried to kill Lord Fel'annár and kill *me*."

Voices stirred once more, even as Llyniel stood, eyes overly bright in the half-gloom at the back of the hall. She had already known that Fel'annár was alive, but the confirmation brought relief that manifested itself in a long, wavering breath. Miren squeezed her hand.

"You were not fit to rule, Thargodén. We all know that. If there was one thing Or'Talán did right, it was forbidding your marriage to that Silvan slut. You were a duteous prince and accepted your lot. You chose duty over love, didn't you? Turned your back on her, didn't you?" Band'orán smiled as he moved towards Handir and Rinon. Turion tensed.

"It's over, Band'orán," said Thargodén.

The cool, controlled Royal Councillor, the astute uncle, the brilliant mind ... it all snapped, and yet no one would say it was so from the tone of his voice.

"It is over when I say that it is, nephew. This Council is over. This *rule* is over."

A sepulchral silence. Disbelief, shock. As it began to fade, black-clad guards converged on them from all sides of the hall and panic took hold. Screams from all around them. The dignitaries crouched low, tried to hide behind the benches they had been sitting on, while the captains drew their blades and formed a circle around Pan'assár and the king. Dinor elbowed a distracted captain, crouched and turned, freeing himself and fleeing behind Band'orán's personal guard. In one swipe of a knife, his hands were free.

Pan'assár watched, counted their numbers, noted their weapons. He glanced at Gor'sadén, read his lips.

Kah Warriors.

Pan'assár raised his voice over the din. "Dishonour even in this, Band'orán? You were never a Kah Warrior. You cannot be a Master."

"Oh, but I *am*, Pan'assár." He pulled open the black robes of council that he wore, threw them to the ground, revealing the black tunic below, and the purple sash that contradicted Pan'assár's words. "Perhaps you would put me to the test, see for yourself."

"It would be my pleasure."

"One I do not grant." Band'orán's smile turned into a sneer as his eyes slipped to Thargodén at the commander's side. His heavy collar of office winked and glinted in the candlelight, sash caressing his thighs as he walked. Turion, Handir and Rinon inched backwards, sideways, and Pan'assár commended the captain, knew he was aware of the danger.

A lone voice shouted out from the back of the Hall. "This is outrageous! This is—" An arrow pierced the elf's chest, and the lord fell backwards with a thud, a scream. Silence descended on them all.

Band'orán walked up to the king's empty throne and regarded it thoughtfully. Then he turned, felt the edge of the carved wood against the back of his legs. He sat, lifted his head. And then he leaned back, crossed his legs and turned to his left; looked at Handir. "That was very well done, Prince. I didn't think you had it in you."

Handir stared back at him. "You can't kill us, Band'orán. There are many still loyal to Thargodén. They will not condone it. You will always rule amidst opposition. You will be ousted, in time."

"Ah, but what a time it will *be*." He smiled.

Handir shook his head. He turned to Pan'assár, wondered why he didn't attack. And then he heard it: the creak of wood over to his left. Pan'assár and the captains did not have bows, but the rebel guards did, and they were trained on Lord Aradan.

The councillors around him inched away, eyes searching for an unguarded door, some way out, but there was none. They were united now in their loyalty to Or'Talán, in their fear that they, too, would be targeted. The dignitaries at the back of the hall cowered behind the benches. They crept along them and to the sides, though they knew there was no way out.

"You were always a thorn in my side, Aradan. Had it not been for you, King Thargodén would never have returned from his lovesick wanderings."

"Band'orán. Don't do it. Your sentence will be harsh, but you can avoid execution. Stop now." Thargodén stepped forward, until Pan'assár grabbed at his forearm.

Handir added his voice to the king's. "He's right. Don't throw your life away. You can take the Long Road ..." Handir couldn't take his eyes off his mentor, his dear friend. Aradan's eyes were heavy with grief, helplessness, love and loyalty. He bowed, and with a soft smile, he turned away from his apprentice, from his king, and to his wife and child. Thargodén clenched his jaw, fury and wrath surging through his blood.

"Please!" Miren shouted from the benches, Llyniel holding her back. "*Mercy!*" Her voice cracked. Band'orán smiled sadly.

With a flick of his jewelled hand ... the archers lowered their bows.

Thargodén closed his eyes, and Handir swayed where he stood. "For pity's *sake!*" he shouted, eyes too full. He searched for Llyniel, who stood taut and trembling, Miren unable to move beside her.

Pan'assár, Gor'sadén and the king surged forwards, but Band'orán held out the palm of his hand and shouted over the din. "Stop, or your princes are forfeit."

Pan'assár did, eyes watching the rebel guards as they lifted their bows once more and this time, they trained them on Handir and Rinon.

"Band'orán!"

He turned, gleeful at the king's desperate voice.

"Your life, Thargodén, in exchange for your sons. And I wonder what you will choose. Duty over love? Love over duty?"

"Like you, Band'orán?" asked Thargodén. "You chose, too, didn't you? Chose the throne over your love for Canusahéi. You chose power over love."

Pan'assár glanced at Gor'sadén. He knew what the king was doing: distracting Band'orán from his plan by baiting him with the past, angering him and waiting for him to make a mistake. *Well done, Thargodén.* He signalled behind his back as he caught Turion's gaze, the captains inching around, towards the princes, three others backing away, out of the Hall in search of reinforcements.

"I had no *choice!* It was Or'Talán that took her from me." He was cracking. Pan'assár could hear it in his voice, see it in his wide eyes.

"He did it to protect me. To protect Lássira. He fooled you, Band'orán. He lied to you, told you he would accede to your demands, but he had a plan."

"You are a lying *runt*, a spoiled, lovesick failure!"

"It is the truth. He was always quicker than you. Always better. You were the failure, Band'orán, and you couldn't stand that, could you, *uncle*?"

The black-clad figure was shaking, lips twisted and eyes bulging. The Three stood before him, Or'Talán was speaking through his son's lips. How? How had they escaped the flood pit? No one ever had. All his plans, obsessively thought out, ruthlessly executed ... they had all led to this day. But Band'orán had made just one mistake.

He had trusted Sulén and then Huren to kill the bastard. Or was he Or'Talán incarnate?

One mistake, and here was the king, standing before him. Not dead.

He felt himself sliding, grappling to the edges of his fraying sanity, on the verge of unravelling ...

"It's over, Band'orán," said Thargodén. "Step away. Surrender your weapons. You are under arrest for the attempted murder of King Thargodén and Lord Fel'annár. For the murder of King Or'Talán and Lássira of Abiren'á."

Band'orán turned to a guard, one short signal and bows tensed. Rinon launched himself at Handir. He heard arrows clatter across the table where they had been standing, shattering oil lamps and toppling candles. An archer sighted the king and a small blade flew from Gor'sadén's hands, sank into his heart.

Handir watched from the floor as his scrolls caught fire. Someone was pulling him away, even as the flames caught on the heavy drapes behind and made their way upwards.

Band'orán drew his swords, his guards rallying around him, Kah Master and Kah Disciples. All he had to do was angle around until he was at the doors and from there, to the courtyard beyond the palace. He would be safe there, for the Dark Road was open, and his army awaited. Still, the captains of the Inner Circle were blocking his way.

Pan'assár strode towards Band'orán. He wanted to slit his throat, but two illicit Kah warriors jumped before him. He fought them, one eye on his prey, watching as he held his sword up over Huren who lay at his feet, one arm held out, palm towards his chosen lord. But Band'orán drove his sword straight through it, pinning it to his chest, and then pushed the blade through his heart. Pan'assár killed his last opponent. He caught Band'orán's gaze and shivered at the gleam of satisfaction he saw there.

Another group was upon Pan'assár, and Band'orán fought his way towards the captains before the great doors with half of his warriors behind him. With a cry, they surged forward. Alpine Kah Warriors, Alpine captains—they had once fought together and now, they fought each other. Dignitaries and councillors ran as far as they could from the fighting. Shouts, screams, yells from the warriors, cries of pain and warning. Llyniel called out to her father, crouching low against a far wall, but he daren't move.

Nearby, Gor'sadén beheaded a guard and then turned, faced another and gutted him. He searched for Pan'assár, found him, knew what he wanted, but Band'orán was already on the other side of the room, too close to the door.

"Pan'assár!"

The commander turned and followed Gor'sadén's line of sight. He killed one, too easily. The second was more skilled, but it was only moments later that he, too, fell dead at his feet. Pan'assár followed Gor'sadén's line of sight, only to be confronted once more. Three of them this time. They were kind enough to afford him a salute.

Pan'assár ignored them, raised both blades and moved forward, straight at the one in the middle.

Dead.

He turned, projected. He disarmed one, tripped him, swivelled left and cut through the other's shoulder, ignoring the shriek of horror.

No projection. They had the technique, but not the power. No Dohai, he realised.

Thargodén and Rinon fought side by side. Handir was nowhere to be seen, but Rinon did not seem worried.

The captains killed Band'orán's illicit Kah Warriors, just as they themselves fell to the warriors they had once commanded, the ones who had supposedly left in search of safer lands with their families.

It had all been a ruse.

A whoosh overhead and the flames engulfed Or'Talán's sigil. Incandescent strips of the once lush fabric rained down on them. Pan'assár watched them fall, like burning stars over the Xeric Wood. He had avenged his brother in part, and the past was the present, the burden lighter but not gone. He turned at Gor'sadén's call.

"The door! To the *door!*"

Band'orán was there, fighting and backing away, surrounded by his warriors. Pan'assár ran towards Gor'sadén and then dispatched the last of Thargodén's opponents, but by that time, Band'orán had gone. Gor'sadén, Thargodén and Pan'assár ran, and behind them, Rinon, Turion and the surviving captains.

Inside the Council Hall, the smoke was heavy and choking. Melu'sán and her retinue staggered out of a side door together with the other panicked dignitaries. Lords and ladies, coughing and screaming, while Miren and Llyniel inched towards where Aradan still crouched. Only the wounded warriors and rebels were left, but it was still dangerous.

Smoke billowed around them, and Narosén called, arms out for them to follow.

Erthoron, Lorthil and Aradan staggered towards them, holding up their robes and sidestepping the bodies, making for the now unguarded doors.

~

THE KING, prince, commanders and captains ran through the deserted corridors, through the open doors, out into the bright sun and staggered to a halt upon the steps that led down into the courtyard. On their right was an army of Kah Warriors in perfect formation. Black robes, grey sashes and silver helms gleamed in the early evening light. Their ranks grew towards the back, the last of them emerging from a door in the ground.

The Dark Road.

How had Band'orán discovered it? And then Pan'assár realised. The Outer City Barracks, where the Shadows trained. That was Bendir's command. Indeed there he was, missing no more. He stood, clad a general, watching his troops fill the entire right flank of the courtyard. He had corrupted an entire unit of his army. Shadows, loyal spies turned rebel Kah Warriors.

Opposite them on the left flank, a desperately forming army populated the lines, still pulling on armour as they scrambled to Esta'hen's orders, stunned at the sight before them. Where had they come from? Had they not left months ago? Did they truly mean to fight those they had once served with? Long shields leaning against their legs, they pulled on their harnesses, strung their bows, loosened sheaths, eyes darting from the grey-sashed rebel army to Pan'assár. They were outnumbered two to one, and the enemy were Kah Warriors.

Pan'assár turned to Thargodén. "My king, will you fight?"

He straightened, Or'Talán's sword in his hand. He grasped it tightly. "I will avenge my father, Pan'assár. I will fight, and I will kill Band'orán."

Pan'assár nodded. He wanted to kill him himself, but Thargodén's claim was stronger than his own. He watched as the king made for Esta'hen, relieved him of command and stood before their barely two hundred warriors. Pan'assár and Turion watched the enemy army before them while Thargodén turned to his humble group.

"It falls to us, warriors. Lord Band'orán killed our great king, my father. He has brought war to these lands, a war between brothers. He must be stopped."

They shifted uneasily, eyes on the army before them, and then back to the king.

"I know what you are thinking. We are outnumbered two to one. They are Kah. But heed me. They are traitors. They fight for gain, for renown. They do not fight for good, from the heart." He thumped a fist over his chest. "And we have Lord Pan'assár; we have Lord Gor'sadén, Kah Masters. We have truth on our side. We stand for justice, and so help me, if I have to give my life for such worthy causes, I will. And if I must die, I would do so in this most loyal and brave of companies." Thargodén's eyes swept over them all. "For Ea Uaré, for Or'Talán and the dream he began. May it never be sundered!"

The warriors yelled, swords held high, and Thargodén turned to the fore. Pan'assár's gaze lingered on him. He gave a slow nod. With Gor'sadén on his other side, and Rinon and Turion on the outer flanks, they watched as the last of the enemy warriors emerged from the ground.

"The Silvans will come," murmured Gor'sadén.

"Not for me, Gor'sadén. They will not ride for me."

"No. Not for the Alpines. But they will ride for Fel'annár. For the Warlord."

Thargodén turned to him, saw the conviction in his eyes, and then his gaze dropped to the Ashorn at his belt. He reached for it, sucked in as much air as his lungs could take, and he blew for as long as his breath lasted. Soon, though, he knew it would all be gone.

That he would be gone.

22

RETURN OF A WARLORD

"From a new dawn, a Warlord will rise."
Book of Apprentices: Sebhat

~

"Thargodén." Band'orán's voice echoed around the courtyard. "King no more! Yield to me and there will be no battle. Your sons will not die and your people will not be slaughtered. You can save them." He opened his arms, a paternal gesture.

"Come!"

Thargodén's face hardened until it was frigid steel and he stepped forwards, a breeze catching on his now dry cape. "I will not."

Band'orán smiled. "You have no army. They have all gone. What stands before me now is nothing but a five-minute practice session for my Kah Warriors. You cannot win the day, nephew. You know this."

"Do I? These elves who were once soldiers in my army, these traitors—illicit Kah—they have no soul, Band'orán. Their hearts are as black and charred as yours. No honour. You cannot rise victorious if you have no soul. Your defeat is as sure as your own death this day, by my hand. In your moment of peace, Band'orán, it is *my* face you will see."

Band'orán faltered, and then anger flared like a conflagration over his black army. A deep breath, one last, desperate clutch on his mind. But the fibres were unravelling, coming apart. He could feel it, like slipping from a high ridge. He had brought himself back from the edge so many times, and yet today, it no longer seemed to matter. He let go and felt the last threads detaching themselves. He had his army, had Thargodén at his mercy. He no longer needed to hide what he was, how he was. Bendir stepped up beside him, and on his other side, Dinor, his hair half shorn away but alive. Angry.

On the far side of the courtyard, Pan'assár called to his host of two hundred loyal warriors, only fifty of whom were archers. "Take aim!"

He heard them prepare at the back, while a line of warriors formed before the king. Anchoring their long shields on the ground, they braced behind them. Gods but they would be skewered even before they could charge, realised Pan'assár. And still there was no answering call from the Ashorn. They needed the Silvans if they were to win this fight, but Fel'annár had no experience rallying troops, not on this scale.

Even if he had managed it, it would surely be too late for them.

"*Ready!*" he called, as if a mighty army stood behind him.

Captain Bendir's order from across the courtyard was almost synchronous, and the black army readied their swords, blades rippling down the lines of Kah Warriors, like the wave of some metallic tail.

"Fire!" shouted Pan'assár.

Arrows shot over their heads, bound for the enemy lines and even as they reached back for the next arrow, the warriors raised their shields, creating a roof for the king and commanders. Arrows slammed into wood. Some clattered away, some sunk into flesh. Another volley sailed into the air, just as the enemy bows were loosed. It was time to move or they would all be shot to death where they stood. These armies had once been one, they shared the same tactics, and the element of surprise was unlikely.

"For *Or'Talán!*" shouted Thargodén.

They surged forward, each with their last, chosen words flying from their lips. They ran headfirst towards the black and silver mass, archers still firing from behind. They would soon join the front line, shoot at a shorter range. The black army sprinted towards them, its warriors lighter, faster, more prepared.

Pan'assár and Gor'sadén rushed into the fray first. One thought of Or'Talán, while the other sent a plea for help—to Fel'annár, to Aria, to whoever would come. Thargodén, Rinon and Turion followed with what was left of the fractured Inner Circle.

Thargodén hefted Or'Talán's mighty sword over his head, proud at last to feel the great king's weapon in his hands. It lent him strength in this, his last battle, the final moments of his life. He would face death knowing that his father had loved him. That he had not betrayed him, that Lássira perhaps was waiting for him.

But their soldiers were falling. It was only a matter of time before they were surrounded and killed. Thargodén knew this. They all did.

Two of The Three were wreaking chaos before them. Together, they worked like some steely machine, like the cogs of some complex contraption. Their movements were almost a perfect complement to each other, almost because Pan'assár was compensating on Gor'sadén's left, sweeping wider that way than the other. It was still mesmerising, still too dangerous for most. The Kah Shadows were slow to engage them.

The shouting, yelling mass of elven warriors who had once fought as one, now killed each other in the name of their lords, for honour or for gain.

But then, over the roaring, bellowing warriors and the incessant clanking and thudding of weapons, a single minor note wailed upon the air. It struck a chord of something deeply atavistic—something only the blood understood.

The Ashorn.

A deep and rumbling groan, and then a violent clank. Thargodén whirled around to face the distant gates to his left.

Chains rattled, cogs whirled and then a violent boom. A lull fell in the fighting. Scattered shrieks sounded from fallen warriors, but all eyes were on the open gates. The sounds of battle were replaced by the marching of many boots stomping forwards, the clink of wood against wood, metal against metal, and then three hundred Silvan warriors formed up before them.

At the front, at the very centre, was surely Or'Talán.

Fel'annár's eyes were green, far too bright, and his silver hair was twisted, braided and beaded. An Alpine, a Silvan, decked a Warlord, painted a leader.

Behind him, a host to terrify the most hardened of warriors. They were wild and they were primal, defiance glittering in eyes that were all the shades of the forest.

There were shouts of disbelief from the high balconies and windows of the palace, its citizens hanging as far out as they dared, voices almost panicked. "What sorcery is this?" they cried. Were they friend or foe? And when the battle began, who would they charge at? Band'orán or Thargodén?

Band'orán's mind was searching, desperate for how he had failed to anticipate this. The Silvans and Alpines had been close to civil war. He had planned it all so meticulously, and it had worked. Why had they ridden to the aid of the Alpine king? How had the boy rallied them, convinced them to work for their enemy? The thought that he had misjudged Thargodén's son took hold and his anger deepened, sunk into his soul and twisted it. He had had him at his mercy, and still, he had escaped—stood there like a king.

Bendir was rearranging the army, regrouping and organising it, and Band'orán spoke fast and urgent to him. Thargodén's ragged warriors were before them and the host of Silvans to their right. It was time for a change of strategy, and the Kah Warriors hurried into their new positions. An arrowhead of archers facing the Silvans and the nearest walls to the right. Behind the tip, two fronts—one looking forwards, and the other to the left and the king.

Band'orán knew his army could take the Silvans, but still, he needed a backup plan. He needed to get to the king, use him as leverage should the battle not go to plan. Bendir would look after the Silvans. He would finish Thargodén for good.

The king stared at the Silvan army, a powerful surge of energy running the length of his spine. These strange warriors fought for *him*. They had always been there, camouflaged under foreign garb, unrecognised skill, at the beck and call of Alpine captains. But how had he allowed it? How had he failed to understand this prize asset? And it was his son who led them. He turned to Pan'assár, saw some hidden grief there. But so too, was there admiration. Finally, he turned to Gor'sadén, and he saw pride—love.

And then he heard the whisper from the nearby Evergreen Wood, reminding him of his return from grief. It seemed an age ago.

Welcome, lord.

He felt Gor'sadén and Pan'assár straighten at his side, and then he heard Rinon from behind him.

"What the *Hell* ...?"

"That is the Warlord, Rinon. Your brother."

"*Ready!*" The gritty, prolonged shriek of Captain Dalú from afar.

There was an answering noise, deep and breathy. Silvan archers prepared at the rear. Gor'sadén could not see them, but he knew they were there, briefly wondered at the tactic they would use. Then he spotted more, high up on the walls. They spread out, knelt, sharp eyes surely calculating the distance to the black army, bows the length of any elf. Gor'sadén's eyes shifted to the rebel archers. Their short bows would not reach them up there.

He spoke to Pan'assár, but his eyes remained trained on the archers. "Long bows."

Pan'assár narrowed his eyes and then looked at the Warlord while he answered Gor'sadén. "That was an excellent tactic."

Before the Silvans, two lines of long, wooden shields, and behind them, at the very centre, were Dalú and Fel'annár, The Company at his shoulders. Dalú turned to the young Warlord, watched as he contemplated the mass of warriors before him. His strategy had been sound, Dalú's scepticism unfounded.

Fel'annár half-turned to Dalú, nodded.

"Aim!"

The creak of skilfully crafted wood, colourful feathers between strong fingers. Hands tightly curled around standards held high—the Grey Bear, the White Oak, the Fire Fox and Silver Deer—ready to unfurl in the breeze, ancient witnesses to the bravery of their descendants.

"Fire!"

Arrows whispered through the air, met enemy bolts high above, and then they took cover as they rained down on shields. The standards were driven into the ground, swords drawn.

"Fire!" yelled Dalú again. Another volley, another shower of thick arrows. Like serpents of death, they whooshed through the air, seeking to even the odds. The archers on the battlements were firing down on the enemy, picking off as many archers as they could. A group of black-clad warriors broke off, made for the stairways up to the crenellations. They didn't have much time, but they *could* even the odds a little.

Fel'annár thought he heard the whisper of something ancient and then soft words rolled from his tongue.

"For Lássira."

The Company yelled them out, words merging with Dalú's cry to battle. "Lássiraaa—*charge!!*"

A sea of yelling, shouting Silvans sprinted forwards, tribal skirts and paints, braids flying around them like ribbons in the breeze. Amongst them, a grey-haired Alpine in breeches.

The line became an arrowhead with Fel'annár at the fore, a sword in each hand, and beside him, Dalú and Idernon. A three-pronged attack, and Band'orán's army was ready for it. To the right, the last of the King's men inched left, towards the charging Silvans, but a part of the black army broke away and charged towards them.

The last of the arrows were loosed from the walls, but they were soon gone and fell to blades. Voices waxed louder the closer they came until, with a collective roar of anger and bravery, they collided. An exhale, a deep heaving breath, and the thud of bodies against armour, the clatter of swords, blades shrieking.

Silvan warriors fell. Kah Warriors fell. The press of friend and foe was too close, so close it was hard to swing a sword, so they used pommels, elbows, heads until there was distance enough to use their blades. Fel'annár felt The Company around him. They knew to steer clear of his swords.

Dalú yelled as he fought, Angon always close by. Fel'annár battled his way forward, rallying the troop, regrouping them and deploying others to places where the line had been breached. All the while, The Company stayed as close as they could. The Kah Warriors were good, better than most, and the Silvans were hard-pressed to defeat them one on one. Instead, they fought in twos and threes, just as Dalú had instructed, as Fel'annár had commanded.

The Warlord slashed and parried, felt a blade glance over his cuirass, felt nothing at all. His longsword arced right and cut through a nearby warrior, while his left hand drove his shorter blade into the back of another. Before long, he fell into a rhythm.

Kill, observe, deploy.

He glanced to the right, to the other, smaller battle. "Salo!" he shouted, gesturing to the struggling group. They were being pushed back. The lieutenant rallied a small number of warriors and sprinted towards them, but there was no time for Fel'annár to watch. It was still too close quarters, but damn it all, he could not see Gor'sadén, could not see the king.

He felt the Dohai stir in his chest, felt its warmth in his limbs, and he released it, slowly, rationing his strength, channelling the force through his arms and legs. Strange, he thought as he fought, because these Kah Warriors knew the moves, executed them well enough, but they did not project. There was no Dohai, a fundamental flaw in their training—one he took full advantage of.

WHILE THE BATTLE RAGED OUTSIDE, Handir fumbled with an ornate chair sitting against a wall. It was the only thing he could find in this sea of panicked, terrified civilians who had nowhere to go.

Smoke lay heavily in the air, and if the fire in the Council Hall was not doused, they would all be forced outside, into the line of fire. He dredged up recent memories of the aftermath of the Battle of Tar'eastór, when he had learned at his Master's shoulder, watched a king reforge his realm.

Handir stepped up and steadied himself on the padded surface of the chair. He held out his hands. He had once seen Damiel do this in a similar situation, had been struck at how dramatic this posture had been. As if he prayed for rain, Handir held his arms out and up, and then he spoke, just as he had heard Pan'assár and Gor'sadén do with their warriors.

"Listen to me."

A lull in the din, but still there were noisy pockets of shouting elves. He turned to them, held his hand out for them to quieten. They did.

"Listen to me. We must do our part to safeguard our people. We are not warriors, yet we are skilled in our own ways. We work together now. That fire must be extinguished. Are there any engineers here?"

"Here!" shouted one elf, arm up.

"Your name?"

"Peldor."

"Peldor is in charge of the fires. Heed him!"

The voices were rising again, and Handir held his hands out once more.

"I need the kitchens to produce enough sustenance for our warriors, for the wounded. Who has experience leading a household?"

"I do." A defiant voice, unmistakably Silvan. Lady Miren.

"Miren."

"I will do my part, Prince."

Handir nodded respectfully at her, turned back to the crowd.

"We have corrupt councillors to find. I need a military leader, someone to organise the search and detention until our warriors can deal with the traitors."

A short woman stepped forward, voice powerful, face utterly strange. Lerita.

"Leave that to me, Prince."

Handir stared back at her. He knew who she was, had always thought her an academic. But her face was sharp and harsh, and something told him she should not be denied. He nodded.

"The rest of you take refuge upstairs. Make rooms ready for the wounded, should the Healing Halls be overrun. Light hearths and prepare clothing. Do what you can, but stay safe."

There were no more shouts, just urgent muttering as the people flocked to Peldor, Miren and Lerita to help. Others climbed the mighty stairs while the lines were formed to bring water from the springs into the Council Chambers.

Erthoron, Lorthil and Narosén stood beside Aradan, near the half-closed grand doors of the palace, eyes on the prince. Handir could not rid himself of that terrible moment in which Band'orán had toyed with them, made them say goodbye to him thinking he would be killed. Handir had realised then just how much the councillor meant to him, like Gor'sadén to Fel'annár, he thought.

Handir approached, nodded at Aradan. "The other councillors?" he asked.

"Those with other skills have joined your effort, Prince. Some are in the kitchens, others help Lerita or have retreated upstairs. There has been some strife with those closest to Band'orán but—"

An elbow to his ribs, and he turned to Lorthil, who was gesturing to an elf in a long, black cloak. He was making for the grand stairs, and Handir followed at a distance.

"Draugolé!" The hooded figure stopped, his back to the prince. "Did you think you could spirit away? Are you going to meet with your new lord?" Handir's voice was loud enough to turn heads, and the noise in the foyer was replaced by the sounds of the battle beyond the doors.

Draugolé turned, his confident, placid face now rigid and wary. "Band'orán is not my lord. I was making for my rooms, as you ordered, my prince."

Handir smiled, stepped towards him. Lerita and her two veterans inched behind the councillor. "Of course you were. After all that has happened. After all your lies and your manipulation. Still, you take me for a fool?" He was angry, and then the vision of Fel'annár hitting a mercenary on the Pelagian Queen came to mind. Handir had hurt his hand when he had punched a pirate. This time, he knew what to do.

Draugolé watched dumbly as a ringed fist, perfectly formed and tight, hurtled towards him, too fast to dodge. He fell onto his backside, Handir towering over him.

Lerita stared, stony face cracking into an expression of shock and then satisfaction. "Get him up! Storeroom four!" she bellowed.

Draugolé was dragged away amidst the jeers and yells of the crowds. Someone spat, someone kicked out at him, and Handir gestured for Lerita to go, make sure they did not kill him before he could be brought to trial.

Handir heaved a breath. He watched Llyniel bow at him from the doors, felt the lingering stares of others as they passed.

It had come from the heart, like a fantasy come true. He had always wanted to punch Draugolé.

A Kah Warrior shrieked, blood streaking after his fall. Angon was advancing, Dalú never far. They were close, now, to the centre of battle where the lords fought.

Band'orán cut down a Silvan, brought his sword around and stuck the tip of it into another's shoulders from above, not so deep so that his blade would catch on bone. He killed everyone around him, fast and efficient.

Too easy.

He was good, mused Fel'annár. But that would not stop him. Nothing would stop him on his road to retribution.

Grandfather. Mother. His people. The Forest.

A Kah warrior crashed into Fel'annár but Tensári was upon him in an instant, like a black eagle, all power and steel. Too quick for him to counter, she killed him quickly, searched for another.

And she found him, the one she had sworn she would kill.

Striding forward, Galdith at her back, a Silvan warrior crashed to the ground before her. She had not killed him—Farón had. She stood before him, knowing exactly where Fel'annár was, where The Company fought. She knew that Galdith was behind her.

"I will have your life, traitor." She struck a stance all Ari'atór were taught, from the first day they were allowed to hold a blade at the tender age of twelve. She could see his shock, knew that he thought he had killed her, that he could kill an Ari'atór with Dream Vine.

"It's not personal, Ari'atór. I couldn't allow him to become the Warlord because he would have obeyed the dictates of Thargodén. That king is weak but Band'orán will take us back to the days of glory."

"By enslaving your people?"

"No. Pan'assár already did that. I would speak for the Silvans, make them great once more. I would teach them of the Kah and we would be invincible before the enemy."

"You know nothing of the Kah. You were never a warrior, Farón. Warriors don't turn on their brothers, don't drug them and deliver them to their enemies. Warriors don't betray the trust of those who took it upon themselves to train you, to mentor you."

Farón frowned as he struck a guarding stance, followed her as she circled him. "You speak of Lainon?"

Tensári bared her teeth at him, blue eyes on fire. "Did you feel remorse? Did you falter at all when you gave him over to Band'orán? Lainon gave his *life* for Fel'annár, *not* so that you could squander it."

Farón's eyes flickered wide. He shook his head, even as he parried her first downward attack. "I didn't know. If I had, I may not have done that."

"You know now. Your ignorance will be the death of you."

Another attack from the side, so vicious Farón staggered but soon righted himself. He attacked his opponent, fast and precise, and scored a blow across her arm. She hissed, wheeled away and turned back.

"You can't beat a Kah Warrior alone, Ari'atór. I don't wish to kill you."

She smiled a grim smile, took up a high stance. "You are nothing but a would-be Warlord, one the Silvans do not wish for. Did you think they would accept you after your treachery? Did Band'orán tell you that they would? You are weak, vain, power-hungry but above all this, you have no honour."

She lunged forwards with three heavy strikes, full of ire and vengeance. He parried them and then he stepped on a fallen sword, his leg wavering. He reeled sideways, righted himself, only to find the tip of her sword at his neck. He daren't move, but chanced a question.

"Who are you?" He watched as her bright blue eyes flared.

"I am Tensári. Divine Protector. I sentence you to death."

He only had time to widen his eyes before the frigid steel pierced his flesh, heard as it cut through his windpipe. Tensári watched, knowing that her back was covered. She waited, did not look away as Farón gagged and gurgled, a wave of red soaking his front. He crashed to the ground, and she turned, nodded her thanks to Galdith and threw herself back into the fray.

"Left! Front!" called Fel'annár to any who could hear, anyone free to help the warriors who were struggling. He heard Dalú seconding his order, and he turned.

"Salo! Henú!" Fel'annár shouted again. Dalú repeated again and slowly, they pushed towards where Gor'sadén and Pan'assár danced the Kal'hamén'Ar, the field always empty around them. Behind them, Fel'annár had caught a glimpse of the king and prince still alive, but where was Turion?

Fel'annár could see the pattern. Band'orán wanted the king, was sending large numbers of troops in his direction. He wondered if he had given the order to kill him or capture him. But in order to do that, they would first have to face the Kah Masters.

Pan'assár swept sideways, killed two, but was soon back, as close as he could get to Gor'sadén and still fight. Fel'annár could see the slight imbalance, how he sometimes needed to correct his footwork.

"Dalú!" shouted Fel'annár. He gestured to the main battle, an order to lead them.

Dalú nodded. He watched Fel'annár as he inched closer to the commanders. Soon, he was within the sight of the enemy, who had so far failed to take the commanders down.

And then Fel'annár saw it—or had he felt it? They widened the space between them, enough for Fel'annár to move forward and breach the gap, make it even. Then there were three, whirling and swirling, arcing and ducking, spinning and slicing, twisting and kicking.

Invincible.

Fel'annár briefly caught the king's eye as he circled round, saw the crown prince fighting at his side and Turion at last. But as he fought, he realised that something was wrong. They were being surrounded, cut off from everyone else. A gully was forming around them, widening.

"We're being isolated."

"Hold steady," said Gor'sadén.

And he did, but as he wielded his blade, his eyes searched for Tensári, for Idernon. He found them, pressing against a growing wall of warriors. He knew Idernon understood the tactic.

An arrow whizzed past Fel'annár's cheek, thudded into a captain behind him. Another embedded itself in Pan'assár's pauldron.

"*Sniper!*" shouted Fel'annár. He heard Dalú yelling from across the slowly widening gap. Another arrow clattered off his forearm.

"To the Warlord!" Idernon's warning split the air as they pressed harder, cutting down the enemy, slowly pushing towards Fel'annár and narrowing the divide as more Silvans flocked to the cause.

Then Angon was through, ran towards them, fought beside them, and behind him, Dalú and Idernon. Fel'annár killed another, felt Gor'sadén stagger sideways, compensated for the gap between them. Tensári was running towards them, sword high, yelling some Ararian curse as she crashed into the circle of combat.

Pan'assár stumbled and fell to the ground beside him, then a clash of swords meeting at the crossguard. From the corner of his eye, Fel'annár saw Dalú's painted face, just before he took the head of a warrior. He nodded curtly at Pan'assár, who was back on his feet, an arrow through his shoulder.

And still, more arrows came, one after the other.

They were tiring, couldn't keep up the frantic rhythm much longer. Something had to change.

"No. Father! Turion!" Rinon's desperate cry.

The king had fallen sideways, far enough from the line for the enemy to surround him, cut him off from the rest.

Pan'assár killed one and turned enough to see him, see Or'Talán as he was set upon by Sand Lords.

"To the king!" shouted Gor'sadén, moving closer to Fel'annár, compensating for the gap Pan'assár left as he lurched backwards. He gave a last glance at his brother of old, a goodbye in his eyes. He ran towards Turion and Rinon, helped fight off their opponents and then ran for the surrounded king. He remembered the Xeric Wood, how they had been left without backup, how the king had perished.

He would not let it happen again.

With a mighty roar, Pan'assár broke the circle, and one after the other, the black-armoured warriors fell, under some unnatural strength that had lent itself to Pan'assár. He had only been able to watch Or'Talán die that day, but today, he would deliver his son, or he would die trying.

Rinon fell with a gasp, an arrow in his upper leg. Angon lurched forwards, parried a downward strike meant for the prince's chest. But he was not quick enough to turn and meet the Kah Warrior behind him. He felt the impact on his upper back, felt the fire as the blade cut through leather and cloth, skin and muscle. He knew that it was fatal.

He fell, and looked up to the churning skies. He saw Prince Rinon looking down at him, confusion in his eyes. Confusion and admiration.

"Win that bet, Prince. Win it for us all."

He was rewarded with a determined nod, three words, the last Angon would hear in this life. "Safe journey, Warrior."

Angon closed his eyes and made for Valley.

"Angon!" Dalú's desperate cry. He ran forward, crashed into Pan'assár's remaining opponent and then skidded to a halt. He fell to his knees, wide eyes wavering and watering at the death of the one he thought of as a son.

The Kah Warriors around the king had thinned to almost nothing and any stragglers were cut down by Gor'sadén, Pan'assár and Fel'annár. They were safe for now, and Fel'annár cast his gaze over the battlefield. The numbers had dwindled greatly, and black no longer dominated.

"Dalú!" he called, then felt him at his side, eyes wet, jaw clenched. "One last push, Captain. One last push and we have them." Fel'annár clapped his hand on his shoulder, felt his sadness, his exhaustion. The captain jogged unevenly away, rallied the remaining Silvan warriors and pushed back into the dwindling enemy.

From afar, amidst the shadows of distant buildings, Band'orán, Bendir and Dinor watched in silence.

The king had been cut off, all but dead. But Pan'assár had reached him and rallied the others. The tide was turning, and the king was still alive. Fel'annár was still alive.

Band'orán surveyed the field, littered with the dead, with mud and blood, stray limbs and strewn weapons. His Kah Warriors all but vanquished. How had he lost? He had sat upon the throne of Ea Uaré, had all her rulers at his mercy. He had felt himself king at last.

But *The Three* had returned, and his eyes lingered on Fel'annár, on Or'Talán. He had tried to rid himself of his brother, tried not to love him. Still, that indomitable flame had haunted him, always would. He loved him. Hated him. He backed away, turned to his right. But Barathon wasn't there.

It was Captain Bendir, with Dinor at his side. They nodded. It was time to leave.

∼

Fel'annár killed his last opponent and then doubled over, desperate for breath. He rested one hand on his knee, trying to fill his heaving lungs. Beside him, he heard the Masters.

Exhausted.

He turned to his right, to Gor'sadén who would not look at him. Instead, he held himself up with his longsword, eyes closed. A heavy hand landed on Fel'annár's shoulder.

Pan'assár.

But when Fel'annár turned, caught his gaze, he started. Those cold, blue eyes were warm and wide, no longer shuttered, despite the broken arrow through his shoulder. The lines around his brow had gone and in their place were smooth skin, bright eyes. Fel'annár knew what it was.

Peace.

He slowly stood, a grimace fixed on his face. His eyes surveyed the field. Galdith was cradling his arm, Sontúr leaning over him. Ramien sat close by with Carodel while Idernon and Galadan stood over them, watching. He saw Tensári, too, helping a nearby warrior to stand.

His eyes travelled over the dead and wounded warriors, over the distant barracks and then the palace itself. Handir would be up there somewhere, safe.

And then his eyes stilled. There, close to the stables and the Healing Halls, was Llyniel, a black robe covering her, hair tied back, face smudged with dirt. They crossed gazes. He saw her relief, felt her, strong in his mind.

Not far away, Dalú and the Silvans knelt around Angon's still form. Their brave, irreverent rebel, the elf who had died for the freedom of his people. He would be honoured by them, by Rinon, whom he had saved.

He squeezed his eyes shut, still denying his mind access to his body. He could not see to it, not yet. There was so much to be done. He startled, opened his eyes to the sound of distant shouts. Someone was anxious, calling the alarm.

"Find him! Find Band'orán!" He thought it was the king's voice.

Warriors were running around him, eyes searching, but Fel'annár closed his, concentrating on the voice within. He knew where it came from, and he turned his head slightly.

He runs.

The Evergreen Wood, hidden forest. It was coming alive. He could feel it in his mind, like a heaving, broiling sun; expanding, tightening. Opening his eyes slowly, he saw the grieving warriors, the lost warriors staring at those who had once been their brothers in arms, their dead and butchered bodies the undeniable evidence of what they had been driven to, what they had done.

Fel'annár knew who was responsible.

He saw Canusahéi, Handir's mother, lonely queen. He saw Handir's suffering, his spite and pain as he looked at Fel'annár, all those months ago. He saw Pan'assár's disdain, his cruelty towards those he thought had betrayed his brother. And he saw the suffering of the Silvan warriors, treated like slaves by Alpine leaders who were told it was the right thing to do, the *Alpine* thing to do. And yet here they lay, side by side. Dead. Equal.

He saw Lássira's vibrant face, her Bonding Braid; saw Thargodén, the tears in his eyes as he remembered her, no braid in *his* hair. Band'orán had killed her, too.

The shouts barely broke through the building crescendo in his mind, the call ever more desperate. He needed to leave. The battle was over, but the Dohai was not spent. Instead, it pulsed inside him, ready to burst as it never had before.

Come, lord.

"Fel'annár." Idernon's voice beside him.

Opening his eyes, he turned. His friend staggered backwards, a startled cry crossing his lips. The Company stood. Pan'assár stood, and Gor'sadén turned to his Disciple, the king and Rinon close by.

A leafy, breathy sigh, of relief, perhaps, that the Forest Lord had answered. But the slow exhale lingered and then deepened, into a bass, droning chant. So loud, Fel'annár wondered if the others could hear it. A lone note, a throbbing vibration that shook the ground beneath him—or was it him that shook?

Forest Lord. Forest Warlord.

The battle had not ended. It had only just begun.

His scalp seemed frozen as his eyes roved over the battlefield. One by one, those who could stood and stared. His honour stone danced in the air to his right, and everything he saw was tinged with green, blue and purple. He saw it all, as clearly as he ever had, despite the fireflies that flitted before him, around him.

Gods, but the suffering Band'orán had brought. The death of Or'Talán and Lássira. The grief of a lonely king, of Amareth. Families sundered, a whole people enslaved.

His eyes rested on Narosén. The Ari stood leaning on his staff, eyes blazing wide. Suddenly, he was all that Fel'annár could see. Aria's light in his eyes. It flared, and he saw her, standing before him. The acorn of the forest, the emerald of Or'Talán—the same one that hung from Thargodén's finger. They would be united, once Band'orán had gone.

He runs.

Fel'annár wasn't sure if Narosén said it aloud or in his mind, but it made no difference.

"Band'orán has escaped."

He turned to Idernon, felt like a reed in water, and his own lips were moving. "He can't escape me. He can't escape the Evergreen Wood."

"It is forbidden," said Dalú.

"Not to me, Captain. I have been invited."

He wouldn't understand. None would, save for The Company, the commanders. His mind sharpened, focussed.

The Evergreen Wood. Band'orán. *Not* retribution.

Restoration.

"You can't beat him alone, Fel'annár." Gor'sadén limped towards him, stopped some distance away. In his chosen father's eyes was a plea to remain, the surety that he would not.

"I'm not alone. Not in there."

Fel'annár turned, strode away from Dalú, Pan'assár, Gor'sadén and The Company. He brushed past the king, Rinon and Turion. And then he broke into a run. As he approached the palace, he veered right, towards the forest behind. He ran faster, through ornate gardens and to the tall gates that barred entry into the Evergreen Wood.

They were open.

A trumpet blasted in his mind, power flared in his blood, and he was sprinting, could no longer feel his feet, arms pumping, hands cutting the air before him.

Stop him.

Behind, Gor'sadén and Pan'assár tried not to lose sight of him, even as The Company streaked past them. Others followed, too. The king, Rinon, Turion. But some force was aiding the Silvan, lending him a preternatural strength they could never match.

Gor'sadén didn't know how long they had run for. It seemed an age to him and his aching leg, but there were lights in the distance, lights and shouting. He saw the backs of The Company, strode towards them, made a place for himself and Pan'assár amongst them.

There, not far away, was Fel'annár, his back to them. He saw the same light he had seen over the citadel of Tar'eastór. The same power, only then he had seen it from a distance, not like The Company. It droned in the air, emanating from his Disciple, lifting his hair in a graceful dance as lights whipped around him, clothes undisturbed.

The Ber'anor had sensed his prey, and now, Gor'sadén knew he would need all his strength, that and more, for the battle to come.

BAND'ORÁN, Dinor and Bendir ran.

There were no paths in this virgin forest. The way was knotted with roots, strewn with stones. They jumped over bushes and ferns, and all the while, the two captains would glance at Band'orán between them. They ran for their lives, but if they had had a choice, they would have run away from him.

A storm was coming, slowly brewing around them. Band'orán

looked up to the cloudless sky, frowned, but he couldn't stop until he reached the cliffs. If his elves were not there, then he would not stop, he thought. Instead, he would fly. It was an enticing idea.

His foot caught on a root. He stumbled but was soon running again. A yell from his left and Bendír had fallen. He turned right—no Dinor.

He slowed, turning, eyes darting to his captains even as he backed away. Band'orán didn't understand.

Bendír, knife in hand, was shouting and slicing at some snake that had wound its way around his ankle. Something fell away, but the snake continued to climb.

Not a snake. A root.

A whispery echo, the lash of a whip, and a vine tangled around Dinor's waist. He yelled, tried to reach for his knife, but his arms were caught. He staggered this way and that, a pathetic, boneless thing caught in a wooden embrace.

Band'orán looked down. He saw the inert loops and ridges of the roots below him, before him. Then they were writhing inside the sodden soil, interlacing and protruding, like fish riding the crests of waves. He stepped backwards.

The wind was rising, the storm approaching, enough to blow his hair across his face. He batted it away. From the corner of his eye, a black-green root reared from the ground. Dagger in hand, he slashed at it. It fell away and then whirled around. He swivelled the blade and cut through another. His feet moved, avoiding the larger roots until he stood on flatter ground, littered with pine needles. They crunched under his boots.

Someone was crashing through the foliage, and he turned, his two throwing daggers ready in his hands.

The storm had come.

∽

FEL'ANNÁR SLOWED his pace through the Evergreen Wood until he came to a halt before a carpet of living roots.

He heard the blades before he saw them. Fine steel hurtled through the air. He brought both his swords up, deflected them, sending them into the bushes on either side.

A captain stood on his own two feet, but Fel'annár knew that, should the roots around his waist disappear, he would crumple. He was caught fast, blade nowhere to be seen, and his eyes were wide and wild, petrified. Nearby, another stood. He almost fell as he tried to free himself of the roots around his ankles. He, too, had been disarmed.

Fel'annár covered the final steps that separated him from his prey, just beyond the struggling captives. He was infused with the Dohai. But he felt something else join that power.

He stood in the shadows of greatness, under a leaf-spangled canopy. This Evergreen Wood that defied the call of winter, its majestic green, its scent of bark and loam—it all seeped into him, stirred him. So much power that he shook, muscles unaccustomed to the strength.

Images came to him of a giggling, kicking babe, a proud mother, dead mother looking down. He saw a colourful dawn, air in inert lungs, life where there had been none.

And then his eyes rested on Band'orán; saw his oily black robes undulating and rippling around him. He was untethered. Too fast, too skilled to be shackled by the trees.

Fel'annár stepped forward. He heard a scream in his mind, raw and primal. It was a memory he had been too young to recall. But the forest said it had wept that day, for a daughter bound for greatness. They said her bane was here.

Queenslayer.

The lights engulfed him, seized him, streaked around him, everywhere. They begged for movement, pleading with him to kill.

Band'orán's glittering eyes stared, half-petrified, half-angry, one sword in each of his murderous hands. "You can't beat me, demon. You are a Disciple. I am a *Master*."

"In that, too, you are dishonourable. When did the rot start, *traitor*?" Fel'annár did not recognise his own voice. It sounded deeper, too far away from his own mouth.

Band'orán smiled. "What does it matter? I killed your mother. She would have made a good queen. Too good."

"And you kill everyone who is good, that could be better than you. You destroy anyone who garners loyalty because you have none. You are a bereft soul seeking the love you never felt. I never thought I would pity my mother's murderer. But so help me, Aria, I do."

"Spare me your stupidity, boy. You are a child playing wargames, but this is a cruel world, Silvan. Now come, and beat this Master if you can."

"And yet you dared step inside this ancient forest. Here, you are not master. *I* am." The whirlwind of light around Fel'annár pulsed as he stepped closer to Band'orán. The lord stepped backwards, and Fel'annár heard the Evergreen's mocking voice.

Coward.

How they wanted him. He could feel them, barely restrained, waiting for a sign that Fel'annár had finished with him. This was not the Deep Forest. This was something darker, something unforgiving.

The ground rippled, bulged, and then from it, roots and vines broke, rising into the air, taking Dinor and Bendir by the arms and legs. They shrieked, and Band'orán flinched. Trees bent forwards, groaning and creaking, closing in on Band'orán, judging him for his deeds.

"Who are you?" asked Band'orán, eyes on the trees and Fel'annár.

"I am Lord of these forests. They seek retribution, for there were always trees. When you killed Lássira, when you tried to kill me—they were witness to your evil. They do not abide your presence."

Band'orán smiled as if he stood before a child. "Then come, Tree Master." Two swords swirled and arced, skilful, graceful.

Fel'annár took up his guarding stance, slower. A droning pulse in the air, the creaking and groaning, the bass hum he had never heard before. He heard gasps behind him and prayed they would not come too close.

Wait. Not yet.

Band'orán's eyes were everywhere, around him, back on his opponent. Then Fel'annár was moving, cutting into the air before him until his swords were descending on Band'orán, and they fought. First one and then the other gained the advantage, but they did not stumble, never lost balance despite the uneven ground over which they danced.

Fel'annár did not feel the pain as his opponent's blade sliced over his arm, did not hear the gasp of pain his own blade wrought from his opponent. The lights no longer mattered; sounds and shouts from behind were muted. He heard nothing, nothing but the whisper of wind upon leaves. Calm and soothing. It was the silent world of a Kah Warrior, drawing from the sizzling, pulsating energy of the forest around him.

Forest Warlord.

Fel'annár turned away, too fast for Band'orán, and then he lunged. He was parried, but not fast enough to avoid the tip of his blade sinking into the space between his opponent's shoulder and arm. Not deep enough to kill.

Deep enough to enrage.

One, two, three, *strike*. Parry. Start again.

One, two. Stop and move. Now. Feet swift over the ground, hands a flurry of movements he knew so well but fuelled now by raw, untethered energy.

A gasp and a growl, and Fel'annár pulled his sword back viciously, tip bloodied, but Band'orán still stood.

One, two, three, circle. He was dancing the Kal'hamén'Ar, Master versus Warlord. And yet the Master had no projection. No Dohai.

Band'orán fell, shortsword slipping from his right hand, landing far away. He rose as if pulled up by a string, wiping his mouth on his sleeve. He flipped his longsword into his right hand, and with his left, he reached inside his robe. "Gor'sadén has taught you well. But it's not enough, Silvan. You can't kill me. I, who was born to be *king*. I, who have killed women, children. I, who broke your father's pathetic heart, had your mother stabbed to death."

The forest lights blazed blindingly in wrath, leaves hissing fury at their prey that was denied them. They pleaded with the only one who could grant it.

Kill him.

Fel'annár ignored the distant screams and shouts. He struck a high stance and moved in for the killing blow. Band'orán dodged to the right, and Fel'annár knew that he had him, swung his shortsword towards his enemy's stomach. But then, he could see Band'orán's hand racing towards him from the left.

Misdirection.

He swayed backwards, too late, and a puff of fine purple powder streaked across his face. It engulfed him, settled in his eyes. He screwed them shut, staggered to the left; felt searing pain, and he was down on one knee. He opened his eyes despite the agony, and dread wrenched from him a cry of horror.

He could not *see*.

Band'orán had blinded him, had violated the most sacred laws of the Warrior Code. Now, he was at his enemy's mercy.

He needed to get up. Band'orán would move in for the killing blow any moment now. The trees screamed, screeched, and their boughs swayed violently. Creaking wood, hissing leaves and the ground beneath his enemy reared upwards. He could hear fast, heavy breaths, a sword through the air, but not yet close enough to kill him. Band'orán was fighting with the trees, battling with the wrathful wood, branches reaching, indiscriminate save for the Warlord.

"Fel'annár!"

He could hear Idernon, Gor'sadén, Sontúr, yelling at him from further away. He half-turned his head in their direction, knew that they were fighting their way in, that the trees would not stop for them. "Stay away!"

Heavy footsteps. He threw himself sideways, rolled and stood, circling, blades held out clumsily. The screaming would not stop, from the trees, from The Company. He couldn't hear the voice ...

Stop!

The rustle of cloth, heat. Something heavy cut through the air louder. He jumped backwards, lost his balance and crashed to the ground. Gods, but his eyes burned.

"*This* is Or'Talán's grandson? If he could see you now, he would disown you."

"But he can't. Did you kill him, too?" asked Fel'annár, breathless as he stood slowly, faced the voice, wavering blades still before him.

"Would you care if I did?"

It was a good question, one there was no time to consider. The screams had subsided, the forest's voice clearer.

Focus. See.

But he couldn't. It was all dark. But at least he knew where his enemy stood.

"Fel'annár!"

"Stay away, brothers. It's too dangerous."

A breath, not his own, and heat coming towards him. Band'orán moved, so fast that Fel'annár staggered sideways, with barely enough time to parry the downward sweep of a blade. Band'orán was toying with him.

"*Or'Talán* was good. Better than me. Much better than *you*." Band'orán's next attack was meant to finish him. Fel'annár parried, once, again. Shock waves rippled down his arms. How had he known where the blade was?

He turned, sure that he faced Band'orán.

Focus. Feel. See.

Heat, sound, touch. The nearer Band'orán was, the hotter, the more acute the buzzing sound in Fel'annár's mind. He no longer heard the cries from The Company, didn't even know if his eyes were closed or open, but he could see patches of colour, like painted fog, swirling and mixing together. Some patches were darker than others. He turned to the dark grey, struck a stance and lunged forwards.

His long blade clanged against Band'orán's.

The colours spiralled, blues and greens, and then there it was again. The shadow amidst the lights. He turned left, swivelled one sword, pulled his other back.

Faith.

Fel'annár flew forwards, blade glancing over his opponent's. He felt the heat as it turned left. He faced it. A back stance, a closed stance, feign, feign. Fel'annár lunged towards the shadow, felt the sting of sharp metal over his cheek. Not deep.

Intentional.

A guarding stance. He watched the shadow move. He turned with it.

"I could have killed you there."

Fel'annár ran for the shadow once more, but stumbled, almost fell when Band'orán sidestepped. He turned fast, swords before him.

See.

And then the lights pulsed, no longer a fog but shapes, clear outlines. Trees and plants, roots dancing in the air. Green, blue, but almost all of it purple. He saw the shape of his enemy, saw his blades.

"You were good, brother. Used to be the best but now ... look at you. Staggering around like a drunken fool."

But Band'orán's goading no longer meant anything to Fel'annár. The shouts from The Company were distant, the screaming of the trees dampened, and he concentrated on the buzzing, droning sound in his mind, constant, steady unless he moved. Then it would pulse and flare.

He surged towards the shadow, saw his enemy's surprise in how he parried a little too late. Sparks of blue speckled across his strange sight and he whirled sideways, blades following, one and then the other. His feet felt sure beneath him. He could see Band'orán's form, dark purple, almost no colour. He saw a blade hurtling towards his face, and he parried, heard it slide down his blade's edge, up to the very guard. He pushed, muscles quivering. He sidestepped, staggered and then threw himself to the floor, twisting out of the way, watching the killing stroke sink into the ground. It bought enough time to stand, breathless and gasping.

But Fel'annár was not finished.

He took up his guarding stance, slower. He called on the trees, heard the creak and groan of their reply, the bass hum as the two captains were hoisted aloft. People gasped somewhere behind him.

And then Fel'annár held his blades high and waited for his opponent to mirror the move. He did.

A high stance. A *final* stance. With his Master's words in his mind, Fel'annár turned full circle, blades angling, changing paths, impossible to predict.

'You must not only see it. You must feel it.'

Band'orán brought his blades up, too slow, and although Fel'annár could not see it, his grey eyes widened. He saw the legendary move too late, and he cried out, braced for impact.

Enha'rei.

But no limb fell to the ground. It took Band'orán a moment to understand. And then he heard it, the heavy thud of a Royal Councillor's collar, the envy of all jewels, marking service to king and land. It lay sprawled upon the still undulating forest floor, chains severed, the acorn and emerald of Ea Uaré flaring on a streaking light.

The lash of something hurtling through the air. Fel'annár knew what it was. He twisted sideways and then stood fast before his opponent, feet wide, blades out to his sides. Band'orán stood rooted, shocked that he was still whole, utterly petrified, wordless, almost boneless as the vines hurtled towards him. Too slow, and they slashed at ankles and wrists. Fel'annár watched impassively as another circled Band'orán's bare throat.

Wait.

The forest held its breath. Fel'annár wondered what he would see in his enemy's eyes. Would he see wrath? Fear? Acceptance? It was only now that he realised he had won, though it did not feel like victory.

He was blind.

With his enemies held fast, the forest stilled and Fel'annár felt the approach of others, felt the nearness of his father. It was Thargodén who moved past him.

"You have been tried and condemned for conspiracy to usurp the throne. You have brought us to civil war. You attempted to murder your king and Lord Fel'annár. You did murder King Or'Talán and Lássira of Abiren'á, and I wonder ... if your own son fell at the hands of the father he always loved." Thargodén took a step closer to the spread-eagled lord, eyes searching, but finding no denial.

Behind him, the two rebel captains made one last, futile attempt to escape their bonds, but all they could do was watch. Thargodén lifted Or'Talán's sword, and then tilted it sideways, ancient runes catching the forest's lights, shining in Band'orán's wide eyes.

'Your life, for love.'

The king stepped up to the bound and stretched elf. His uncle. Bane of his life and his land. He spoke softly, only for his prisoner and Fel'annár. "I told you, Band'orán, that it would be *my* face that sends you across the Veil—my father's blade to see it done. Remember it well. May you never find yourself on the other side. For you, eternity ends today."

Thargodén placed Or'Talán's sword against Band'orán's throat and sliced sideways. A ceremonial death by the hand of a king. But he did not press the blade all the way in, did not sever the airway.

And then he stared into the shocked face before him. He saw the horror of impending death, the question in his eyes. Why had the king held back?

Thargodén turned to Fel'annár, saw his tightly closed eyes, a purple tinge over the eyelids. He screamed at himself not to reach out, not to succour his blinded son—not yet.

"You have earned the right." He stepped away, stood beside his son and watched in fascination as one hand rose before him, palm up. With one swipe towards the canopy above, Fel'annár released his hold on the forest.

Now.

Dinor, Bendir and Band'orán were lifted off the ground, hoisted high into the boughs, a victorious trophy for the world to see. Behold the enemy, how he is vanquished at last. The voices of the sentinels echoed through the forests, to the Old Oak of Lan Taria where a queen had perished. It journeyed on then, to the most distant, driest trees of the Xeric Wood, where a king once sat scribbling in his journal.

The captains shrieked and screamed, and Band'orán would have joined them, but all he managed was a wet gurgle.

Fel'annár stepped back, and the forest seemed to exhale. But the delicate sigh rose, higher and higher until it was an avenging scream. Blood ran down Band'orán's body, leeching into the purple of his sash. Then the vines were squeezing and pulling. The forest flared, a conflagration of lights, and the people were running, eyes on the trees and then the distant palace. But the commanders, Turion, Rinon and The Company held fast, arms out as the wind buffeted them mercilessly.

Fel'annár turned from the slaughter, walked back the way he had come. The king walked beside him and behind, Band'orán, Bendir and Dinor were ripped apart, limb from limb until all trace of them was gone.

THE GROUND beneath them still trembled, but the vivid, blinding colours had waxed soft, playful even. They still flared and sparkled, whirled around the boughs, but they were no longer streaks of terrifying lightning. They were colourful ribbons at a Silvan thanksgiving, soft and mischievous, no longer dangerous. The threat had gone, and in its place, it seemed to rejoice, to revel in the aftermath of its killing frenzy.

They would never forget what they had seen. They knew it had torn their enemies apart. The Company, the commanders, Turion, even Rinon with an arrow through his leg—they had all fought it, desperate to reach the duelling elves beyond, desperate to kill Band'orán themselves for using the vilest of weapons, the most dishonourable art of the blinding powders. Tensári had stood as close as she dared but had not drawn her sword, had not defied the forest as the others had. And their struggle had been futile. The forest was stronger, could have killed them, had that been its wish.

They watched as two figures emerged from the rippling veneer. Father and son. King and Forest Warlord. The Company, commanders and prince stared for a moment, their swords drawn, severed roots all around them. Further away, still behind the open gates, Captain Dalú and a host of Silvans stood watching.

Fel'annár stopped, wavered, felt a hand under his elbow as he sunk to his knees.

Sontúr rushed forwards, ripping a strip of dark cloth from his own cape, a flask of water in his other hand. "Let me see."

"No."

"Open your eyes, Fel'annár," said Galadan from behind him.

"I can't ..."

"Trust me. Open them."

And he did. Sontúr repressed the shudder, the gasp that had collected at the back of his throat. "Hold still. I'm going to flush them ... water, I need more water!" He heard running feet, saw Thargodén standing over him, an object in his hand.

"This was what Band'orán threw in his eyes." Sontúr reached for it, took the hollow piece of bamboo in his hands. He smelled it, and then again.

"Hedgeberry, and something else ..." he poked his finger into the hollow, brought it out and rubbed the powder between his fingers. It was fine but abrasive. "Gods, where is that water!"

Someone fell to their knees beside him. "There's more coming!" Galdith's rasping voice.

Tensári and Idernon stood before the kneeling warlord and healer, the rest of The Company, even Pan'assár, forming a shielding circle around Fel'annár and the two healers as they worked.

Sontúr crossed gazes with Galadan and waited for him to take hold of Fel'annár's head. Tilting it backwards, Sontúr poured water into the flickering eyes, watched them well and the water run purple. He knew it would be a painful process, tried to block out Fel'annár's stifled cries of agony. When his flask was empty, he reached for another Galdith held out for him. When at last it ran clean, he wrapped the strip of cloth around Fel'annár's now closed eyes and Galadan tied it at the back.

"It's not permanent, Fel'annár. You are not blind, I promise."

A brave nod. He collected his feet beneath him.

"Come." The king's voice.

On his feet, Fel'annár straightened as much as he could. He stepped forward, swayed and stopped. Walked again, unsure of where. And then a commanding voice and the people opened a path before the king of Ea Uaré.

"Follow."

The strange play of lights had not left him. Faceless shapes, dark blotches—it was all he could see. But he felt The Company behind him, Gor'sadén at his side. And then the gritty voice of Dalú sliced into the air.

"Hail the Warlord!"

"Hail!" It was a cry to Aria, a deeply felt word of thanks, of utter joy because they were free at last. Free of Band'orán and everything he had done. It was just as they had said. A warrior would come to set them free, and that day had come.

"Hail!" they shouted again. And then another voice, deep and clear. Pan'assár.

"Hail King Thargodén Ar Or'Talán!"

"Hail!" The warriors shouted from further afield, even those who had fought for Band'orán, those who sat tied hand and foot in the courtyard beyond. For mercy, perhaps.

As they walked towards the palace, Rinon watched the mage in grudging respect, for his father was alive, was king once more. He had fought in the ways of the Kal'hamén'Ar, had commanded the Silvans, commanded the forest. Even now, he navigated the stairs as if he could see, but Rinon could not hear the softly spoken orders that Gor'sadén gave him from just behind.

Beside the limping prince, Pan'assár walked tall. He had atoned, his brother avenged. His last memory of him was no longer the agonised screams but that strong, noble face that had colonised a land and been loved for it.

Gor'sadén's hand remained at the small of Fel'annár's back, lending what strength he could as they made their way inside the palace. There, Thargodén's eyes swept the still smoky halls. His people moved with purpose. Some led struggling elves away, whilst others carried bundles destined for the kitchens, or up the grand stairways. And then he saw Handir, shouting orders. They crossed gazes.

Handir's eyes landed on Fel'annár, knew he could not see him, see the shock in his own eyes. He turned his questioning gaze on the king, who gestured with his head that he should follow.

Joining the tattered, haggard warriors, Rinon clapped him on the shoulder, pride in his eyes. "He's gone, brother."

Handir's eyes widened, his lips dared a tentative smile. Taking the fore, he led the party to the grand stairway. They passed Lord Erthoron, Lord Lorthil and Lord Aradan. Narosén stared at the blinded Warlord. They bowed, watching as the party continued upwards, towards the very top of the palace, to the royal suite itself.

Every room had been prepared, every fire lit, every bath filled. Handir opened the door to a room close to his own. Inside, it was warm.

Gor'sadén relinquished his hold on Fel'annár, watched as he walked towards the window, wondering how he knew it was there, how he could see blindfolded. He tried to quell his outrage at Band'orán's ultimate act of dishonour, told himself he was dead, that he had suffered, and then he remembered Sontúr's words.

'You're not blind ...'

Running feet, a startled servant, steadying the pile of towels in her arms. Llyniel stood in the doorway in soiled and crumpled robes, horror and denial on her face. Her eyes filled, hand shaking. Idernon reached out, squeezed her shoulder tight. She straightened, breathed and wiped at her eyes. She closed them, and when she opened them again, they were not the despairing eyes of a distraught lover but the steady eyes of a Master Healer.

Thargodén, Rinon and Handir bowed, but Fel'annár didn't see it. His mind was on the Evergreen Wood beyond the window. As the door clicked shut, his royal family gone, Gor'sadén approached him, The Company and Llyniel watching.

"Well? Has your duty to Aria been fulfilled?"

Fel'annár had become the Warlord and united the Silvan warriors. He had vanquished Band'orán. But trust had been deeply wounded, the army all but ruined. What would it take to rebuild loyalty? To unite the Silvan and Alpine people? What would it take to reforge a kingdom, make it a better one? He turned to where he knew Gor'sadén stood, to his real father.

"It has only just begun."

He turned back to the window, the hail to the Warlord still echoing in his mind. It had been a scream to the heavens, to the Gods themselves. It had surely reached the farthest stars upon the firmament, perhaps even across the Veil.

Had Or'Talán heard it? Had Lássira heard it? They had fallen along Band'orán's road to power, to revenge, for things Fel'annár still did not fully understand. They said Or'Talán had tried to help Lássira, and he wondered if he would ever know their story. And then he thought that perhaps they would tell him themselves, one day, when he, too, crossed the Veil and met them at last.

One day.

EPILOGUE

A pale hand reached up. Long, elegant fingers on a strong hand, a warrior's hand, dry from weeks of travel through the harshest of territories. Unfiltered sunlight beat down on black robes, glinting off overheated steel, leeching the liquid from his flesh.

So thirsty.

He reached out, reached down, drove his hand into the shallow well until he felt the hot water. He dug deeper, felt it cooler. He immersed both hands, up to his forearms, then stayed there for a while. Bright eyes, immortal eyes, stared at the murky surface, at his own reflection. This was what he had come for.

Water.

It was what his people needed and did not have. It was his gift to them, in exchange for what *he* needed most.

A home.

And he would take it, when the time was right. He would not make the same mistake that his brother had. When everything was in place. When every plan had been executed, every order fulfilled; only then would they converge on their new lands.

He sat up, bare forearms wetting his clothes, and his lovely eyes turned south to the distant haze of green. It was not yet the end of this vast sea of sand, land of his mortal forefathers. But he would leave it, soon enough, and enter the forests of his mother's land. Eternal lands, fat with water, ripe with meat.

Beautiful, just like him.

He smiled and stuck his hands back into the water, water that flowed beneath the arid land and away. Southwards, to the still distant wood, infusing roots, feeding Sentinels.

And the Sentinels awoke.

Far away, on the last floor of the royal palace, the Warlord, too, stirred from his long, healing slumber.

He sat up, reached for his eyes, felt the cloth across them. He pushed the bedclothes away from him. A rustle came from nearby. He felt his bond with his Connate stir in his mind. He stood, reaching out to steady himself on the back of a chair. The fire was back in his eyes, pulsing, flaring, and he listened.

Something was coming, travelling on the wind—or was it the water? It rushed under the ground, pooled between rocks, oozed from crevices and soaked the land; the arid lands of the Xeric Wood.

And then the Sentinels called. A deep rumble from the north, the brush of tainted flesh, unnatural blood. Something beautiful and something horrific. He knew that canticle, the meaning of its lyrics.

Beautiful. Monster.

THE END

The Silvan Book V: Destiny of a Prince. Coming soon.
Visit here to receive updates:Visit here for updates: https://landing.mailerlite.com/webforms/landing/t4b8j8

FROM R.K. LANDER

If you enjoyed the story, please consider reviewing. It would mean so much to me.

And if you are on Goodreads or BookBub, would you share your thoughts with friends and followers?

The Silvan is an ongoing saga, so if you would like to keep abreast of the latest news on upcoming releases, or simply participate in the discussion, why not join find me on Facebook or Twitter.

You can also check news by subscribing to my blog at rklander.com.

ACKNOWLEDGMENTS

As always, my unwavering gratitude to the mighty M.Y. Leigh. I am also privileged to have the best developmental editor on Earth, Andrea Lundgren.

I would like to thank my incredible team of ARC readers over at R.K. Lander's Company. What a wonderful job we have done together. Special thanks go to Adrian Lee, Ana Pérez, Bruce Sutton, Claudia Linquanti-Sue, Chris Edwards, David Witko, Donna Navarro, Evelyn Ziegenhagen, Hermina Speksnijder, Jen Smith, Kadie Gotcher, Ken Edmondson, Kirsty Kilpatrick, Marilyn Wilkinson, Sharon Willis, Shelly Suter, Sherrin Eiffler, Simon Prebble, Singa Nga.

I would also like to thank A.J. Fraser-Brown, Carolyn Langen, Charity Wiggins, Dale Whitley, Devin Vandermeer, Ellen Roddy, John Melton, Kate Ferraro, Lesley Walsh, Paul Zawacki, Susan Peters and Tim Carter.

R.K. LANDER

- facebook.com/rklwrites
- twitter.com/rklwrites
- instagram.com/rklanderwrites
- amazon.com/R-K-Lander
- bookbub.com/profile/r-k-lander

www.ingramcontent.com/pod-product-compliance
Lightning Source LLC
LaVergne TN
LVHW040130080526
838202LV00042B/2857